Hector Trog

GW00838912

by P. A. Booth

hectortrogg.com

First published in Great Britain in 2014

Abas UK Ltd, Beech House, 48 Eastfield Road, Barton-upon-Humber, North Lincolnshire, DN18 6AW, England, UK.

ISBN 978-1-909745-00-1 (hardback)
ISBN 978-1-909745-01-8 (softback)
ISBN 978-1-909745-02-5 (audiobook)
ISBN 978-1-909745-03-2 (ebook)

MORE IN THE SERIES

Hector Trogg: Fell Heights
fellheights.com

Hector Trogg: Fell Deeds
felldeeds.com

For Jenny

CHAPTER ONE

Flight

Hector Trogg looked from the little that remained of his father's car to the tall policewoman stood in front of him.

'It wasn't me!' was all he managed to say, although he realised it sounded a little feeble.

'Well, of course it wasn't you dear,' said the policewoman. 'Eleven-year old boys don't have access to explosives.'

'Don't think he hasn't asked,' muttered Kate, Hector's thirteen-year old sister.

'There's another person coming to talk to you and your Dad and Mum, they'll explain it all,' said the policewoman kindly.

Kate furrowed her brow and then shook her head.

'Dad will do his nut; he polishes it almost every day; it's almost new,' Kate announced.

'Do you think Volkswagen will give him a new one, it is under warrant?' asked Hector.

'The word is warranty, Hector,' said Kate, unkindly, 'And given that one of the wheels is in the farmer's field next door and one of the seats smashed through Mrs Urwell's lounge window, we will be hard-pressed to claim that the car was hit by a sudden bout of very aggressive rust.'

Kate was like that; clever, but annoying.

An hour or so later they were all sat in the kitchen, as this was one of the few rooms that had not lost any of its windows. A fat man with a nasal voice was explaining that it was all related to the inheritance. Just two weeks earlier Kate and Hector had been amazed to find out that several million US dollars had been left to them by a distant relative in America called Irvine Deeds. The money was in a trust fund, and they were not allowed to spend any of the fortune until they were twenty-one years old.

It seemed as though the money had been left to Kate and Hector so as to upset all of Irvine Deeds' closer relatives, who had expected to receive the money themselves. The fat man explained that while Mr Irvine Deeds had gone to great trouble and legal expense to ensure that his will could not be challenged in the courts, he had forgotten to be clear about what would happen if Kate and Hector were both murdered. There were a large number of Mr Deeds' relatives scattered throughout the world, and any of them might be behind the attack, the fat man explained. From now, until they were twenty-one, they were at great risk.

'Brilliant!' exclaimed Hector. 'This will be really exciting.'

'No, it won't!' complained Kate. 'We could be killed!'

'No. Whoever tried to kill us made the bomb beep as we got into the car. I'm sure they are going to give us a sporting chance,' explained Hector.

The fat man groaned and put his head in his hands. 'The problem is,' he explained, 'your father's side of the family, I mean Mr Deeds' relatives, are...'

Hector and Kate looked puzzled.

'Well, they are diverse,' the fat man went on.

Hector and Kate continued to look puzzled.

'They come from a wide variety of backgrounds,' the fat man tried again.

Hector and Kate looked even more confused.

'I think what Detective Inspector Smithson is trying to say,' said Dad with a sigh, 'is that quite a number of my more distant relatives have not led blameless lives.'

Hector's look of puzzlement grew even more extreme, but Kate worked it out.

'They're crooks,' Kate explained.

'I'm afraid so,' said the Inspector. 'Big ones, and your trust fund is worth millions, although quite how they really hope to get their hands on it I don't know.'

Hector's unshakeable belief that everything would turn out alright meant that he had a good night's sleep. Kate fell asleep worrying. The following morning things got even better, at least from Hector's perspective.

The police had raided a flat and discovered more plots to murder them, while a man walking his dog had fallen into a large hole that turned out to be the start of a tunnel someone had been digging under their house. Both Kate and Hector were kept off school for the day in a house full of workmen and police. By 10am Hector had broken the controls on a police car when the officer allowed him to play with the lights and the siren.

Hector was pleased it was the officer who got a good telling off, not him. When the Inspector had finished shouting, he informed Hector, Kate, Mum and Dad that they needed a sudden holiday. Apparently, some of their inheritance could be used for this sort of thing, and so Dad hired a plane and a pilot.

'Brilliant! I can't believe it. Dad's hired a plane! I hope I get to fly it, or at least be the rear gunner,' Hector said, as he ran around the room in excitement.

'You don't hire a plane, Hector, you charter one,' said Kate in her most annoying voice, 'and of course there won't be a rear gunner's seat.'

Hector did not even bother giving his sister a shove. Today had been brilliant fun, and tomorrow they were going on a surprise holiday, missing school for another day.

The family spent a frustrating evening in two bright, clean but small hotel rooms. The rooms were joined, which did little to ease the sense of confinement. Kate felt as if they had been sent to prison; a feeling heightened by the presence of two armed police officers in the corridor. For Hector, this just added to the excitement.

Hector's next day was even better, because the plane did have a rear gun, as well as guns at the side. Kate looked sour; annoyed that her brother had been correct. Mum and Dad looked flabbergasted. Mum kept asking the pilot how old the plane was, while Dad just looked dumbfounded at the propellers attached to the giant engines. Hector suspected that he had not yet noticed the guns.

The pilot explained that the plane was usually just flown in air shows, except for a recent trip to Africa for something more exciting. The charter company was really sorry, but the normal plane had been grounded and this was all they had.

'We cannot fly in that,' said Dad, after a very long look at the aircraft.

'I am very sorry,' said the pilot waving some paperwork, 'but it is airworthy. It's legal.'

'Is it safe?' Mum asked.

'I think so,' the pilot declared confidently, 'although if you want to wait until the weekend I'm sure we can sort out something else.'

Dad turned to the two police officers, both of whom looked as bewildered as he felt.

'We were told to get you here safely,' said the smaller of the two officers, 'I can't say I expected to have to make decisions about aircraft. It does look old.'

'True,' said the other officer, 'but certificates of airworthiness are not easy to get for old planes. It will have been very well maintained. Plus, these planes safely transported lots of bomber crews. Personally, I'd give it a go. It'll be a flight to remember.'

'There has got to be a risk to waiting for another plane,' the smaller officer added.

Once the luggage was aboard, the engines spluttered and then roared. The plane did not really take off. It rattled along at increasing speed until it ran out of runway and a slight dip in the land left the aircraft without any other options.

Kate and Hector were used to the boredom of long flights, but this one was different. It was cold, very noisy, and in places rather grubby. However, it was anything but dull. They were sat amongst their luggage, and so both got out warmer clothing. Mum reluctantly let them explore, and it did not take them long to discover that there was no kitchen, drinks or food. There was no toilet either. There were parachutes, however, together with extra ammunition for the guns. Hector and Kate took one of the parachutes back to show Mum and Dad.

Kate discovered there was a hatch at the back of the aircraft you could open. She could have jumped straight out. She was sure she and Hector would never have been allowed to explore if Mum or Dad had known about the hatch.

Hector spent considerable time aiming the rear gun at imaginary aircraft. He reluctantly allowed Kate smaller turns, and they both had fun yelling 'bandits at two o'clock', aiming just in front of the enemy plane, and watching the pretend fighter go down in flames.

Kate discovered how to load the gun, and even where the safety catch was. Hector was very keen to fire the gun for real. Kate thought firing live ammunition was a mistake, and this eventually led to an argument. They both retreated back to Mum and Dad in a sulky silence.

Some time later Dad put down his book and mentioned that he needed the bathroom. Kate told him about the hatch, and this led to a spirited debate as to whether Kate and Hector should have ever been allowed to explore. A few minutes passed before Dad returned from the hatch saying that it was the most dangerous toilet he had ever visited.

'Show me these guns,' said Dad, beckoning Kate and Hector.

Mum sat in the cold and noise with her newspaper, trying to remain as warm as possible. They were a long way into the flight, and she felt as if her body temperature had lost a degree with each passing hour.

Her mind turned to the guns. Aircraft like this were used for displays, but she was sure they would not have ammunition for the guns. The more Mum thought about it the more uneasy she felt. Why take an aircraft like this on a huge trip to Africa? As she tried to imagine possible scenarios the only one that seemed realistic was that it had been used for something illegal. The pride the pilot had in the aircraft made her suspect that he had been the one to fly it down to Africa.

'Out of the frying pan and into the fire,' said Mum, summarising her worries that they were now in a bad situation. Dad, Hector and Kate had returned from the rear gun and were sat around among the bags.

'I think it will be fine,' said Hector, 'It's still in the air. It hasn't crashed or caught fire yet.'

'Thank you for those thoughts Hector,' said Dad, although he did not sound grateful at all.

'At the very least this is a rather odd plane charter company,' Mum went on, 'Providing an aircraft as old as this, and one with ammunition is extraordinary. And what where they doing flying something like this to Africa?'

'Well, we're in the air now. We just have to hope it all goes well,' Kate said, 'I can't see what else we can do.'

Kate was about to continue, but found her attention drawn to Hector, who was looking intently out of a window. Kate got up to look as well. In the distance behind them there appeared to be aircraft.

There was a bang from the front of the aircraft as the pilot emerged from the cockpit.

'Ahh, good,' said Dad, 'I have a few concerns. There seems to be ammunition for the guns.'

The pilot glared at Dad and then looked down.

'I don't ask about things like that in case I don't like the answer,' replied the pilot in a loud voice as he walked down the plane towards them.

'Hang on,' said Hector, 'aren't you supposed to be flying the plane?'

'Yes, I am. Sorry,' said the pilot as he picked up a parachute, 'but there are some fighters on our tail.'

'How the hell did we attract the attention of the Air Force?' Dad yelled, starting to get angry, but noticing that the pilot was now stood by the door ready to leave.

'It's not the Air Force. They're very old planes. They're freelancers, and I suspect they've been stolen from collectors,' said the pilot as he opened the door and the sound of rushing wind grew louder.

'You've got to be kidding!' exclaimed Mum.

'Please don't give me the whole "this cannot be happening to me" thing,' said the pilot unkindly, as he turned to jump.

'I don't think you should do that!' shouted Hector.

'Why ever not?' grinned the pilot with an evil look on his face as he turned back to face everyone, 'Too young to die are you? Too frightened to use a adult parachute because it will undoubtedly kill you? Or is it just not fair? Well, well...why not?' The pilot jumped.

'It's because that's the parachute Kate and I have been playing with,' said Hector to the empty space.

Dad partly closed the door and they all watched the pilot fall as he disappeared as a speck behind them.

The pilot confidently pulled the rip cord, and was at first confused to see a series of knots and then the remains of a sticky sweet appear, followed by a ribbon tied in a neat bow. The horror and true seriousness of the situation hit him. He scrambled madly for the reserve chute finding only scraps of material, some of which had been cut into animal shapes. The pilot was still scrambling madly when he disappeared from view. His parachute did not appear. He was just a dot, plummeting downwards.

'Can I fly the plane?' asked Hector.

'No!' said Kate.

'It's not up to you,' retorted Hector, 'I've flown lots of missions on my computer.'

'Yes, and they all end up with your plane in a heap of flaming wreckage,' said Kate.

'What about the parachutes?' Mum asked, looking at Dad, who seemed horror-struck.

'I think we'll die. We've no idea what to do. Maybe adult parachutes will flip over if there is only a child's weight. I just don't know.'

'We could strap Kate and Hector into the same parachute,' Mum suggested.

'They might shoot us as we drift down,' said Kate.

'I think we'll be plummeting too quickly to shoot,' said Dad, 'It requires training. We've just seen the pilot fall to his death. We could be next.'

Just then there were loud bangs as bullets hit the plane.

'You're in charge of the rear guns, I'll fly,' shouted Mum, as she pushed Dad towards the rear of the plane, and set off for the cockpit herself.

Kate and Hector each went to the guns at the side. Kate immediately took aim and let off a few rounds. All of their earlier play suddenly had a purpose. She could see two propeller type planes, and a single jet she thought was called a Hawk.

'Mine's broken,' said Hector, 'it won't work,' and for the first time he felt a panic rising in his throat. Dad's gun had not fired a round either.

'You need this catch to be here,' explained Kate pointing to the side of the gun. She then ran to the back of the aircraft to help Dad, just as a volley of bullets ripped a hole in the fuselage. Next, Kate ran to the front of the plane to tell Mum to fly in circles.

'We can shoot them with the side and rear guns, but it is harder for them because they have to line us up.' yelled Kate.

Hector could not help but feel a certain admiration for his sister. Kate was good in a crisis, even if she did always take the biggest slice of cake when allowed anything more than a nanosecond's head start.

Soon there was a regular rattle of all three guns. Kate was careful and determined, while Hector was having the time of his life firing anywhere. He could not be sure what sort of planes the two propellor aircraft were, but as far as he was concerned they had to be Messerschmitts. He should have been starting his maths lesson at school, sitting next to pooty Collins, but instead he was in an aerial dog fight to the death with two Messerschmitts and a jet fighter. Their plane veered wildly, the guns rattled, there were explosions as bullets hit their aircraft, and a small fire had started near the cockpit. As far as Hector was concerned, this was as exciting as life could ever be.

Aiming was easier than Kate and Hector had expected, but the problem was that the plane kept changing direction. Sometimes there was a larger, deeper rattle, and it sounded as though Mum had found the forward guns. The lights kept going on and off, and Hector thought it was because the electrics had been hit. Kate guessed that it was because Mum did not know which buttons did what. Her suspicions were confirmed when the radio was turned on full and they were all blasted with hits from the sixties.

As the Beatles sang 'All you need is love' at full volume, Dad and Hector had their first real success, and the jet fighter exploded. Yet, even the deafening radio could not drown out the thuds and explosions as the rounds from the other two fighter aircraft hit. There was now a growing hole in the fuselage next to Kate, and as Hector glanced up and down he could see other holes. It was only a matter of time before the two fighters either hit them or something vital in the aircraft. Things were getting desperate. Either they were not hitting the remaining two fighters, or their bullets were not enough to do any real damage. The two fighters were having problems lining them up as Mum flew this way and that, but sooner or later they would succeed.

In addition to the endless chorus of 'All you need is love,' the thud and bang of bullets, the roar of the engines and the increasing wind noise as yet more holes appeared everywhere, there was now a regular deep thud that shook the whole aircraft. Either something was seriously wrong, or Mum was lowering and raising the wheels and other bits of undercarriage as she attempted to turn the radio off. Suddenly they turned sharply to port and started losing height and speed. Whatever criticisms they might make of Mum's flying, they had to admit she was difficult to anticipate. Then Mum came running out of the cockpit.

'Kate dear,' she yelled, 'would you like to have a go. I seem to have turned one of the engines off.'

Hector took his chance and dashed forward. He was going to fly the plane. This was his opportunity. He ran forward just as a hail of bullets tore fresh holes in the walls, floor and roof of the middle portion of the plane. Very soon, Hector thought, it will all be portions; small, chopped-up bits of plane falling from the sky.

Hector had just got himself into the seat and pulled back on the stick when bullets hit the cockpit sending a frightening spray of debris everywhere. He pushed the working engine to full throttle and compensated for the yaw with the rudder. Yet, they were still going down. Just then Kate arrived and began looking at the buttons. She turned the radio off, withdrew the undercarriage into the plane and was soon working on getting the port engine started again.

'I'm going to weave about,' yelled Hector, just as he pushed the stick forward and the plane lurched down.

'Got it,' yelled Kate, and the port engine roared back into life.

'Brilliant Hector,' Kate yelled as Hector pulled the plane sharply up, and they saw the bullets whistle underneath the aircraft, 'I'm off to help Mum.'

Mum had found Dad knocked unconscious, and worse than that, they were running out of ammunition. Mum, it seemed, had fired both side guns madly until all the ammunition was spent. Only the rear gun had a few bullets left, and that was only because the gun had become too hot to use. The only good news was that one of the pursuing fighters had part of a wing missing, and seemed to be weaving, as if the pilot did not have full control.

Kate slipped into the rear gunner's seat and was pleased to find that the gun had cooled down. She noticed the large hole in the very rear of the plane. Kate took aim at the undamaged fighter. She had a calm, steel-like determination as she fired, but the fighter pilot had seen it coming and pulled up sharply, taking him out of the line of fire, and moving him further back from them. The damaged fighter had disappeared, but the remaining pilot seemed determined.

Kate fired the smallest burst she could manage just as the fighter pulled to the right. She quickly aimed a fraction in front of the fighter and fired a longer burst, but the pilot had pushed the stick forward, in a manoeuvre that made Kate think he must have his stomach in his mouth. She waited until he brought his guns into line and then fired again. So close! So close!

Kate decided to wait. He had to line up again and she would get him eventually. Now she understood what she had to do; just wait until he was lining up, trying to keep his aircraft straight and level. He dodged and pulled left and then right. Finally, he lined them up. Kate fired a longer burst, but it was soon over. The long burst turned out to be a very short burst. The ammunition was spent. The fighter was still in the air.

'That's it! We've no more ammunition,' Kate yelled to her mother, who was tending to Dad as he lay on the floor. She turned to see the remaining fighter moving closer in. Hector was still weaving about, but it was a big plane. Without the fire from the rear and side guns to keep the last fighter at bay there was nothing to stop it getting close and finishing them all in a hail of bullets.

'The parachutes, the parachutes!' yelled Mum.

Kate grabbed a parachute, pushed it into the hole at the very end of the plane and let it fall as she held onto the harness and pulled the rip cord. It billowed it out and was ripped from her hands, becoming a sudden frightening wall the pursuing fighter had to avoid. Kate rushed to get the next parachute. She pushed it into the hole again, held on to the harness and waited for the fighter to line them up once more. Just as the fighter swung into a direct line with them Kate pulled the rip cord and the parachute expanded, before being ripped from her hands once more. Again, it billowed out into a sudden flapping wall the fighter had to turn hard to miss.

It was a brilliant bit of innovative thinking; superb adaption; magnificent make do. Yet, Kate knew that it would work only as long as there was a ready supply of parachutes. Time was running out. Their last hope was fading. If only Hector could push the plane into a suicidal dive and yet pull out just in time to land safely then all would be well. Yet, the plane's wings simply would not manage. They could not out-dive a fighter. The wings could not pull the plane out of a vertical dive when they had so many holes in them.

Kate felt a hot wave of panic. She had to do something different, but she also had to keep pushing the parachutes out of the hole at the end of the plane. What she needed was a smart bomb like the ones in the computer games, but they did not exist; they were fantasy. As Kate pushed the last parachute into the ragged hole at the end of the plane she felt a sense of hopelessness. They were not going to make it. The fighter pilot was too clever; he knew what he was doing; he knew they had run out of ammunition; he was waiting for the right moment to fire a final volley of bullets into their stricken plane and send them all spinning to their deaths.

As the last parachute exploded out into a fragile but, for the fighter pilot, huge advancing wall, Kate huddled down, clutching the side of the aircraft. The plane pulled up; it rose and slowed. Then it rolled to starboard and then pitched down, leaving Kate feeling as though her stomach was trying to get out through her throat. Kate knew Hector was trying everything. He knew things were desperate. He would have guessed that the ammunition had run out, if only because of the absence of a reassuring rattle of return fire whenever the fighter's shots ricocheted through the plane.

Then it happened; the final rattle of gunfire that would destroy the plane, and destroy them all. The plane lurched upwards and slowed. There was a huge crunch as the plane began to disintegrate. The rear of the aircraft where Kate clung huddled partly exploded, and then buckled and groaned. Yet, to Kate's surprise she was not spinning down. She could not hear the crunch and splinter of the plane as it continued to fall apart. There were no bullets spraying in, just the sound of the engines and the wind. Even stranger, Hector was yelling in triumph.

'What happened?' yelled Kate.

'I think Hector managed to reverse the plane into the fighter,' Mum yelled back.

'You can't reverse a plane,' shouted Kate.

Yet that was exactly what Hector had managed to do. He was trying to avoid the fighter, but by pulling up sharply he had slowed the large plane. The fighter had simply run into the back of them.

'I think the fighter crashed into the rear of our plane,' yelled Kate.

'Yes,' shouted Mum, 'radical braking. Your father has managed to get several cars to run into the back of our car at roundabouts. It's probably genetic.'

'Is Dad OK?' Kate asked. It seemed strange, but when death seemed imminent, even her father laid in her mother's arms was something she could ignore. Now she was worried.

'He has muttered a few things. I think he's just hit his head.'

'Kate dear,' shouted Mum after a pause, 'things don't look too good. When I said parachutes I was rather hoping we would parachute to safety. It never occurred to me that you'd use them as a weapon. Are there any left?'

Kate just shook her head. Their problems were definitely not over. One engine was on fire and the other was leaving a dark trail of smoke across the sky. Added to this, Kate had just noticed that there were other planes around them. She raced forward to the cockpit. The best place for her now was at Hector's side.

Hector, rather annoyingly, was in a very good mood.

'It's a Typhoon,' he explained.

'What?' questioned Kate.

'It's a Royal Air Force plane,' said Hector, pointing to the plane on the starboard side. 'Fly by wire, carbon fibre.'

Hector's wild unfettered enthusiasm and simple joy at being near a Royal Air Force vacuum cleaner, that by some accident of design could fly, left Kate feeling exasperated.

'And that one,' said Hector, pointing to their port side, 'is another type of jet fighter, but it's not British. I think it's american. It might be a Raptor. They've got vectored thrust. That means the power is directed.'

'Hector,' shouted Kate, 'why is this good?'

'I think they're here to protect us,' explained Hector. He went on to demonstrate his enthusiasm by waving wildly to both of the pilots. As far as Kate could see they were waving back.

'You don't think they're a bit late,' said Kate, 'in case you hadn't noticed the last plane that was trying to shoot us out of the sky was rammed by the highly dangerous pilot I'm sitting next to. It wasn't shot down by those two, and the other one that was trying to kill us might come back.'

'No,' said Hector, still wildly cheerful, 'that old fighter would never dare attack with these two jets near us.'

This was undoubtedly true. Unfortunately, there was very little either of the planes could do to help them stay in the air. They were losing height; the fire in the starboard engine was getting worse and spreading down the wing. When Kate looked at the starboard wing she could see that quite a bit of it was missing.

The good news was that all of the port wing was still there, even if there were quite a few holes ripped in it. The even better news was that Kate could see that the two jet fighters were leading them to an airfield. It had bright lights and what looked like a lot of fire engines judging by the blue and red flashing lights.

'Oh no,' thought Kate, 'Hector loves fire engines, he'll probably die of happiness before he lands the plane.'

As they neared the airfield Kate could see the roads surrounding them were crammed with cars and people. They had all stopped to watch their stricken, flaming aircraft attempt its desperate landing.

Kate spent the next few seconds looking over the controls. She tried to ignore the fact that the starboard engine was now fully alight and had stopped spinning completely. She decided to lower the landing gear early so that if she got it wrong she would have time for another attempt. She did not think there was any possibility that Hector might turn the aircraft around for a second attempt at landing. They only had one chance!

Nothing happened. Kate knew she picked the correct controls because she had raised the landing gear earlier after her mother's eccentric time in the cockpit. Kate moved the switch to lift the landing gear up and then pressed the switch down again.

'Come on,' shouted Kate in frustration, as she desperately waggled the switch back and forth.

Kate looked around the cockpit at the holes, tattered cloth, smashed glass and shattered metal, and decided that her attempts were futile.

Hector had seen the problem and reassured Kate that he landed his plane in the computer game without any landing gear lots of times. At first this had simply been because he forgot to put the landing gear down, but later he landed without landing gear just because it was fun. The main thing, he explained to her, was not to hit the ground too hard, but to skid along. A tumble and spin on the ground was always something that lost you points.

'Well,' said Kate, 'at least if you crash this you won't lose any points. Your head may no longer be connected to your bottom via the middle part of your body, but at least your score on the computer game won't go down.'

Hector spotted the sarcasm but ignored it. This was brilliant; this was better than the best daydream he had ever had; better even than the ones in religious education lessons. He was about to crash land a real plane and he was unsure whether to concentrate on the controls and the task at hand, or whether to carry on trying to count fire engines.

'Hector,' yelled Kate, 'you're looking at the fire engines. Concentrate on landing the plane you buffoon. If I live, and I have all my limbs, I'll buy you a really big model fire engine. And in case you haven't noticed the port engine is now on fire as well.'

'Oh great!' exclaimed Hector, as visions of a brand new favourite toy swam the into view in his mind's eye, alongside the real vision of the rapidly approaching runway. He snapped back into reality because the plane yawed to one side as Kate lowered the flaps. Not all of the flaps worked, and Hector had to stretch to reach the pedals for the rudder.

The concrete was racing below. It looked hard and unforgiving. There were flashing blue lights all around as the fire engines raced along beside them.

The landing was brutal, but relatively quick. Hector flew along the runway for quite some way before making contact. He did not stall the plane, but he certainly made it lose a lot of its speed before it finally made contact with the concrete runway. There was a crunch as they hit the ground, followed by a horrible deafening scraping noise that filled the whole aircraft.

'See,' said Hector cheerfully as the fuselage scraped to a halt on the runway concrete, 'I said we'd survive.'

'Yes,' said Kate, 'and I said you always land in a heap of flaming wreckage, and you have.'

White spray filled the air as the fire engines poured foam on the burning wings. Men were suddenly breaking into the aircraft. Kate and Hector were quickly wrapped in fireproof blankets and carried to waiting ambulances.

'Who are you? Where are we?' asked Kate, looking round for Mum and Dad. The men did not seem to understand her. Hector realised that they did not speak English, and so decided to speak slowly and loudly.

'Do - you - have - any - cakes?' he yelled at them.

Minutes later Kate and Hector found themselves in a large airport building, in a strange land, with hostile natives, no real law, and nothing sensible to eat. They had landed in France.

Dad was taken off to hospital in an ambulance with Mum. Kate and Hector were assured that it was just a precaution.

It was two hours later when, in front of an impromptu gathering of several hundred people, Kate and Hector had been presented with medals. Hector repeatedly said that he would swap the medal for a ride in one of the fire engines, but either the local French dignitaries did not understand him or they did not believe him.

The ceremony went on for about fifteen minutes, which in Hector's view was approximately fourteen minutes too long. He liked the applause and congratulation, but he did not like the speeches. Kate had to endure an annoying Frenchman who kept patting her on the head. Added to this Hector kept hissing threats about what he would do if his model fire engine did not turn up soon.

It was not until almost 9 o'clock that night that they heard that Mum and Dad were safe and well. Dad had received a nasty blow to the head, and the hospital had decided to keep him in for observation.

They also heard from Inspector Smithson. His message was that a special security nanny would be arriving to keep them safe.

CHAPTER TWO

Mrs Warp

A security nanny. What on earth was a security nanny? This question went through Kate's mind again and again. The crowd had departed. The dignitaries had left. Kate and Hector had been sat in a corner of a large police office.

They had been told, in faltering English by a very tall French policeman, that they would be taken quickly and quietly to a secure house. The words discreet, quiet, hidden, dark, all seemed to swirl around whatever was planned next. The police were hushed, and now and then one of the policemen would glance over at Hector and Kate.

Hector had been very disappointed at the idea of being bundled into a small car and smuggled off to an anonymous house.

'It's a good idea Hector,' Kate had assured him, 'We need to disappear somewhere safe.'

Hector's glum mood lightened slightly when the blue reflected flash of police lights danced around the grey office. There was a sudden bustle and urgency. It was apparent that many people had just arrived. Kate and Hector were beckoned outside. Kate could not believe her eyes.

'What happened to discreet?' she asked.

It was a motorcade. It was their motorcade! Hector was in raptures. He counted no less than seven police cars; all with their blue flashing lights on. There were two vans, the insides of which could not be seen. There were four police outriders on motorbikes. In the very middle of the motorcade was a large heavy S-class Mercedes limousine. Hector guessed at once that it would be bullet-proof.

Once inside the Mercedes, Hector went straight to the middle arm rest. If there was a mini refrigerator with some chocolate that was where it would be. It was exactly as he hoped; there as even some milk. Better than this was the noise when the motorcade began to move. All of the police cars seemed to have turned on their sirens. It was deafening!

Kate on the other hand was horrified, not just by the lights and sirens, but by how close the cars travelled together, and just how quickly they moved. It was fast, very fast, bordering on reckless.

While Hector experimented with every button he could reach, and managed to turn the air conditioning to very hot, very cold, completely off, and something resembling a gale; Kate noticed that the anonymous man in the passenger seat had a gun on his lap. The problem, she mused, with having so many people surround you with guns is that only one needs to be an assassin. Indeed, the perfect cover for an assassin had to be someone working for security; someone with a reason to carry a gun. None of these thoughts made her feel any more relaxed.

After twenty minutes of their journey the driver managed to disable all of the buttons within Hector's reach. Kate was relieved, as it had felt as though she was riding on the inside of a very plush but erratic hair dryer. Hector was growing bored. He had eaten his way through everything he found in the refrigerator, played with every button and control he could reach, and wiped his chocolate covered hands on the immaculate leather interior of the Mercedes. The milk he had spilt was still soaking into the seat.

That was the annoying thing about Hector; he was nearly always happy; very happy! Plus, he looked, as he so often looked; like a labrador that has been thrust into a chocolate and jelly filled fridge only to be pulled out grubby, full, and still eating the last thing he'd managed to get his teeth into.

The motorcade veered right into a winding tree-lined drive. Grass-level lights illuminated the gaps between the trees, revealing an immaculate paper-flat lawn stretching away into the darkness.

As the lights from the château came into view it was apparent to Kate that the French authorities believed that discreet could still be grand. The man in the passenger seat with the gun turned around and spoke for the first time in a thick accent both Kate and Hector found difficult to understand.

'There are guards around the perimeter, but there will only be one person with you,' he explained, 'This will be the security grandmother.'

Kate understood this to mean that the security nanny was already waiting for them. She was, for the first time, impressed with Inspector Smithson's speedy arrangements.

As Hector and Kate got out of the car armed French police peered out into the inky dark of the night, their machine guns at their hips as they tried to look as important and tough as they could. The sirens were no longer blaring but the lights on all of the police cars were still flashing. It made Kate feel anxious. It made Hector feel important, and he grinned as he bounced on the balls of his feet.

'Oh hello dears,' came a very English voice, 'I'm Melinda Warp. I am here to look after you.'

In front of Hector and Kate stood a middle-aged woman. She was slightly plump and only a little taller than Kate.

'Are you the security nanny?' asked Hector, in a tone that exuded disbelief.

'Yes,' smiled Mrs Warp, 'that's right.'

'But I thought you'd be an Olympic athlete, or a Kung Fu expert, or mud wrestling champion or something like that,' Hector blurted out in the same slightly disrespectful tone.

'Well, I'm sure I can do all of those things,' said Mrs Warp, 'but first we have to get you up to bed.'

The thought of bed and sleep after such an intense and exhausting day seemed to sap the little energy remaining in Kate and Hector. As she walked towards the château's doors Kate was surprised to see the motorcade gone. She had not really noticed.

Hector's sleepy attempt to persuade Mrs Warp that he had a special exemption from cleaning his teeth signed by the UK Prime Minister had no effect, as she clearly did not believe a word of it. Nor would she be persuaded that, despite crash-landing a burning plane, he was really quite clean and did not need a shower.

Hector could barely remember the shower, and it was just a few minutes before he was drifting off to sleep in the warm comforting bed. Kate, despite the worries that swam around her head, soon followed Hector. Mrs Warp's kind smile was the last thing both Hector and Kate saw that day.

It was the same kind smile Hector saw in the morning. The curtains were open, the sun streamed in, but best of all there was a breakfast tray. Hector had never been allowed breakfast in bed; this was brilliant! Kate was equally surprised, but not as pleased. The idea of prising Hector from a bed where he had glued himself in with jam was not appealing. Nevertheless, Kate was pleased that her and Hector were in the same bedroom. It was reassuring to see her little brother after the frightening events of yesterday.

'Mrs Warp, when will we see Mum and Dad?' asked Kate.

'Very soon dear,' said Mrs Warp, 'They are going to let your father out tomorrow.'

Kate could see Hector looking to the window. The bright sunshine of a brilliant spring morning might just as well have written in the air 'please explore the château'. With five floors, if you included the cellars, and large grounds, the château was an open invitation neither Kate nor Hector were going to ignore.

Just fifteen minutes later Kate's worst fears were realised, as Hector had managed to get the contents of every little pot of honey, jam, marmalade, margarine and butter onto his face, hands, arms, hair, the bed, the sheets, and even a portion of the wall behind the headrest. As Mrs Warp dragged him out, Kate could even see some jam on one of his feet.

Kate ignored Hector's shouts for help as Mrs Warp made him wash in the shower. Kate went to the window and looked out over the sunlit lawns and paths. She felt her spirits rise.

Once Hector was out of the shower and getting dressed, Kate asked Mrs Warp about the gardens. Mrs Warp began to describe various plants and trees in much more detail than was needed. As Hector struggled with his socks, and Kate's conversation with Mrs Warp continued, Kate sensed something unusual about Mrs Warp. If asked she would not have been able to explain her feeling; it was just a feeling. Mrs Warp was odd.

Kate and Hector's clothes appeared to have been washed and dried in the night. Once they were dressed, Mrs Warp was quite happy for them to explore and enjoy themselves. They started with the cellars, which were a great deal less exciting than they expected. They were full of junk, rubbish and abandoned furniture. One room was locked, and although Hector was excited by the possibility of mystery and adventure, these lively expectations were soon doused by Mrs Warp, who informed them that it was the gardener's room.

They worked their way up the different floors, finding nooks, hidden rooms and grandiose areas for entertainment. There was an air of decay, painted over with a new layer of synthetic hope. It was a monument to an era passed, but a fantastic place for hide and seek.

A short time later Kate was hiding on the second floor. She could hear Hector's taunts as he advanced up the main staircase. The problem, Kate had discovered, was that so many of the rooms were poorly furnished. They were large, but there were very few places in which to hide. Hector's confidence that he had her caught, cornered, and that he was closing in, was justified.

Kate slithered up the banister, trying to press her weight down using her hands so that her feet would not make the floorboards creak. The top floor was much smaller and only had three rooms, but it was her last hope with the advancing, gloating Hector stumping ever upwards.

Kate opened one of the doors, gripping the door handle much more tightly than was necessary, to discover a small cupboard full of coats and old clothes. She quickly buried herself in a smelly pile of discarded curtains.

Kate could feel her heart beating as Hector's heavy tread reached the top floor. It was only Hector, and nowhere near as dangerous as the previous day's events, but it was still thrilling and jangling and breathtaking. It was something of a disappointment to hear Hector's voice exclaim in awe, rather than gloating threat.

'Wow,' said Hector, 'I can see everywhere,' Then he shouted, 'Whatever you do Kate, I can see you.'

Kate did not hesitate. The game was over, Hector had definitely discovered something.

As Kate scrambled out from under the curtains, through the landing and on through the next open door, her jaw dropped as she took in the vast array of television screens, all of which showed different views of every single room in the château.

'This is awesome,' said Hector, whose line in hyperbole was un-rivalled.

Kate, however, was gripped, not by the vast array of television screens, but by the surprising window, which had handles around its side. It was made, not of glass, but of polythene. It flapped gently in the wind. Outside the window Kate could see the beginnings of a huge rope slide.

'Wow,' said Hector, following Kate's gaze, 'let's try it now!'

'I really don't think you should,' said Mrs Warp as she entered the room, 'For one thing, it is far too dangerous, and for another, it is time for lunch.'

'Then why is it here?' asked Hector.

'It is there so anyone can escape if things get tricky. After all, this is not a normal house.' said Mrs Warp, her usual kind smile returning.

Lunch turned out to be a vast selection of salad, meats and fruits. There were supposed to be sausages, but they had been taken, Mrs Warp explained, with a glance to the young man who had appeared at the kitchen door.

The man began to talk in French, and both Kate and Hector were surprised with the apparent ease with which Mrs Warp slipped into what they assumed was fluent French. Mrs Warp turned to Kate and Hector.

'Do you like dogs?' asked Mrs Warp, 'only our gardener has been looking after his uncle's dog. His uncle died two days ago, and no one wants the dog. You could play with it in the grounds this afternoon if you liked.'

'His name is Bandit,' explained the gardener in a thick accent, 'And he is a terrible thief.'

'Does he keep getting caught?' asked Hector.

'No, it's the fact that he keeps stealing things,' explained Mrs Warp, 'and he has just been caught with the sausages that were for lunch.'

A young chocolate brown labrador appeared in the doorway, complete with a permanently happy look.

'Ahh, you are soooo cute,' exclaimed Kate, rushing to cuddle the dog.

This was what Bandit did best. He seduced his victims, stole their food, and then looked cute again so he would be forgiven. It was a constant cycle of looking cute, stealing and eating. Bandit was very good at it. He could already tell that the young female would forgive him easily, while the boy had a sticky look which, at the very least, would mean he would be good to lick.

In the garden that afternoon Bandit was more than fun. He was a runner, a jumper, and great at hide and seek. In fact, he was too good. He just used his nose. Kate noticed that when Hector went to hide while she covered Bandit's eyes, Bandit would follow the exact path Hector had run, even if Hector had gone in zig-zags. Following a scent was just easy for him.

Bandit found other things he was not supposed to find. Hector and Kate did not know that police officers, trained by the French Special Forces, were positioned in the garden in hides dug into the ground. They could not be seen, but Bandit could smell them, and their holes in the ground were his favourite toilets. Every time

Bandit trotted off to the toilet there would be a yell of complaint as a French police officer emerged covered in dog wee.

Some of the French police officers thought the whole thing was very funny, but these were generally not the ones that Bandit had used as a toilet. By late afternoon there was a gathering of police officers on the drive. Some of them wanted to get rid of Bandit, while others still thought the whole thing was funny. Kate and Hector sat with Bandit between them watching. One officer seemed to be claiming that someone had stolen his lunch, and the glances in their direction told Hector and Kate that Bandit was head of the suspect list. To be fair, Kate reflected, Bandit would be at the top of anyone's suspect list.

Bandit was leaning on Kate, and Kate could see that Hector was leaning on Bandit. As Kate watched an exceptionally tall man with a suitcase approach the police officers, it occurred to her that Bandit was with them now, and she rather liked the idea. Bandit was probably not much use in a tight spot, but if they were murdered by an assassin Bandit would probably make sure the assassin went without lunch.

The tall man was now walking towards them, removing his hat.

'So this is the Hound of the Baskervilles?' he asked, smiling, 'My name is Gary Rhodes,' he continued in an Australian accent, 'and I'm here to provide some information.'

'Are you a police officer as well?' Kate asked.

'No, no, well not really. I work for the Australian Government. I need to talk to you inside.'

A short time later they were in the kitchen with Mrs Warp, Gary Rhodes and, strangely, the gardener. Kate and Hector began to suspect that he was really a police officer as well.

Gary Rhodes explained that he had already seen Kate and Hector's parents. He had news; there was an Australian assassin, known commonly as Sludge, on their trail.

'We think he was in England on his way to you there, as he can't travel on normal aircraft flights,' said Gary.

In answer to Hector's unspoken question, Gary produced a photograph of a short, stumpy man with a misshapen face and no hair.

'He is too easy to identify, and far too large.'

'He looks tiny,' exclaimed Hector.

'Yeah,' replied Gary, 'he looks tiny in the photograph. He is really six and a half feet tall, but very broad, which is why he looks small in pictures. He is incredibly tough, strong, tenacious...well terrifying actually.'

'He looks like a troll,' said Kate as she took the photograph from Hector.

'Yes, and he's about as bright as one. He grew up in Australia's toughest institutions for young offenders, where he terrified the staff. He left aged thirteen when he stole a car belonging to the head of security. They were rather pleased, as he had taken to thumping holes in the walls and had began to experiment on the main beams supporting the building. He's about thirty-two now, and has survived five shootings by various police forces around the world.'

'What?' exclaimed Kate, 'He's like a vampire; he can't be killed.'

'No, no,' said Gary reassuringly, 'He's been lucky in part, but he is also very tough.'

'If he is that large, and he looks like a camel's bottom, why haven't you caught him yet?' asked Hector.

'We have, several times,' said Gary. 'The police in Singapore caught him first. If you include the seven with life-threatening injuries, twenty-nine officers managed to wrestle him into a police van. Not the largest coppers, but very brave. They were exhausted, but then had to watch while Sludge just punched a hole in the side of the van and ran off.'

'We, that is the Australians, caught him when he was foolish enough to catch a scheduled flight home on a fake passport. In fact, you might like to see the passport.'

A photocopied sheet was pushed towards Kate and Hector showing a lopsided figure with long hair and a frilly hat. The passport was in the name of Mrs Hemingway. Both Hector and Kate laughed.

'Yeah, stupid wasn't it,' said Rhodes, 'and Sludge is stupid most of the time, but don't underestimate him. I tell you, Quantas don't want to see Sludge again. We surrounded the plane with troops, all with machine guns. He came quietly, but broke out that night. The usual subtle approach, straight through the wall. Some idiot decided that Sludge would break a normal wooden bed, and so they gave him a steel, reinforced bed that he couldn't break. Well, we happen to think that Sludge was strong enough to break that bed as well. He didn't try to break it, however, not when a steel, reinforced bed makes such a good battering ram. The armed guards got there just as he broke through the wall. He threw the bed at them and then some of the rubble from the wall he'd just demolished. Some of the bricks he threw went so fast they took out part of the next wall. Sludge ran in among the guards, knocked them out, and for good measure, bent their guns.'

'Clever,' the gardener muttered in his thick accent.

'Why is that clever?' asked Kate.

Mrs Warp explained, 'Well, by running in among the guards it made it difficult for them to shoot him. They could not shoot without possibly shooting one of their colleagues.'

Mrs Warp then turned to Gary Rhodes, 'How close is he?'

'He's here. He got a small boat from England. The boat owner asked him to pull it onto the beach, but Sludge misunderstood and pulled it eighty metres inland. You can see his footprints. He stole a car and drove down across France. Sludge is a dreadful driver, and stole a different car after each of the six accidents he had. As far as we can tell, he's been joined by a Chinese gentleman called Mr Tick. We think Mr Tick is supposed to increase the team's average IQ, but adding a senile sheep would do that.'

Gary Rhodes did not stop for tea. It was as if he was eager to get away; aware that they were already doomed; reluctant to have the opportunity to get to know and possibly like them.

Tea was a somber affair. Kate had hidden behind a door and listened to Gary Rhodes briefing a senior French officer. He kept emphasising how fast and strong Sludge was. He was trying to impress upon the man just how many people Sludge had killed, and that while he was undoubtedly dim, he could be resourceful in a fight. The French officer, however, dismissed a good deal of what Gary Rhodes told him. The Frenchman was either well-prepared or surprisingly complacent.

Things turned ugly when Gary Rhodes suggested that there was a spy in the French police, and that not everybody in the French force could be trusted. Kate had eaten her tea in silence, trying to digest more than the iced buns.

Once alone with Hector, Kate explained everything she had heard. Hector, as usual, seemed quite unperturbed.

'I expect we'll have to fight Sludge,' he said casually.

'Hector, he'll murder us in an instant. And, there is a spy. Someone on the French side could be helping Sludge.'

'Yes, I think it's Mrs Warp,' said Hector, 'She has a gun, some explosives and a box marked piano tuning kit in her handbag,' He then added in his most casual tone, 'I should think she was too closely watched last night, and tonight will be the night she does us in.'

'Hector, how could you think that, she's been really nice. She's looked after us, and made nice meals, and just been nice,' Kate trailed off.

Hector was looking smug. He was miming shooting and blowing up.

'Oh no Hector, what are we going to do?' Kate whimpered as a feeling of hopelessness engulfed her.

'Nothing,' said Hector, 'I've already done it. I've nicked the bomb and the gun and hidden them under your bed.'

'Why my bed?' exclaimed Kate.

'Well, I didn't want the blame if they're found,' explained Hector, as if it was the most reasonable thing in the world.

Hector began to act rather strangely at bedtime. He cleaned his teeth and had a shower without an complaint.

'You're not a French boy pretending to be Hector are you?' asked Kate.

'You'll see,' replied Hector in an undertone.

After Mrs Warp left them Hector triumphantly revealed that he had managed to smuggle Bandit up to their room. He also had a spade and axe he had taken from somewhere downstairs. Kate sat on the floor, and she and Hector cuddled Bandit, who sat passively, but apparently happy, between them.

'We'll see Mum and Dad tomorrow,' said Hector, and Kate smiled, feeling reassured for the first time.

'I don't want the excitement to stop.' Hector confessed.

'You just think we'll survive and everything will turn out right,' Kate observed.

'Yep!' said Hector.

They sat in silence for a while, before turning to a discussion of what to do tomorrow. Hector was convinced there would be hidden tunnels. He was sure Bandit could sniff them out. Kate was beginning to laugh. There was something infectious about Hector's wild and utterly unrealistic optimism.

Eventually, Bandit settled down in the gap between the beds. Hector and Kate climbed between the crisp, clean sheets. It appeared as though their beds had been changed. Kate believed this was down to Hector's disastrous breakfast in bed.

Their sleepy talk soon turned to conspiracy. Kate and Hector were for once agreed; they should keep Bandit. Hector had a range of thoughts on how Mum and Dad could be manipulated, deceived and emotionally blackmailed.

Hector's favourite plan was to convince Dad that he should take up clay pigeon shooting. They should then claim Bandit was a highly trained gun dog. Kate pointed out that gun dogs were for retrieving birds that had been shot, and clay pigeon shooting did not involve shooting real birds.

Kate favoured emotional blackmail. She believed they should emphasise the shock and fear the attack on the plane had caused, following on from the bomb attack on Dad's car. Bandit was a source of security, and if Mum and Dad did not want them to grow up emotionally scarred they should allow them to keep this source of warmth and hope.

Hector privately thought it was the best plan, but could not agree on the grounds that his sister had thought of it. He suggested variations on his ideas as he and Kate spoke in the darkness, over

Bandit's increasingly loud snores. Neither he nor Kate could recall slipping off into a deep sleep.

There was a shot from the grounds. Kate woke first, wondering whether she had imagined the sound. It was dark and silent as Kate looked around for a clock. There were more shots and these woke Hector. Kate and Hector looked at each other through the gloom of the darkened bedroom, and then got out of bed and ran to the window.

There was shouting in French and then two bursts of automatic gunfire. After this there was an eerie silence that seemed to last for minutes, but only lasted seconds. Then there was frantic shouting followed by three explosions.

A huge squat figure was running across the furthest lawn towards the house. Sludge had broken through. He was coming to kill them.

Beneath them another figure had emerged from the house. The gardener was running towards Sludge, clearly aiming a gun. Sludge saw him, dived to his left, rolled and shot. The gardener slumped to the ground.

Next, Mrs Warp ran across the lawn. She had a strange sort of run, like someone who has had running explained to them, and even seen diagrams, but never actually practised it. Sludge fired twice, but he must have missed because Mrs Warp did not stop. Mrs Warp then pulled something from her pocket and threw it towards Sludge. Sludge could be seen to half-grab it, push it away, and then scurry around the other side of the fountain in the centre of the lawn. The brief flash from the hand-grenade Mrs Warp had thrown showed that she had adjusted her direction and was now heading towards the fountain. Sludge rolled around the edge of the fountain and fired a volley of shots, none of which hit Mrs Warp.

Sludge launched himself across the fountain, and was clearly surprised, judging by his yell, to be hit hard by Mrs Warp. They fell, thrashing into the water of the fountain. Mrs Warp hit Sludge again and again, while Sludge replied with blows of his own.

'She's amazing, how does she do that?' Hector asked in awe.

'I think it's because she's not fighting Sludge, as Sludge would beat her in a fight,' said Kate in a tone of horrible realisation. 'I think the French have repelled Sludge but been betrayed, and that man she is fighting is trying to save us from her; he's trying to save us from Mrs Warp.'

'Oops,' said Hector, 'let's go downstairs, but take the gun.'

A short time later they were downstairs. Kate and Hector had quickly dressed. Kate had the gun tucked into her shorts. Hector had unwisely hidden the bomb in his underpants. Bandit had followed them down, hoping to join in the fun. As expected, Mrs Warp was already back in the kitchen.

'Everything's all right dears. I think that Mrs Sludge has left us alone for the moment.'

'You didn't kill him then?' asked Hector.

'No, I tried, but she's, he's, she's, he's, surprisingly strong,' said Mrs Warp in her usual, calm, pleasant tone.

'Now, let's have you two off to bed,' she added, smiling reassuringly.

'Shouldn't we get help for the people that have been hurt?' Kate asked.

'Is Burt hurt, Burt hurt, Burt hurt?' Mrs Warp asked.

'Sorry,' said Kate, confused. 'I don't know who Bert is?'

'There is no Burt here, ear, bear, fear, vinegar,' said Mrs Warp, shuddering slightly.

Kate noticed a fizz and a crackle, and then Hector tugged at her arm and was pointing to Mrs Warp's legs.

They had holes in them, and lower holes had water seeping out.

'She's a cyborg,' yelled Hector, just as Mrs Warp lent forwards, gripped the kitchen table and crushed the thick wood to splinters.

Kate saw Hector dash around the kitchen and open a small door.

'Hector, what are you doing, run!' yelled Kate.

There was a burst of machine gun fire as Mrs Warp's chest opened to reveal two barrels with flame flying from each one. Mrs Warp reached for the fridge to steady herself and pulled it to the ground. As the fridge contents rolled to the floor Bandit took his chance, and threw himself head-first into the food.

Kate and Hector ran for the stairs, and scrambled up. At the first landing Kate paused to turn and look. Hector hit her hard in the side with a half-shove, half-rugby tackle.

'Keep going, keep going,' he yelled.

It was lucky they did keep going, as moments later a volley of machine-gun fire ripped through the place they had been standing. Mrs Warp was staggering about firing. Most of the bullets were exploding into the staircase, sending wood splitters flying everywhere. Mrs Warp's right arm began revolving wildly, making it difficult for her to keep her balance, there were sparks coming out of her neck, and a small fire had started near her bottom. Mrs Warp was definitely not human.

Kate stood transfixed as Mrs Warp advanced towards the stairs still firing. As her foot reached the first step she stopped firing and spoke. She still had the same smiling face, but her voice was very different; she sounded like a robot with a cheap speech synthesiser.

'Would you like a cup of hot chocolate, is that why you came downstairs?' asked Mrs Warp.

'Go away,' yelled Kate, just as she noticed that Hector was missing.

Mrs Warp began to advance unsteadily up the stairs. They were creaking and groaning, which was not surprising given that most of the top step had been shot away by the machine guns in Mrs Warp's chest.

'This will do the trick,' yelled Hector, appearing suddenly with the axe he had taken earlier.

Hector began to chop at the tattered top step. The creaking grew louder, and as Mrs Warp was just four steps from the top, the whole staircase gave way. Mrs Warp fell, briefly. Her hand caught the edge of the landing as she fell, and amazingly she held on to the rest of the staircase with her other hand.

Hector advanced with the axe.

'Don't do that,' said Mrs Warp, in her robot voice, 'I want to tuck you in.'

'Rip our limbs off more like,' said Hector, as he raised the axe once more.

'No Hector,' yelled Kate, 'You can't cut nanny's hand off.'

'She's not a nanny; she's a murdering robot on a mission to kill us!' Hector exclaimed.

Mrs Warp smiled and looked from Kate to Hector. Kate was momentarily lost in thought.

'Fair point,' said Kate, 'Get on with it.'

It took quite a bit of chopping to remove Mrs Warp from the landing, but her hand finally came loose and she and the stairs fell. As if to underline her robot credentials, Mrs Warp never once cried out or complained. When she hit the ground she picked herself up and muttered something in her robot voice about making hot chocolate. She fizzed, crackled and disappeared into the kitchen with her bottom still on fire.

Hector and Kate slumped onto the floor of the landing. Only now did the question of what to do next hit them. They were stuck in a French château with no way down from the first floor, and a mad murdering robot was making them hot chocolate.

'What about the servant's stairs?' asked Hector, 'Really big houses like this have servant stairs, don't they.'

'No, not here, I think they must have removed them, probably security,' Kate answered. Kate buried her head in her hands.

'Oh no Hector, what are we going to do?'

'It'll be all right,' said Hector, 'we seem to have been given a sporting chance.'

'Oh yes,' replied Kate sarcastically, 'a mad robot that intends to give us hot chocolate and then murder us, and just in case we escape another madman is on our trail who can thump holes in prison walls. Very sporting!'

'Why don't we shoot her?' asked Hector.

'Have you seen the number of holes in her already, and they have made no difference,' said Kate, despondently.

'No,' said Hector, 'but water might. How about you shoot her and I'll use the fire extinguisher.'

'OK,' said Kate, 'but watch out for the machine guns in her chest.'

'I think she's out of ammunition,' said Hector with a shrug, 'She shot loads and loads..,' Hector stopped as Mrs Warp appeared once more.

Mrs Warp's bottom was no longer alight, but she seemed to be fizzing and crackling more than before.

'I have put the milk in the microwave dears,' said Mrs Warp in her robot voice. 'I will climb the outside of the building and find some sheets you can use to climb down.'

Mrs Warp disappeared into the night, and Kate and Hector raced upstairs to stop her getting through any of the windows. They ran from room to room to see where she was attempting to climb.

'Hang on,' said Hector, 'she can't climb, she only has one hand.'

'Oh yes she can,' said Kate, who was looking out of one of the windows.

Hector joined her, and to his horror saw that Mrs Warp was climbing the building using just one hand. One finger would dig into the corner of the building then another finger would extend further and get a higher grip. Mrs Warp's hand was anything but normal. The whole thing looked bizarre and revolting. Mrs Warp was moving slowly but inexorably up the outside of the château.

'Shoot her Kate,' yelled Hector, as he rushed to find a fire extinguisher.

When Hector returned Kate had emptied every bullet into Mrs Warp, whose eyes were now flashing red and blue.

'Good shooting dear,' said Mrs Warp in a robot voice.

Hector aimed the fire extinguisher and emptied it all over Mrs Warp.

'Oh dear, these cardigans never fall back into shape once they've been soaked,' said Mrs Warp, in the same robot tone.

Hector stepped back, convinced that nothing would stop Mrs Warp. Kate flashed past just as Mrs Warp reached the window, and hit her hard on the head with the blunt side of the axe. Mrs Warp wobbled and more sparks flew out. Kate hit her again and again.

Suddenly there was a whir and a slump as Mrs Warp's lights went out.

'Thank goodness,' groaned Kate as she sat on the floor. 'If she comes back to life we'll use the bomb.'

'We can't,' said Hector, 'I put it in that time safe.'

'Time safe?' questioned Kate, 'What time safe?'

'The one in the kitchen,' replied Hector, 'I put the bomb in and selected the time I wanted it to be kept safe.'

'There isn't a time safe,' said Kate.

'Yes there is,' retorted Hector, 'between the fridge and the chopping board.'

'Hector, you idiot, that's the microwave. You put the bomb in the microwave,' said Kate with incredulity.

'Well it's not my fault, it didn't look like a microwave; it didn't have a Start button,' explained Hector.

'That's because it's in French. Are you sure you didn't start it?' asked Kate.

'Sure, but Mrs Warp did for the hot chocolate,' said Hector slowly.

'Oh no!' wailed Kate, 'we're trapped!'

'We'll be OK,' said Hector confidently, 'Most explosives will not go off in a microwave.'

'How do you know this?'

'I looked it up on Google. All the boys at school know what will explode in a microwave. C4, the plastic explosive, is really safe.'

'Are you sure?' Kate asked, her confidence returning.

There was a bang from downstairs as the microwave exploded.

'What was that?' Kate asked.

'I think it was the microwave exploding,' replied Hector, 'but it was only a small explosion.'

There was another bang and then a rushing noise. Kate turned to glare at Hector.

'It's started a fire, hasn't it?'

'Let's go and have a look,' Hector suggested.

'Are you a complete idiot? What sort of person advances towards the flames when things are exploding?' Kate declared rather than asking, as there were more bangs and the roar from the rapidly spreading fire began to grow.

'The rope slide!' bellowed Hector, as they both rushed for the top floor.

Once they had burst into the room on the top floor they discovered several sliders. Hector and Kate took one each and pushed off. It was strange after the panicked rush to the slide to be drifting through the quiet night making hardly a sound. Good rope slides are kept slightly loose so that the person using it naturally slows down near the end of the rope. Kate and Hector were surprised to find themselves slowing down high above the ground. Before they knew it they had landed on a platform high in a very large tree. Two surprised French policemen were asking them questions in French.

'Something's gone wrong,' Kate explained.

'Are you sure?' asked one of the policemen in a thick accent.

'Yes,' said Hector, 'Mrs Warp, but we've fixed it.'

'Fixed it?' questioned the police officer, just as the fire in the château exploded through its windows.

The police officers looked at the château in horror, and then one of them began talking into his radio. The other policeman began hooking Kate up to a harness looped over another rope slide.

'Bandit,' shouted Hector, pointing to the ground.

There he was, trotting happily along, seemingly unperturbed by the ball of flame the château had become. Kate watched him as she was pushed off, down the second rope slide.

Once Kate reached the end of the slide she could see several police officers, some with machine guns. Surprisingly, Inspector Smithson was there, along with another man, who appeared to be in charge.

'I am Inspector Mason. Where is Mrs Warp?' asked the man in a French accent.

'In the château, but there is something you should know,' stuttered Kate, 'She's a robot. She tried to kill us.'

'Impossible,' said Inspector Mason, 'She would only protect you. She is programmed only to help. She is the finest example of French engineering. But, if she is lost, destroyed...it would be tragic. Are you sure?'

'Yes,' said Kate, 'I think she was just outside the château when it exploded, when the fire burst out.'

'Then she may have escaped,' said the French Inspector.

'She went rather wrong. She started firing the machine guns in her chest,' Kate tried to explain.

'Ahhh, but she is worth millions of Euros, there will be hell to pay if she is lost. We must pray she has not been too badly damaged,' said the French Inspector shaking his head.

They all turned to look at the burning château.

'This was our best safe house. It cost many millions, and it has been destroyed. How did it happen?' the Inspector continued.

'I don't know,' said Kate, keen to minimise her role in the carnage.

They all stood in silence in the still night, with only the crackling of the château as it burned, the orange glow spreading out over the lawns to meet the blue flashes of the police cars on the perimeter.

Bandit arrived and sat next to Kate, just as Hector slid down the rope slide.

'Hello,' said Hector, in his usual cheerful tone, 'Don't worry about Mrs Warp, she was a mad robot assassin, but we did her in eventually.'

There was silence. Hector noticed that the man who seemed to be in charge was staring at him in an unfriendly way.

'Did her in? Did her in? You destroyed Mrs Warp!' yelled the French Inspector.

'It wasn't easy,' Hector declared.

In the stunned silence that followed Hector decided the Inspector needed an explanation.

'Well, Mrs Warp already had some holes and water in her, I saw it leaking out. I chopped off her hand with an axe when she was clinging on to the landing. Kate shot her when she was climbing up the building and I sprayed more water into her using a fire extinguisher, and then Kate sort of finished her off by hitting her on the head with the blunt part of the axe.'

'That was an accident,' Kate said weakly.

'Yes, she meant to use the sharp end,' Hector added in an attempt to be helpful.

Inspector Smithson had started to wave frantically behind Inspector Mason's back, trying to tell Hector to shut up. Hector completely misunderstood this, and carried on.

'The château caught fire because I put a bomb I found into the microwave in the kitchen,' Hector explained.

'You put a bomb in the microwave?' asked the French Inspector, in a constricted voice.

'I found it, but I thought the microwave was a digital safe, and I was trying to stop old Warty Warp getting it,' said Hector.

'Old Warty Warp,' shouted the Inspector, 'was trying to protect you! She was on our side! You hooligans! You vandals.'

'Now, I understand you're upset,' said Inspector Smithson, 'but I am sure Kate and Hector were doing their best. They need our help and protection.'

'Protection!' retorted Inspector Mason, 'Maybe you could persuade Sludge to protect them; he'll be dead before sunset. Who is more dangerous, Sludge or these two hooligans? They've managed to burn down our top safe house and destroy an indestructible robot, who was incredibly expensive and highly sophisticated. Mrs Warp was almost perfect, the secret engineering pride of France, and your hooligans finished her off with an axe?'

'They are two young children who need a good night's sleep and our help,' said Inspector Smithson in a measured tone.

Inspector Mason stormed off.

'Don't worry,' said Inspector Smithson, 'I'll sort something out.'

CHAPTER THREE

The Camp

Kate, Hector and Bandit were escorted to a police van by two grim-faced police men. From the look of it the van was used for moving prisoners. It soon set off, and judging by the flashing blue lights, they had an escort of police cars ahead and behind them. Kate found a small window, and gazed with disbelief at the burning château, as the movement of the van brought various policemen and women into silhouette against the roaring flames that were tearing the château apart.

At one point she thought she could see Inspector Mason ranting at Inspector Smithson. Everything seemed to have made him angry; the burning of the château, the destruction of Mrs Warp, and lastly Bandit's attempt to wee on him just before they left. Bandit had simply trotted up happily, lifted a leg and urinated. Inspector Mason had jumped back amazingly quickly, and then began shouting in French.

Kate was pleased that Bandit was with them, despite the trouble he had caused, and soon Hector was also cuddling their new dog. His insouciance was calming. Kate was feeling shaky. She found it hard to keep back the tears, while even Hector's cast-iron belief that everything would turn out alright had several Sludge-sized dents in it.

Bandit, on the other hand, was feeling a mixture of contentment and excitement. He was content because he had two admiring young humans who were cuddling him as if he was the most important thing on earth. He was excited because he suspected the van might be taking them towards food, and possibly even a warm fire; although hopefully not as warm as the château.

The journey continued into the night, made seemingly longer by the absence of any information about where they were going or how long it would take. After an hour Hector had drifted off to sleep, his head laid on a snoring Bandit. Kate, on the other hand, found it difficult to sleep. She kept turning over in her mind just two ideas. The first was that it was difficult to tell friend from foe. She had assumed the pilot on their chartered plane was helping them, and yet he turned out to be an enemy. Likewise, her and Hector had believed Mrs Warp to be another assassin, and yet she had been there to protect them.

The second persistent thought that bothered Kate was that they had narrowly escaped death twice in the space of just two days. If this carried on then, at some point, they would not be lucky; things would not turn out just right. An enemy who could not be stopped and would not give up would eventually succeed. She felt waves of hopelessness wash over her, just as they had when their plane was almost shot down. She cuddled Bandit just a little bit harder, and was rewarded with a soft hiss as Bandit passed wind.

Suddenly, the van braked hard, lurched left and then right, and continued at a slower pace. Kate looked out of the thick glass of the window and saw soldiers and armoured vehicles. When the van came to a halt it was a soldier who opened the door and addressed her as mademoiselle.

Moments later another soldier introduced himself as the commanding officer, Colonel Bertrand. In polished English, he explained that they were now in his care. It was apparent that this new responsibility was troublesome and unwelcome for him, but this man prided himself as a gentleman, and manners dictated that he should be hospitable. He explained, as kindly as he could, that they would be guarded in the prison block, and that this was because it was as hard to break in as it was to break out.

Colonel Bertrand had earlier given orders that the children were to be separated from the dog they had picked up, but the father in him, faced with Kate's tears, and Hector's defiant stare, could not see it through. They were, after all, two frightened children, away from their parents and being pursued by a fearsome killer. Finally, it was the soldier in him that issued the discreet and slightly unofficial order that Sludge should be shot on sight. A gun-battle could be faked after the event if need be.

Kate and Hector's cell had been hastily improved with some pictures, plush bedding and a jug of water. The door to their cell remained open, but it was still a night in the cells. Outside their cell were two soldiers with machine guns.

Their sleep was further delayed by the arrival of a small man wearing a raincoat and a short, oddly-styled beard. He insisted that they tell him about everything that happened to Mrs Warp. He was quite kind to begin with, but as he heard more Kate sensed that he was angry with them. It had already dawned on her that this man was probably one of the people who had built Mrs Warp. She started to describe the various injuries to Mrs Warp as accidents, but Hector interceded and unhelpfully provided all of the details about how they had chopped her hand off, shot her, filled her with water and then smashed her head in using the blunt side of an axe. The man left muttering to himself, although Kate noticed that the two soldiers were laughing.

Hector thought that the two soldiers were probably special forces, and Kate suspected he was right about this. They did not look quite as neat as the other soldiers, and unlike the French police, they made no effort to appear tough. It was as if they had no need to show off or pose; they knew what they were. The other surprise was that they both spoke good English. The taller one introduced himself as Andrè, while the smaller soldier was called Pierre.

'Can I go to the toilet please?' asked Hector.

'Well, that all depends,' said Pierre, 'Are you going to blow it up, set fire to it, or use it properly?'

Hector laughed, 'That wasn't my fault. The château just caught fire.'

'You need to understand,' said Andrè, 'that we are here to protect France from you. And by the way, châteaux in France do not just burn down.'

'Unless,' said Pierre, 'you take the bomb you've hidden in your pants, place it in the microwave oven and turn the oven on.'

'OK, then they will catch fire,' said Andrè.

'I think we should let him go to the bathroom Andrè,' said Pierre, 'He does not look like he has a bomb in his pants this time, and there is always a chance that the dog is not the only one in this dangerous group who uses people's legs as toilets.'

'I've not done a wee on anyone,' declared Hector laughing.

'Stay back,' yelled Pierre as Hector approached, 'I know how dangerous you are.'

It was obvious to Kate that Pierre and Andrè had been well briefed, and their natural confidence made her feel safer. As Kate settled down to sleep the noises from the camp drifted through the window, intermingled with the occasional sound of Andrè or Pierre speaking into their radio microphones.

There were snatches of conversation from outside their window; footsteps; the occasional distant sound of cars and lorries being driven; doors being opened and closed. It was the scrape, grumble and grind of a place that never truly sleeps. Kate found it an un-welcome intrusion into uneasy dreams.

'Great' was the first thing Kate heard when she woke in the morn-ing. Hector was bouncing around the cell, while Pierre and Andrè looked on, tired but amused.

'We can explore this French Army camp,' said Hector, 'I bet they'll let me drive a tank if I turn the charm on. Bang, bang, bang, boom! I could fire the gun!'

'Now I can see why we have to guard him,' said Pierre.

A short time later Andrè and Pierre said goodbye, to be replaced by two more soldiers. They were escorted to a bathroom in another building with a shower. They were given clothes donated by fami-lies living in the camp.

Kate and Hector were returned to their cell for breakfast, which was brought to them by a man with a facial twitch. Hector sus-pected he was a prison guard, as he clearly had difficulty with the notion that he should be nice to anyone in a cell. The idea that they should have a dog caused him further anguish. He kept shouting two or three angry words in French, before reverting to a much softer and politer voice. It all made no difference, as neither Kate nor Hector understood a word. Bandit, on the other hand, may have understood more.

Kate and Hector were just tucking into a very welcome breakfast of breads and cold meats when there was a shout. The guard jumped back and began to yell in French. Bandit had tried to wee on the man's leg. Hector was beginning to see a pattern. If Bandit did not like someone he approached wagging his tail, and then urinated on their legs. When the shouting started he would run a short distance and then deploy the giant brown eyes and slightly regretful face, before bouncing on to his next target, which was usually food.

Sure enough, Bandit sat at his feet, waiting for an accident with the breakfast tray. Hector, it seemed, was his current best bet. Bandit's judgement was flawless, as just a minute later there was a shout as a man ran into the cell, causing Hector to tip the tray just as Bandit hoped he would.

'You come, you come quickly. Vite, vite!' shouted the man.

Kate and Hector did as they were told and ran to follow the man. They were taken across the camp to an office where Colonel Bertrand was talking to someone on the phone. Both Kate and Hector were quickly informed that this was someone very important from Paris who wanted to speak to them. The phone was put onto speakerphone, and a man with a near-perfect English accent addressed the room.

'Your safety is very important to us. In France the rule of law is paramount. We do not tolerate assassins and killers, and we will make any dispute involving the dark forces of the criminal underworld our battle. It is for the love of our heritage, our traditions, and the love of France that leads us to this bold and brave position. We will not fail you, the innocent, no matter where you come from, and no matter who you face. Only in France..,' the voice continued.

Kate could see another man in the room reflected through a mirror. He was looking at Colonel Bertrand and rolling his eyes, while Colonel Bertrand quietly shrugged his shoulders in a manner that suggested weary resignation. Kate began to see why, as the speech just went on and on.

'How long?' whispered Hector.

'I don't know,' whispered Kate in reply.

'How long?' asked Hector again more loudly, causing Colonel Bertrand to silently indicate that he should remain quiet.

A short while later the experienced father in Colonel Bertrand had seen the danger; there was almost no chance of Hector remaining silent. Colonel Bertrand was looking frantically at the other adults in the room; their various military ranks seemed to dissolve as the collective problem built.

It was one of their special forces guards who lent forward to look at the phone, and pressed the mute button. The Colonel then had his own idea, and pointed Hector towards another part of the rambling room that contained a large tropical aquarium. Hector was immediately transfixed and moved towards the brightly coloured fish as if dragged by gravity. Kate was not so fortunate, as Colonel Bertrand made it clear that she was to stay by the telephone in case she was needed.

While Hector studied the fish in the tank, the Colonel would occasionally press the Mute button on the telephone and utter a few words of agreement, before pressing the button again so that the important person in Paris could not hear them. Hector returned to the Colonel holding a large black plastic screw, only to be waved away imperiously by the same man that had fetched them to the Colonel's office just a few minutes earlier.

'But it came off,' said Hector, 'and it's very wet.'

The Colonel gave a stifled yell as he realised what Hector held in his hand. The pool of water spreading throughout the office was obviously coming from the aquarium. The Colonel silently grabbed the plug from Hector, dashed towards the aquarium and began trying to stem the flow of water. The plug would not fit back in, and soon everyone in the room was trying to either stop the water from leaving the aquarium, add more water to the aquarium, or catch the fish using the small net so they could be saved in a bucket.

Hector moved back to the desk to join Kate, as it seemed like the best place to watch the crisis unfold. One man was bitten by a small fish, while another seemed to have a spine embedded in his hands. The splash of water, the yells, and Colonel Bertrand's frantic instructions as they all tried to save his prized fish collection, drowned out the never-ending speech emanating from the telephone.

Just when Colonel Bertrand thought the situation could not get any worse he saw movement out of the corner of his eye. He turned and watched, in what seemed like slow motion, to see Hector lean forwards and release the mute button on the telephone.

'Could you stop a minute please?' yelled Hector, 'Colonel Bertrand is fighting a shark.'

'No, no, no,' said the very important man from Paris over the speakerphone. 'I think you may be mistaken. The Colonel is a very brave man, but he does not fight sharks. You must be Hector, is that so?'

'Yes, I am,' spluttered Hector as he raced to explain. 'But the Colonel is fighting a shark. It's a small shark in his aquarium. You see the plug came off in my hand and all of the water began to spill out. So the Colonel and his men pressed this button on the phone so you wouldn't be bothered as they tried to rescue the fish. But it's getting so noisy in here that there's really not much point in you just droning on and on because the Colonel and his men aren't listening.'

There was a moment of stunned silence before Colonel Bertrand gathered his wits.

'Gosh,' said Colonel Bertrand, 'what an amazing imagination you have Hector. It's wonderful that you can be so creative after your frightening experiences of the last two days.'

Suddenly, there was a crash as the sides of the aquarium broke under the weight of a soldier leaning in while trying to catch the fish. A wave of water sloshed into the office. The Colonel dived forward, and urged his men to catch the fish floundering on the floor.

'What was that?' asked the voice on the phone.

'It was the sound of the aquarium breaking,' said Hector.

There was a yell and a crash.

'That was a man treading on the fish and slipping,' said Hector keen to keep up his commentary.

Then there was a blue flash and a terrific short explosion.

'That big bang was something electrical getting ruined by all of the water in here,' said Hector unhelpfully as the Colonel let out a muffled yell of frustration. 'And that's the Bertrand getting angry.'

The next silence was longer than the last. Eventually, the man from Paris spoke in a new icy tone.

'It seems that Hector's imagination is not quite as productive as you make out Colonel. You are supposed to be looking after these children, not tending your office ornaments.'

'I'm bored,' said Hector,' I'd like to ride in a tank, and I'd like to go to a cake shop with my dog Bandit. Is there a zoo near here?'

'What a good idea,' said the man from Paris, evidently still annoyed. 'Bertrand, take the boy, the girl and their dog to a patisserie in a tank, and let him drive where it's safe. Then, take them to the zoo.'

'But it may not be safe,' objected Colonel Bertrand.

'You are a soldier Bertrand, or are you an office cleaner? Make sure it's safe,' said the man from Paris ending the call.

The finality of the click as the phone line went dead seemed to stop everything in the office, with the possible exception of the dripping water. Colonel Bertrand looked around at the chaos, while everyone else in the room looked at the Colonel.

Some time later Kate and Hector were playing happily on the swings not far from Colonel Bertrand's office. It seemed strange to Kate that soldiers would want swings, slides, see-saws and a small play fort in their barracks. Later she saw children and mothers, and guessed that the soldiers' families stayed at the camp.

Yet, they were the only ones playing. Kate noticed several children gesturing towards the play area, but their mothers shook their heads and took their hands to guide them away. It was as if Kate and Hector were indecent; somehow infected with danger.

While Hector had already forgotten about the damage and chaos he had brought to Colonel Bertrand's office, and was simply enjoying the swings, Kate found herself confused. On one hand it sounded like an exciting day ahead of them. On the other, Hector had once again broken things, moaned, and got exactly what he wanted. There was something very annoying about that.

In addition, the Colonel's concerns about their safety seemed genuine. She suspected that the self important man from Paris had ignored the Colonel simply because he was angry with him.

On top of all of this they still had not seen Mum and Dad. Just thinking about the last time she saw them moved Kate close to tears. She was worried about Dad; maybe his injuries were worse than she and Hector had been told. Kate wanted to cry and hold Mum. Most of all, she wanted to be with them; to be safe. Of course, she knew rationally that they were safer with the French police and special forces, and yet Mum and Dad and home was all she really wanted.

Kate wished she and Hector had never inherited the money. She wished Irvine Deeds was not related to them. She wished she could give the money to the horrible people who were trying to kill them. She wished she was in school doing something trivial, such as thinking of a way to get Hector to agree to watch the film she wanted to see tonight, rather than something involving cars or planes.

An odd thought then struck Kate. She realised that she did not know how much money she and Hector had inherited. All she knew was that it was more than a million pounds. However, from Inspector Smithson's comments it sounded like it was much more than just one million. Maybe if they publicly gave it all to charity they would be safe; maybe their mad, distant relatives would call off the assassins.

Her thoughts were interrupted by a yell from Hector and the sound of a large engine. The sun shone and the wind blew the clouds into dazzling swirling patterns, but all were eclipsed by the arrival of the tank. It had metal tracks, a turret and a gun. If it was possible to die of happiness then Hector was in mortal danger. Hector's heaven on earth was definitely on track.

Just a minute or two later Kate discovered that the surprising thing about the tank was that it was very small and cramped inside, especially compared to how large it was on the outside. In addition, it seemed to have all manner of sharp corners, edges and protruding stalks from which small but painful injuries could be received.

Kate did not want to admit it, but she was quite excited by the idea of a ride in a tank. Her surprise and delight grew more when she was invited to be the first to drive it.

'Great,' shouted Hector,' I can fire the gun. Bang, Pow, take that, Bang.'

'Who can we shoot? Who can we shoot?' Hector continued as he bounced up and down.

The soldier who had helped them into the tank explained in impressively clear English that they were going to the firing range first, and then they would go to the cake shop in an armoured car. After the cakes they could go to the zoo. However, the Colonel had ruled out any chance that Kate or Hector might be allowed to drive on the roads, and the firing range was to make up for that.

As they made their way out of the camp the rumble and grind of the engine and tracks made everything else recede into the background. Kate was surprised to find she was allowed to drive. Of course, she had been told that she would get to drive the tank, but the confidence the soldier showed in her, allowing her to drive along the narrow roads of the camp, was still something of a revelation. Nevertheless, the soldier's hands were never far from the steering yoke.

'What sort of tank is this?' asked Hector.

'LeClerc,' replied the soldier.

'You're a cleric?' Kate clarified.

'LeClerc, yes,' repeated the soldier, 'Main battle tank.'

Hector did not know what a cleric was. Kate, on the other hand, was completely puzzled as to why the tank should need a vicar. The LeClerc main battle tank is just called LeClerc, and the French do not routinely people their tanks with priests. As it happened the soldier was not religious, although he might have ventured a prayer that they would get through the next hour without any major damage.

As they followed the track out of the camp up the gently sloping hill to moorland above, Kate had a chance to look around at the bewildering array of lights and dials and buttons and knobs. Hector had found the controls that allowed him to move and position the gun, and was already yelling bang, pooow and boom, interspersed with shouts of 'enemy at 2 o'clock,' and 'take that'.

After about fifteen minutes they reached a plain, with their tank on a slight hill. In the distance Kate could see a number of tanks and burnt out lorries. The soldier explained that they were to be allowed to fire one shell each at any of the targets, but then began to drone on about what they had to do and the best way to hit the target.

Hector paid attention. He appreciated that in a computerised tank you had to know what you were doing to fire the gun, and he was determined to fire the tank's gun. He asked several questions, clarifying the steps needed to load, aim and fire the gun.

Kate tried to feign interest in the long ramble about trajectories, tanks and shells and how these affect accuracy. Hector, on the other hand, made no attempt whatsoever to look interested as soon as he had worked out which controls did what. Accuracy was for those without talent. Clearly, if he fired a shot it was going to hit; that was the way of the world, or at least the way of Hector's world. Hector was brilliant, in Hector's opinion, and it was the only opinion that mattered.

'Wow, a moving target,' yelled Hector while looking through the gun sights and pointing. 'This is going to be great.'

'Are you serious?' asked the soldier, 'If there is something moving we cannot fire.'

'Why not, he's got his gun pointed at us,' replied Hector.

The soldier let out a resigned sigh, and took a look through the gun sight.

'Ohhh,' was all he managed to say before a massive explosion rocked the tank and threw him to the floor.

'Oops,' said Hector. 'I think this is for real'.

The soldier indicated to Kate that she needed to get their tank moving, but Kate was ahead of him, and already they were picking up speed. He began yelling something about a tiger into the radio.

'Tiger?' questioned Hector.

'An old German Tiger tank,' the soldier replied.

'No,' said Hector, looking into the gun sights, 'there are three of them.'

'You two have some terrible enemies,' the soldier said, as another nearby explosion rocked their tank, and he began to shout into the radio again. Next, he armed the main gun and told Hector to move over so he could aim.

'No,' said Hector, 'this is my go.'

Before the soldier could reply, another explosion rocked them, and the soldier turned to tell Kate to vary her course more.

'You want me to zig zag?' she shouted.

'No, but not so straight, and do not keep an even speed,' he said, just as Hector muttered 'Got ya'.

'No!' the soldier instructed, but it was too late. Hector had fired.

'You've wasted one of our shots,' the soldier said angrily.

'No, I haven't. I got him,' declared Hector.

Moments later the soldier had seen the wrecked tiger tank for himself, and loaded the other shell. Hector was already tracking one of the other tanks.

The next few minutes were fraught, as Kate took them behind hills, slowed and accelerated. Explosions echoed around them, some closer and some not so near.

'They are not very good' said the soldier, 'but they can still get lucky.'

'He's tipped over, he's tipped over,' yelled Hector suddenly. It was true, one of the Tiger tanks had run up an embankment and toppled over. 'They must be real idiots.'

As if to wake them from Hector's confidence, another blast rocked the tank, and this one was much, much closer. The tank lurched to the left.

'It's going to the left' yelled Kate, 'I cannot go straight or right.'

'They've damaged our tracks,' said the soldier. 'They've been lucky'.

Then, bit by bit, the tank slowed to a halt.

'We are sitting geese,' yelled the soldier, 'get out!'

'Sitting ducks,' Kate corrected, as Hector briefly reflected on just how annoying his sister could be at times.

'Too late, the Tiger tank is here,' said Hector, looking through the sights.

There was a boom, and then silence.

'Got it,' said Hector, in the same matter of fact voice he used when completing a well-known level on a computer game. The soldier let out a long sigh. Then he started talking into the radio, as Kate and Hector heard the squeak and rumble of arriving French armour.

Kate and Hector exchanged looks. Hector grinned and Kate looked worried. They had survived again, against all the odds. Hector thought about school, and how much fun he was going to have telling his friends about all of this. Of course, some would not believe him, but there might be newspaper reports.

'That doesn't look like our tank,' said Hector, just as the soldier took a look himself.

'Leopard. Leopard tank. It is a Leopard,' he stuttered, a look of shock on his face.

'Any more shells?' Hector asked quickly.

'No no. We're dead. Where did they get a German Leopard Tank?' the soldier said to no one in particular.

'They've been stealing old planes from collectors. Maybe they stole the tanks from collectors,' said Hector, in a matter of fact tone. Hector believed the tank's armour would protect them against anything.

Kate began pressing all of the buttons.

'What are you doing?' asked Hector.

'Causing a distraction, or at least trying to,' said Kate.

'Too late, all too late,' said the soldier, shaking his head.

As if to confirm the worst they heard the boom of the leopard tank firing its killing shot, and they all crouched a little lower.

After a moment or two the soldier looked up, and Hector looked through the sights.

'The tank's on fire. Something must have gone wrong,' said Hector, just as he saw a familiar figure walking towards the burning tank. It was Pierre, and he was holding some equipment.

The soldier looked through the sights and muttered something about a Eyrx anti-armour missile. Then he slumped to the floor shaking and cried a little. Kate put her hand on his shoulder as he muttered things in French.

'What's an ear-wax missile?' asked Hector.

'Eryx not ear-wax, you idiot,' Kate answered, 'and show some sympathy.'

'Don't worry,' said Hector patting the soldier on his arm in a cheerful and utterly insensitive way, 'this happens to us most days now, and we always survive. Actually, I quite like it.'

'Hector,' Kate exclaimed, but she could not decide what offended her most; the way he ignored someone else's distress, or his wild and utterly unjustified optimism.

'Well it's simple, isn't it,' Hector explained, 'I've decided there is a God and he wants me to get to that cake shop. Come on, I bet Pierre's got a car. I hope it's a sports car.'

Hector continued to mutter as he got out of the tank. 'Maybe he'll let me drive. After all, I didn't get my go at driving the tank. It's not my fault it's ruined. Kate was driving, and she went very fast.'

As Hector walked from the tank he caught sight of Pierre. 'Pierre, Pierre! Sorry the tank's ruined.'

'Get down!' yelled Pierre, and Hector was roughly pushed to the ground by another soldier who had run up from behind.

'We have to wait until the area is safe,' said Pierre, as the sound of a helicopter grew louder.

Hector realised that his hopes of driving a fast sports car from the scene of a tank battle straight to a cake shop were not going to be realised.

CHAPTER FOUR

Cakes

The man from the British Consulate looked worried. Keith Chatterton moved his face in a way that suggested he was about to speak, but had then decided better of it. He kept this up for some time, with Hector's almost unflinching gaze adding to his discomfort. He was used to dealing with people who had lost their holiday money, or needed to repatriate the body of a loved one after an accident or heart attack.

Yet, here he was in a small patisserie, opposite two children who had recently destroyed several tanks. When he agreed to work for three weeks in France to cover for holidays this was not what he expected. The assignment was supposed to provide some experience of day-to-day consular activities in France, and yet here he was in a cake shop, surrounded by regular and special forces soldiers, with two armoured vehicles outside. When he had arrived they were loading extra ammunition for the heavy calibre machines guns on the armoured cars. It all looked very serious.

At first he introduced himself to Hector and Kate. They seemed quiet, but that was to be expected given their recent experiences. His warmth towards them had faded somewhat when he read the hastily-prepared French report. Hector was described as, 'Pleasant, polite and energetic, with an aptitude for machinery, bombs and weapons,' The report went on to praise Hector's ability to quickly identify threats and his willingness to act without hesitation when using whatever he found to hand in the most violent way possible.

It also described Hector as 'easy to underestimate,' pointing out the speed at which he had mastered both the controls of the plane he crash landed and the tank gun he had so recently fired. Keith Chatterton believed the high regard in which the author of the report evidently held Hector probably betrayed the author's background, as someone who more often appraised soldiers or special forces candidates.

Kate was described as, 'Mature, likeable and attractive. Calm in a crisis,' The report also said she displayed characteristics suggesting the same high degree of intelligence her brother possessed. As he read further Keith Chatterton could see that author of the report clearly did not rate Kate as highly, stating that she displayed no inclination towards violent action. The report went on to describe Kate's part in recent events, including the fact that she had probably gunned at least one plane out of the sky, and had demonstrated skill and calculation in navigating a tank during the recent battle. The report also praised her 'sensible use' of the blunt end of an axe head when dispatching a suspected assailant, commenting that the sharp end can so easily become embedded in the attacker's skull making further assault more difficult.

Keith Chatterton could not understand how anyone who had recently shot down a plane, finished someone off with an axe and then driven a tank with some skill in a real encounter against four other tanks could not be considered at least potentially violent and dangerous. He suspected that the person who wrote the report was as myopic as the sports teacher at his school who had written that he had no aptitude for football, the day after he had scored a hat-trick for the B-team and been awarded Man-of-the-Match.

'Mr Chatterton I presume,' said Colonel Bertrand entering with a guard of two soldiers. Keith Chatterton was completely on the back foot. Nothing had prepared him for this, and he stuttered and stammered a reply.

'Mr Chatterton, please, I do understand this is all a bit out of the ordinary,' Colonel Bertrand continued, 'As soldiers we are used to guns, bullets and violence, but even we are taken aback by all of this.'

'Right, yes' stammered Chatterton while glancing around at the bright and attractively tiled walls and floor, 'I am sorry, no, I mean yes, I am grateful for the bravery of your troops in repelling the attack,' he continued, lapsing into official speak, before continuing in a more honest tone, 'I've read the report, but I do not under-stand why. To be honest, I don't understand any of it.'

Colonel Bertrand quickly explained the situation, and Kate was surprised by how much he knew about her and Hector. He even knew the name of her school. He also explained that the tanks had been stolen from a farm, where they were kept by a collector. The farmer and his wife had been found dead. The men in the tanks were believed to be French, from Marseille. They were known criminals, who appeared to have been given money and other in-ducements.

A common theme, according to Bertrand, was the use of weap-ons, aircraft and vehicles stolen from collectors. He explained that in some ways it was a clever strategy, as there were many collec-tors who had all manner of old weapons, including ammunition.

It also became apparent to Kate and Hector that the document Mr Chatterton had been reading was a report on them. Colonel Bertrand apologised for the poor English, commenting that it was rushed and a little rough and ready.

Chatterton explained that he was there to make sure Kate and Hector were safe, and the Colonel explained that they were not safe, but he was doing all he could.

'Shall we all take afternoon tea?' said Colonel Bertrand. He saw their surprised faces.

'We may be in France, but tea can still be found,' the Colonel continued.

A short time later they were all sat around a small table, with the soldiers guarding them partly hidden by a mass of hanging flowers and other plants. It was a peculiar sight; a boy, a girl, an Army Officer and a well-dressed man in his thirties sat in a French cake and pastry shop surrounded by heavily armed troops, with the door guarded by two armoured vehicles.

Colonel Bertrand poured tea and explained how impressed he was by Kate's composure under fire, and Hector's indefatigability.

'Did anyone die?' Kate asked.

'Well, you have to remember that they had come to kill you. They had money, we think they had been taking illegal drugs, and they would not have hesitated. One person died in the tank that turned over. Everyone in the tank shot from the shoulder-launched weapon died,' said the Colonel.

'I think Pierre fired that,' said Hector.

'Yes, he did well. He is very brave,' the Colonel replied.

'Did I kill anyone?' asked Hector in a small voice.

'No, Hector. You saved your sister, and I should say with her driving she saved you. You also saved the men on the range. They only had one missile,' said the Colonel kindly.

'Were they injured in the tanks?' Hector asked in a slightly more confident tone, 'The ones I shot'.

'No Hector,' said the Colonel kindly, 'they all died.'

'Sorry,' said Hector, and for a moment he looked quite lost.

'Hector, they killed themselves,' said Colonel Bertrand, 'They were set on murder, they killed a farmer and his wife. They could have tied them up and left them, but they murdered them instead. They took a tank onto a firing range and tried to kill you, your sister and the soldiers on the range. They had already signed their own death warrants. If you hadn't hit them the helicopters that arrived moments later would have torn them apart.'

Hector looked worried and Kate put her hand on his shoulder. Hector felt shocked. What he did not say, but could not stop thinking about, were the pilots who had died. It was the first time that it hit Hector; he had already killed, but he had not given it a moment's thought. It had been like a game. Now it felt more real and more frightening.

'Hector,' continued the Colonel, 'it is good that you are worried about someone dying. It is not a good thing that anyone should be killed. Very few of the men under my command will ever have to kill anyone, and almost all that do find that it troubles them. It should have never fallen on your shoulders, and for that I am very sorry. But remember, you did not seek them out. You were having a treat with your sister and they tried to kill you.'

Chatterton was warming to Kate and Hector, and beginning to realise that whatever their extraordinary experiences and background, they were not the violent sociopaths the misleading report had suggested.

'Hector,' Chatterton said, 'I have no experience of guns and tanks, but you were the one who, just by chance had the means of stopping these people. Is this correct Colonel?'

'Oui, quite correct.'

'And, had Hector paused, or turned away scared or missed, then there would probably have been several dead soldiers?' Chatterton continued.

'Yes, definitely. There's nothing a soldier can do against a tank. Several were shot at. It was a miracle that we only had one small injury,' said the Colonel.

'So, some stupid people effectively killed themselves, and if you hadn't acted Hector there would be several families in the camp, and maybe elsewhere, who would be preparing funerals for husbands, brothers, fathers. The Colonel is quite correct, it is a big thing, but think of the people who didn't die, and think about them sat with their families tonight, unharmed and happy.'

Colonel Bertrand nodded a quiet thank you. There was a pause. The only sounds were a quiet radio playing, the breathing of the soldiers and Hector slurping his tea.

'How did these people know that Kate and Hector were in a tank?' asked Chatterton, gaining in confidence.

'We think there are at least two sources, one French and one British,' said the Colonel, 'We really do think this, we are not just saying there is a British source to even it up and escape any embarrassment.'

'What's a source?' asked Hector.

'Someone who is leaking information to the criminals,' Chatterton explained.

'The plan now,' said the Colonel, 'is to clear the camp of some families and staff, take you back there and wait for an attack. If no attack comes you will go back to England.'

'No zoo trip then?' asked Hector, 'The important person in Paris said we could go to the zoo.'

'The important person in Paris; you remember Hector the one who was speaking when you ruined my aquarium? Well that person; the same one who you told about me not listening to his call because I was rescuing fish, getting me into all of that trouble? Yes, Hector, you remember? Well, he might be the source, the leak,' said the Colonel. Kate could see Pierre and Andrè grinning at each other.

'The important person will not expect me to take you to the zoo after the attack today, so that is exactly what I will really do,' said the Colonel.

'We will make it look as though you have returned to the camp. In a while, I want you to get into the armoured car and out of the other side into the small car that is waiting. You will go with Pierre, Andrè and Mrs Warp.'

'Mrs Warp!' exclaimed Kate, 'I thought she was dead.'

'There is more than one Mrs Warp,' Colonel Bertrand explained, 'And this time, because of the malfunction, I want both of you to have a remote override.'

The Colonel presented them each with a small round disk with a red button on it.

'All you have to do is press the button and Mrs Warp will obey your next command no matter what it is,' said Colonel Bertrand.

A noise outside drew Kate's attention. There was activity; two people were speaking with the soldiers.

'Ahh, but this is why we are really here,' Colonel Bertrand said with a huge smile on his face.

Hector looked to the window.

'Kate, Hector,' said Colonel Bertrand to attract their attention, 'I have some generally good news. Your father is much recovered, but he has suffered a small amount of brain damage.'

Hector just stared at the Colonel, while Kate felt as though her chair had suddenly been dragged from under her, allowing her to slip into the underworld.

'It is not so bad,' said the Colonel quickly as he saw their reactions, 'but this is why you have not seen him. However, he has still not completely recovered. People who have head injuries can feel depressed sometimes for months afterwards. He may also be more bad tempered.'

'More bad tempered?' questioned Hector, 'How is that possible? When our outhouse was burgled, and Dad saw two men with iron bars breaking in, he chased them all through the park, even on the cycle path.'

'There isn't a cycle path in the park,' Kate corrected, 'I think you mean like a psychopath. That's how everyone describes him; a deranged psychopath.'

'Well, your father is very welcome to chase burglars around the local town here, I would enjoy the spectacle,' said the Colonel. 'However, the key thing is that we must all be patient and kind and understanding, even if he is a little angry about things. Remember, he has been very worried about you, and your mother has been ringing me almost every hour.'

The four of them sat in silence for a minute while Mum and Dad displayed their passports and were checked for weapons, made their way past the guards, and then through into the small cafe.

Kate immediately ran to hug them both. She was followed just after by Hector, who felt unsure what to do, until Colonel Bertrand gave him a firm push. Mum was in silent tears while Dad had a very grim and set look on his face.

It was Mum who first broke the silence.

'Thank you very much for looking after them,' she began, speaking to Colonel Bertrand. Keith Chatterton quickly introduced himself, and then sat down again.

'Mrs Trogg, you have two clever, resourceful and very brave children. In the latest attack, it was your children who saved some of my men,' said the Colonel, as Kate and Hector both went red, basking in the praise, and yet embarrassed by the attention.

'There's been another attack?' asked Dad.

Colonel Bertrand explained what had happened on the tank range. Mum listened in open-mouthed horror as the Colonel described events. Again, Kate was surprised by how much Colonel Bertrand knew. The Colonel again lavished praise on Hector and Kate, and it was then that Dad really spoke for the first time.

'What the hell were they doing in a tank?' he shouted, staring straight at Colonel Bertrand.

The Colonel took a deep breath and explained that it was a treat to distract them, that he had incidentally been ordered to do this, but also that a tank was normally a very safe place to be.

'Not on a bloody battlefield it isn't!' Dad shouted, continuing to stare aggressively at the Colonel, 'You were supposed to be protecting them, not asking them to man the guns because everyone else was off cooking and cleaning.'

The Colonel paused again, and then started to explain that he could understand that it had been a horrible time, and that Dad was worried and angry. However, he had to appreciate that there had never been a case of anyone stealing old tanks and attacking an army firing range before.

'I don't give a damn about your weak excuses,' Dad yelled, picking up a cream cake from the table and throwing it at the Colonel.

'Dad!' exclaimed Kate.

'Trevor!' pleaded Mum.

Thick dollops of cream splattered the Colonel's otherwise immaculate uniform. Hector could see Andrè and Pierre trying to conceal their grins.

Colonel Bertrand had obviously decided to take another pause and a much deeper breath. He looked down at his uniform and flicked a blob of cream away. Unfortunately, the blob jetted through the air and landed on Dad's arm.

Dad flew to the counter and picked up two more cakes and hurled them at the Colonel. The Colonel's temper had finally snapped, and while muttering something in French, he hurled one of them back.

Mum and Kate were looking on in horror, but Hector was suddenly back in his element. He had missed the food fight at school between two of his friends just by accident, but now was a chance to make up for that big style.

Hector darted for some cakes and began to hurl them at Andrè and Pierre, hoping to get them into the fight. Dad and the Colonel were throwing food at each other, but they both really meant it, as if this was the only way they could avoid getting that little bit closer and throwing punches.

To Hector's disappointment neither Andrè nor Pierre retaliated. Some of the other soldiers, who took some pretty impressive direct hits with parts of a baguette and some pastry nibbles, looked like they were considering it, but Hector noticed a warning raised eyebrow from Pierre and all resistance faded.

It was Chatterton who eventually intervened, pleading for peace and common sense.

'All of you have had the most extraordinary and stressful time. No one has died. I think we need a break.'

'How can anyone die, we're only throwing food,' said Hector, with his usual spectacular bad timing. There was silence as everyone looked at Hector, and it felt very different to when the Colonel was praising him.

Pierre then intervened, explaining that the zoo would be a good place to be together as a family, and suggested they cleaned themselves up. The cafe owner was just appearing with paper rolls, looking angry and muttering about payment in broken English.

'Will we be safe?' was the only thing Dad managed to say.

'I don't believe you are safe anywhere,' said Pierre, 'but a false trail is being laid back to the camp and that will help. Several of us will guard you.'

'Do you have experience of this?' Dad asked, his face stern.

'We will do our best, and yes we have experience,' said Andrè, 'My colleague here just destroyed a tank with a shoulder launched missile while under fire from a machine gun, so our best is, how you say, not bad.'

There was a pause before Dad seemed to sag.

'I'm sorry,' he said, 'I should be grateful. I seem to get cross very easily.'

Colonel Bertrand said nothing, but walked out past Dad, while laying a hand on his shoulder.

'He has had quite a tough time too,' Pierre said once the Colonel had gone.

As they made their arrangements to leave Hector noticed that Andrè had several pictures of the aftermath of the food fight on his mobile phone. Even Hector appreciated that they would soon be distributed around the camp.

Hector and Kate had little problem crawling through the armoured car and out the other side into the small Citroen hidden from view. Dad and Mum found this a surprising and cramped introduction to Hector's and Kate's new world.

Worse was to follow. As soon as they were in the car a small old man got into the driving seat and explained using grunts and rapidly spoken French that they should all get down and cover themselves with blankets. There was a smell to the car, and Kate wondered if it was more commonly used for moving goats or other small livestock.

The car took several attempts to start, and sounded more like a large lawn mower than a normal vehicle. It lurched forward, and the bumpy trip to the zoo began. Nothing could be seen, but the old man's driving seemed erratic and at times alarming.

It was strange that their family reunion should continue in a moving car under the blankets, with the smell of petrol and goats. The sound of the road rushing just inches below poured through a couple of rusting holes in the bare metal floor.

'Trevor, I know you think they have not done well, but I couldn't believe it when you started a fight,' said Mum, in a tired tone.

'I didn't start a fight, I just threw a cake,' explained Dad.

'And Hector,' Mum continued, 'you didn't need to join in. Your father was very angry, and we've both been very worried, but you had no excuse. That was just bad behaviour. I expect you to apologise to Colonel Bertrand and his soldiers.'

'Yes Mum,' said Hector in his resigned tone.

'Well there's one good thing,' said Kate, 'Dad and Hector have got to be the only people on earth who have ever taken on the French special forces with cream cakes and pastry nibbles.'

As the conversation continued, Kate was struck by how much Mum and Dad knew. They had clearly been kept fully informed. Dad said very little, while Mum kept alternating between being angry and tearful. She was obviously surprised they were not gibbering wrecks, but also relieved that they were not full of bullet holes or wrapped in bandages.

When the car eventually stopped, and they were told to remove the blankets, they found themselves on a narrow street between old buildings. Kate and Hector were both surprised to be let out onto the street with no guard. They were even more surprised to see Mrs Warp round the corner and walk smartly towards them.

CHAPTER FIVE

Zoo

'Oh,' said Kate, a look of horror on her face as Mrs Warp smiled in that friendly, reassuring way she could instantly produce.

'Hello Kate. Hello Hector,' said Mrs Warp, as if nothing at all had happened to her in the past. Hector reflected that in fact nothing had happened to this Mrs Warp in the past. It was another Mrs Warp they had mercilessly destroyed with water, an axe and a bomb in a microwave.

Mrs Warp introduced herself to Mum and Dad. She immediately put them at their ease, just as she had Hector and Kate when they had first met her.

'Mrs Warp,' Kate tentatively asked, 'Do you remember meeting us last time?'

'Oh yes dear. I have all of those memories, but not the very last ones.'

'Good,' said Hector quickly and firmly.

'But, I have been filled in on everything that happened,' Mrs Warp said, turning to look Hector in the eye.

'Oops,' said Hector.

'I'm really sorry,' Kate began.

'It does not matter at all,' said Mrs Warp kindly. 'It was a misunderstanding on your part, and a sort of malfunction on mine. It could happen to anyone.'

'It couldn't happen to me,' Hector muttered to Kate, 'I don't run on eighteen volts.'

'Hector, shut up,' Kate hissed.

'And my eyeballs don't flash different colours,' added Hector.

'I bet you wish they did,' Kate whispered.

Hector did not respond, not least because he had just launched into a rather active daydream where he was terrifying the religious studies teacher and some of his classmates with his blue, white and red flashing eyes.

Mum and Dad both looked puzzled. They clearly did not understand the use of the word malfunction.

Once inside the zoo, Kate and Hector caught sight of Andrè and Pierre. They were dressed as zoo staff, and both were picking up litter in different places.

Mrs Warp was very good at small talk, asking Mum and Dad about themselves, and chatting about the zoo. When Mum asked about Mrs Warp she simply explained that her job was security, and she was good at it because she did not look like a minder. Kate saw Mum and Dad exchange looks. It crossed her mind that they had no idea how strong Mrs Warp was. Kate rather hoped that she did not still have the machine guns the other Mrs Warp had fired so wildly.

The first half an hour was spent wandering around looking at the animal enclosures, all of which appeared too small to Kate's eyes. The zoo was large, with many trees and shrubs creating a green view in almost any direction. Nevertheless, it had an unfinished feel to it, as if every addition had been yet another plan and another load of concrete.

Mrs Warp was very good at chatting. She asked questions about Mum, Dad, Kate and Hector, and seemed to have an encyclopaedic knowledge of the animals in the zoo. Indeed, Kate suspected that was exactly what she had; an encyclopaedia added to a chip in her head, or wherever her brain was really located.

It was not long before Kate was quietly bored, while Hector's restlessness was rather more obvious. There were only so many amazing south american giant rodents that can be amazing.

Hector nudged Kate, and she was just about to shove him back, when she realised that he was trying to tell her something. Hector had the Warp emergency override in his hand. Just as she was wondering what he was up to, Hector moved to the side of Mrs Warp and whispered something. Hector knew Mrs Warp had extraordinary hearing and that even muttered commands would probably be understood.

'Oh, look at that armadillo,' said Mrs Warp in her light conversational tone, 'such a large nose, it's almost as ugly as you Mr Trogg.'

Mum and Dad both paused and looked a little surprised. Neither said anything, but it was obvious they were confused by the turn the conversation had taken.

As Mrs Warp continued speaking, as if nothing unpleasant had been said, Hector fell back to walk beside Kate. It was Kate's idea to tell Mrs Warp to walk like a Chimpanzee. Hector did not sidle up to her this time, but whispered the instruction as if he was talking to Kate, while pressing the emergency override button at the same time.

Mrs Warp immediately altered her gait so that she walked like an overweight sailor with knee problems. It was not quite the effect Kate had hoped for, but then she remembered that Mrs Warp's run was rather odd as well.

'Are you all right?' asked Mum when she noticed Mrs Warp's walk.

'Oh, yes, quite all right,' Mrs Warp replied, 'Gosh, look at those parrots. They are colourful.'

'Suggest we stop for an ice cream,' muttered Hector while pressing the emergency control.

'I think we should all try an ice cream from that kiosk,' said Mrs Warp, pointing to a brightly coloured wooden stall that masked a range of very modern refrigerators. The range of ice creams was astonishing.

Kate glanced at Hector and muttered her approval.

Mrs Warp refused an ice cream. Hector and Kate knew why. For some reason, Mum decided not to have one either.

There was a light breeze as they all lent against the rail next to the Rhinoceros enclosure. The sun was warm, and Hector felt content. Kate smiled at him and he knew she felt the same; relieved that the world was returning to normal, except for the fun they were having with Mrs Warp.

As ever, Hector's feeling of contentment quickly gave way to boredom. He muttered a command and Mrs Warp suddenly grabbed Dad's ice cream and thrust it on the top of a passing man's head.

'Hector!' Kate hissed, as the only one aware of who was really responsible for what had just happened.

The man said nothing for a few seconds, clearly stunned by the assault, and then launched into a tirade in French. Mrs Warp did nothing but smile back and say a few calm French words in reply. Mum and Dad exchanged looks, while Kate's initial disapproval gave way to laughter.

'I would like to have a look at the fish,' said Mrs Warp, 'They have some extraordinary specimens here.'

Mum and Dad agreed automatically, as it was quite clear that their thoughts were not on the next exhibit or animal. Once inside the aquarium, however, Mrs Warp began to provide volumes of information on each of the fish. Dad was genuinely interested, while Mum continued to look concerned.

Kate bought some peanuts with money she got from Mum. When the opportunity presented itself she gave them to Mrs Warp, pressed her command button and instructed Mrs Warp to hide the peanuts in her pocket. Dad and Mum had just been looking in fascination at a poisonous octopus with blue rings, and even Hector had not seen Kate's quick trick.

'Watch this,' Kate whispered to Hector, before she pressed the command button and muttered an instruction while walking alongside Mrs Warp. It was surprising to see the packet of peanuts partly emerge from Mrs Warp's pocket to be ripped open by her apparently normal but quite unearthly hand.

Mrs Warp took one of the peanuts in her fingers and flicked it at a man on the other side of the room. It went like a rocket, hitting him hard. He yelled and held his forehead, before looking around to see what had hit him.

'Hop over to him like a frog and tell him off in French for making a noise,' Hector muttered while pressing the control.

Everyone in the hall had stopped looking at the fish in the tanks, and was staring first at the man, and then at Mrs Warp as she hopped towards him. The man looked bewildered, and then angry as Mrs Warp lectured him as if he were a child, using words neither Kate nor Hector could understand.

'My god, the woman's mad!' Dad exclaimed, none too quietly.

'Can we leave?' Mum asked.

'We haven't seen the crocodiles,' Hector protested.

'Hector, this woman is potty. She might not be safe,' said Dad.

'We shouldn't leave until we're told, as the people guarding us will not know about it,' suggested Kate.

Dad reluctantly agreed while Mum just looked worried. Kate and Hector, however, were trying hard to conceal their grins. It was Hector who made the mistake of looking his sister in the eye. They burst into laughter, but it was Mrs Warp who told them off.

'Come on you two,' said Mrs Warp, 'it is not nice to laugh at that man. He may have been loud, but he was hit rather hard.'

'Sorry,' said Kate, trying to contain her laughter.

'Oh look, Piranha,' said Mrs Warp, as she headed towards another tank.

'They don't look that dangerous,' said Hector.

Mrs Warp went into a long explanation about how Piranha could attack much larger animals than themselves because the shoal acted together. It was when she reached the point of explaining about the size of a Piranha's jaw that Mrs Warp surprised everybody, by bending back the mesh protecting the tank and reaching in to grab a fish.

'Hector!' Kate whispered accusingly, convinced he was responsible.

'Not me,' hissed Hector, 'I haven't done anything.'

Hector, Kate, Mum and Dad tried to look interested as Mrs Warp spoke at length about the Piranha she held in her hand, while everyone else in the aquarium looked between Mrs Warp and the gaping hole in the Piranha tank.

'That's fascinating,' said Dad, 'but I'm getting hot in here. Could we move on?'

Mrs Warp replaced the Piranha, but then appeared to be bitten when her hand was in the water. She showed no pain, and reached in with her other hand to remove the fish. As they walked out Kate looked at the reflection in a large tank, and saw people approaching the hole Mrs Warp had created. She glanced at Mrs Warp and noticed that the very end of one of her fingers was missing.

After they had left the aquarium, they headed for the enclosures with the big cats. Kate continued to instruct Mrs Warp to flick peanuts at people. She chose victims a long way off, and in this way her party could not be suspected. There was a wonderful whizzing noise as the peanuts rocketed off towards their targets. Mrs Warp was very accurate, but the peanuts could be seen to curve in the air slightly. Often they would just miss, but produce a marvellous thwack as they hit glass, wood or brick nearby.

The other strange thing was the way in which Mrs Warp could continue a conversation. She did not hesitate in her speech when she received an instruction, retrieved another peanut and fired. Yet, her conversation and behaviour, while outwardly normal, was unusual after a while. It seemed as though she had a wide set of rules governing social behaviour, but not all were applied at the best time.

There were a number of small puddles of water scattered about the enclosures that had been recently cleaned. Mrs Warp would take Dad's hand and guide him around them, much as some ancient gentlemen might take the small hand of a delicate young woman in a large Victorian dress for fear that she might faint and fall.

The other problem was that Mrs Warp would bow to some people, and curtsey to others using an imaginary dress. These people seemed to be selected at random, and it only happened about every six or seven minutes.

After about half an hour Hector was becoming bored and annoyed. He felt upstaged by Kate's wonderful peanut flicking trick. It was funny, but he decided to bring it to an end. He pressed the command button and muttered to Mrs Warp to sit down and organise a meal.

Mrs Warp promptly sat down in a puddle, removed her wig, and began to wave it and shout. 'Excuse me, excuse me! Are there any animals we can eat?'

'Hector, what have you done?' Kate hissed, alarmed that everyone was looking at their group.

'Nothing. I didn't tell her to sit in a puddle and wave her wig. I didn't know she had a wig,' said Hector, moving swiftly from concerned denial to hysterical giggles. This set Kate off, and they moved away to sit on a bench as Mrs Warp continued to shout in English.

'You! You over there,' said Mrs Warp loudly, while pointing at a very hairy man who was heavily overweight, 'You look like you've eaten a few of the animals. Which ones taste best? Come on, speak up? Look, here have some peanuts and then tell me.'

Mum and Dad joined Kate and Hector on the bench, keen to move away from the utterly bonkers Mrs Warp. She had started to splash her hands down into the puddle to attract more attention, as if that was needed. After a while even Mum and Dad were overtaken by the giggles.

'You! Yes, you! Slobber chops,' yelled Mrs Warp pointing at a sad-faced man, 'You've clearly had too many pies, so you probably know which animals taste best. Which one should we kill and eat?'

Five minutes later, everyone was still laughing while Mrs Warp had started to sing and speak in German. It was at this point that Mrs Warp was approached by a man Kate immediately recognised, although he seemed to have shaved off his silly beard. He was the person who had quizzed Kate on her first night at the army camp. He was one of Mrs Warp's creators.

Mrs Warp got up and walked off to a nearby building. She entered and disappeared. The man approached and it was obvious he was very angry. He introduced himself to Mr and Mrs Trogg, and explained that Mrs Warp was not human, and that Kate and Hector had command buttons. He believed they had abused these, and issued silly commands. Mum and Dad seemed more surprised by this than by Mrs Warp's behaviour.

'Mrs Warp is here to protect you,' the man said to Hector and Kate while shaking slightly, 'She is mostly bullet proof, immensely strong, well disguised. The previous model defeated the world's most feared assassin, and yet you two ruined her. You already have your teeth into this one and there hasn't even been an attack.'

The man then handed Mum and Dad a command button each, together with a warning that Mrs Warp would not question or carefully consider any command. He explained that letting her get on with it was the best approach, and that the command buttons were only for dire emergencies where Mrs Warp had some sort of error.

'If you keep on abusing the command button I might just change sides,' said the man to Hector and Kate as a parting shot.

Ten minutes later Mrs Warp was back, cleaned up slightly and smiling as ever. Mum and Dad had just about finished telling Kate and Hector off. Kate managed to distract them both by explaining how strong Mrs Warp was, and how she had managed to successfully fight off Sludge.

'The thing is Dad, she's bullet-proof and stronger than Sludge,' Kate explained, 'We've got to keep her with us, enjoy the zoo and not draw attention to ourselves.'

'I see,' said Dad in the tone he reserved for the final killing blow, 'and you two have been helping us to keep a low profile have you?

Making sure we don't stand out? Ensuring that we are difficult to spot?'

There was silence.

'Sorry,' said Hector, for about the tenth time.

'Sorry,' said Kate, 'It just seemed very funny.'

'Well, let's do our best from here,' said Mum, drawing things to a close.

Dad decided they would go to the reptile house, as this was inside and made them slightly harder to see. Nevertheless, some people openly pointed at them as they made their way to the brightly coloured concrete building.

Hector noticed that Mrs Warp kept looking around, as if she was checking for danger. The problem now was that as her head moved her wig did not always follow. He nudged Kate and pointed it out. The two of them lapsed into giggles. Yet, as they entered the reptile house, Kate saw a worrying small blue flash from Mrs Warp's leg.

'Mrs Warp, what can you tell us about this crocodile?' asked Dad.

'Well, the notice says it is a nile crocodile, but I believe it is a salt water crocodile from Australia,' explained Mrs Warp.

Then to everyone's horror she prized back the glass window with her unearthly hands, set it to one side, and climbed in with the giant crocodile.

'Now, as you can see it is completely still,' explained Mrs Warp, moving closer to the giant reptile, 'Normally, they lie still until they get close to their prey. It will use its amazingly strong tail and whole body to propel itself suddenly forwards. Its jaws are very strong, and it will grab a kangaroo, sheep, deer or whatever it can and drag it into the water to drown it.'

'Mrs Warp,' said Mum, looking around to see how many people were watching, 'do you think you should get out in case it attacks you?'

'No, no, it's quite alright. If anything it will be anxious about me entering its cage. It is a very large crocodile, but it will still be unhappy about being approached. Now, if I take hold of it...'

Mrs Warp half-dived and half-fell on the crocodile, and managed to get on its back as it began to thrash about.

'As you can see, it is unhappy,' shouted Mrs Warp above the noise of the splashing water and thumps as the crocodile's tail hit the side of the pool, 'but once I get hold of its jaws I will be able to hold them shut. This is because the huge muscles that are used to clamp the jaw shut on its prey completely dwarf the muscles used to open the jaw.'

Mrs Warp had lent forwards and was sliding up to the front of the crocodile. She clamped just one of her hands around the front of the giant beast and it stopped struggling.

By now, a number of people had gathered to watch. Some thought it was a show, but others clearly appreciated that this bedraggled, middle-aged woman was unlikely to be employed by the zoo to mud-wrestle one of the largest salt-water crocodiles in captivity. They were the ones looking on in open mouthed horror.

'Mrs Warp,' said Kate, 'I really think we should leave. We are attracting attention,' Kate could also see that someone had rushed outside and, from the little she could see through the open door, appeared to be speaking to a member of staff at the zoo.

Mrs Warp stepped forwards, but as she did the crocodile struggled free and then lunged forwards to bite her left arm, ripping her blouse. What happened next drew gasps of wonder and horror. As some of the water splashed about earlier dripped its way back into the green pool, Mrs Warp took hold of the great snout with her free hand and simply opened the crocodile's jaws. As it pulled back she smacked it hard on the nose, and then climbed out of the tank.

Just then two zoo staff arrived and seemed to quickly reach the conclusion that the crocodile had barged open the glass panel and tried to grab a visitor. They spoke quickly in French, and judging by their manner were very apologetic. When another visitor began to speak, and seemed to be claiming that the lady had opened the tank, climbed in, and even wrestled the crocodile's jaws open, the zoo staff gave him withering looks of disbelief, and returned to apologising to Mrs Warp.

Dad, Mum, Kate and Hector all exchanged looks. Keeping a low profile was going very badly.

A short time later the crowd had dispersed and they were all looking at the different snakes. Dad, Mum and Kate were all rather pleased that the snake house was quite dark. Only Hector was praying that something else exciting would happen. He was being guarded by a disguised robot that had wrestled a huge crocodile, and in truth he was proud and wanted more.

'Mrs Warp, you must not lever off the front of any of the tanks,' said Dad, just as they reached an enclosure with a huge anaconda.

'Very well,' said Mrs Warp, before walking off.

'Where's she gone?' asked Mum, looking down the corridor where Mrs Warp disappeared.

'What do we do now?' asked Hector, disappointed that Mrs Warp had not wrenched the front of the tank off and attacked the giant snake.

'Oh! There she is!' exclaimed Kate, pointing at the anaconda's enclosure.

Mrs Warp had opened the tank from the back, and was climbing into the murky pool. She waded across and grasped the snake, just as it was waking up.

'As you can see,' said Mrs Warp in a voice muffled by the glass, 'this one is very large, and has eaten in the last day or so. You can see a pronounced bulge.'

'What did she say?' Kate asked.

'Don't worry,' said Mrs Warp, as she waded forwards and used one of her bizarre hands to push at each of the corners of the steel-frame holding the glass until she forced it open. Dad rushed to hold the heavy glass and lower it to the floor so it did not break.

'That's better,' said Mrs Warp, 'You should be able to hear me clearly now.'

Again people began to gather, as young children pointed excitedly at the lady wrestling the snake. Mrs Warp continued to explain how snakes, like the constrictor that was wrapping itself around her, lurk in trees, dropping onto their prey, biting with their large fangs, and then wrapping themselves around the animal, squeezing and squeezing every time the poor creature breathed out, so that it would eventually suffocate.

Some onlookers were speaking in French and gesturing to Mrs Warp to get out of the tank. They were clearly fearful and confused about a middle-aged lady stood in the middle of a murky pool with a giant snake. Mrs Warp walked forwards with the snake so they could get a better look, addressing them in French.

The snake was clearly becoming more agitated and active. Mrs Warp kept unwrapping it as it coiled around her. Through all of these struggles she kept up her commentary.

Eventually, however, the long, powerful snake was too much for Mrs Warp. She was stronger than it, but there was a lot of snake, and she lost her footing, sinking below the surface of the water with a plop. There was splashing and writhing, and the body of the huge snake moved and coiled around its attacker.

'Dad, you've got to save her,' Kate declared.

'Save her?' Dad questioned, 'how can you be sure the snake's female?'

'No, I mean save Mrs Warp!'

'Why? She attacked the snake,' said Dad, plainly, 'She's only a robot, the snake might drown or crush me. In any event, my money's on Mrs Warp.'

'Yeah,' Hector chipped in, 'she doesn't need oxygen.'

Kate nodded, and reflected on the fact that she had finished off the last Mrs Warp with an axe, and so she probably should not get too upset about this one being in a death struggle with a giant snake.

As the snake and the submerged Mrs Warp thrashed in the green slimy water, onlookers shouted, children cried and were led away from the appalling scene. Some spoke about helping. Others ran to get help. The Trogg family, however, watched with indifference.

Suddenly the trashing stopped. There was a pause, with only the sobbing of some of the shocked onlookers breaking the silence. Then, with the force of Poseidon emerging from the oceans, Mrs Warp rose up, clutching the head of the snake and about a meter of body in one hand. She had simply torn it in two. The other part of the snake was held in her other hand.

'Told you,' said Dad, in a matter of fact sort of way.

There was an angry outburst in French, and the Trogg family turned to see the two staff who had been so apologetic following the crocodile incident. More staff were arriving, some with tools that looked as though they might be for restraining snakes. Kate reflected that they probably did not have anything for sewing a snake together after it had been ripped apart.

A short balding man with stubble and bottle-bottom glasses began shouting at Dad, who seemed remarkably calm.

'I'm very sorry, but I do not speak French very well,' Dad explained. The man paused and gathered himself.

'Why did you allow your senile old mother into the tank with our largest snake?'

'She's not my mother, and she's not senile,' Dad replied.

'She's just got a small fault,' Hector added, 'I think there's some water in her legs.'

Fortunately, Hector's incomprehensible contribution was lost as the staff collectively noticed that the snake was in two parts. Only the slow drip of water in the humid room broke the silence. They were all staring at Mrs Warp, who had the head and about a metre of the snake in her left hand, and the beginnings of the rest of the giant snake in the other.

'I think it's dead,' said Mrs Warp in English, 'I'm afraid it fell apart,' There was more astonished silence before Kate heard Hector muttering.

Mrs Warp then began to press the two parts of the snake together as if trying to fix it. Worse, she started giving it mouth-to-mouth resuscitation. However, she seemed confused about whether to concentrate on getting the snake back in one piece, or focussing on getting it to breathe again. Kate suspected that Hector had muttered a command to repair the snake while pressing his red button, and it was not going well. The bald man who appeared to be in charge was starting to look at Dad again when Mrs Warp became excited.

'Oh, oh, it's getting better,' said Mrs Warp, shaking the two halves, 'Has anyone got any glue?'

'How can you say that she is not senile?' asked the bald man.

'I've got to admit, it's difficult to sustain,' admitted Dad after a pause.

One of the other men began to speak in French, and it was apparent that he could not work out how anyone could tear an anaconda in two. The bald man summarised the problem.

'How did she tear the snake in half?'

'It's not really in half,' Hector unhelpfully explained, 'because if it was in half both bits would be the same length.'

'Hector!' Mum admonished.

'We did it in maths. The snake is in two unequal lengths,' he said, placing the emphasis on 'unequal'.

'Hector, please be quiet.'

'But, it was a long snake,' said Hector undaunted, 'Mrs Warp, can you show us the longer dead bit?'

Mrs Warp threw the head of the snake to the bald man, who caught it in both hands, and then began to drag the rest of the giant snake out of the water. The staff looked on in awe, quite unable to comprehend the situation. They had people behaving badly sometimes; people who smeared food on their children's faces and tried to get animals to lick it off; people who came in drunk; and even the odd idiot who tried to get into a cage. They had never had anyone who had simply torn a large, dangerous animal in two. There was nothing in any of their training that really told them what to do.

'Right,' said Dad in an attempt to seize control, 'I am very sorry indeed about your snake. I really have no idea how it happened. Maybe we should leave now.'

'You broke into the enclosure and killed one of the most valuable animals,' said the bald man.

'Now, that's not fair,' said Dad, 'my mother-in-law simply leant against the tank and it gave way.'

'Oh Brilliant!' muttered Mum, 'You've made her my mother.'

There was silence as the group of staff looked from Dad back to the cage, where the bent and ripped metal showed clearly that the tank front had been ripped or pushed outwards. The bald man approached the cage and pointed at the bent metal.

'It does not look as though it simply gave way,' he said.

'Well, once it gave way and she slipped inside then obviously we had to rip the front out to rescue her,' explained Dad, weakly.

'How did you rip out such strong steel? How did you tear the snake in half?' the bald man said, as he began to look around for crowbars and any other weapons the family might be hiding.

A short time later everyone was sat in an office waiting for the police to arrive. The office was brightly painted, most probably by someone with a severe eyesight problem. The paint on the walls looked smart and new, but the electrical sockets, shelves, filing cabinets, coffee maker and even a pair of shoes appeared to have been painted in the same mad spree. Only after a while did Kate notice that one of the panels in the wall was really a glass window that had been painted over. Small holes had been scraped in the paint, presumably so the staff could peep out.

The bald man wanted to have them arrested for breaking into two animal enclosures and killing a large snake. He seemed resolute, and did not want to hear about further excuses. He certainly had no interest in the wild idea that they were hiding from assassins. Hector's contribution had not helped their cause.

Other staff arrived to look at the Trogg family, and then nod in confirmation. It seemed as though their previous misdeeds were catching up with them. Eventually, the man who Mrs Warp had assaulted with the ice cream turned up to identify her, together with a number of people who had seen her sitting in a puddle. When the very hairy man turned up this seemed to trigger something in Mrs Warp, and she began to point at him as well as bob up and down.

'He's escaped. You need to put him back in his cage,' announced Mrs Warp in a carrying voice.

'I think I'd choose the planes, guns and near-death experiences to this,' moaned Dad, 'What I should have said was that we were on a holiday for people with mental health problems, and that we needed to get back urgently for medication. But, after this even that story wouldn't work.'

'Look on the bright side,' said Mum, 'Mrs Warp broke the rules, not us.'

'Mrs Warp did what she did under Hector and Kate's direction,' hissed Dad.

'Yes, and they may not be criminally responsible, and we didn't know,' suggested Mum with a tone that suggested advancing desperation.

'I think the best thing is to say we are very sorry, explain that Mrs Warp is not human, and offer a large donation,' suggested Dad, 'They may be angry, but I'm sure there is something they are planning to build that we could offer some money towards.'

'Like a new snake!' suggested Hector, who had been eavesdropping.

'No Hector!' said Dad, making it quite clear that further help on the ideas front was not needed.

Andrè and Pierre turned up, but this did not help. They were dressed as staff, but no one knew them. This added to a mysterious day, and there was no way the bald man was going to accept the argument about pressing security concerns.

Dad approached one of the staff who they had not seen before, explained that he wanted to make a donation to the zoo, and took out his bank debit card. Ten minutes later the bald man was taking a more relaxed view. Hector could hear Dad using words such as 'cruel,' and 'unforgivable' and suspected he was speaking about the snake's death.

Twenty minutes later the police arrived. After a brief conversation one of the officers recognised the cards Pierre offered them. They soon had the police on their side, and things were even more relaxed. Everything was being blamed on Mrs Warp's psychiatric problems, Dad was offering to apologise personally to the man she had insulted and the one she had squashed an ice cream into, and Hector had deployed his large smile so that he could try on both the zoo keeper and police hats.

Cups of coffee were being handed round, and Hector was just building up to asking whether he could feed the lions, when the door opened briefly and shut again. Only Hector saw the metal ball roll in, so he quickly picked it up and with a few steps and one swift movement threw it into the next room. It was as if time had slowed down, and everyone had turned to look at him as he ran the four paces across the room.

'It was probably only a toy one,' said Hector, as the door was slammed shut and then partly smashed by an explosion that tore through the next room.

Everyone stood still, except for Pierre and Andrè, who had been already moving towards Hector even as he had been speaking. Hector had been pulled roughly to the floor just as he uttered his last word and the grenade went off.

They all looked at the holes made by the shrapnel in the door, and then at a man in the blue shirt who had blood spreading across his arm. Andrè and Pierre were already pulling guns from their jackets and yelling at everyone to get down. Seconds later a volley of automatic fire smashed the windows.

Andrè and Pierre both seemed to jerk and wave their arms. There were loud bangs and flashes as stun grenades went off outside, and Kate realised that Andrè and Pierre had just thrown them. Kate could see that Andrè had something small in his hand; he was pressing it and shouting clearly in French. Mrs Warp ran straight to the door and fearlessly out to meet whatever awaited. Pierre had a radio in his hand and was speaking quickly.

There was a strange silence for about ten seconds. Kate reflected that this was Mrs Warp's purpose. She was fearless, possessed inhuman strength and was ultimately expendable. If she was destroyed there would be no funeral and no relatives to comfort.

Kate heard a scream from one of the zoo staff, and although she glanced in the direction of the cry, she could not help but be drawn back to Andrè and Pierre. They took no notice of the woman who had begun to cry; they seemed almost calm. Kate glanced again and saw that one of the policemen had a large amount of blood around him.

Pierre was speaking into his radio again, as to Kate's horror two figures vaulted through the smashed windows and made straight for the two remaining policemen, both of whom had guns drawn. Andrè and Pierre were shouting at the policemen, one of whom had fallen backwards. Then there was a bang and a hiss as one of the attackers was hit square in the face by the powder from a fire extinguisher.

'Hector! Hector! They are on our side,' yelled Pierre.

'Oh, are they?' replied Hector, in his cheery voice, 'Sorry!'

The soldier covered in powered muttered something that sounded like 'imbecile' as he wiped the powder from his face.

There was so much going on. The zoo staff were tending to someone else who had been injured, Dad was reassuring Mum, several people were crying. Only Hector seemed in his element, imbued with a firm belief in his own invulnerability.

'Vite, Vite!' came a cry from outside, and Pierre urged Hector, Kate, Mum and Dad to rush forward out of the door towards an armoured car waiting just beyond a door in the zoo perimeter wall.

'We can't leave these people,' said Mum, pointing at the zoo staff.

'They will be guarded. Now go!' shouted Pierre, grabbing hold of Mum's wrist and propelling her through the door.

'Get her into the armoured car no matter what happens!' Pierre barked at Dad.

While Mum and Dad ran ahead, Pierre and Andrè ran on either side of Kate and Hector. Kate noticed that Andrè had hold of Hector's jacket; his other hand clutched a gun that was pointing at the ground. Then she realised that Pierre had hold of her jacket. His hand dug into her back when their strides were not in time.

Despite the forced run, Kate glanced back at the shattered office just as two loud cracks rang out. Kate turned to see Mum twist and fall to the ground. Kate opened her mouth to scream but nothing came out. Hector yelled a guttural animal howl just as the fist in Kate's back pushed her on and up, past her fallen mother.

'Drag her,' yelled Pierre to Dad, just as Kate realised that she had turned back to look at her mother, and was herself being dragged. Hector shrieked a furious 'no,' as he too was dragged away from his mother. A crimson bloom was spreading across Mum's chest and she seemed to be gasping for air, while Dad's face was a sea of blood.

CHAPTER SIX

Escape

The world went dark as they were bundled into the armoured car and the door was shut. Hector immediately went to open the door again, but Mrs Warp's voice rang out.

'No Hector. You must stay.'

'We've got to help,' insisted Kate, while giving the gloomy Mrs Warp a defiant stare.

'You are the primary targets. Pierre and Andrè will stop helping your parents and protect you as soon as they know you are there.'

The inhuman and brutal logic felt like a blow to the stomach. In order to help they had to restrain themselves and do nothing.

'But they've been shot,' shouted Hector at Mrs Warp.

'I know, I heard it on the radio. Wait a moment,' said Mrs Warp calmly, as gunfire rang out nearby.

Kate glanced around for a radio, but then realised that Mrs Warp almost certainly had a radio built into her, and that Pierre might even have been speaking to her when they were trapped in the zoo office.

'Your mother has been hit near her armpit. There is an entry and exit wound and no damage to the ribs,' said Mrs Warp.

'Will she be alright?' asked Kate.

'Yes. Your father has been hit in the mouth by some shrapnel. He has lost some skin and possibly a tooth. He will recover.'

'But his face was covered in blood,' Hector declared.

'Head wounds always look bad. Your father will recover,' said Mrs Warp, just as her legs gave another nasty flash of electric blue.

'They are trapped in a building under gunfire,' Mrs Warp continued, 'we must leave.'

They were ushered to the front of the armoured car and Mrs Warp gestured for Kate to take the driver's seat.

'Why?' asked Kate.

'I cannot drive,' said Mrs Warp.

As Mrs Warp explained the controls, Hector noticed that the gunfire had become heavier. There were explosions and occasional bangs as small fragments from the blasts hit the armoured car.

Kate set off with a lurch, but they had only moved ten metres when an explosion blew out a wall on their right, scattering their path with debris. A car drew alongside and bullets hit their vehicle. Kate instinctively turned away from it, and through the hole in the wall. Judging by the cages, they were back in the zoo. To make matters worse, some of the animals were roaming free. In fact, they were rampaging in terror. Kate reflected that this made the animals more dangerous.

'Are there any weapons?' asked Hector.

'No'.

'They've got weapons,' said Hector in a calm, factual way, while looking through the tiny window at the rear of the armoured car at the gang chasing them.

'Oh, it's Sludge!' said Hector, in the same cheery tone he would use if recognising a friend.

'Do they have rocket launchers or grenades?' asked Mrs Warp, who was still standing calmly by Kate, as if coaching her during a first driving lesson. Hector noted that one of the strange things about Mrs Warp was that she did not sway and bump as the armoured car charged through the zoo. Her iron grip on the hand rail beside her meant that she did not move at all relative to the vehicle.

There was a bump as the car behind hit them.

'Sludge has jumped off the car onto our car,' said Hector.

'Oh crickey,' muttered Kate as fear for her own safety finally loomed above all of her worries for Mum and Dad.

'It's quite all right, there is no way he can break in to this car,' said Mrs Warp in her best reassuring tone.

'Why should he?' asked Hector, 'I should think he's attaching the explosives above us right now.'

Kate braked hard. There was a bang as the car behind hit them, and Sludge fell from the roof in front of them.

'Brilliant Kate!' yelled Hector, 'Now run him over.'

'Yes, dear, it's a good idea,' encouraged Mrs Warp.

Kate spun the wheels and crunched the gears as she set off in pursuit of the now running Sludge. He had a head start and kept changing direction, which meant that Kate had to turn sharp corners, most of which she managed only by bouncing off the buildings. Hector was impressed by the amount of damage his sister was causing.

'The car isn't following us anymore. I think you ruined it Kate,' yelled Hector.

There were more turns, slides and horrible crunching noises as Kate changed gear. Hector was surprised by how fast and fit Sludge was. As they charged around the zoo they gained on Sludge on the straight, but lost ground whenever he changed direction and they had to turn a corner.

'There's something wrong. I think I've damaged the way it goes,' said Kate.

'What?' asked Hector.

'When it's in number 3 it doesn't go,' explained Kate.

'Oh, you've ruined the gears,' said Hector, who had nurtured an interest in vehicles for a long time. 'Just use two and four and skip gear three.'

They were now in a part of the zoo that did not have any cages or enclosures. As Kate rammed the armoured car around the next corner they discovered a dead end. As if prayers had been answered, Sludge was cornered.

'Brilliant!' declared Hector, 'Squash him and kill him!'

'Hector! That's murder!' Kate objected.

'Kate!' Hector admonished in desperation, 'you're as bad as Mum and Dad. Why do you think this is difficult? You've just been trying to run him over. Either squash him now or wait until later, when he rips our heads off.'

'I think Hector's correct,' said Mrs Warp, 'we should squash him.'

Sludge was trying to climb the walls. There were no windows or doors to smash through, but his attempt to climb a drain pipe merely pulled the pipe off the wall and left him in a heap.

'Look at him. It's not fair,' declared Kate.

Hector had began to complain that Sludge was not fair either, but Mrs Warp found a button that operated the loudspeaker on top of the armoured car.

'If you surrender,' said Mrs Warp as her amplified, but thin voice bounced off the walls, 'then you will live.'

'No he won't,' said Hector, equally amplified, 'I thought we were going to squash him,' It occurred to Hector that on moral issues Mrs Warp was broadly programmed to follow the last opinion she heard.

It occurred to Sludge that there were at least some in the armoured car that wanted him crushed and killed. Sludge was not clever, but even he could detect a life and death debate when it was broadcast over a loudspeaker. He ran towards the armoured car and dived right under it.

'Reverse quickly!' yelled Hector, 'Wiggle about. The wheels might squash him.'

Kate slammed the armoured car into gear and began to reverse just as Sludge was emerging at the rear. There was a dull thud as he was hit and run over, followed by a crunch as the armoured car connected with the building on the left hand side and was partly spun around until it was firmly wedged in the tight alley, with the front of the vehicle embedded in the building on the right hand side.

'We're jammed between the buildings,' Kate announced, almost as if it was nothing to do with her.

'Sludge is running away,' said Hector, before adding, 'He's stopped. I think he knows we're stuck. He's coming back.'

'Oh no, he knows we were trying to run him over,' said Kate in a tone of desperation.

'It's worse than that Kate,' said Hector cheerfully, 'You did run him over; just now, when you were reversing. He'll kill us anyway. I don't think it makes any difference.'

They watched as Sludge climbed on top of the armoured car.

'Can he get in?' asked Kate.

'No,' said Mrs Warp.

'I bet the explosives are still on the roof,' said Hector, cheerfully.

'Hector!' complained Kate.

Mrs Warp made straight for the rear door. Once outside she clambered inelegantly to the roof. Strangely, there was no sound, just an unexpected thump from the rear as Mrs Warp landed with Sludge on top of her.

Kate and Hector looked through the open door in fascination. Clearly, Sludge was taken by surprise. He expected to land on top of this middle-aged woman and then return to the task of killing the children. She was supposed to be unconscious or dead, not gripping him by the throat and asking him to surrender.

Sludge hit her hard in the face with his fist. Mrs Warp hit him back. Sludge struggled to break free from the grip she had on his neck. He twisted round, broke free, jumped up and kicked Mrs Warp with all his might in her stomach.

It was at this point that Sludge noticed the open door into the armoured car. He lurched towards it, and towards Hector and Kate. Mrs Warp grabbed his leg with her left foot, which closed around his leg like a hand. Sludge had a hand on the door frame. Kate shot forward and slammed the door on his hand.

There was a yell of pain from Sludge, just as Hector marvelled at how his sister could be so afraid, and yet still be so aggressive. Sludge pulled the door open again only to be hit hard in the face with the end of a pole Hector had just found.

'I'm going to kill you!' Sludge roared in pain and rage.

'You were anyway,' said Hector in a tone that Kate noticed was still casual, but now edged with fear.

Sludge lurched forward again, but then fell, with a cry of pain. Mrs Warp had kicked him in the groin. Her right leg had extended well beyond its normal length so she could reach him. Clearly, Mrs Warp did not fight fair.

Mrs Warp dragged herself towards Sludge, and then gripped him with both hands. He was panting, clearly trying to recover some control.

'You can surrender now and you will live,' said Mrs Warp.

Unfortunately, this seemed to galvanise Sludge, who reared up like a huge snake, picked Mrs Warp up, and then threw her towards the ground. Mrs Warp extended one of her legs and hit Sludge hard in the stomach. Yet, this time he was ready. He grabbed her leg and swung her around and around. It struck Hector as he scrambled away from the armoured car, that Mrs Warp might be immensely strong, but she was not immensely heavy. Sludge finished his swing with a heave, catapulting Mrs Warp towards the roof of the nearest building.

Mrs Warp hit the wall with a thump, failing to quite reach the roof. She then moved at surprising speed towards Sludge using both her arms and legs. Sludge was ready, and neatly side-stepped her charge, taking hold of her head and trying again to fling her onto the roof. It was only on his third attempt that he managed to catapult Mrs Warp up onto the flat roof of the nearest building.

Sludge turned, ready for the kill. He was fed up with this job. It was very well paid, but had been unexpectedly difficult. Now he could finish it, collect the rest of his pay and disappear.

Unfortunately, disappear was exactly what Hector and Kate had done. Sludge scanned the surroundings; they could not have gone far. He checked inside the armoured car and to his horror there was his bomb, ticking, ready to go off. Sludge turned and ran. There was an almighty explosion. Sludge was thrown to the ground as debris rained down all around.

After a minute Sludge picked himself up. He felt angry and shaken, but managed to cover his head as more small bits of debris thudded to the ground around him. He could not hear a thing. His left arm and back were splattered with blood from a number of smaller bits of shrapnel. Furious, he resolved that even if he was not paid he was going to kill those children.

Kate and Hector had watched Sludge from the roof of one of the buildings in the alley. Now, they too were sheltering from the debris of the explosion. They decided to remain on the roof. Hiding seemed the best option.

'Good idea,' said Mrs Warp, 'stay hidden.'

Finding Mrs Warp was not necessarily a bonus. Her head appeared to have been dented or squashed. It was fortunate that Sludge could not hear very well. The blue sparks she was emitting from her left ear were more of a problem; Sludge soon spotted them.

Kate and Hector had no problems clambering onto the armoured car and then up the drainpipes onto the roof. Mrs Warp was on the roof because she had been thrown there. Sludge, however, was just too heavy, and the armoured car was now in pieces. Every time he attempted to climb one of the drainpipes it came away from the wall.

It was not long before Hector began to pull faces at Sludge. Although Kate initially disapproved, her confidence grew, she felt safer, and she could not help herself; she joined in. Sludge was a killer, a violent criminal, and not someone given to self-control. Children goading him and pulling faces left Sludge incensed.

Sludge began to kick the walls. Even his returning hearing did not lessen his temper. He picked up debris from the explosion and hurled it at Kate and Hector. His aim was surprisingly good, and Hector in particular had to duck on several occasions.

Amazingly, they were having fun. Mrs Warp even joined in with some bizarre insults of her own. She called him a 'pot diddler,' and a 'pancake slice'. Hector and Kate had no idea what these meant, but it all added to the general enjoyment.

'Mrs Warp, have you used your radio to tell Pierre and Andrè where we are?' Kate asked.

'Yes dear. They are in a gun battle with little ammunition left. They cannot help us.'

Just as Kate started to worry about how things would turn out, two rough looking characters rounded the corner and called to Sludge. After a brief conversation, it was immediately apparent what they were going to do. They handed Sludge a gun and prepared to give him a leg up onto the flat top of the building.

The mood had quickly moved from fun back to dangerous reality. Only Mrs Warp could save them now.

'Oh good!' said Mrs Warp, as two lionesses appeared at the entrance to the dead end.

'Great!' Kate exclaimed.

'Good luck with the killer cats!' yelled Hector, still immersed in a gloat-filled glow of happiness.

Sludge had been about to climb the building, but suddenly his associates had other things to worry about.

'Sometimes,' said Mrs Warp, returning to her encyclopaedia mode, 'big cats from a zoo can be more dangerous than completely wild ones. You see, animals in the wild are often cautious or even afraid of humans. Once they become used to us, however, this fear can leave them, and they can be more willing to attack.'

Hector decided to ignore Mrs Warp's decision to include herself in the human race.

'Why don't you explain that in French, to the nice people below,' said Hector, 'it might panic them.'

'Good idea,' said Kate, as Mrs Warp began to speak quickly and quite loudly in French.

'Come on kitty!' yelled Hector, 'Din dins. Come and get the tasty criminals.'

Mrs Warp's explanation, together with Hector's obvious gloating, panicked Sludge's new best friends. They backed away, leaving Sludge in front. The lionesses stood for a minute watching.
Kate and Hector could not understand the rapid French from
Sludge's helpers, but they could guess.

Sludge was calm, even as the lionesses moved to opposite sides
of the alley and began to approach. There was more panicked
speech, but not a sound from the lionesses or from Sludge. He was
looking at his gun. It was small, and unlikely to stop a lion according to Mrs Warp. It appeared as though Sludge had reached the
same conclusion.

In one swift movement Sludge turned and shot one of the men
in the leg and the abdomen. He completely ignored the cries of
shock from both men, simply picking up the one he had injured
and hurling him towards the lionesses after a short run.

As the lionesses converged on the injured man, Sludge walked
slowly out of the alley, wholly impervious to the screams and cries
for help. He did not appear to be looking at the giant cats. Both
Hector and Kate were amazed at his calmness, and horrified by his
ruthlessness. They turned away to look at Mrs Warp.

'Sludge is running off. We need to get to the other side of the
zoo,' said Mrs Warp, 'There is support there.'

'What about the escaped animals?' asked Kate.

'I can defend against some of them, but large animals might
push me over and crush you,' said Mrs Warp.

'We'll have to travel from rooftop to rooftop!' Hector announced, completely failing to hide his excitement at the prospect.

Twenty minutes later Hector's hopes were much lower. It was nowhere near as exciting as he expected. There were some buildings
that were joined together, and they could move from roof to roof.

This had allowed them to move well clear of the lionesses. For others, however, they had to check for animals, climb down, and then climb up to the roof of the next building.

For Hector and Kate this was quite easy. Mrs Warp lowered them down using her extendable arms, and gave them a push up onto the next building once they had all quickly crossed whatever space was between the buildings. Getting Mrs Warp onto the next roof proved more difficult. For the lower buildings it was comparatively simple. Mrs Warp extended her arms and pulled herself up. The taller buildings presented difficulties. Usually, Kate and Hector could find something to hold onto as Mrs Warp gave them a push. Mrs Warp, however, could not be helped; she was too heavy. Hector marvelled that Sludge managed to throw her onto a roof.

Some animals did wander past, but mainly harmless ones such as goats. A leopard appeared when Mrs Warp was climbing up onto one roof, and it paid her a great deal of attention. Hector had annoyed Kate by repeatedly saying 'Cool, just cool' over and over again. He continued saying this even when she pointed out that the leopard could probably jump up and kill him if he attracted its attention.

Their adventure improved when they reached the lion cages. Mrs Warp stopped to inform them that their parents were safe. The good news was that their attackers were dead or had fled. The bad news was that there were still some gunmen in the zoo, and that Mrs Warp had been instructed not to radio over her position in case their communications were being monitored. In other words, they were on their own. She was only to give their location if they needed immediate rescue.

'I'm fed up with climbing over every building,' said Kate, 'I'd like to be rescued.'

'What happened? What happened?' Hector demanded.

'Pierre and Andrè stopped firing back to give the impression that they had completely run out of ammunition,' explained Mrs Warp.

'Is that dangerous?' asked Kate.

'Yes, of course,' interrupted Hector, who had now become a military strategist, 'the attackers can approach the building and throw grenades in.'

'You are correct Hector. However, the attackers rushed the building,' said Mrs Warp, 'Most were shot. One has been taken prisoner. From what I heard over the radio two of the attackers rammed a car through one of the doors and Pierre and Andrè were taken by surprise.'

'Are they alright?' Kate quickly demanded. She had been worried for her parents, and just assumed that Andrè and Pierre would come out in one piece.

'Yes, thanks to your father. Apparently, his raw aggression is frightening. Your father was only armed with a large office stapler, but had to be pulled off the last gunman,' Mrs Warp explained, 'I do not know the whole story, only what I gleaned from radio messages.'

The mood had lightened as they made their way across the roof to the next building. There was a delay when they spotted snakes in the gap between the buildings, but Mrs Warp threw small bits of gravel from the flat roof of the building to drive them away.

The next building was more of a problem. It was a huge cage for the gorillas. The top had a slight slope. Kate and Hector had no problems stepping from bar to bar. Unfortunately, Mrs Warp kept slipping and falling over. At one point her foot slipped through the bars and jammed. It took a couple of minutes to free her. The major problem was that Mrs Warp did not seem to be able to hold on to metal very well.

After a while Kate and Hector took to dragging Mrs Warp across the roof constructed of bars. It made a terrible racket, with a metallic clang every time her head hit a bar. There were also scraping and other odd noises from Mrs Warp. She seemed to be saying that they were 'terribly kind,' but it was all drowned out by the clanging and scraping.

The gorillas had not escaped, but one male had climbed up and followed them. He seemed to be evaluating the threat they posed, although he might also have been simply curious.

Hector was just muttering that they were nearly there, when Mrs Warp came to a dead stop. A hand had emerged through the bars and clamped around one of her legs. Kate saw the problem first.

'What shall we do?' she asked.

'Just pull,' Hector suggested, 'Mrs Warp is very tough.'

The tug of war that followed was not only noisy, but witnessed by a family who had taken refuge in a viewing area. A man, who Hector assumed was the father, was shouting up in French. He clearly could not understand why Kate and Hector should be dragging a middle-aged lady across the top of a cage. Mrs Warp shouted back in French.

'I've told him that it's quite alright,' said Mrs Warp, 'but I don't think he agrees.'

Hector decided the situation needed his diplomatic touch.

'We're English! English!' shouted Hector, as if the English normally dragged their relatives across the tops of zoo cages.

By now, the gorilla had let go of Mrs Warp. He was still curious, but content to let Hector and Kate drag her a bit further. The man was trying to speak in English.

'It's OK,' said Hector, 'she's had a bit of a malfunction.'

'Alright,' said the man after a pause, 'Who is she and what is wrong with her?'

'Errm,' said Hector, confused about how much he should divulge, 'She's my grandmother. She has problems balancing on these railings and so we thought we'd drag her.'

'I think this is not right,' said the man, 'She is old, it will hurt her.'

'It's no problem, really,' said Hector, suddenly getting into the swing of an explanation and even a little humour, 'She's old and confused. She dribbles and she has trouble standing up anyway. These bars are very difficult for her. In fact, this is the fastest she's moved in ages. I think she quite enjoys it. Even the head banging seems OK. If we could just play her some of that heavy metal music she'd probably enjoy it even more. She's quite safe.'

'No, no! You will hurt her, you must stop,' said the man, just as Hector made the mistake of releasing Mrs Warp and standing up to listen.

'I can't hold her. She slipping. Hector! Hector!' yelled Kate, as Mrs Warp slid away with a horrible scraping noise as she tried to get a grip.

There was a brief second of silence after Mrs Warp slid head first over the edge of the cage, followed by a crunch as she landed. Kate, Hector and the gorilla looked down. Mrs Warp was impaled on iron railings.

'Oops,' said Kate.

There was a scream from one of the onlookers. The father was saying something in French again.

'Don't worry. Don't worry,' said Hector, 'It really doesn't matter. We've got several grandmothers. This one is a replacement for the one who died last week.'

'She appears mort, errm, dead,' said the father in faltering English.

'I know,' said Hector, 'She's the second one we've ruined. But it's OK. As I said, we've got lots more.'

'Hector! Shut up!' Kate demanded, 'You sound like a mad dictator who kills off old people.'

'Sorry,' said Hector, 'I thought an explanation would help.'

'Hector! There isn't an explanation that gets you past dragging an old lady around and dropping her off a building.'

'OK,' agreed Hector, 'What do we do now?'

As they paused for thought the gorillas began to make noises. Hector spotted the problem. A snake had appeared and exposed its black mouth in a threat. The man, who had just been leaving the shelter of the viewing enclosure to help Mrs Warp, quickly retreated.

'If Mrs Warp still works she might be able to protect us,' Kate reasoned.

'If she's completely ruined we'll get the blame again,' said Hector.

The snake was approaching Mrs Warp, and Hector had an idea.

'Mrs Warp?'

There was a crackle, a blue flash and a mechanical robot-like voice said, 'Yes dear?'

'Oh!' said Kate, 'We've heard that voice before,' remembering the time when Mrs Warp had produced machine guns from her chest.

'If you can reach that snake, could you tear it in two?' said Hector, 'I think it's poisonous'.

One of Mrs Warp's strange arms shot out, grabbed the snake, which bit her to no effect. Her bizzare hand moved and she separated the head from the body. Mrs Warp achieved this with just one hand, and Kate was not sure which looked more frightening, Mrs Warp, or the snake, which she believed was a very fast, aggressive and highly venomous black mamba.

Kate and Hector made their way across the top of the cage. They dropped down to the roof of a lower building, and from they were able to climb down to the ground.

'Mrs Warp,' Kate began as they approached her, 'you're too heavy for us to lift off the railings. Could you use your extendable arms to push yourself off, and then we can try to steady you?'

Mrs Warp crackled as her arms extended to the floor. She pushed herself free, accompanied by the sound of scraping metal. Hector and Kate took some of her weight as she leaned towards them, but it was too much, and they had to jump back as she landed in a heap.

Mrs Warp looked quite pleased with herself. She said nothing, but smiled her pleasant, reassuring smile, as if she had just prepared an attractive salad for everyone towards the end of a warm, sun-filled afternoon. There were a row of puncture marks starting at her head and moving in a diagonal down her body. In addition, her head hung to one side.

Hector could see inside her head and noticed that it contained a lot of machinery and wires, which he assumed were for facial expressions. He had suspected some time ago that her brain was not in her head. He harboured the same suspicion about his school form teacher.

'I think the guy who made her will go nuts,' said Kate.

'Yep,' Hector replied.

They stood staring at her. Hector began to look around.

'We could say they were bullet wounds,' Kate suggested.

'The bullets would either still be in her, or there would be holes where the bullets went out the other side,' said Hector, 'They're army people; they know what bullet holes look like.'

Hector reflected that this was the best he and his sister had ever been. They were in a pickle, and they were reasoning sensibly, and not blaming each other.

'Sorry I let go,' said Hector.

'We'd probably of dropped her at some point anyway,' said Kate, lapsing into giggles. Suddenly, it was the funniest thing in the world. Death might be close at hand, but dropping Mrs Warp from the top of the gorilla cage was very funny. They were in so much trouble after they destroyed the previous Mrs Warp with water and an axe, and now they had done it again. They knew they could not be seen laughing after what looked like the most appalling mistreatment of a middle-aged lady. They both understood that the French family would be watching them. They should not attract any more attention. They needed to be calm, kind and sensible. They needed to look serious and concerned.

Hector and Kate laughed until they cried. The French family looked on in horror at the two murderous English children and their apparently dying grandmother.

Once Kate and Hector had recovered enough to think, Kate spotted a store that sold pastries.

'How does that help?' Hector asked, confused.

'Well, this is France,' Kate explained, 'They are bound to cook the pastries in the little shop. There will be some dough. I bet it's a similar colour to Mrs Warp.'

A short time later they were in the shop pushing dough into the holes in Mrs Warp, and then jamming as much as possible into her neck in an attempt to get her rather loose head to sit straight on her shoulders. The pastry was an excellent colour match, and when Kate and Hector stood back it was hard to spot where the holes had been.

'As good as new,' said Kate.

'Except that her head is slightly squashed, and she has a robot-voice.'

'Except for that,' agreed Kate, 'but we can put that down to the fight with Sludge'.

'Oh, and the blue flashes,' said Hector.

'And the hair,' Kate added, before lapsing into giggles again.

'We could replace that with a big pastry,' suggested Hector.

'It really looks good though,' said Kate, admiring the places where dough had been forced into the holes.

'Yep,' Hector agreed in his most cheerful tone, 'no one will know about our slight accident where we dropped her off the top of a gorilla cage onto some spiked railings.'

This set Kate off again, and they tumbled out of the pastry shop with Mrs Warp clanking along behind them.

Hector mused on how much Mrs Warp cost, and how much damage they had done. He even wondered whether they would be charged for destroying two Mrs Warps.

'I think we should be careful,' said Kate, in a sudden change of mood, 'There may still be some of the gunmen about, and the animals.'

Hector agreed and unhelpfully added that Sludge might even be close. Neither he nor Kate believed Mrs Warp would now be a match for him.

As if to accompany their sudden change of mood, a helicopter approached. They both watched as it grew larger and the rhythmic thumping of the rotors louder. Suddenly, gunfire rang out, clearly aimed at the helicopter.

'Over there! There!' Kate said hurriedly, pointing to where the gunfire was coming from on the ground, approximately two buildings away. Kate and Hector instinctively moved away from it, round the corner of the next building and into the path of two soldiers. The men lowered their weapons and glanced briefly at Mrs Warp as if looking for confirmation, and then at Kate and Hector. They were safe.

A few minutes later they were in a circle of armoured cars. There were soldiers everywhere, and more helicopters arriving. Dad and Mum were sat to one side with a medic each dressing their wounds. Kate and Hector had rushed over to them to receive brief hugs before being shooed away by the medics.

Pierre and Andrè gave them each a hug. Pierre seemed to be limping, while Andrè had a gash on his cheek and red marks around his neck. It looked to Hector and Kate as though some of the fighting had been very close and personal.

'Oui!, Oui!' said Pierre, motioning for another soldier with clothing to come over. Kate and Hector were quickly fitted with large, bullet-proof vests. Both were surprised at how heavy they were. It provided a vivid reminder that the danger was not at an end.

'Oh no!' said Kate, as she spotted the furious-looking man they believed to be Mrs Warp's creator. He was marching towards them with a certain intent. Colonel Bertrand seemed to appear as if by magic. He was clearly warning him to keep his temper.

'What have you done?' the man demanded.

'Nothing,' said Hector, almost instinctively.

'Monsieur Ballingrow, I am sure the damage was all in the line of duty, wasn't it Kate,' Colonel Bertrand prompted.

'She got in a fight with Sludge,' said Kate, 'She was very brave, and saved us,' Kate added, realising that Mrs Warp's success reflected on her creator.

'She's been in a hell of a fight,' said Colonel Bertrand, 'She has done well. You can be pleased.'

Ballingrow still looked furious. Mrs Warp smiled pleasantly. Hector and Kate exchanged relieved glances. They had got away with it.

'I don't think it helped that you caused damage earlier, before the fighting started,' said Ballingrow, looking between Hector and Kate.

'We're sorry,' said Kate, 'but we didn't do anything else,' Mrs Warp had turned to look at her, but her neck made a nasty grating noise as it turned.

About ten metres away there was a man speaking in French and pointing at Kate and Hector. It was the father and the family who had witnessed the accident at the gorilla cage. He paused, and his wife appeared to be helping him with some English words. Hector and Kate felt as though the floor was slipping from beneath them, although she noticed that Pierre and Andrè were trying to conceal grins.

'They dragged, errm, the lady. They traverse the errm top of the cage,' said the father, and he mimed Mrs Warp being dragged along and her head banging on the bars. Mrs Warp turned her head again, accompanied by the horrible grating noise.

'French please,' instructed Ballingrow, Mrs Warp's creator.

'Non, English please,' commanded Colonel Bertrand. Whether this came from a desire to see fairness, with everyone included in the conversation, or whether it was because Bertrand hoped it would limit what the man with the family could say, neither Kate nor Hector knew.

'Her head was, errm, how you say, errm, bashed in.'

'What?' exclaimed Ballingrow.

'They dropped her onto, errm, spikes,' the man continued as Mrs Warp's creator grew redder and angrier. The man mimed spikes going into his body.

'It was an accident. She couldn't hold on, so we dragged her. We didn't mean to drop her,' said Kate, now a little tearful.

'Then,' said the father with the family, 'they laughed. She was, errm, stoook, errm, impaled and they could not stop laughing.'

'She does not look as though she has been impaled,' suggested Andrè, as Colonel Bertrand nodded furiously in agreement. Hector was deeply pleased that they had filled in all of the holes. Kate, on the other hand, was beginning to worry. She knew that dough would grow or rise. She had a feeling that the warmth from Mrs Warp's machinery might have started the process judging by the bumps she could already see.

'I am not sure this account is entirely reliable,' suggested Colonel Bertrand, taking his moment to undermine the father and bring things to a close. 'It was a tough battle, and there are no holes or signs that she fell on any spikes.'

Colonel Bertrand trailed off as the father of the French family approached and pointed at Mrs Warp's face. There were bumps;

definite bumps. Her creator looked at her neck, where a large swelling was beginning. The dough had begun to rise.

'What is this?' asked Ballingrow, as the bumps appeared even more visible. This demand, and the long pause that followed, was a cue for Hector, who decided that his diplomatic skills were required once more.

'Well,' he began, as Colonel Bertrand visibly sagged, 'we filled her with dough.'

'What?'

'Dough! You know, the stuff you make bread with,' said Hector, 'because she was full of holes.'

'Why?'

'Because it seemed like a good idea, and her head was a bit loose. It was already a bit wonky, but once we'd dropped her off the gorilla cage her head became really wobbly. Then her voice went. But we tried our best,' he continued defiantly as Ballingrow turned from red to crimson, 'even when the gorilla grabbed her we gave it everything we had in that tug of war. I thought she'd fall apart.'

'You filled her with bread and used her for a tug of war?' the man shouted.

'Well water ruins her, and we didn't want any more to get in. And she already had some water in her. We thought it would cheer you up if she looked normal,' Hector went on.

'Looked normal! Looked normal, but was really full of holes and bread dough?' Ballingrow shouted.

'Yes, well you got very cross last time. We thought you'd go off like a banshee on a bad night.'

'Hector, Hector, really,' said Colonel Bertrand, as Pierre turned away to hide his laughter, 'I think this is enough detail.'

'No, no, no!' shouted the outraged creator, 'Let us have everything. What else did you do to her you little monster?'

'Well, Kate did some of it,' Hector said instinctively, while instantly regretting it.

'The anaconda wasn't my fault,' said Kate as their final defences fell apart.

'Anaconda, anaconda!' the man screamed.

'We didn't make her get in the pool and wrestle the anaconda,' said Hector defiantly, 'And she spent ages underwater when she was fighting that crocodile.'

'I told you this one isn't waterproof!' Ballingrow shouted at Bertrand.

'Look,' said Hector, 'she's fought a really big crocodile, wrestled and killed a giant snake, fought with Sludge really well, so she's bound to be a bit bashed in.'

'A bit bashed in!' Ballingrow repeated in a scream, 'So you thought you'd finish the job and drop her off a huge cage onto metal spikes, eh?'

'No, no more,' said Colonel Bertrand, but now the father of the French family had started speaking in French. Hector and Kate waited patiently for the next damning piece of evidence.

With the shouting and dispute no one had noticed a huge helicopter pilot approach behind Pierre. The muffled complaint from a man he pushed roughly out of his way attracted everyone's attention.

Pierre turned around, just as the pilot produced a gun. There was a shot. Pierre gasped and fell. It was Sludge.

Sludge quickly levelled the gun at Kate and fired. Even as Sludge fired the shot, Pierre rose up from the ground, covered in his own blood, and launched himself with his legs like a missile, hitting Sludge in the throat with his fist. The force of the blow knocked Sludge back and Hector could see shock on Sludge's face. As Sludge choked and coughed, the gun fired again into Pierre, as Colonel Bertrand hit Sludge on the hand to knock the gun free.

Sludge, still coughing, turned and ran, bowling two soldiers over. Kate was on the floor looking for her own blood. Mum was screaming. Hector could see a hole in Kate's bullet proof vest. Andrè was holding Pierre's head and shouting for a medic. Pierre had closed his eyes. The argument over Mrs Warp was over.

When Hector looked back on that day he could remember nothing more of it. He did not even know when or how he went to bed. At least Kate had been with him. At least the vest had saved her.

CHAPTER SEVEN

Irvine

The following two days were as sombre as they were overcast and damp. They had been welcomed into the camp for the first time. Other children had played with them and let them join their games. Hector was repeatedly run to exhaustion by two brothers who adored tig. Kate enjoyed painting, but found it hard to settle to anything for long. The mood of fear in the camp had been replaced by an unspoken kindness; unspoken in part because of the language barrier.

Kate had time to reflect on this. When the worst happened; when brothers and fathers were lost, then fear retreated. Pierre had not been the only soldier to die.

Dad spent a lot of time with Colonel Bertrand. Andrè had even joked that they were getting on so well him might take them cream cakes, but even his normally boundless joviality disappeared as quickly as it arrived. Everyone was trying to be cheerful, but everyone was struggling.

Kate and Hector were back in the prison cells at night, guarded by new soldiers from another camp. Andrè seemed to be in charge. The cells, the watchfulness, the guns and a general attitude of grim determination made their temporary bedrooms as unwelcoming as a dark corner in a giant spider's cave.

On the second night after Pierre's death, just as they were preparing for bed, they all stopped in surprise as they heard Dad's furious voice bellow from Colonel Bertrand's distant office. Andrè ran to discover the problem, but returned shortly afterwards.

Kate could hear some words and had already worked out the cause. Dad was shouting down the phone at the people who controlled their trust fund. He wanted money to give to Pierre's family, as well as the families of the other soldiers who were lost.

'...died saving my children, at least we can look after his children...I don't care about the rules you pointless idiot...make it happen...well say we damaged something very expensive, anything. Are you deaf, or are you pretending not to understand?'

The whole camp had gone slightly quieter as those who understood English listened and translated.

Dad went on to issue some fairly graphic threats about what he would do when he returned to England if the trust fund did not release the money. Some of these threats involved a sink plunger, and at one point he was shouting about buying a shotgun. Andrè returned to the cells with a grin on his face.

'I don't know why the Colonel lent him the phone. They can probably hear him in England without it.'

It was the first time Andrè had really seemed like himself since Pierre had been lost. One of the soldiers asked Andrè what was going on. Kate assumed that the gabble of French was a translation or summary. The soldiers were all smiling, and then they laughed.

'I said,' explained Andrè, turning to Kate, Hector and Mum, 'that he doesn't need a gun. You should see how dangerous he is with office equipment.'

Dad had become quietly popular. It was well known that he had taken part in the fight despite being injured. His unconventional approach might have been a cause for amusement, but his bravery had won him respect, as had his desire to do what he could for the families. His fight with Colonel Bertrand, who even Hector appreciated was a popular commanding officer, was not forgotten, but had been entirely forgiven.

Now, they had just one difficult day left before they returned to England. They had no idea how they were going to return; it was a secret even to them. Despite everything, Hector was desperately hoping it would be another old plane with guns and parachutes. He really liked the idea of an aerial gun battle followed by some skydiving.

The funeral service the following grey morning was held in a small, modern church. Pierre's family were at the front, and the benches full. Pierre's wife was easily spotted. She was shaking while crying silently, and did not seem to take anything in. Her face was wet and red. Pierre's two children were not crying, but looked shocked and bewildered rather than tearful. They seemed to be a little younger than Hector, and stayed close to their mother. It was as though tonight's nightmare was unexpectedly realistic, and they had yet to wake up.

Hector did not think Pierre would have children, but he did not really know why he was surprised. Maybe this was why Pierre had been so kind to him. Just yesterday he had been introduced to both children, but everything was in French and so he had not understood who they were.

Hector understood funerals; the men looked grim and everyone else cried. Hector was determined not to cry. He was going to be factual. He was going to remain detached. Hector had to think factually and detach himself from his feelings.

Hector had liked Pierre. He had been funny, brave and kind, but he was a soldier, and soldiers sometimes get shot. Mum was crying and Dad looked very solemn, but it was probably just expected. Kate could be expected to turn on the waterworks, but in reality there was little point. Pierre was gone. They should be practical about it and cut out the wailing, although even Hector felt it was probably best if he kept this view to himself.

Hector thought Pierre was a real daredevil, very unlike the comic-book characters who bounced back from every calamity and so had nothing really to fear. Naturally, he would miss Pierre. He had been kind, and he was a hero. Hector thought about the shock on Sludge's face when Pierre launched himself at him. Pierre had been so fierce and fearless. Pierre had saved them all, and would not now be there for his children.

Hector remembered when he first met Pierre, when the special forces soldier said, 'Stay back, I know how dangerous you are.' Hector thought about Pierre's smile when he was teasing him. He remembered Pierre's mock outrage that Hector had burnt down a château by putting a bomb in the microwave. Hector also remembered being asked if he was going to use the toilet properly or blow it up. In all the misery and fear of their first night at the camp, it had been Pierre and Andrè who made him feel safe. He could almost hear Pierre's laugh.

They were singing now. Hector did not sing, except in the shower. In any event, this was all in French.

The music blossomed and the chorus grew, as shafts of sunlight burnt through the windows into the church for the first time. The ground tilted slightly and Hector swayed and fought to catch his breath. The tears came.

Lunch was a sombre affair in Colonel Bertrand's office. Pierre's wife had been invited, but had decided to go straight home after the service.

Dad had been irritated to be called off to answer two phone calls. He seemed more irritable than usual, but curiously more in control of himself. The wound in his face was covered with a giant plaster, but the bruising had spread to his right eye, and the whole right side of his face still appeared swollen.

After the second call Dad returned to announce that the trust fund was now in his sole control, with the court overseeing it. It turned out that the solicitors in London had been thoroughly frightened by any involvement with a family being hunted by a killer like Sludge. None of the London law firms were prepared to take it on.

'Are you sure about this?' Colonel Bertrand asked Dad as he glanced out of the window, clearly referring to an earlier private discussion.

'Yes, given all they have been through they deserve the facts,' said Dad.

A short while later a short, slightly plump man in a loose-fitting suit came into the room. He had a round face, with a thin moustache and balding head.

'Mr Wilkins, welcome,' said the Colonel, standing to shake hands, 'You are looking very well.'

'The diet's killing me; I want to turn cannibal between meals; and none of my clothes fit me anymore, and you said dieting was easy after the first two weeks,' said Wilkins in a distinctly southern american accent.

'I lied,' said Colonel Bertrand with a smile.

'Hey, it's good to meet you folks,' said Wilkins, turning to face Mum and Dad, and clearly ignoring the fact that the Colonel was about to introduce him. 'I'm Dave Wilkins, FBI in the US of A.'

Dave Wilkins sat down and immediately began reminiscing about Pierre. It was obvious that Pierre had been widely known, and Dave had liked him.

'I wouldn't be here if it wasn't for Pierre,' Wilkins continued, 'He was there at that little event when our countries' interests did not completely coincide. Pierre was the one that suggested we all put down the guns and ignore our orders. Bright guy. Got the job done.'

'We seem to have catapulted through top secret and straight into politically embarrassing,' said Colonel Bertrand, with a raised eyebrow.

'Hell yeah, well at least this is all cleared,' said Wilkins, waving a sheaf of papers.

Dave Wilkins continued to talk. After a while Hector began to wonder if he had a special oxygen supply in his bottom, because he rarely appeared to pause for breath. Hector also spotted that although Dave Wilkins expressed sorrow about Pierre, as well as the ordeal Kate, Hector, Mum and Dad had been through, he did not really seem very sorry. It was all exciting events and gossip to him.

Hector's study of the endless Dave Wilkins was interrupted by the arrival of two men with a large machine.

'Mr Wilkins suggested that we should all be scanned,' said the Colonel, 'There is always a chance that one of us has a tracker or some other bug implanted.'

Once the machine was assembled and they all took turns to step into the large airport-like doorway, Dave Wilkins continued to talk about how advanced some tracking technology had become. Even Bandit was brought into the room and scanned.

'Irvine Deeds used some of this technology on the people he was keen to keep tabs on,' said Wilkins.

'You think some of his relatives may have picked up his tricks?' asked Dad.

'No, we know that Irvine Deeds was the one who set Sludge on you,' said Wilkins, and he even paused while everyone absorbed this information.

'Well, that's daft!' said Hector, 'He gave us all of that money.'

Wilkins smiled, while Colonel Bertrand looked puzzled.

'Prepare for a story of money, murder and deception,' began Wilkins.

'Yes,' said Dad, evidently impatient with the theatrics, 'I imagine money, murder and deception covers roughly ninety percent of what the FBI deals with.'

'Ok! Ok!' said Wilkins, holding his hands up, 'Irvine Deeds made Hector and Kate the sole beneficiaries of his will and let his relatives know about it. He made sure it was legally watertight. Deeds was worried one of his relatives might have him killed, and with his relatives and the sort of company Irvine Deeds kept that isn't hard to imagine.'

Dad was giving Wilkins the 'I know all this' look, but Dave Wilkins was not a man to be easily hurried.

'Irvine Deeds had connections all over the world. He was connected with a lot of dodgy business dealings, and people who crossed him often ended up beaten up and sometimes dead. We have a lot of evidence on him. We can link him directly to at least four killings; two of them where he pulled the trigger, but there is never enough to get a conviction.'

'Last year one of my colleagues got wind of some insider trading. This is using private market information. You know the sort of thing; something good or bad has happened to a company and their share price is about to go up or go down, and Irvine Deeds knows this before everyone else, so he starts buying stock or short selling.'

'Deeds showed up on some market analyses. He was getting too lucky too often, so lucky in fact that he could have won the lottery as many times as that old crook Mugabe in Zimbabwe. We managed to get a judge who understands math to let us bug his phones and all that stuff. Boy, did we strike gold. Deeds was right at the centre of something much bigger than we suspected. I know how much you inherited, and let me tell you that it's a tiny fraction of the money he really had stashed away in all sorts of foreign companies.'

By now Hector was bored, but Kate was several steps ahead.

'Deeds faked his death, didn't he?' said Kate.

'Smart girl! Deeds died in a helicopter crash at his ranch. He knew he was about to be arrested. He had an idea of how much we had on him, and so he got real drunk and started flying his helicopter around. Wow, what a mess. Of course, it wasn't really Deeds, but a relative some of his thugs had kidnapped a week earlier. Bloodstream was full of alcohol and sedatives. The DNA matched and we bought it. We thought he was dead. Now we know he isn't, and we still can't work out how he got the guy he killed to take off.'

Now, Hector was interested.

'So, does that mean we have to give the money back?' Hector asked.

'Wow, wow, hang on,' said Wilkins, 'he had a legal agreement to be executed if he was declared or even suspected dead. He was really scared of being assassinated. It was not a normal will. It was watertight. Besides, Deeds can't pop up in a court to challenge his own will after faking his death, because we've got a cell waiting for him.'

'Are you saying that Irvine Deeds is the one trying to kill us?' asked Dad, 'because it still doesn't make sense. Once we are dead he still will not get the money.'

'Well, that's the interesting thing,' explained Wilkins, 'he doesn't want you all dead, least I don't think so. He wants to kill one or two of you so that whoever is left will be in the desperate position of not wanting to lose anyone else. It's a tactic he's used before.'

'I don't understand,' said Hector.

'Hector,' said Kate, returning to annoying mode, 'Deeds had a will that gives everything to us so he wouldn't be killed by his relatives. He faked his death to escape the FBI and however many decades of prison he was facing. He didn't mean us to get his money. Now he wants it back.'

'That's right,' said Wilkins, 'He tried to get some of it out, but it was blocked because the bank got the news very quickly. Well, everyone got the news, it was a big fireball on a big ranch. He probably assumed he could beat you up until you gave in. I think Sludge has been a bit too over the top for Deeds, however, as this zoo incident has attracted international news teams. Sludge was supposed to kill one of you, not start a war. The pilots who shot you up in that plane were supposed to kill one of you and allow the others to parachute to safety. Sludge seems to have forgotten his orders.'

'Could we give him the money now so he'd leave us alone?' asked Mum.

'Yeah, I think that would have worked except for two problems. Deeds hired Sludge, and that's the first problem. I'd like to talk a bit about him in a moment. The second problem is that Deeds is dead; I mean really dead this time. He used some contacts he had in the Mexican drug gangs to get him out of the USA. Unfortunately, he trusted the wrong people. One of our agents was there, got photos, DNA, the works. So you can't negotiate with a dead Deeds,' Wilkins finished, evidently enjoying his poor joke.

At this point Wilkins took a sip of his coffee and Colonel Bertrand used the tiny pause to explain a little more about Sludge.

'We know him as Sludge, but he first worked for some gangs extracting money in Australia under the name of Paul Simmons. Sludge developed an image; once you give him a job he will get it done, even if it takes him a year. He cannot be called off. He will not stop even if the person who gave him the job tells him to stop. His reputation in the criminal world is built on his madman-like determination. He charges millions per hit plus expenses. Even the criminals are afraid of him, and they never argue about his expenses. Having him on your tail has been like having a death sentence, but then the people he has killed in the past have not had an army to protect them.'

'Hey come on Bertrand,' Wilkins interjected, 'what about some of those jobs in africa?'

'They were not the most professional,' said the Colonel, 'This time there is a real determination to get rid of Sludge. Governments are united on this. We have a lot of cooperation.'

'Yeah, but also some leaks,' said Wilkins.

'So,' Dad began, 'is this about protecting us or getting rid of a killer even governments fear?'

'A bit of both,' said Wilkins, 'plus the French have nailed their colours to your mast.'

'What does that mean?' Hector asked, turning to his mother.

'It means that the French Government has said they will protect us. If they fail, it's...,' but Mum trailed off.

'If we fail it devalues the French Government in the eyes of other nations,' explained Colonel Bertrand, 'This is good because it means we will not have a problem with getting what we want; you know, resources, agreement to do things, that sort of thing.'

'I don't like being the bait for the trap,' said Dad to the Colonel, 'as I know I've mentioned.'

The Colonel sighed and shrugged his shoulders, then Dad explained that he wanted to run over the issue one more time, as they had clearly discussed it previously.

'You can take on a different identity and move to another country,' the Colonel explained, 'but Sludge has millions of dollars and we know he will not give up. He will track you through your money and through your contacts with friends and relatives. It will take him a while, but he will find you eventually, even if he was not getting some of his information direct from leaks in the French and British Governments.'

'He will also have informers in the US,' Wilkins chipped in, 'with the money he's got it wouldn't be a problem and we know he knows people.'

'Your other option is to live in a prison,' the Colonel continued, 'It could be made into quite a nice prison, but it would still feel like imprisonment. Plus, I think Sludge would still eventually find a way of attacking.'

'Finally, you could go with the option we have discussed at length. You can return to England, apparently rejecting the help offered to you. You can make an amateur attempt to hide, to make sure the wait is not too long, and then Sludge is killed or captured when he attacks. Yes, to a degree you are being used as bait, but the other approaches just delay the day when he finds you. When you are defending someone or something, time and complacency are great enemies. You do not want a period of years in which Sludge might eventually track you down. It gives him so many days when he might turn up.'

There was silence. Mum looked at Dad, and Dad looked back. Mum winced, as she now often did given the huge bruising around her ribs. Kate felt a pressing weight, as if she had just been told they were to wait for the executioner and hope he made a mistake. As she reflected on this she realised that this was almost exactly their position; the executioner was Sludge, and they had been told not to delay.

Hector felt cheerful. True, he had been frightened, but only briefly. He had also felt very sad about Pierre. Yet, when it came to him, Mum, Dad and Kate it always seemed to work out one way or another. Even when Mum and Dad had been shot the wounds were not too serious. A return to normal life would be too dull to contemplate.

He was praying for another aerial dogfight; maybe he and Kate would be trained to fly fighter aircraft because this was the thing Sludge would never expect. His other alternative was a return to England in a submarine. He relished the prospect of nerve-racking moments as they were tracked by the hunter-killer Sludge would have stolen. The thunderous explosion of a near miss, the screams of fear, the hiss of pressurised water powering in, followed by panic and a miraculous escape. He was also hoping for some sort of firefight when they reached dock in England.

Hector and Kate had been interviewed before the funeral by an English lady about how they were coping. Hector had guessed that it was a psychologist and decided to be frank. Despite the bad things that had happened, this had been the best week of his life. His only real complaint was that he thought he deserved more medals. He always believed that people would be pleased when he was open and honest. However, the psychologist seemed unimpressed as she repeatedly underlined the words, 'paucity of medals'. Nor was she interested in his complaints that he did not have more medals as the French authorities were sulking just because he had destroyed two Mrs Warps and a large château.

Hector now wondered whether he could talk Colonel Bertrand and Andrè into allowing him to use a machine gun. When the inevitable gunfight at the docks back in England started he could leap down from a container, right into the middle of the baddies, and spin round, shooting them all.

'Hector, Hector! Are you paying attention?' It was Dad, ruining a top-notch daydream.

'Mr Wilkins, please continue,' said Dad.

'Sludge is the person who unites the various agencies; FBI, CIA, French Secret Service, MI5 and MI6 in the UK. Your plane, the one he tried to have shot down, then that ridiculous attack on the zoo, well these things can't be hushed up. Politicians are asking who he is, and why he's at liberty.'

Wilkins paused, looking from person to person, clearly pleased that he was once again the centre of attention.

'You'll have all of our intel. If you give us the location we will watch from overhead and give you live feeds.'

'No,' said Dad, 'if you have a leak then Sludge will know from your surveillance that we are better prepared than we appear. We want him to think that we are just hiding, having lost faith in any government.'

'But, we would like the intelligence,' It was Andrè. Hector and Kate had not even seen him enter the room.

'Good to see you again Andrè,' said Wilkins, but with a very slight difference in tone that suggested he was not at all pleased.

'I have a file here. This is some of what we know. There's other stuff we don't want to commit to paper,' said Wilkins, leaning in with a conspiratorial air.

'We've known for some time that Sludge is close to being the top hit man in the world. He's strong, brave, resourceful and fast, but if brains were dynamite he wouldn't have enough to blow up a balloon. We've always suspected that he's guided by someone else and now we've found out who.'

Wilkins produced a photograph of a woman who appeared to be about forty-five or fifty years old.

'This is Marie Maga. She's originally from Poland, but defected on an athletics tour during the Cold War. Quite a looker in her day, and she's been married to two very nasty big-time crooks. Bright girl. Got a first class degree in Chemistry. Never finished her Ph.D.'

'Sludge trusts her with his money, safety, everything. She organises things for him, plans it all, gets the weapons. Stealing planes and weapons from collectors was her idea. We even think she's calmed him down a bit; made him that bit more professional; knocked off a few rough edges. She's got people all over the place on the payroll. She knows how to blackmail and threaten. She's about as trustworthy as Irvine Deeds, may God rest his stinking, rotten soul.'

'Why does Sludge trust her?' Kate asked.

'Because, she's his Mom,' Wilkins declared, with the flourish of an overconfident card player revealing his winning hand, 'She's his biological mother. Gave him up when he was born, not the maternal sort I'd guess. We think his father was some thug who worked for her first husband. How the hell she found him after he'd been adopted in Australia and then guided so carefully into the Australian Youth Justice System, I just don't know. Probably bribery and blackmail.'

'So, they have brains and brawn,' said Dad.

'And, they have intel,' said Dave Wilkins.

There was a pause as Dad and Colonel Bertrand looked at one another.

'OK,' Dad said with a sigh, 'I agree. Awful plan, but the best we've got.'

'So officially, you have rejected all help and you will leave to-morrow in disgust,' said Colonel Bertrand, 'My report, and the report Mr Wilkins submits, will say that you intend to hide in the UK, convinced that Sludge will never find you.'

'Dave,' said the Colonel, turning his attention to Wilkins, 'I do not mind what you say once things are settled, but I will find out if you submit a second more secret report that lets anyone in your country know about the unofficial support. It would have a great impact on cooperation, and friendship, I do...'

'OK, OK, I know when I'm being threatened,' said Wilkins with a smile, 'I'll report a falling out and nothing else.'

A short time later Wilkins was gone, while Kate and Hector were in the Colonel's outer office, as there was no one to escort them back to the jail. Hector could see Mum with the Colonel and Pierre's wife. Both seemed to be crying, while Colonel Bertrand looked very tired, and Dad was out of sight. Hector hung on to Bandit and hugged him a little bit more.

It seemed a lifetime since Hector had ruined the Colonel's aquarium and flooded his office. Despite the shouting, the bangs and the anger at the time, the sun had seemed a good deal brighter. Now all they had to look forward to was a return to a dismal, wet England from a grey, leaden France.

CHAPTER EIGHT

Trains

Hector's dreams of flying lessons, dogfights and yet more excitement were dashed the next day.

'By train, really? Awwww.'

Hector's mood improved slightly when he discovered that they were to leave camp by helicopter. He found himself, for the first time, wondering where his luggage was. It only took a few moments for him to remember that it was all destroyed in the crash landing at the airport.

Two heavily-armed Gazelle helicopters were already in the air by the time they boarded. Two more helicopters sat in bright sunshine with their rotors spinning. It was supposed to look like an exercise. He and Dad were in one Gazelle, and Mum and Kate were in the other.

There were no goodbyes; these had been said earlier in the prison block. They were dressed in army fatigues, although both Mum and Dad had a small backpack with normal clothes.

The take off was swift, but they stayed close to the ground, skimming the tree tops. For Mum it was horrifying, even worse than the pain of climbing into the helicopter. For Kate and Hector it was electrifying.

After ten minutes of heading south, they banked heavily, turning north-east. Everyone appreciated that this made them very hard to follow from the ground, but only Hector and Kate enjoyed the ride. The helicopter would move unexpectedly up or down, depending upon the currents of air it hit. The pilots were confident and experienced, but to everyone else it felt unsafe. They raced ever forwards, following the contours of the land, and Kate even saw one of the leading helicopters fly underneath the electricity lines between pylons.

Hector decided that this was the only way to really enjoy countryside; at high speed, just above it. He looked down to see meandering lanes, hedge-rows, hills, ponds, streams, lakes, woods and houses racing past. He thought about how much better this was than flying high, walking or even cycling, which was one of his favourites.

All the helicopters were heavily armed, but the two lead helicopters were the main protection. Hector could see the heavy, aircraft grade machine guns, as well as quite a few tubes. He pointed these out to Dad who explained that while the forward tubes probably fired missiles, the rear tubes fired bright, hot flares or chaff. The flares distracted heat-seeking missiles, while the chaff was supposed to confuse radar-guided missiles, and consisted of many tiny strips of metal.

There was drama fifteen minutes into the flight, with chatter between the pilots. Their helicopter banked heavily to the right, and Hector saw the others go in another direction. Now they were even lower, actually flying between tall trees.

'What is it? What is it?' Hector demanded.

'Strong radar I think,' said Dad, 'my French isn't good, but I think one of the pilots thought it was close to a lock on.'

'Wow, what's a lock on?'

'I think it's where the signal is strong enough to indicate that the helicopter is being tracked, ready for a missile to be launched.'

With that Hector heard small bangs from their own helicopter, and saw what looked like dust emerge from some of the other helicopters, and then bright, red flares.

'Brilliant!'

'No, it isn't brilliant Hector,' said Dad suddenly angry, 'I just hope it's standard procedure and not something more sinister.'

As the minutes went by their height increased to just above the tree tops. Hector had worked out that if they were flying between trees it made them a more difficult target. Any missile would most likely collide with a tree and explode before it reached the helicopter. It must also make tracking by radar more difficult.

Hector looked out expectantly. He was not just looking for a missile, he was hoping there would be one heading towards his helicopter. Maybe it would hit a tree, but knock out the pilot and copilot with its explosion. Obviously, he would have to take the controls. He had never flown a helicopter in a flight simulator, but he was sure it would be easy. With luck, he could crash land it on the enemy. It would mean more damage to French state property, but they were not going to give him any more medals so there was nothing to lose on that score.

For Hector, the end of their helicopter flight was as unexpected and disappointing as the joys of the flight. The two Gazelles with the family put down in a large farmyard. There were soldiers in the buildings keeping watch. The other two helicopters stayed in the air circling. Andrè said a quick hello and took the keys to an old taxi. Everyone crammed in, with only Hector asking why they could not fly all of the way to the train station.

From what Hector could see, the French railways were clean, fast and efficient. The food was good and everything worked as it should. There were no old guns or parachutes left in a corner; no curious doors from which shady figures could emerge; no flickering lights or unexplained and dangerous stops. He hated the French railways.

Kings Cross Station was grim. There were lights at the windows and students walking past with backpacks and guitars. Hector had long ago given up on the wonders of being up after eleven at night. Midnight held no allure. He had stopped moaning about not being able to see the Harry Potter bridge and the trolley in the wall. A return home on the train had been the last thing he had expected.

There had been a surprising moment earlier when Hector had pointed to a man on another platform, and in a loud carrying voice announced that he had a false moustache. Everyone looked, and then Hector pointed to another man and then another. In fact, they all had false moustaches, and appeared to be on a night out on the town. Fortunately, they were not in the slightest bit upset by someone pointing at them. Unfortunately, Andrè was furious that Hector had yet again drawn attention to himself. Andrè had expertly guided them through customs and immigration without passports and without fuss, and here was Hector undoing all of his good work.

The 23.30 to Leeds. They were due to get off the train at Newark at around one in the morning. Andrè insisted they wore hoodies so faces could not be easily seen. This even applied to Dad, who said that he would rather be dead than seen in a hoodie. Andrè had pointed out that dead was still a strong possibility, and so Dad had given in, although not before he had pointed out that there might be little difference given Hector's ability to announce himself to the world.

The plan, always the plan. Andrè had said anonymity was the best cover, and the plan was to stay out of sight while others laid false trails. They wanted Sludge to find them, but not too soon. They needed time to prepare the trap. Andrè wanted two months.

Two cars had crossed through the Channel Tunnel with the markers that Sludge and his associates had presumably left attached. The driver of one of the cars carried Mum and Dads' mobile phones. They were travelling to Cornwall in England, and Perth in Scotland. Mum used to have relatives in Perth, and so there was a family connection. Cornwall had always been a popular holiday destination. Both cars would lose their trackers once they reached their targets. The cars would then be sold on to local car dealers, just in case other trackers were attached.

Kate had to remind herself that the plan was not to avoid Sludge forever. Dad had been given the hiding forever option before their meeting with the man from the FBI. He explained this in hushed tones during the train journey across France. Once the lifestyle of living like a prisoner and never contacting friends or relatives again was explained, it had been quickly rejected.

The plan was to find a place to hide. A place where they could prepare for an assault. Given that someone was leaking information hiding was not really a long-term option. The story was that Dad had rejected all help from the security services, and this fitted well with Dad's huge public argument with Colonel Bertrand in the cake shop. Information was being leaked, and so false information was fed into both the French and British police and armed services. Only the heads of the British and French secret services knew the truth. Nothing was on computer. Nothing was written down.

The plan was to make Sludge think they intended to hide forever. The choice of Lincolnshire, just twenty miles from their original home, was not the brightest, and so Sludge would find them, and they would appear ill-defended. A better hiding place would extend the period of time when Sludge and his helpers might appear. They needed Sludge to believe they were poorly prepared, and that their only plan was to hide, but they did not want a two-year timescale in which Sludge might pop up.

Andrè's grim determination was like a faint, ever-lasting beacon in a dark storm. Sludge was going to fail, and Sludge was going to die. Andrè was going to kill Sludge, but Kate suspected that Andrè also intended to show Sludge he had failed. She even feared that Andrè might torture Sludge given a chance. On the other hand, his determination was reassuring. She had no doubt that Andrè would risk everything to save her and Hector and Mum and Dad. It was very personal, and her family was the prize.

Once the train started to move Hector quickly disappeared to the First Class carriages to see if there were any biscuits he could snaffle. Andrè was angry; as ever, the world was Hector's playground. When he returned empty-handed, Hector deployed his most appealing grin when asking if he might be allowed to drive the train, even for a very short time. Hector was endlessly annoying, but adults could not see it. The guard even said he would ask, and Kate managed to steel herself and maintain her silence. What she wanted to do was point out that this small boy had recently crash-landed a real plane, destroyed a German tank, and was perfectly capable of leaving any train in a heap of smouldering ruins.

Yet, the burst of energy the moving train supplied soon dwindled. Hector was asleep thirty minutes later, quickly followed by Mum. Kate noticed that Dad was more awake. He had changed since his talks with Colonel Bertrand. He seemed calm, but in charge. He did not always agree with Andrè, but he was more reasoned and less angry. Kate suspected that Colonel Bertrand had pointed out that, however unfair, the dangerous situation his family were in was just the way it was, and he could either lose his temper and storm about, or act like a leader and think about the options. Dad often questioned Andrè about why things should be done this way or that, but he did not resist. It was as if he was stor-ing things away, ready for later.

One of the surprising things Kate learned was that Andrè was completely confident that they were relatively safe alone. Sludge also had problems with intelligence leaking, and apparently he had made it very clear to those who fearfully worked for him that he had to be the one who killed the children. In addition, he wanted the whole family, not just Kate and Hector. Irvine Deeds might have wanted just one or two members of the family killed, but Sludge felt his reputation as an efficient killer had been damaged. He was going to restore it by wiping out the whole Trogg family in a single attack. He did not want a piecemeal approach of one kill followed by another that could last years. He was paid by some of the most ruthless people in the world, and his survival depended on them believing that no one could hide from him. Kate fell into an uneasy sleep.

The next day, Kate remembered Newark North Gate train station, even though she could not remember falling asleep on the train. The station was old fashioned, with large car parks all around the entrance. She remembered being sleepy. There were some men there. Andrè knew them, but they were English. The large, old-fashioned clock showed one o'clock. She had no memory of leav-ing the station, nor of going to bed.

Hector and Kate woke at almost the same time. They were in a small bedroom with wallpaper that had been painted white. Mum brought them both a drink of water.

'Where are we?' asked Kate.

'In a safe house. One of the terraced houses opposite the station,' said Mum.

'How long will we stay here for?' Hector asked, already concerned that he might become bored.

'About an hour. After breakfast and a shower we can leave.'

Two hours later they were in a builders van on the road towards Lincoln. Hector had just about forgiven Kate for throwing cold water over the top of the shower, but Kate was still feeling resentful about the ointment Hector had mixed into her toothpaste. Without doubt the best thing was that Bandit was now with them. Apparently, he had been in a cage on the train. Now, he was allowed on the rough seat with both of them.

Kate and Hector assumed that Bandit was so happy because he was with them. In truth, he was happy to be cuddled. Happy to be with the main contingent of his pack. Happy to be next to someone who his nose told him was hiding a packet of sweets. Happy to be out of that cage and on a comfortable seat more befitting of his importance and status. Most of all, however, he was happy to breathe the air of a Lincolnshire spring, even if filtered through the van's heating system. The air had a wealth of smells. The ones he recognised were exciting. The ones new to him were intriguing.

'Where are we going?' Hector asked.

'To a place called Rothwell, near Caistor,' Andrè replied, 'We have to meet someone there, and they will tell us where we are going to stay.'

'Why can't they just tell us on the phone?'

'We have to be very careful with communications,' said Andrè, 'They can be intercepted. We do not want to be found until we are ready.'

'I've just had a thought,' said Kate, 'Why not set up a place for us to stay and for Sludge to attack, but we can be somewhere else. What's wrong with that?'

Andrè laughed. Dad turned around and smiled lopsidedly as best he could with his heavily bruised face.

'It is a good idea,' said Andrè, 'but we have already thought of it. If you and your parents hide, we will still have to protect you there, just in case Sludge discovers where you really are.'

'Also,' Dad chipped in, 'We're fairly sure Sludge will not attack until we have been sighted. He will not want to attack somewhere if we only seem to be there.'

'But you are quite right Kate,' said Andrè, 'There is another house being set up to appear as though it is the one where you and Hector will be staying. Our hope is that Sludge will attack that house. It is the job of a few people to make it look as though you are staying in Cornwall. Calls your mother and father make will be routed through there to make it appear as though you are a long way from Lincolnshire. If we are lucky Sludge will attack the Cornish house, and some people will be waiting for him and his friends.'

Dad went on to explain that there had been a difference of opinion between the heads of the British and French secret services. The easily-agreed compromise was to go with the British plan to set up a honeypot house in Cornwall, but also to go with the French plan to make the place where Hector and Kate were really hiding also a trap for Sludge. The French thought Sludge was too experienced to be fooled by the British distraction. The British thought they could pull it off. A case of French or English wine rested on whether the British could succeed.

'For once,' said Andrè, 'I hope we are wrong and the British are right. I know one of the British guys on the Cornwall job. Very professional.'

'Kate, Kate, it's the Queen's birthday soon,' said Hector, making it quite plain that he had been listening to no part of the conversation. He had just lifted his head from a brochure entitled 'Presents Galore'.

'I'm going to send her a fake stubble kit,' Hector declared.

Kate considered a riposte, but as ever Hector's ability to be so unexpected left her unable to construct a sensible reply. This was unfortunate, because Hector was keen to explain all the uses the Queen might have for a fake stubble kit, including a scenario where the Queen was the country's top MI6 agent.

Once around Lincoln, Kate could see more green hedgerow and less road. She felt relieved, as if she was coming home. Of course, they could not return to their own home. Now, that was all in their past. She wondered when she would be able to get the things from her bedroom. Strangely, she longed for her bicycle.

It seemed very strange that they should have been in France for just a few days, and yet with all that had happened it felt like years. Home, school and friends seemed a lifetime away. Not for the first time, she wished she and Hector had not inherited Irvine Deeds' money.

Kate could see the toll it had taken on her parents. Mum was hunched, moving slowly and carefully because of the bruising to her ribs. She was putting a brave face on things, but Kate knew she was worried. Dad's face looked less swollen now, but was black and purple with bruising. If anything, Dad had calmed down. He seemed more measured in his reactions to events.

Hector, as ever, was just annoyingly cheerful. She had overheard a conversation about Hector's comments to the psychologist. It did not surprise her at all that Hector thought it had been the best week of his life. The psychologist thought Hector was putting on a front; deep down he was terrified. Kate thought that deep down Hector really had enjoyed almost everything, and probably hoped every week would be the same. Hector believed he was immortal and so had nothing to really fear.

Kate was woken from her thoughts by the sight of daffodils in the verge on both sides of their path. The bright, yellow flowers lined a curving road that swept down into Rothwell. It was cut into the landscape from centuries of use. As the spring sunshine filtered through the trees Kate felt her hopes rising.

There were farm buildings and houses to the right, with a small stream running in front of them. Ahead was the Blacksmith's Arms. The prospect of lunch in an English public house felt like an escape to heaven. It was as if Kate had grasped at a lifeline and been hauled into the most luxurious of safe havens.

The wait outside the Blacksmith's Arms was an unpleasant shock. It was as if Kate had been shown the door to freedom and safety, only for it to be slammed shut. She and Hector were to wait in the van. Mum and Dad also had to hide, as their injuries made them memorable. It was important that they did not attract attention, or prompt curiosity and questions.

Hector complained, although his attention was drawn to a machine gun Andrè had given Dad. In fact, he had not so much as given it to Dad as pulled the cover off, pointed out the safety catch and just to make sure shown Dad the business end of the weapon.

They were in Lincolnshire. They were home, and yet they were waiting in a van like prisoners, while the guard went to the pub. Kate could hear the mumble of conversations, the chink of plates, glasses and cutlery, as well as louder exclamations and laughter. All she wanted was normality, safety, a pleasant meal, a game of I-spy with Hector, a little bit of boredom, pleadings over puddings, even a squabble and a telling off. Kate just wanted to breathe normally and be normal. It felt like a very special kind of torture.

The waiting was eased when Dad told them about a man called Nickerson, who had owned much of the village of Rothwell. He had numerous wives, but his real claim to fame was he was the only man ever to have been shot by a serving British Home Secretary. Apparently, someone called Willie Whitelaw had accidentally shot him while hunting.

Andrè reappeared with some sandwiches after fifteen long minutes. They were shared around, and Andrè got in and drove smartly away.

'Well done on the food,' said Dad.

'It was a bit difficult,' Andrè confessed, 'I said you were all French and had learning disabilities and so you could not come in. They said that you would be very welcome, and not to worry.'

'And what did you say?' Dad asked, in an accusational tone.

'Well, I had to think of something,' said Andrè, clearly embarrassed, 'so I said you were not like normal people with learning disabilities. I said your problems were severe.'

'And?' Dad prompted, with a hint of a smile playing on his lips.

'I said you were extremely incontinent and you would use all of the seats as a toilet.'

Hector and Kate collapsed into gales of laughter. Dad rolled his eyes in exasperation.

Andrè explained that they had found somewhere almost suitable. They needed somewhere away from other people, so that when they were attacked no one else could be involved. It was also important that they were not easily spied upon. The retired MI5 agent he had met described their new home as the best they could manage in the time available.

Dad was reading through the details Andrè had handed to him when he got into the van.

'It's called Rothwell Hall,' said Dad, 'It has grounds and fields of two hundred and twenty acres, including a small golf course, a lake, a swimming pool, a tennis court, parkland and woods.'

'Sounds brilliant,' said Hector, who was already planning on building his own boat and a massive tree house in the woods.

'The swimming pool has a fun slide and a range of exciting inflatables. There are some drawbacks. It has a hefty rent, and the owner of the house, Dunbar Hellstone, lives in the east wing. We get the rest of it. Apparently, Mr Hellstone is an Earl.'

'That means he likes tea not coffee,' explained Hector. Everyone ignored this, as the depths of Hector's confidence and ignorance were far too great a challenge when the future looked so exciting.

'It comes with a housekeeper,' Dad continued, 'A Mrs Katherine Wells. There is also a secretary called Ms Rogerson, and two groundsmen, both called Mr Hepstall. Apparently, the contract has been negotiated so that we can make engineering changes to the house and grounds, although why it says that when it is bound to be a listed building I don't know. Except for the money, it sounds quite good,' Dad finished turning to Andrè.

'Well, my friend just told me that Dunbar Hellstone needs the money, but is a difficult man,' Andrè explained.

'Who cares,' said Hector, 'we can explore forever and no school.'

'That's not quite true,' said Mum, 'You cannot return to school but we are going to get a couple of local teachers to give you lessons.'

'I would prefer at least a month first,' said Andrè.

'Yes!' said Hector, 'Far too risky. You can't trust teachers. Most of them are trolls.'

Dad looked at Hector with raised eyebrows. Hector deployed his winning smile. What this hid was a myriad of burgeoning plans, including nights in the woods, boats, secret passageways and there just had to be an abandoned mine.

It was a very short distance from Rothwell to Rothwell Hall. There was a large stone wall marking the boundary with the road. The gravel drive that swept into the grounds passed between two brick towers, each the height of a two-story house. Fifty metres on there was a large gatehouse. The drive ran straight through a huge archway in the house. As they drove towards the gatehouse Kate could see arrow slits in the walls to either side. She knew from her history lessons that this was not just an entrance. It was a medieval defence; a killing field, where robbers, invaders or other unwanted guests could be slaughtered.

The gates were open and the portcullis up. They drove straight through, and on into the wood beyond. Large beech and ash trees were scattered amongst giant, crashing waves of daffodils. Bandit had started to whine and wriggle.

'I think he needs the toilet,' said Kate.

They stopped and Bandit dodged the lead Kate was trying to attach, and burst into the woods. He crashed through the first wave of daffodils to be rewarded by the panic, squawk and flap of a startled bird taking flight. He paused briefly to mark a tree, delighted to be ruffled by a strong breeze bringing new scents, before racing on, plunging into a muddy ditch.

Bandit could hear his name being called. It hardly stirred his curiosity, not when weighed against the heaven he now had to explore. Kate and Hector were chasing, which was just fantastic. He could lead the whole pack into exciting adventures.

Yet, as he stopped to mark another tree, a figure dived from behind it and seized him by the scruff of the neck. He yelped in shock, and struggled to free himself. Then he caught the smell. It was Andrè, breathing quite hard. It was time to use the large sorrowful, brown eyes.

Once Bandit had been dragged back into the van, the stink of the mud he had discovered in the ditch hit them all. All windows were opened. Only Bandit liked his new perfume.

The drive through the grounds to Rothwell Hall was longer than any of them expected. It meandered through the rolling hills of the Lincolnshire Wolds, past a number of small lakes and ponds, before opening up to reveal a wide parkland valley, with an imposing red brick hall next to a long lake, over which willow trees seemed to hover.

As they descended into the valley they could see that Rothwell Hall had three white domes. The Hall was three stories high, except for the domes, each of which added a further level. Dad informed them that it dated partly from the Elizabethan period, although it was largely rebuilt in 1938, all of which meant little to Hector. The last part of the drive was lined with smaller trees, bursting with pink blossom. As they emerged into the larger gravel area in front of the Hall everyone looked, expecting to be greeted.

Ten minutes later Dad appeared from around the back of the Hall with a stout woman in her sixties. It was Mrs Wells, the housekeeper.

'I am sorry,' said Mrs Wells, in an accent that reminded Kate of holidays in Cornwall, 'Ms Rogerson was supposed to be here. In fact, I think that will be her and Lord Rothwell now.'

They all followed Mrs Wells' eyes to the drive. A Range Rover was making its way at speed long the drive towards them.

'I am pleased you're here. I am sorry, but I've not been told anything about you,' Mrs Wells continued, 'everyone calls me either Kath or Nana.'

'I'm Kate, and this is Hector.'

'And we're hiding here from some criminals who are trying to kill us,' Hector added.

'Hector!' Mum admonished.

'But it's true,' Hector protested, 'Mum and Dad got their injuries in the attack at the zoo.'

'Oh my word!' said Nana quietly, 'You were at that zoo in France.'

'Hector, is there anything you can't blab to the world?' Dad asked in an annoyed tone, before adding, 'Think more, speak less.'

'Hello, hello,' came a voice from a man with a pudgy face and bouffant hair, 'I'm Dunbar Hellstone, Eleventh Earl of Rothwell, but if that's a bit of a mouthful then just my Lord is acceptable, or Lord Rothwell.'

'Hello Dunbar,' said Dad, clearly unsure as to whether the pompous display was for amusement or whether the man was serious, 'I'm Trevor Trogg, and this is my wife Sarah, and my two children, Hector and Kate.'

Hellstone glanced at the bruised faces, and then his eyes lingered on the scruffy van and the mud-encrusted, but happy dog.

'I will need payment ASAP,' Hellstone said, before turning his back and walking into the Hall, while adding 'They'll show you around'.

Mum and Dad exchanged glances. Hellstone's rudeness had clearly annoyed Dad.

'Mrs Wells, errm Kath, could you show us around?' Dad asked, before turning to the other woman Hellstone had not bothered to introduce.

'You must be Ms Rogerson?'

'Yes, I'm Lord Rothwell's secretary.'

'Would you mind distracting the children by showing them the swimming pool? Andrè, I know you want to have a look round, would you mind taking the dog with you?'

The swimming pool was not what had been promised. It was dark and grim, despite being strangely clean, as if it had been scrubbed endlessly by a sleepless psychiatric patient. It echoed to a sinister drip.

The large fun slide, as it had been described, was nothing more than a piece of plywood propped against a wall. The exciting inflatable was a small ring with a swan neck. It did not appear to be large enough to support a small pot plant, let alone anyone sitting in it.

Kate and Hector looked at each other. They were stood with Ms Rogerson in the opening between two large sliding doors. Both were thinking similar thoughts. Mr Hellstone was clearly as mean as he was pompous. The grey, dank pool was a very long way from the mediterranean retreat both of them had heard about.

The gloom and stillness were suddenly shattered by a crash and shouts. Kate, Hector and Ms Rogerson turned around to see Bandit in full gallop towards the pool.

Bandit knew all about swimming pools. He was not allowed in them, but they were just like ditches or ponds, but warmer. Plus, someone would always try to get him out, and that was a great game. All he had to do was swim around until he got caught, and then deploy the big sad eyes and look sorry.

'No! No!' shouted Ms Rogerson, putting her hands down to ward him off and moving to block his jump into the pool.

It took only a neat sidestep to evade her legs, but Bandit's second-rate steering meant that his bottom bounced off her shins. The splash as Bandit rocketed into the water was accompanied by wails and flailing arms as Ms Rogerson valiantly fought to defy gravity. She toppled slowly, but energetically into the pool.

Dad arrived just after Andrè, to find a furious dripping Ms Rogerson climbing out of the pool, while Bandit and Kate were engaged in a tug of war with the already punctured fun inflatable. Bandit appeared to be trying to drag Kate in, and Kate seemed unconcerned about whether she would win or lose.

'Kate, Kate! Please! We've just arrived and you're behaving worse than Hector,' Dad pleaded.

As he ended his appeal Dad saw a completely naked Hector running from a pile of clothes en route to joining Bandit.

'This will not do!' shouted Ms Rogerson.

The pool was still unwelcoming and dark, but Bandit had brightened it up.

After her unwelcome dip in the pool Ms Rogerson disappeared to find clean clothes. Kate and Hector were less fortunate, and Mum had to ask Mrs Wells if she could find any clothes for them.

'Oh, you are a naughty pair,' scolded Mrs Wells, although she did not sound very angry. Hector and Kate were already warming to her.

'What should we call you?' Kate asked.

'Well, most young people who have stayed here have called me Nana.'

Nana went on to explain that a lot of people rented the Hall, but they never stayed long. Dunbar Hellstone, the Earl of Rothwell, drove everyone away. The more Nana spoke the more Kate and Hector felt they could trust her. She had a down-to-earth quality and a kindness. For some reason Dunbar Hellstone was the great regret of her life, but they did not know why. She could not like him, but there was something in her that still loved him.

'There's no living thing that Dunbar has ever shown any sort of consideration for, with the exception of his parrots,' explained Nana, 'Ever since he was nine he's kept parrots, even sitting up through the night to nurse them when they've been ill. Of course, when they died it was everyone else's fault.'

'You don't like him, do you?' Hector asked, displaying his legendary lack of tact.

'Well, that's a difficult one. I was his nanny originally. I was nanny to him as well as his brother and sister.'

'Do they live here?' asked Hector.

'No, he's driven everyone away. Dunbar went to Stowe School. Didn't have many friends. Decided to become a teacher. Made it to headmaster at a school in Yorkshire. The only head ever to be locked out of his own school by a rebellion of students and staff. Hated him they did.'

'If he's so difficult,' Hector ploughed on, 'why hasn't he sacked you?'

Nana laughed, and then turned away.

'Sorry,' said Kate instinctively, while glaring at her brother, 'Hector isn't very tactful'.

'Oh, don't you worry about that,' Nana laughed, 'Dunbar's father, Magnus Hellstone, he was a fine man. Everyone loved him. When he realised what Dunbar was like he made sure, through the family trust that owns the house, that Dunbar can't sack any of us. Now, now, now, Hector Trogg, you're as rude as you're sharp, aren't you?'

Nana gave Hector a penetrating stare, while pulling out a box of cigars from a pocket, before hurriedly putting it back again.

'Should we call him Mr Hellstone, or Dunbar, or Lord Rothwell?' Kate enquired.

'If you want to please him call him Lord Rothwell. If you want to annoy him, call him Mr Hellstone. If you want to see him explode and rocket skywards call him Dun Duns. His brother used to call him Dun Duns, usually just before a big fight.'

Hector laughed. He already liked Nana.

'However,' Nana went on, 'Your Mum and Dad look like they've got a mountain of troubles, and so I think you should call him Lord Rothwell for the moment.'

Nana took them up to their room on the second floor. Again, Hector and Kate were sharing. The Hall was large, imposing, but slightly uncared for. Nothing looked new or refreshed. It was as if life and love had long since departed the Hall.

Their bedroom was enormous, with two large windows, one of which included a door onto a balcony. There were two surprisingly modern beds, and everything smelled clean and fresh, with just a hint of the neglect from the rest of the Hall. The views over the lake, with the hills rising beyond, were spectacular.

Sheep littered one side of the lake, with great herds of trees seeming to hem them in. The trees looked like giants marching down to the lake. Some had the bright green of new spring leaves, while others were still bare. Kate recognised them as beech and oak; the same as the trees in the park near, what was now, their old home.

The lake had a distant island, crowded with scots pine trees, and Kate knew immediately that Hector would be desperate to visit it. There was also a smaller island nearer the Hall, but this seemed to be man made, consisting of rocks. It had an ornament or small statue at its centre.

Flapping and noise attracted Kate's attention to a large aviary. It contained a number of brightly coloured birds. It was near the shore, next to a neglected boat house. Even from a distance Kate could see that the wood of the boat house was rotting. It almost looked as though it was surrendering, as different colours of paints fell away against the onslaught of burning sun, wind and withering rain. It needed reinforcements, but none had come.

'I think you should both have a shower and get off to bed,' said Nana, 'You can explore tomorrow. If you like you can leave the curtains open. There's no one who can look in. You can rest easy. No one will disturb you tonight.'

Hector and Kate looked at one another as Nana closed the door. There was excitement in the exchanges, but they were both dog tired. Kate and Hector knew that they needed an undisturbed night's sleep, and Nana had promised them that. Neither of them could know that Nana was quite wrong, and that an unwelcome visitor would walk between them as they slept.

CHAPTER NINE

Otto

The moon hung over gathering herds of giant trees. They seemed to have slipped a little closer to the lake, as if they were trying to get a better view of the events that were about to unfold.

The curtains to Kate and Hector's bedroom were open wide. It was three o'clock in the morning, and even the birds in the aviary were quiet. The moon slipped behind a thin cloud, just as a figure stepped onto the balcony.

He took his time. There was no rush; no need to feel hurried. The pleasure of a job done well. He was someone who enjoyed almost everything he did. He cared little for anyone else and kept no tally of the number he had killed. Not for a moment did he reflect upon the pleadings or cries of those at his mercy.

He stepped confidently through the open window, and strode into the gap between the two beds. In one slept a boy with blond hair and an innocent face. His eyes were moving under his eyelids. He was enjoying a last dream.

In the other bed was a girl, who seemed to be slightly older. Her blond hair covered part of her face. She was still, breathing deeply. Both girl and boy were asleep, and this would make their murder so much easier.

But which to kill first, that was the problem. A cry from one might wake the other. Best kill the one who seemed to be in the lightest sleep.

He walked back, and then around both beds, surveying each child. An easy kill, they were the best. The boy was moving now, in a vivid dream no doubt, and so he would be the first to die. The girl was in a deeper sleep and would react more slowly. It was decided.

He walked back to the gap between the beds. It was the place where he could kill both quickly and easily. He readied himself, but then paused. There was a problem. Both children were far too large. If only, if only they were smaller.

'Got you!' shouted Kate, as Hector woke to see his sister illuminated by a full moon holding a surprised and unhappy cat.

It was an unpleasant shock, but the cat quickly adapted to his new situation. The boy and girl were definitely too large to kill, but there had to be some possibility they might feed him.

The girl began to stroke him, and he felt his legs buckle. She released the grip on his neck, and the boy joined in the stroking. The cat had made up his mind. He liked both of them and decided he would spare their lives, at least for a while. Nevertheless, it was imperative that he was fed immediately.

Hector and Kate continued to stroke and fuss the cat. It had a long, luxuriant coat, and clearly enjoyed attention. The cat was on its feet now, pacing between them, rubbing itself against both Hector and Kate. It was a large cat with a giant, bushy tail.

It did not take long for both Hector and Kate to agree on a small adventure to the kitchen. The cat even seemed to like being held. Kate cuddled it close as they ventured out onto the dark, shadowed landing.

Bright moonlight streamed in through so many windows, only to be swallowed by endless dark wood panelling. Hector thought it odd that he only noticed the hideous tartan carpet when lit by moonlight. They crept past the wooden benches in the wide hallway, through all of the wooden arches, on towards the stairs.

The first set of stairs creaked, and Kate hissed at Hector to walk near the edge of the stairs so the wood would move less. On the second set of stairs there was a surprise. The glass in a door allowed them to see into the rooms used by Dunbar Hellstone. There was a dim light, and from what they could see Lord Rothwell's rooms were considerably better furnished than the rest of the house.

The stone and tile of the ground floor felt cold on Hector's feet. As Hector glanced into the drawing room a face looked back at him from the gloom. He stopped and looked again into the room, only to see a statue he had mistaken for a person. The Hall had the slow tick of an old house with a ghost or two, and in truth Hector adored it.

The cat became excited once in the kitchen, and wriggled from Kate's grasp and jumped down to the floor. Hector opened the huge two-door fridge while Kate found a saucer. The cat paced and meowed restlessly. In the cat's opinion control and patience were for hunting, they were of no help when you were waiting to be fed.

Kate and Hector stroked the cat as it lapped the milk. Once it had finished and began to complain again, Hector opened the fridge to get some more milk. This was a mistake.

In its life at the Hall the cat had tried on several occasions to get into the fridge. It had ham and cooked chicken. It had cheese and cream. It smelled of heaven. Unfortunately, Nana was too fast, and the cat had never got within a metre of the open fridge door. Now, however, he was in the company of two new people, and they trusted him.

The cat rocketed around Hector's legs like a toy snake on a string. He leapt onto the second shelf, crouched down and took a bite out of the cooked chicken.

'Hey!' Hector yelled, moving to grab the cat. The cat moved further back, jamming himself behind the chicken, determined to eat as much as possible before he was dislodged. Hector could not reach to the back of the large fridge, and Kate could not get a grip of him either.

After five minutes of 'here kitty, kitty,' enticements and threats the cat had not moved an inch. He was, however, a good way through the side of the chicken. Worse, he was flicking his tail about, showering the fridge and all of the food with fine ginger hair.

Ten minutes on saw Kate and Hector sat on chairs, starting to get cold. The cat was still eating. For all they knew he might keep eating until he exploded.

'I've got a plan,' said Hector.

'So have I,' said Kate.

'Mine's best,' said Hector, while moving to the sink. He picked up the plastic washing up bowl, which was full of dirty water, and hurled it at the cat and the fridge.

'Oh brilliant!' Kate exclaimed.

'Well, cats don't like water.'

'Now you've ruined all the food,' said Kate.

'Well, if that's a problem, why didn't you come up with a better plan?' Hector asked in an accusational tone.

'I did,' replied Kate, 'I realised that we could just move the chicken. Then some clot went and threw dishwater all over everything.'

Kate and Hector sat in silence for another minute while water dripped down all of the food in the fridge. The cat gnawed doggedly on through the chicken, quite unperturbed by the water.

'I've got another plan,' suggested Hector.

Kate gave him her withering look, the one she reserved for times when he had got them into lots of trouble.

'We could sneak into Hellstone's rooms and swap his food for the food in this fridge.'

'And, do you think his rooms will be locked or unlocked?' asked Kate, pointing out just one of the glaring holes in Hector's plan.

'Might be unlocked.'

'Do you think he is likely to have exactly the same food?'

Hector thought for a moment.

'Well, he might have a chicken that hasn't been chewed by a cat,' Hector ventured.

Kate looked at Hector, and then back at the cat, who seemed to be working his way through one of the chicken's legs, and then burst out laughing. This set Hector off, which was unfortunate, as it was exactly the moment when the door opened and a torch was shone on their faces.

'I might have known,' said Andrè, 'A midnight feast.'

'No,' said Hector, 'we were getting milk for the cat.'

'Which cat?' asked Andrè, who could only see the children and the light spilling from the open fridge.

'The one jammed in the fridge eating the chicken,' said Kate, pointing and lapsing into giggles.

'Why did you let it in the fridge?' asked Andrè, moving to look at the cat.

'We didn't,' said Hector, 'it moved like a rocket on rails when I opened the fridge door.'

'The fridge is broken,' said Andrè, 'There's water dripping everywhere.'

'That was Hector,' said Kate.

Kate believed that you should never rat on a friend, but Hector was her brother so it did not count. Hector gave her a stare.

Andrè glanced at the plastic bowl on the floor and then at Hector. The train of events immediately became obvious; he had a mental picture of Hector flinging dishwater at the cat.

'Have you ever considered thinking before you act?' asked Andrè.

'Well, we're all in trouble now,' said Kate, in a move to include Andrè in the guilt and thus enlist his help in covering up the crime. Andrè looked at her in silence for a few moments.

'It's your choice. You can confess and apologise tomorrow morning to Mrs Wells, or wait until I explain what I found,' said Andrè.

'He was going to help us until you decided to blackmail him,' hissed Hector as they walked up the stairs back to bed. Andrè had put the cat out through a low window, and was some way behind.

'We need to say that we thought the cat was ill, but we didn't want to wake anyone because they're all so tired,' said Kate, 'That way we look noble.'

Hector stole a glance at his sister but said nothing. As far as he could see all of the food was ruined, and they had been caught redhanded. He and Kate looked anything but noble.

The next morning Hector and Kate were woken by Nana with a cup of milk each and some toast on a tray.

'You've slept in a bit,' said Nana.

'Oh, I'm really sorry,' said Kate, quickly remembering the events in the night.

'Yes, yes,' said Nana dismissively, 'I gather you've met my cat, Otto.'

'We didn't mean to ruin all of the food,' said Hector.

'Oh, your Mum has gone to the shops. They've had some good news. Just say sorry when you see her then it'll all be forgiven.'

'Your cat, Otto, he just shot into the fridge and...' Hector stuttered.

'Really?' said Nana, 'Now, I've said it's all sorted. Stop worrying. As for Otto, I know him well, and he's more than capable of turning a small act of kindness into a major robbery.'

'Will you tell him off?' Hector asked.

'No point,' said Nana, 'He's got so many crimes to his name he can't remember five minutes ago let alone last night's smash and grab. It's all in the distant past to him.'

Hector was about to go on, but Kate gave him a look. They were out of trouble, off the hook. There was no reason to keep going over last night's misadventure.

Once dressed and downstairs Kate found Andrè and Dad sitting in the kitchen. They seemed pleased.

'Sorry about the food,' said Hector.

'Yes, it was particularly stupid,' said Dad, although he didn't sound at all angry, 'I think Otto is quite capable of finding his own food.'

'What's the good news?' Kate asked, keen to change the subject.

'Sludge's mobile phone has been identified,' said Dad, and he gestured to Andrè to explain.

'He has three mobile phones,' said Andrè, 'We have the numbers for all of them. One of the thugs who died at the zoo had them written down in a flat. I'm amazed he had them, but they have since tallied with sightings. The policewoman who searched his house was smart enough not to try the numbers. Mobile phones show your position. We can track him.'

'Can the police just arrest him?' Hector asked, feeling relieved but also disappointed that their adventures might be nearing an end.

'Oui, if he kept them turned on, but Sludge is far too experienced to do anything so stupid. There's a team on their way to the area, but I'll be surprised if they find him. He will turn one phone on, use it and then turn it off. However, we can monitor all the messages left and read all of his text messages.'

'What this really means,' said Dad, 'is we can relax. We know he is in Scotland. He turns them on once or twice a day. We will know when he is getting closer and we can be careful then.'

Kate was about to ask more questions when Bandit bounced into the kitchen and made a dive for the cat's food dish. He was smartly grabbed by Dad and marched outside again, although not before he had managed to snaffle all of Otto's food. Bandit was soaking and stank of mud. He seemed to be very pleased with himself. Nana volunteered to wash him.

'If they get washed quickly I find it puts them off after a while,' said Nana.

Bandit and Otto had already met. Otto had decided to charge and hiss at Bandit. Nana believed this was on the grounds that Otto had an alphabetical approach to new relationships. Most smaller animals moved straight to C for caught, which was a short phase that inevitably progressed to D for Dead.

For larger animals Otto started with A, for aggression. If this did not produce the desired effects then he moved on to B, for bloody-minded, relentless harassment, eventually through to E for enemy, a phase characterised by simmering resentment and hatred. The E for enemy phase could last a long time, not least because it meant that the dog, cat or whatever had managed to skip D for dead. It took a long time to reach F for friend, and this was a transitory and unstable phase. A return to the D for dead phase was always lingering at the back of Otto's rarely exercised mind.

Bandit had been excited by the charge from Otto. Yet, despite being slightly afraid, he clearly enjoyed the whole thing. The fear had added to the joy. Bandit danced about, and then charged back. Otto knew you could intimidate larger animals and kill smaller ones. Bandit was disappointingly large and disappointingly difficult to scare. Worse than all of this, Otto's food dish was empty and Bandit looked like the number one suspect. Otto was still very full from last night's chicken, but that did not mean anyone else could take the food he did not want.

There was no doubt in Otto's mind, getting rid of Bandit was going to be a major task. To intimidate a larger animal you had to frighten it; leave it uncertain about when the next worrying attack would come; you needed to depress the thing, and leave it desperate to escape. Otto knew all about evil campaigns of bullying, and yet Bandit appeared immune. He was cheerful, as if he enjoyed almost every moment of every day. Breaking Bandit would be a major task, although seeing him dragged off to be washed was a singular pleasure. Otto decided to watch Bandit's bath, and play with the rivulets of water as he was soaped and rinsed.

Mum arrived back driving the van with bags full of shopping, just as a large Mercedes articulated lorry turned up. As the rear doors opened a number of men appeared, all blinking in the sunlight.

They spoke only French. Kate and Hector gathered that they were a technical team. Only the British driver knew where they were.

After a brief lunch a control room was established in one of the upstairs bedrooms. Discreet ariels were placed on the roof. Some of the men disappeared into the grounds with backpacks full of electronic kit.

'Booby-traps!' declared Hector, 'Things to blow Sludge sky-high.'

'If we have booby-traps who are they most likely to blow up?' asked Dad.

'Sludge!' declared Hector, incredulous that the answer might be anything else.

'No, you fool, us!' said Dad, 'Or the people who work here.'

Dad went on to explain that the grounds were being rigged with cameras and movement sensors. They would be monitored from France. Hector's annoyance at being contradicted by Dad was lessened when Andrè gave him a watch, and then a belt with a metal buckle. There was a watch and a locket for Kate. All of them were small, attractive and could be used to monitor their position.

'I can monitor where you are all of the time,' said Andrè. 'Your father and mother can monitor your position in an emergency. It is imperative that you never take them off. If you do something you should not do, or you do not tell the truth about where you have been, I will not report you to your parents. This is too important; it is not about little sins.'

Andrè explained that he would teach them about hiding and evasion. They would be taught about how and when to attack, but not how to fire a gun.

Hector was annoyed, and this got worse when he discovered that they would be told how to sabotage a gun as well as defuse explosives, but firing a gun had been ruled out by Dad. It was made more aggravating when they discovered that Mum and Dad were going to be taught how to fire guns. Even Nana had signed up.

'I have fired shotguns before and I thought it might be fun,' said Nana, 'In any event, I've been told I don't have to take sides, but all the bullets will be coming this way and so I thought I'd send a few back.'

'Does Lord Rothwell know?' Kate asked, 'I wouldn't have thought he would agree to all of this.'

'The way to Dunbar's heart is cash,' said Nana, and then she looked down as if she had said something indecent.

Hector and Kate decided to retreat to their room. It was suddenly all too busy. For Kate is was an unwelcome reminder that the threat and fear had not left. Hector was still annoyed about his exclusion from gun training.

As they approached the main staircase in the Hall both of them glanced through the glass doors into Lord Rothwell's luxurious rooms. There were sofas and great animal skin rugs over a thick, new carpet. Lord Rothwell was on the phone, and his voice drifted out.

'I tell you Hugo, I've had to accept a pretty rough lot. The woman looks like she's been beaten up by her husband, while the husband seems to have lost in a fist fight. Face like bruised melon,' said Lord Rothwell.

'They've come along with some sort of French social worker. Plus, they've got two children, and the less said about them the better. There was a time, Hugo, when children died working in factories, and I think that would be the best place for these two. Country's on the slide, Hugo. It's all social workers and sados like the lot I've had to let in. The father virtually has loser tattooed on his forehead.'

Kate gripped onto Hector's arm. He was heading towards Lord Rothwell's rooms.

'No Hector,' she whispered, 'Revenge. Served cold.'

Hector relaxed, although his face remained fierce.

'Revenge,' agreed Hector.

Kate and Hector spent some time discussing various wild schemes to trouble, inconvenience, wound, shoot, blow-up or otherwise murder Dunbar Hellstone, the Eleventh Earl of Rothwell. The more they planned, the more complex the schemes, the more fanciful the ideas, the more impossible it all seemed. Hector had taken to pacing their large room.

'Hector, sssh. Hector, be quiet!' hissed Kate urgently.

Hector hurried over to the window. Kate was listening in to Andrè and Dad who were outside two floors below.

'He wants a huge amount of extra money,' said Dad.

'Just pay it,' said Andrè, 'Money is the least of your concerns.'

'I know, but the Eleventh Earl of Rothwell sets my teeth on edge,' said Dad. Andrè laughed and there was a pause.

'You have to be a friend to him,' said Andrè, 'He's a risk and we need to keep him onside. Pay him what he wants and ask for a guided tour.'

Dad sighed and agreed. There was a long silence.

'Yes,' said Dad with an air of a decision being made, 'being nice to Dunbar cannot be as bad as being shot. I should stop moaning.'

'I think by the end of the tour you might be praying for a sniper,' said Andrè, and the two started laughing again.

'What do you really think our chances are?' asked Dad after a long pause.

'I don't know. I really don't,' said Andrè, 'We have to hope the British get him. Some of the guys in the British Special Forces are very keen to put a row of holes in him.'

'And if he makes it here, what then?'

'Fifty, fifty.'

'He's that good?' asked Dad.

'Yes, he's good,' said Andrè after a pause, 'I've never faced anyone as dangerous, determined and relentless. I would plan for a long and happy life if I were you, but make sure you enjoy the coming days just in case.'

There was another long pause, and Kate began to wonder whether they had walked off.

'OK, I agree,' said Dad.

'About Hellstone?' questioned Andrè.

'No, that's fine, I mean about Kate and Hector. We've got to give them every chance.'

'It's a double-edged sword, but it is what I would do in your shoes. These are extraordinary circumstances.'

Kate and Hector looked at each other. Neither had any idea what Dad and Andrè had just agreed. Both of them, however, understood the fifty, fifty comment, and it was a sobering reminder of their situation.

As Kate and Hector went down to the kitchen Hellstone appeared from his rooms. To Kate's amazement Hector was very polite.

'Good afternoon Lord Rothmere.'

'Rothwell, it's Lord Rothwell,' barked Dunbar Hellstone.

'Sorry,' said Hector, trying to perfect the sad injured look that served Bandit so well.

Lord Rothwell stormed away, and Hector glowed and turned to smile at Kate. Dunbar Hellstone was a man with a giant key in his back, and Hector was going to turn it.

'It sticks in my throat to say it Hector,' muttered Kate, 'but that was brilliant. He's so touchy.'

'I bet he's a screamer,' said Hector.

'No,' disagreed Kate cheerfully, 'he'll have a deep, outraged bellow.'

'OK,' said Hector, 'I bet you. Loser has to jump in the lake.'

'You're on.'

Lunch was a cheerful affair, made better by Dad's announcement of a surprise. Nana served everyone, and insisted that Mum sit down and relax. Nana did not smile, but radiated pleasure. She clearly adored having a family stay, and judging by the looks she gave Dad she knew all about the surprise and approved wholeheartedly.

Andrè was late, but seemed pleased with the progress the visitors from France were making. His only bad news was that the man who would be staying on from the French team was not popular. His name was Henry, but his colleagues called him something less attractive. Apparently, he was not much use, but considered an asset in a live battle.

After lunch they all went to the front of the Hall. Standing there was a brand new silver Jaguar XJ Diesel Portfolio. Dad explained that it had been ordered by someone who had then cancelled the order, and so it was immediately available. It seemed as though the money had its benefits. Beside the Jaguar was a large Toyota double-cab pickup. Attached to the back was a trailer, with a small sailing yacht.

Kate had only tried sailing once, but had been addicted from that first experience. Her eyes widened, before she ran and hugged Dad. Hector was almost as pleased. Already he had passage to the island and his plans were expanding by the second. Kate had a boat, maybe he could have a submarine, possibly with torpedoes. He would make Bandit first officer.

'Hector,' said Dad, calling him over, 'I've decided that you and Kate should be taught how to fire a gun.'

'Yes, yes!' Hector shouted, punching the air.

'Hector, I don't approve of guns. They bring misery, and the way some people worship them frankly gives me the creeps. Nor do I think children should ever be allowed to use them, but we are all at huge risk and I don't see why you and Kate shouldn't have a chance to defend yourselves.'

'Brilliant, brilliant, brilliant!' Hector shouted as he bounced on the spot.

'Yes, well,' said Dad, aware that everything he had just said was wasted on Hector, 'Andrè thinks Sludge will not expect us to arm you and Kate. It might give us all an edge, assuming you don't shoot us by accident.'

Hector now appreciated Andrè's double-edged sword comment, and assumed the conversation he had overheard was about whether he and Kate should be taught to use guns.

Kate and Hector headed into the Hall. Kate had been given a wet-suit and was going to change. Mum was going to give her a sailing lesson; their turn being trained by Andrè was later. Hector was going to have a lesson with Andrè now. He had been told to wash his hands and change into some rough clothes Nana had provided. As they got to the door Lord Rothwell appeared.

'Hello,' said Hector, 'I'm really sorry about getting your name wrong.'

Lord Rothwell stopped and looked at Hector.

'I'm always slow at school. I'm bottom at everything. I can't remember things,' Hector went on.

'Right, I see,' said Dunbar Hellstone, 'I suppose there has to be some allowances.'

'Thank you Lord Brothmell,' said Hector.

'No, no, it's Rothwell,' Hellstone corrected.

'That's what I said, Brothmell.'

'Look, it's Rothwell, Rothwell, not Brothmell. I'm The eleventh Earl of Rothwell, not someone who provides soup!'

'Sorry, really sorry,' said Hector, 'Actually, I was wondering, what do you do?'

'What?'

'What's the point of you?' Hector asked, 'policemen and women catch criminals, firewomen and men put out fires and other things, teachers bore everyone to death, what do Lords do?'

'What do you mean, what do Lords do? You idiot, we make the country work. We are what makes England England. We are history; past and future. We are the embodiment of a feudal system that has adapted to make a country great. We're the reason you have clothes on your back, food on the table and you're not dying of disease' said Hellstone, his tone rising from shouting to screech.

'Wow,' said Hector, 'So you're like a super farmer, and you're a hospital doctor, and you're fantastic with a sewing machine so you can mend clothes.'

'No, no, no,' screeched Hellstone, 'other people do those things. Lords make it all work.'

'Do you do the timetables, and ring people up and help everyone?'

'No, you idiot, it's about history and culture. It's about place, and where people belong.'

'So, you're like oil; a sort of lubricant,' declared Hector, 'Or are you like a secretary who organises things,' his innocent face still firmly in place.

'Idiot, idiot! You stupid, brainless idiot!' screamed Hellstone, before revolving like a damaged train on a turntable and storming off.

'That wasn't an accident. You did that on purpose, didn't you?' said Kate, trying to hide her admiration.

'Yep,' said Hector, trying to hide a swelling feeling of superiority, 'And remember to jump in the lake; he is a screamer.'

Hector suspected that pretending to be very dim was a developing masterstroke. Although, he could not imagine how someone like Lord Rothwell might survive as a headmaster; there was a fair chance that the cat would outwit him.

At that precise moment the cat was outwitting the Eleventh Earl of Rothwell. He had sneaked into Hellstone's rooms, chewed through a plastic lid, and was lapping at the cream Hellstone had yet to put in the fridge. When he was full he began flicking it around. A bit of fun, then he would go for a nap.

By tea Kate was exhausted but very happy. Mum knew quite a lot about sailing and Kate walked into the large kitchen after a shower as if she was floating on a pillow of pure pleasure. Mum was still struggling with her wounds, but seemed to move more easily than yesterday.

Hector had enjoyed Andrè's instruction, even though they had started with toy guns. Andrè did not talk too much and got the messages over quickly. They had started with a gunfight, which Hector won because he refused to die when shot, claiming super-human powers. Andrè had managed to get Hector to shoot himself twice, and when Andrè then fired a real gun to show the damage it could do, the message about gun safety began to sink home. They had finished with Hector firing an air rifle at a target.

Lord Rothwell appeared briefly to complain about Otto. The cream was blamed on the cat, as were several 'unspeakable things'. Lord Rothwell stormed off, and Nana was happy to explain.

'Dunbar's happy enough that he keeps the rats down. The prob-lem is that Otto kills the rats and then plays with them, flinging them around. Unfortunately, his favourite place is outside Dun-bar's study, by the windows that reach all the way to the ground. Dunbar will be working there and then suddenly a dead rat will splat against the window, followed by Otto jumping on it. It get's Dunbar all worked up.'

'I'll have to admit though, Otto does always seem to do it when Dunbar's got guests. Not nice. Often the rats have bits missing, and sometimes Otto hurls bits of the rat's intestines at the window. That really annoys Dunbar. He raves until the windows are washed. Well, there's no point until Otto's given up playing with his rat. Clean the window and five minutes later there's more rat's insides all over them. I tell him, you've got to wait until Otto's had his fun, there's no point just cleaning and cleaning.'

'Dunbar is all about show and presentation, and trying to im-press your guest when there's a small mass murderer dismember-ing his latest victim outside your window is rather hard. Truth is,

Otto likes fuss and trouble, and once he discovered that guests plus rat sends Dunbar's balloon up it's like it's one of his treats. When Otto sees cars arrive with guests he rockets off to find a rat. It's not like he understands it all, he just understands enough to know it's fun. Well, except for the rat of course.'

Nana surveyed her audience, all laughing.

'Otto is a little so and so. If he hears screaming he chews the rat's head off and flings it through any open window, and Dunbar always likes the windows open. I used to say it was just chance, but the fact is it's happened too often. Otto does it on purpose.'

'Funny thing is, Otto knows his music. I tried it once. I sneaked in while Dunbar was away and put on the music that he always puts on for guests. Five minutes later a rat hits the window. So I screamed. Guess what. A few seconds later there's a rat's head flying into the room.'

'I think Otto intends to terrify your dog Bandit, but I reckon he's met his match. I bet they're real good friends by next week.'

By five o'clock it was growing dark. The breeze moved the spring grass and the rushes by the side of the lake. The drooping branches of the willow trees swayed, but could not disguise the approaching shapes. Silhouetted against an old wooden fence they moved with purpose and menace.

Otto had caught the scent of these intruders some days ago, and had been hoping for some sort of violent confrontation. Almost all cats enjoy violence when they are winning, but for Otto it was a pursuit to which he was utterly devoted.

Both intruders stopped as they saw the huge, ginger cat. Otto was worryingly relaxed. He was handsome, confident and still. He already had the psychological upper hand. Worse than that he had fast paws, a tolerance of pain, staggering determination and no understanding of compassion or forgiveness. If he had ever appeared in a beauty pageant then when asked 'If you had the chance what would be the one thing in the whole wide world you would like to do?' then while other competitors might have mewed on about bringing world peace and curing sick children, Otto would have confidently announced it was murdering kittens.

The cats had stopped their advance, and now moved back and forth along a line. It was as if Otto had cast a spell and they could approach no further. In reality, this was the threatening stage, where the participants in the coming dust-up try to intimidate their rivals. They were building up the pressure, as well as building up their confidence.

Otto remained still; dreadfully, dreadfully still. He was well ahead on points, and the intruders' confidence was waning. Then there was a bark in the middle distance, together with an advancing thunder of paws. In truth, Bandit was not as frightening a prospect as Otto. The two cats facing Otto did not really stand much chance in any event, but had obviously decided to give it a go. They were going to test Otto and then retreat. There was no need for full-on, panic-fuelled flight. Bandit, however, was changing this equation.

Bandit had several things Otto did not have: considerable weight, extreme velocity, questionable steering and substandard brakes. Leaving aside the huge jaws, the speed and weight alone were enough to convince both cats it was time to flee. Otto had expected a fight and a retreat from the intruders. He could not hope for a screaming flight, with both cats fleeing in fear of their lives. He could only achieve that when he faced a single cat. Bandit, however, had delivered the unexpected. Otto enjoyed panic in his enemies and victims.

Thus, for the first time, Otto began to warm to Bandit. He might be annoying, smelly and a bit of a lunch snaffler, but he was good in a stand-off when you needed a missile. In addition, Bandit was already causing a lot of trouble around the Hall, and Otto liked that. Bandit was undoubtedly an unwelcome usurper, but it turned out he was in Otto's gang, or at least he thought he was. Of course, only Otto was really in Otto's gang.

The cats turned in panic and accelerated to top speed. It was a long way to safety, and they could only outpace the dog for a while. Where did the dog come from? Why was that horrible ginger monster unafraid of the dog?

Otto sat still as Bandit charged past. Otto then stood up and sauntered in Bandit's wake. There was no need to bark when he had a dog. Bandit created panic and chaos, and Otto was really starting to like him. He saw the grey outline of one of the cats rocket up a tree. The fool would stay there and Otto would return to haunt him in a short while.

Bandit was barking. It sounded as though he was near the lake. The other cat had run along a jetty, only to be horrified to discover it ended in water. There was a gate to the wooden jetty and Bandit could not get past it and was barking. Stalemate, for the moment.

Otto hopped on the top of the gate and gazed at his victim. The cat trapped at the end hissed and arched his back. This was all too much for Bandit, who retreated, charged and leapt the gate. In truth, he half-collided with the top of the gate and scrabbled over. It was then full speed to the end of the jetty. The cat fell into the water just as Bandit drew level, before flying on and into the lake.

The cat paddled desperately for the reeds, just as Bandit surfaced and could hardly believe his luck; he had lost a cat and found a lake. How lucky could he be? Best of all, he was washing off the horrible smell of Nana's coconut shampoo.

Otto had no intention of hunting down the cat in the reeds. It would be messy and difficult. A cat could drown in there, even a

water-loving cat like Otto. The cat stuck in the tree was now his
concern. Sleeping just down-wind of the tree seemed like a great
idea. At some point the intruder would sneak down, and Otto
would have the pleasure of bringing about another panic-fuelled
flight.

CHAPTER TEN

Marmaduke

Breakfast brought a surprise. As Kate and Hector headed downstairs Mum was carrying clothes, which they assumed were for them. She did not look happy. Nana's raised voice drifted out of the kitchen.

'I think she's weird. It's not right. She should go.'

Kate and Hector felt shock, and looked as their mother disappeared upstairs.

'I don't want her round the place,' Nana continued, 'I'm the housekeeper and I say she goes.'

Hector and Kate arrived to see Nana stood next to Mrs Warp, and suddenly the object of Nana's objections became clear.

Nana had been told all about Mrs Warp by Hector and Kate. Nana had been fascinated to hear about their adventures, and the two of them spared only a few details.

'If it's not human it should have an on and off switch, like a toaster,' said Nana, while glancing at Mrs Warp and then issuing a mumbled apology. It seemed as though Nana was caught between her deep dislike of this mechanical human, and her fundamental politeness.

'Mrs Warp is very effective if there's trouble,' said Dad.

'Kate and Hector have told me they had trouble with the previous models,' said Nana, while again looking at Mrs Warp as if she was profoundly indecent.

'I see, and what have they said?' asked Dad in a slightly darker and doubting tone.

'The first one broke and went mad, and the second one came out in lumps.'

Dad sighed and glanced at Hector and Kate.

'The first Mrs Warp broke because Hector filled her with water and Kate smashed her head in with the blunt end of an axe,' said Dad.

'Ohhh,' said Nana, sitting down.

'Then Hector burnt down the whole château. There was very little of her left. It was hard for the technicians to work out what had gone wrong,' said Dad, speaking slowly and deliberately.

'The second Mrs Warp grew bumps because Hector and Kate filled in the holes she had acquired with bread dough. She had holes in her because they dragged her across the top of a gorilla cage and dropped her onto a set of iron railings.'

'We were trying to help,' Hector protested.

'I'm sure you were dear,' said Nana, giving Mrs Warp another suspicious look, as Andrè sat down.

'I think it would be a good idea for us to have Mrs Warp. She was a real asset at the zoo,' said Andrè.

'I think she should be in a box,' said Nana, 'You can unlock her when you need her.'

'I would like her to patrol the grounds at night,' said Andrè, 'Maybe you could find a cupboard for her to stand in during the day?'

'There's one in the hall, and it's got power. She can plug herself in,' Nana added nastily.

'Mrs Warp,' said Andrè, 'There are some poachers who have been visiting. The movement detectors will pick them up. I need you to deter them from returning. We need them out of the way.'

'Of course,' said Mrs Warp, in her kind, even tone, 'I'll have a chat when I catch them, and if that doesn't work I'll detain them and call you.'

'Good luck,' said Nana, 'But if it's who I think it is you'll have a job catching them.'

During breakfast Kate and Hector learned that Bandit had annoyed Lord Rothwell by escaping from his kennel and barking during the night. In future, Bandit would be sleeping in Hector and Kate's room.

Lord Rothwell was also unhappy because Bandit had been worrying his parrots. The beautiful birds had spent some of the previous day looking at a salivating Bandit as he eyed them up as a second breakfast. Today, Kate could take Bandit in the boat with Mum.

Hector was to have the morning with Dad and Andrè learning about guns. In the afternoon they were going to cover evasion. Hector's suggestion that these be combined and he could hunt Andrè and Dad with a live weapon produced only silent stares.

Hector enjoyed the training with guns. Andrè had set up a range in a small quarry. Lincolnshire is dotted with tiny quarries. In the past, anyone wanting to build a house simply dug down until they found the stone they needed. There was several of these in the grounds. They were all overgrown, as might be expected of earthworks that could be up to a thousand years old.

Andrè once again illustrated the importance of gun safety by shooting a large ham he had 'borrowed' from Nana. Andrè explained the idea of aiming the gun and then squeezing the trigger until it went off. Dad picked this up quickly, and was soon notching up an impressive number of hits in the centre of the targets. Hector pulled the trigger, and as he did moved the gun. His scores were poor. However, he soon discovered that he could confuse Dad and Andrè about which target he had been aiming at, and managed to claim a number of Dad's better hits.

When they came to rapid fire shooting Dad did not score so well. They had to turn around and hit three targets quickly. Hector was annoyed because he was only allowed to use an air pistol, not a real gun. On the other hand it was a task that suited him better.

Andrè only missed the centre of the target once. His shots in the rapid fire exercise were better than Dad's shots when he had unlimited time to aim. Andrè was full of helpful advice and was good fun to be with.

'I've shown you how much damage a bullet does,' said Andrè near the end of their session, 'This sort of information can make it harder to shoot at someone.'

'I'll be alright,' said Hector, dismissively.

'Hector, be quiet and pay attention,' said Dad.

'Almost everyone has problems shooting at someone. People even deliberately miss and do not realise that they have done it on purpose,' said Andrè, 'I think this is probably a good thing. However, the people we may face need to be shot. My advice is that if you have little time always aim for the middle of the chest. If you have a lot of time and you cannot pull the trigger, and this is where it can be difficult, then shoot them in the lower leg, below the knee. This will cause a lot of pain and probably take them out of the fight.'

'I hope I don't have to shoot anyone,' said Dad.

'We could get you a large stapler if you would prefer to attack with that,' suggested Andrè.

Mum and Kate enjoyed an energetic, if slightly frustrating morning of sailing. There was a brisk, constant wind; the sort that sailors dream of. Unfortunately, they had one of the worst sailors in the world aboard.

Bandit considered himself a natural sailor. Mum and Kate considered him a menace.

Bandit clearly enjoyed himself, and for a crew that needed to practise a man-overboard drill he was a godsend. Bandit would fling himself overboard if he saw anything in the water that interested him. Sometimes he seemed to jump overboard without any particular reason. By the end of the morning Kate and Mum were soaked because Bandit had managed to capsize the boat just by racing to one side unexpectedly while they were tacking against the wind.

They had sailed near the smaller island, and Bandit had jumped out and swam to it. On the island was an ugly head of a man on a small plinth, with hole at the top for water to spout out. It took them some time to get Bandit back in the boat. By the time they were ready for lunch they had not gone very far. Most of their time had been spent rescuing Bandit.

When Kate and Mum returned to the Hall, Hector was in the kitchen being told off.

'You are not to issue any commands to Mrs Warp,' said Dad, 'I still remember what you did at the zoo.'

'I wasn't being rude, I just wanted to understand,' Hector protested.

'What's he done?' Kate asked.

'All I did was order Mrs Warp to undress. I wasn't being rude. I just wanted to see her dials and electronics,' said Hector as he tried to deploy the sweet, innocent face he had seen Bandit use to such good effect.

'And the instruction to dance in the nuddy in front of Lord Rothwell's windows,' said Dad, 'Where did this fit in your open-minded world of innocent discovery?'

Hector was silent. The order to dance naked in front of Lord Rothwell had been the first instruction he had issued to Mrs Warp. He did not think Dad had heard this as well. When she had re-fused he had ordered her to take off her clothes as a first step, and then Dad had appeared. Now, he had been caught out.

'Maybe Hector wanted to see the psychological effects on Lord Rothwell?' Kate suggested.

Dad gave her a withering look. He then returned to looking at Hector, allowing the pressure to build.

'Hector,' said Dad, 'we need Mrs Warp. She is an effective weapon. You really must not mess about with her or break her. Andrè tells me she was a real help in the battle at the zoo. She's fearless, strong and ultimately it does not matter if she dies in a battle as she is not really alive. You must not break her.'

'Sorry,' said Hector.

Lunch was an enjoyable affair. Mrs Warp was in her cupboard, and Nana now seemed happy. While Mum and Kate never wanted to see Bandit in a boat again, everyone else thought their disastrous time sailing with the dog was very funny. Hector's attempt to per-suade everyone that he should be allowed a machine gun to keep under his bed was simply ignored.

'Nana,' asked Hector, 'does the Hall have secret passageways?'

'Ha, well, it used to have, according to what I've heard.'

'So, they've been blocked up,' Hector went on, his excitement rising.

'I'm afraid I'm going to disappoint you there,' said Nana, 'The Hall burned to the ground in 1935. Only the outer walls survived. Even the cellars were gutted. When they rebuilt it everything was redesigned.'

'Wow,' said Hector, 'The walls are really thick. Imagine them falling down.'

'The walls are not that thick, they're hollow,' said Nana, 'They built an inner wall all the way round, and all of the pipes and wires and everything is run through the gaps in the walls. The gap's big enough to walk through.'

'Can we get into the gap?' Hector asked.

'No,' said Mum and Dad in unison.

'Only if you're a plumber or electrician,' said Nana, 'and you look like more of a demolition expert if you don't mind me saying.'

Hector's afternoon was filled with information on evasion. He did not enjoy it as much as the morning's shooting, but he appreciated that it was useful. Kate and Mum had joined them. To Hector's great annoyance Kate, Dad and Mum were all better at hiding than he was.

'It's the singing Hector. You don't realise it, but you hum tunes,' said Kate in a tone that was far too cheerful for Hector's taste.

Things improved for Hector in the last exercise. While Hector found everyone, no one found Hector. This was partly because he cheated and used Bandit to track everyone down. It was also partly because he had run back to the Hall past the parrots, knowing that Kate would use Bandit, but that Bandit's interest in Hector's scent would wane once the birds were spotted.

When he told everyone what he had done Kate accused him of cheating. Andrè reminded her that there was no cheating when you were hiding from someone who might kill you; there was only surviving. Distracting the dog was a good strategy.

When they returned to the Hall for tea Nana was in tears of laughter. She explained that Lord Rothwell had opened the cupboard door in the Hall only to find Mrs Warp standing there asking him if there was anything she could help him with. He had shrieked and was now demanding that Dad explain why a woman was hiding in a cupboard.

'Are you going to tell him Dad?' Hector asked.

'No, I'm going to tell him that she's my mother-in-law and she's a bit odd.'

'Trevor, don't you dare say she's my mother!' Mum demanded.

'Grandmother is a bit odd,' Kate unhelpfully suggested.

'She doesn't run on twelve volts,' said Hector.

'Her hearing aid does' said Kate.

'Grandmother's eyes don't light up,' said Hector.

Dad raised his eyebrows, as if to indicate that they might.

'Trevor!' said Mum, in a warning tone.

'Don't worry,' said Dad, 'I'll think of something,' before disappearing off to find Dunbar Hellstone, the Eleventh Earl of Rothwell.

A short while later Ms Rogerson appeared.

'Lord Rothwell is unhappy with some of the driving,' Rogerson announced, 'Fifteen miles an hour is the maximum speed for the drive through the estate to the Hall.'

'And what's the problem?' asked Nana in an even tone.

'Too fast. Handbrake turns spreading stones everywhere. It's dangerous and it could scare the wildlife.'

'I'm sorry, but I don't drive like that and neither does Trevor,' said Mum.

'Dunbar does though,' said Nana.

'Lord Rothwell is a model driver,' said Ms Rogerson while glaring at Nana. It was clear that they rarely saw eye to eye.

'The day he's a model driver will be when he's been shrunk and left in a toy car,' said Nana, while casually moving a pile if ironing.

'Yeah, I've seen him,' said Hector, 'He drives like a maniac.'

'Hector, this is none of your business,' said Mum, although Hector saw Nana give him a sly wink.

Ms Rogerson was about to continue the argument when Lord Rothwell appeared at the door with Dad in his wake.

'If I could have everyone's attention please,' said Lord Rothwell, 'I wish to apologise,' he added, before turning to face Mum.

'Mrs Trogg, I am so very sorry that I shouted at your mother. I just did not expect to find her in a cupboard. It was such a shock, but I should have controlled myself. I certainly should not have shouted at an old, demented and confused lady. I apologise.'

Mum went deep red, partly through embarrassment, and party through anger that Mrs Warp had been presented as her mother. Mum stuttered a thank you and Lord Rothwell bowed and walked off. Ms Rogerson glanced around the room, as if unsure as to what she should do, and then followed dutifully behind her Lord and master.

Dad held out his hands, as if to say it was an accident. Mum looked furious, and then Kate noticed that Nana seemed to be upset. She was shaking and crying. Hector noticed too, but as Nana turned they realised that she was helpless with laughter. This set Kate and Hector off, and even Mum started to laugh.

'Just out of interest,' said Mum, as the laughter died, 'what will you say if your new mother-in-law malfunctions, starts emitting sparks or demonstrates any of her superhuman strength?'

'Let's cross that bridge when we get to it,' said Dad.

'Actually, it is quite helpful,' said Andrè, who had just entered the room, 'If she is found wandering the grounds at night it will be put down to her old age and confusion.'

'Exactly,' said Dad, pretending that this had been the plan all along.

Some time later Hector and Kate were sat watching a film called 'Keeping Mum' on an old television with a slow and noisy DVD drive. There had been some complaint that there was no television signal. This was because the hills of the Lincolnshire Wolds blocked the signal from the transmitter. Lord Rothwell had satellite television, which was unaffected by the shape of the land. Everyone else at the Hall had DVDs or nothing.

It was a quiet evening, but warmer than usual. The window was open and the air very still. Kate was pleased to be closer to their usual routine. Hector and Kate had never been permitted to routinely watch television, just occasionally. Instead, they were allowed thirty minutes of a film or children's drama on DVD before bedtime. The film was interesting; it had started with a murder. Mum and Dad were occupied and so there was a fair chance they would get to watch more than their allotted thirty minutes.

There was a scream from the grounds, and then yelling and crying. Kate and Hector ran to the window. It was Lord Rothwell. In his hands he was holding a parrot which appeared to be dead. He let out a guttural cry and fell to his knees, as if asking the heavens why the love of his life had died.

'Does he ever stop?' asked Hector.

'He is upset. Maybe he was very attached to the parrot' suggested Kate.

Nana bustled out. To Hector and Kate's surprise she put an arm around Lord Rothwell, comforting him. Kate reflected that in some ways she was still his Nanny; still telling him off and still comforting him.

Kate and Hector were just returning to watch the television when the tone outside changed. There were angry shouts from Lord Rothwell.

'Now don't start that. Always blaming other folk,' said Nana.

'It's his fault! His fault!' Lord Rothwell yelled, and then he swore.

'I don't want that language,' said Nana, firmly.

'Why not? All his staring! All his staring! It frightened Marmaduke to death.'

'Marmaduke was old. He was very old, and he would have died a long time ago if you hadn't given him such a good life,' said Nana soothingly.

The ranting from Lord Rothwell and the calming talk from Nana continued for a while. Kate and Hector assumed that Lord Rothwell blamed Otto, Nana's cat for all of the staring he believed had frightened Marmaduke. After a while, however, the word 'dog' drifted out in a yell, and it was apparent that Bandit was being blamed.

As if on cue, Bandit trotted over. Lord Rothwell was still on his knees with Nana crouched beside him.

'You!' Lord Rothwell yelled at Bandit.

Bandit was quite unperturbed. He sniffed the parrot and at one point gently opened his mouth to take it. Nana pushed him away, but Bandit would not leave. Lord Rothwell looked as if he was going to drop the parrot and strangle Bandit. Just as Kate and Hector thought things could not get worse, Bandit cocked his leg and relieved himself over Lord Rothwell's thigh, prompting a scream of rage.

Lord Rothwell handed the dead Marmaduke to Nana, and while yelling death threats ran to his rooms. He appeared moments later with a shotgun. Nana was yelling for him to stop and shouting at Bandit to leave. Lord Rothwell was opening a box of shells. Kate's heart was in her mouth. As Lord Rothwell loaded shells into the weapon, Hector was racing out of the room to protect Bandit.

As Hector reached the outer door Dad appeared behind Lord Rothwell. He smartly wrenched the gun from Rothwell just as Andrè appeared behind him.

'How dare you? How dare you?' screeched Lord Rothwell.

'Andrè will remove any other guns from your cabinet and we can talk about this tomorrow' said Dad, with a calmness and command that left Hector and Kate gasping in amazement. Dad was usually the one losing his temper.

'I'll call the police,' shouted Lord Rothwell.

'Call them,' said Dad, 'After what has happened they will remove all of your guns. Let's talk about this in the morning,' said Dad, laying a hand on Lord Rothwell's shoulder just as Dunbar Hellstone burst into tears.

Hector and Kate turned off the film they had been watching. It was a good film, but it could not quite match the drama Lord Rothwell provided. They tried to stay out of sight as Rothwell stopped crying and returned to a more defiant attitude.

Nana provided a cup of tea. Lord Rothwell sipped at it impatiently as he paced up and down. Suddenly he stopped.

'Where's Marmaduke?'

'He's gone Dunbar. I'm sorry but he's dead' said Nana kindly.

'I want Marmaduke!' Lord Rothwell shouted, like a toddler demanding a favourite teddy bear.

'It's for the best Dunbar' said Nana, 'We have to let go.'

There was a long pause while Lord Rothwell stared at Nana, as if sizing her up. Nana remained impassive and calming.

'You've put him in the bin, haven't you?'

'He's gone Dunbar.'

'He's in the bin, isn't he?'

'Dunbar, I'm trying to help,' said Nana quietly, although Kate and Hector now appreciated that Lord Rothwell was correct. Marmaduke had been laid to rest with the discarded papers, packaging, dog hair, dust and other rubbish.

'You evil old hag!' yelled Lord Rothwell, before marching off towards the bins at the back of the Hall.

A short time later Dunbar Hellstone, the Eleventh Earl of Rothwell was striding towards the lake with a slightly dusty parrot in one hand and a shovel in the other. It appeared as though Marmaduke was going to get a proper burial.

Nana was cycling off up the drive, into the spring sun as it sank into the trees. Hector and Kate prayed she was not leaving for good.

With all of the fuss and trouble Kate and Hector's bedtime had been forgotten. They had watched the whole of the film they had been given. Dad had spoken to Ms Rogerson to explain that he wanted to renegotiate the contract he had with Lord Rothwell and that he was prepared to offer more money.

Some time later Lord Rothwell appeared and began stalking around the Hall looking for Nana. He was surprised to find Mrs Warp in the same cupboard as last time he had looked.

Nana finally appeared just as Kate and Hector were about to go upstairs to bed. Bandit had already been put into their bedroom to ensure he was out of the way.

'Ohh, you're up late. All the fuss I expect,' said Nana, 'Would you like a cup of milk before bed?'

Kate and Hector followed Nana into the large stone-flagged kitchen, only for all three of them to stop as they encountered Lord Rothwell.

Dunbar Hellstone paced back and forth, clearly furious with Nana. It seemed as though the death of his favourite parrot was now Nana's fault. Clearly, Marmaduke's ignominious burial in the dustbin was Nana's responsibility, but that had been remedied. His grave even had a small wooden headstone with neat writing on a temporary note.

Nana waited. She had years of experience. Her timing was precise. Her methods exact. Her knowledge of Dunbar Hellstone unrivalled. Her main reason for waiting, however, was that she had drunk rather a lot at the Blacksmiths Arms. She was waiting for Lord Rothwell to come into focus.

'The problem Dunbar is that I don't care about whatever it is you're angry about. Animals die, we do our best, but Marmaduke's death was nobody's fault. You always was a troubled child. I can't set sail on your stormy seas and hope to understand you.'

'Why the hell did my bloody father have to protect you? Why? Now you think you can do and say anything you like!' Lord Rothwell yelled through his teeth.

'Your father was kind and wise and a lovely man. If you just tried to be a little bit like him you'd be better than you are.'

'Oh yes. Oh yes. Always had a soft spot didn't you? Always had a soft spot for my pathetic, weak father?' Rothwell raved, while picking up a knife from near the sink.

'Everyone had a soft spot for your father, because he was thoroughly decent. Just like these kids are decent. Just like their Mum and Dad are decent,' said Nana, although throughout her eyes were on the knife.

The situation was decidedly difficult. Lord Rothwell was clearly someone who had a complex and unpredictable character. Yet, just as Kate and Hector were both thinking about how they could leave to get help, Andrè appeared to the side of Rothwell. Andrè smartly removed the knife from his hand.

'How dare you?' Lord Rothwell exclaimed. Andrè looked back impassively.

'Outside!' screamed Rothwell, although neither Kate nor Hector had any idea whether this was an invitation to a fight, or whether the Dunbar Hellstone, the Eleventh Earl of Rothwell was about to try to sack Andrè.

'Of course,' said Andrè, gesturing for Hellstone to lead the way.

Hector shot out, determined to be there when Hellstone was thumped on the nose. Kate followed quickly behind. Nana just tried to focus.

By the time Hector emerged outside, Andrè was blocking Hellstone's wild blows. Andrè was simply catching his fists and pushing them aside. Now and then he seemed to goad Hellstone, and the ferocity of the blows increased. It took only a minute or so until Lord Rothwell was completely exhausted.

'You have thrown a lot of punches,' said Andrè, in a matter of fact sort of tone.

Hellstone looked at him, panting desperately, like a cornered animal that had run several miles.

'Next time you pick up a knife to threaten someone you will be in very serious trouble,' said Andrè.

Andrè then left Hellstone's side, and walked up to Kate and Hector.

'Bed!' was all Andrè said, but he meant it, and even Hector decided to immediately obey.

CHAPTER ELEVEN

An Agreement

Kate and Hector had spent some time after lights out discussing the day's events. Both agreed that Lord Rothwell was potty. They also agreed to be early down to breakfast to see the inevitable fall out from the evening's dramatic confrontations.

The next day they were both disappointed. Lord Rothwell only made a fleeting appearance. He seemed polite and quiet. Breakfast was a strained affair. There was small talk but nothing else. Despite the sun streaming through the windows, it was as if everyone was waiting for great clouds to roll in and thunder to shake the building.

'OK,' Dad suddenly said, standing up.

'Good luck,' said Mum.

'Don't you take any rubbish,' said Nana.

Dad walked out of the kitchen and into the hall, towards Lord Rothwell's rooms. It became apparent to Kate and Hector that a time for a meeting had already been agreed.

Trevor Trogg settled down into a very comfortable sofa in Lord Rothwell's study. He looked out through the windows onto the grounds and the lake. Dunbar Hellstone, the Eleventh Earl of Rothwell sat on another sofa, to the side.

The rooms were luxurious, with deep red and gold drapes hanging from the walls. There were bright paintings of nothing in particular and dark tapestries showing tortured characters. Trevor

Trogg knew nothing of modern art, but he had a feeling these were expensive pieces.

The heating was turned up too high, and the windows were always open a notch. The rest of the Hall froze in winter according to Nana, with only Dunbar Hellstone's rooms heated.

'I am very sorry that I became rather overwrought yesterday,' said Lord Rothwell, 'Marmaduke was a personality and I was very fond of him.'

'Yes,' said Dad, trying to bring to mind the structure of all of the things he needed to discuss.

'I understand you wish to offer more money,' said Lord Rothwell.

'I am considering it,' There was a pause as Lord Rothwell looked at Trevor Trogg.

'Mr Trogg, some of your hoard…' Rothwell began.

'Let me stop you there,' said Dad firmly. He had been coached through this by Nana, Mum and Andrè. They all said he must stay in charge, remain calm and not let Rothwell get into one of his rants. Andrè was particularly keen on Dad remaining in charge of the conversation; Trevor Trogg had reflected on this as he had tried to get to sleep. He suspected that Andrè's favoured option was really dropping Lord Rothwell from a top floor window.

'Legally, we are cast iron,' said Dad, although this was not what he had been advised when discussing the situation with the solicitor on the telephone late the previous evening. He had been told that he needed a further agreement that encompassed loss and damage, including any animals.

'The contract is very broad,' said Lord Rothwell.

'And the payment very large,' said Dad, 'I have been advised that the size of the payment for the facilities offered is likely to be the nail in the coffin for any legal challenge. But this is not what I want to get into. I want you to be as happy as possible with this arrangement. I am prepared to offer an extra thirty thousand.'

'Oh, well, that is generous,' said Lord Rothwell, clearly surprised by the size of the extra payment.

'In return, I want us all to do our best to accept the situation, and that includes the dog.'

'The dog is a nuisance,' said Lord Rothwell.

'Yes, but my children have been shot at, they have crash landed a plane, they have fought off an attack that killed special forces soldiers. The dog has been a distraction for them, and a great comfort.'

'Of course, of course, I understand,' said Rothwell, 'Andrè explained some of this to me last night.'

'You now understand that he is not our social worker,' said Dad, slightly reproachfully.

'Quite, quite, and I appreciate that they have been very brave. I understand this. Of course, there is a great tradition of bravery in the Hellstone family,' said Lord Rothwell, suddenly getting into his flow.

'Yes,' said Dad holding up a hand, keen to head Rothwell off until he had worked his way through all of the business.

'I am prepared to make some further offers,' said Trevor Trogg.

'Oh my, are you, err good, very good, what are they?' said Rothwell, suddenly quite unable to contain himself.

'If any more of your animals die while we are here I will pay for the reasonable cost of a replacement, regardless as to whether it was old age, an accident, the dog, or whatever else. I hope they do not die. We will do our best.'

'Oh, excellent, excellent,' said Rothwell.

'I will pay for electric gates for the end of the drive.'

'In keeping, of course?' asked Rothwell.

'Yes, they will match the style of the existing ironwork' said Dad, careful not to offer a veto on the design in case Rothwell delayed this essential piece of security forever.

'Lastly, I do not intend to return your guns to you until we leave.'

'That is not acceptable! This is my house!' Rothwell exclaimed, his anger suddenly returning.

'Very well, but you should understand that if you pick up a knife again, or appear with a gun, Andrè will act. I believe you know what he is.'

Rothwell stopped. He looked out of the window, clearly gathering himself.

'I am sorry if this seems harsh,' Dad continued, 'but it is very frightening when someone appears with a gun. All of my family have been shot at. I am still recovering from shrapnel in the face. Also, you might reflect that it is in your interests given that Andrè will treat you as a threat.'

'I get the guns back and you get the key,' suggested Rothwell.

'You get the guns back and I get the key to the new lock,' said Dad.

Lord Rothwell smiled. He seemed genuinely pleased. The change surprised Trevor Trogg.

'Well, that's all settled. I am sure we will get along famously,' said Lord Rothwell as he made his way to the drinks cabinet.

'Maybe you could help me a little bit,' said Rothwell, 'I hear your daughter is a splendid swimmer. I open the swimming pool for the odd day here and there to treat the local children. Maybe she could help out?'

'Yes, I suppose so,' said Dad, taken aback. As he pondered this idea Dunbar Hellstone disappeared for a moment. Music began to play through the various speakers hidden in the walls around the room. Dad reflected that this was how it was supposed to go. Now, he had to be friendly with Dunbar Hellstone. The idea did not sit easily him, but his sense of family duty held him in check.

'That's the second movement of Brahms' German Requiem, isn't it?' Dad asked.

'Ahh, an educated man!' Hellstone exclaimed, 'I always put it on when entertaining favoured guests.'

Otto also heard the music drifting through the open windows. He was only about an hour away from his big daytime snooze. Nevertheless, the music called. He changed his plans and went to get a rat. His path crossed with Bandit, and he stopped to sniff him. Bandit also seemed to have a mission, but someone had chained him up.

'I tell you what,' suggested Lord Rothwell, 'I have Ms Rogerson to help me out. Superb at organising this or that. Why don't we split her salary for six months and she can help you as well as me?'

'Yes,' said Trevor Trogg, 'That would be useful, if you could spare her.'

'I can always spare Ms Rogerson, for a friend!' Rothwell declared.

'There is something I wanted to ask,' said Dad, 'I would love to know more about the history of the house and your family. Maybe you could give us all a tour at some point?' This had been agreed earlier. It was Nana's suggestion. It had exactly the effect Nana predicted. Her words came back to him, 'Dunbar's as stupid as he is vain.'

As Dunbar Hellstone, the Eleventh Earl of Rothwell spoke at length about his boring family and their great tradition of heroic acts, a rat hit the lower window with a small thud, on cue, exactly as Nana predicted. Trevor Trogg bit his lip as he tried to look interested in Lord Rothwell's family history. He really wanted to laugh, but he knew he must restrain himself.

The advice from the solicitors was that Trevor Trogg needed an agreement covering the loss of animals and damage. An agreement had been drafted in the night and couriered to Trevor Trogg first thing in the morning. He had a note he wanted Dunbar Hellstone to sign to cement their agreement. He could not afford another tantrum.

Five minutes later Dad was sagging under the onslaught of Hellstone self-aggrandisement. The rat had stopped hitting the window and he hoped that Otto had got bored and walked off, which apparently could happen. More worryingly, he had caught sight of something colourful in the distance near the lake. He prayed his eyes had deceived him. At least the rat threat had disappeared.

There was a splat as the rat's bloody intestines hit the window. It was phase two, as predicted. Otto had not lost interest. 'Damn' Dad thought, it had all been going to plan. He focussed again on preventing Lord Rothwell looking over to the window where red bits of rats' insides were being added by the minute.

'Tell me, Lord Rothwell, which of your ancestors were the most daring and brave, in your opinion?'

Bandit also had a plan. He was going to follow his nose. For a dog a sense of smell is more important than eyesight. If Bandit could have known what it was like to be human his first thought would not have been that colour vision was amazing; it would have been that humans' lack of an ability to smell anything other than socks and smoke was the most terrible disability.

Bandit lived in a world of smells. He knew where Otto had been in the last two days. He could follow him. He could follow Hector or Kate. He could follow anyone. It was like following a string on the ground. It was really easy. He knew what each of the family had been up to because of the smells they had picked up. He knew who had been near who because smells rubbed off from things they touched.

Bandit also knew Marmaduke's smell. He had been right up to the parrot when he lay in Lord Rothwell's arms. He had also smelled him earlier when he was waiting outside the aviary. In the bedroom the previous evening Bandit picked up the smell of Marmaduke and of earth. The smell came from Hector and Kate. It took him a while to work it out, but he believed Marmaduke had been buried like a bone underground.

Bandit did not know where Marmaduke was buried, but all he had to do was follow Lord Rothwell's odour string. The problem was that Bandit had been tied to a stake. A collar had been attached, and the lead was hooked over the top of a pole. Clearly, there was an issue of trust, although why no one trusted Bandit was a puzzle to him.

Bandit had been patient. He had lapped at the water in the bowl and sniffed Otto when he visited. The problem came when Otto trotted past with a live rat. It reminded Bandit that there was a parrot hiding underground somewhere. Bandit decided to wait another minute for someone to free him. This was roughly how long Otto's rat had to live.

At first Bandit tried to walk and then drive away from the pole. Although this cut off his air supply he was fairly sure the post would fall down. The post did not fall down. He barked in frustration, and then pulled and pulled. He ran a little towards the post and then ran backwards and pulled hard. It was almost enough force to break a human's neck, but Bandit's neck was stronger. It hurt as the collar was yanked over his ears, but finally he was free.

It took Bandit less than a minute to find the spot by the lake. There was a small wooden cross with a paving slab over the grave. Bandit knew about graves, albeit vaguely. He understood that humans buried people and sometimes animals. He understood nothing of the sanctity of the grave. He knew nothing of ghosts, of zombies, of the undead or of vampires. All of the beliefs, laws, rules, myths and fears that prevent humans digging in graves were unknown to Bandit. However, even if Bandit had possessed this terrible knowledge it would not have made him pause for a moment.

Bandit was forced to dig in the hard earth at the side of the paving slab. It was strenuous work, but after a while he was able to move into the softer, freshly dug soil. He had to dig further than he expected. He kept reversing, pulling the earth with him out of the hole, and spraying it behind. Marmaduke's scent was very strong now. He could also smell washed clothes.

Finally, his paws pulled at a blanket. He dug more, with the earth spilling down onto the cloth. Marmaduke's scent filled the hole. He dived his head down, gripped with his teeth, and pulled the parrot from its grave by one wing.

If Bandit had been granted the ability to read English he would have noticed that the cross over Marmaduke's grave read, 'Marmaduke, a beautiful and much loved parrot, laid to rest as the sun set on a clear spring evening, with great sorrow and ceremony by Dunbar Hellstone, the Eleventh Earl of Rothwell.' If Bandit had a pen he might have added 'Dug up by Bandit, just after breakfast'.

Bandit was ecstatic. He threw the parrot into the air and caught him. He ran and danced towards the Hall, and threw Marmaduke again, capering with joy at his triumph. It was this flash of colour that Trevor Trogg glimpsed from his sofa in Lord Rothwell's study.

Trevor Trogg had earlier decided to leave the signing of any agreement until later. Otto throwing bits of dead rat at the window as he played with his latest victim was likely to annoy the taciturn Lord Rothwell, but it was not a disaster. On the other hand, Bandit appearing in front of the window throwing his much loved parrot around was likely to kill the whole deal on the spot. This was unfortunate, because at that precise moment one of the windows Trevor Trogg could see was full of brown labrador flinging colourful parrot.

'Lord Rothwell,' Dad began.

'Please, call me Dunbar,' said Lord Rothwell.

'Dunbar, I would really like to hear more about the history of the family and the house. But, not to put too fine a point on it, I might not live. I don't want to be dramatic, but there is a risk. I think it would only be fair if there was a permanent record of our agreement just in case the worst happens. It is a lot of money and in fairness I would not want you to miss out.'

'Oh, yes, yes, yes, of course, yes,' mumbled Rothwell.

'I like to think I am a man of my word, but there's not a lot I can do if I'm in my grave,' said Dad, regretting immediately the use of the word grave, aware as he was that the parrot's grave was now quite empty.

Trevor Trogg produced the agreement. He had hoped to wait a little. He did not want to seem so keen as to appear desperate. The problem was Bandit. Rothwell only had to turn around and he would see Bandit flinging Marmaduke in the air.

'I'll call Ms Rogerson,' said Lord Rothwell, 'We will need a witness to the agreement.'

As Lord Rothwell took the agreement and read it through, Trevor Trogg could see Hector, Kate and Nana advancing on Bandit. Far from appearing cowed and sorry, Bandit looked wildly excited. He ran around in a small circle, looking backwards, ready for the chase to come. Hector darted first, hurling himself in a rugby tackle, head-first towards Bandit.

'My, my, a spelling mistake,' said Lord Rothwell as he examined the agreement and Trevor Trogg prayed he did not glance to his side and see the chase taking place on the lawn.

Andrè was trying to sneak up behind Bandit, but Bandit could smell him, and took off around the lawn, his back legs lower than the rest of his body. Bandit could out-run, out-manoeuvre and out-accelerate any human. Even the world 100 metre sprint champion could not get near Bandit. He was fast; very, very fast and he knew he was fast.

Bandit took off again, rocketing around the lawn, circling everyone who was chasing him. He continued for a second circuit, letting Marmaduke spill from his mouth a few metres in front of Andrè. As Andrè dived forwards to grab the dead parrot, Bandit turned a sharper circle, returning to run just in front of Andrè and snatch Marmaduke. He accelerated, glancing back with a wild look of excitement.

Trevor Trogg watched in helpless horror. The only good news was that Rothwell was still reading and Otto had stopped throwing bits of dead rat. Presumably, Otto was watching Bandit, but almost certainly without Trevor Trogg's feeling of all encompassing dread.

'I'll add a line about Ms Rogerson,' suggested Lord Rothwell.

'Yes, yes, good idea,' said Dad, trying to keep his eyes on Lord Rothwell and away from the riot of colour that was cartwheeling through the air as Bandit flung and capered with Marmaduke.

It might have helped Kate, Nana, Hector and Andrè if they had shouted at Bandit and told him off. Unfortunately, the windows were open, and this was a chase that had to take place in silence. The stern looks and hissed warnings had no effect on Bandit.

'The agreement says I surrender my guns. Maybe we should just miss that out?' Lord Rothwell ventured.

'No, I'm afraid not,' said Dad, on one hand desperate to get the note signed, but on the other sure he had to get it all sorted out.

'I'm really not keen on this Trevor,' said Lord Rothwell, just as Bandit completed another wild circuit of the lawn and flung Marmaduke once more.

'There is a great deal of money riding on it,' said Trevor Trogg, trying to keep his eyes away from the window.

As Lord Rothwell added in a line about his guns being under lock and key, Bandit began to chew Marmaduke, as well as dance and race.

Lord Rothwell began to weigh the agreement. He was looking over clauses, reading bits, muttering things. He gave the impression that he was being very kind in agreeing to this new arrangement, and in accepting a huge sum of money in addition to the vast sum he had already received.

Bandit threw Marmaduke, caught and chewed a bit more. He hoped this would entice them into chasing him. Nana, Kate, Hector and Andrè were now trying to walk in a line towards Bandit. They were trying to trap him near a small walled area with chairs and a table. Bandit waited, his excitement growing. He had already decided to race towards Hector, and then double-back past Andrè, as this would be more daring.

Bandit went. Bandit dodged right. Bandit stopped and went back. Bandit rocketed around Andrè, delivering pure power down and back to drive past him. Andrè dived, his hand outstretched he clipped Bandit's bottom. Bandit rolled, dropping Marmaduke. Andrè lunged forwards towards Marmaduke with surprising speed just as Bandit recovered and dug his teeth firmly into the lower half of the parrot.

Andrè gripped the head of the parrot with his left hand, flailing with his right. He was desperate to keep hold of the parrot and grab the dog, but he did not want a tug of war. He could not win against teeth. Bandit settled back into a rhythm of tugs, his whole body convulsing as he pulled and pulled. Andrè was spread out on the ground and could not get hold of the dog. He muttered something in French as he tightened his grip around the head of the parrot.

Lord Rothwell was flicking through the pages of the agreement now, while Trevor Trogg looked through the window in horror. Andrè was laid on his front on the lawn, his left arm outstretched in a tug-of-war with Bandit. Marmaduke was the colourful rope. Kate was running to help, while Hector and Nana looked on.

Kate's intervention was too much for Bandit. He knew that once someone had him by the scruff of the neck he had lost. He redoubled his efforts, pulling with huge, violent wave-like spasms. Just as Kate reached for Bandit's neck, Bandit fell backwards, partly rolling over.

In a flash he was back on his feet and off. He still had Marmaduke, or at least most of him, as Andrè now had Marmaduke's head. Bandit danced and capered, flinging Marmaduke in the air once more. A battle for the parrot and he had won round one. Hopefully, there would be more rounds.

Lord Rothwell was still ponderously looking over the agreement. Trevor Trogg was very grateful for his host's need to lord it over him. However unpleasant Rothwell could be, he had shed genuine tears for an animal he truly loved. If Rothwell was to just glance up and to his left he would see his beloved Marmaduke, exhumed from his grave, being pulled to pieces by the dog he loathed, with Trevor Trogg's children in close attendance.

Just as Trevor Trogg did not think things could get any worse, something hit the window. It was Otto. He had not given up. The thing Otto was flicking around was a brown-grey colour, and had only a small patch of red. It hit the window once more, before sailing through on the third attempt. The rat's head landed on the pages of the agreement and Rothwell exploded.

'That cat! That cat!'

'No, Dunbar,' said Dad desperately, trying to stop Lord Rothwell from looking towards the window, but it was too late.

Bandit was just disappearing from view, and Marmaduke was thankfully out of sight, although Lord Rothwell was clearly puzzled as to why so many people should be on the lawn, and Andrè appeared to be getting up. There were four people, but no noise.

'I think we should focus on what is important,' said Trevor Trogg.

Rothwell stood up and began pacing back and forth. It seemed as though any small thing could disturb his mood. As he walked back towards Trevor Trogg, Bandit flashed past the window, a blur of yellow, red and green feathers in his mouth. Hector followed just behind, running with his arms outstretched like an egyptian mummy from a horror movie.

'Yes, yes, you are quite right,' said Rothwell suddenly, 'I should sign quickly and then take you on a tour round the grounds.'

'Maybe we could start with the house,' Dad suggested desperately.

'No, grounds first,' said Rothwell, as he strode towards his desk to pick up the telephone so that he might finally summon Ms Rogerson.

Bandit was growing bored. They had stopped chasing him. He settled down in a flower border and began to chew Marmaduke. He decided to eat the claws. This prompted another capture attempt from Hector and Kate, and Bandit happily jumped up and ran around once more.

'I reckon,' said Nana quietly to Andrè, 'that the more we chase the longer he'll take to eat it.'

Andrè was testing the wind, wondering whether an attempt to sneak up on Bandit was worth another try. Instead he and Nana moved to block the view of Bandit from the house. Kate and Hector were called over to join the human fence. They pretended to be taking in the view, while silently urging the dog to chew and swallow Marmaduke as quickly as possible.

Otto was less than pleased. Dismembering a rat was always satisfying. There had been a pleasing yell when he threw the rat's head into the room. Nevertheless, Bandit was clearly having more fun. Otto was not sure he liked Bandit enjoying himself so much. Otto crouched down and stared.

Bandit appeared to have killed Marmaduke, Rothwell's favourite parrot. This also annoyed Otto. He had long planned to kill Marmaduke himself, chew him up and hurl bits into Rothwell's rooms. Somehow Bandit had got there first, and now he seemed to be eating the claws. Otto liked eating claws.

Otto stared and stared. Bandit was too big to kill, and that annoyed him as well. Otto, stood up, stretched, and then turned around to survey the remains of the rat. He put his paw under the main part of the rat's corpse and flicked it hard. It landed back exactly where it had started. He succeeded on the second attempt, and the beheaded and disembowelled rat flew in a less than elegant arc through the window into Lord Rothwell's study. There was no scream and Otto felt an itch deep inside. He could not reach inside and scratch it. It made him want to writhe, to kill, to race; it made him daring.

Bandit was now chewing off Marmaduke's left wing, unaware that he was being stalked. He had checked around for one of the humans, ready for yet another exciting chase. He had no idea that just downwind was a very agitated predator trying to prevent its tail from flicking.

Otto dived, seizing Marmaduke from under Bandit's nose. As Otto went to accelerate away, Bandit's head moved with a speed humans can only dream off. His snout caught Otto's rear end, sending him spinning and Marmaduke flying, quite possibly for the very last time. Bandit charged forwards and Otto snarled and hissed a threat. Yet again, Bandit had achieved a threatening momentum in a fraction of a second. Otto dived away just before he was hit, clawed at the parrot to his side, and was rewarded with an impressive multicoloured wing.

Otto sprinted away with his prize. He might have wanted the whole parrot, but the wing was a splendid trophy. He had triumphed over Bandit and he was determined to eat his prize in full view of everyone.

Bandit on the other hand was not in the slightest bit upset. Fighting over the remains of Marmaduke was right at the top of his list of dream encounters. Bandit adored excitement, and the surprise attack by the cat left him tingling, bouncing and ready for another chase. He liked Otto, and made a mental note not to wee on him.

Andrè looked on with a dull sense of a situation that was always going to get worse just when he thought things were improving. Bandit had managed to flatten a number of attractive spring flowers. He was sprawled full length, chewing Marmaduke, with only occasional glances that betrayed his hopes of another attack or chase.

Otto was in a tree, Marmaduke's wing clearly on display under his front paws. Andrè previously had hopes that Marmaduke would be completely eaten, leaving no evidence. Now Otto had complicated an already difficult situation. He could see no way of getting to Otto, at least not without a gun or a chainsaw.

Hector was well ahead of everyone. He had rushed inside to get a water pistol he had spotted when rummaging through the utility room cupboards. He filled it, ran out past Kate who was on her way inside, took aim, and shot Otto.

'Nice idea,' said Nana, who had started to feel in her pockets for the pipe everyone knew she smoked, but she believed was a secret. 'Unfortunately, Otto likes water.'

Kate appeared a minute later with a bucket of hot, soapy water. Bandit's ears dropped.

'Bath Bandit, come on,' said Kate, advancing towards him.

Bandit looked at Kate briefly, and then took off. He headed towards the woods. Things had suddenly turned very unpleasant. He hated baths.

'Right,' said Nana, 'Give that here.'

Nana took the bucket from Kate and went towards Otto's tree. Otto was suddenly much more alert, and much less smug. He was top notch when it came to looking smug. If there had been an international award for looking smug he could have been a contender. The sight of Nana with hot soapy water was not an attractive one. All of his smugness had deserted him.

'I tell you what Andrè,' said Nana, 'you fling it. I reckon your aim's better than mine.'

As the water was in mid air, Otto turned and vanished down the tree. The wing fluttered from his grasp. He sprang down and moved with amazing speed and agility to catch it, but Andrè was advancing with the little that remained in the bucket. As Otto fled, Andrè picked up the wing and put it in his pocket. He believed the bottom of the dustbin was the best place for both wing and head.

'Good, good,' said Lord Rothwell, pacing towards them. Andrè instinctively placed his hand over his pocket. He was relieved that things were about to calm down. His problem was that he did not appreciate the extent to which things were about to settle to a much slower pace.

Lord Rothwell's tour was a living hell. His interest and detailed opinions on every tree, hill, slight undulation in the ground, the water table, the role of the Vikings and the influence of the Romans, the wildlife, the clouds, different grasses, the effect of the fire that burnt the Hall down and just about anything he could ramble onto, left Andrè and everyone else longing for another desperate chase after Bandit.

'In the lake you can see two islands. Curiously, the smaller man-made island is undoubtedly the most interesting,' Rothwell droned.

'One of my forebears played probably the most important role in the famous Charge of the Light Brigade. As you may know, the captured canon were melted down and the metal used to make this country's highest military honour, the Victoria Cross. My ancestor is the only person to be honoured with a great chunk of one of the cannons. It has been fashioned into that fountain. It is undoubtedly my family's most precious heirloom. A source of great, great pride. You might notice that the noble head bears some resemblance to my own features.'

As Lord Rothwell turned sideways so they could all see the similarities, Kate thought hard about history and the little she knew of the Crimea War.

'Wasn't that a military disaster?' Kate asked quickly, without stopping to think further.

'It was the greatest example of the British officer class doing what their betters told them needed to be done. It was following orders!' declared Lord Rothwell, clearly affronted, 'As I said, he was a key figure. A brave man.'

'He was probably in charge of the compass,' Kate whispered to Hector.

'Dunbar, this has been fantastic. I've been enthralled,' said Dad, 'Unfortunately, it is lunch time.'

'I've really only scratched the surface,' said Lord Rothwell, 'There's lots more to tell.'

'Maybe after lunch,' Mum suggested.

As they sat eating a glorious salad Nana had produced out of no-where, Andrè commented that only the British could celebrate a military disaster and turn a communications fiasco into a source of pride. Dad was fairly sure the French had done something similar. Andrè smiled and then complained that Dad could not possibly understand.

Nana had missed the tour. Instead, she had spent her time re-moving bits of rat from Lord Rothwell's study and windows. She explained that one polite family had endured almost a day and a half of Lord Rothwell's tour.

'There's only one way to stop the tour and that's to hide,' said Nana.

'It seems so rude,' said Mum.

'So is talking until everyone's so bored they'd welcome death,' Nana replied, 'It's your choice, you can stay with the tour for an-other half a day and then hide tomorrow morning, or hide now.'

'This minute?' Hector asked, rising from his seat.

'No, Dunbar always takes at least three quarters of an hour for lunch,' said Nana, 'I reckon you've got at another ten minutes.'

There was silence while Hector and Kate looked at Mum and Dad. Brother and sister knew what was going on. There was an internal struggle between manners on one hand and good advice on the other.

'You have to remember,' said Nana, recognising their dilemma, 'Dunbar is used to people hiding from him. It's part of his world. He thinks he's giving someone a treat and they run away or do just about anything to avoid it. I reckon this is partly why he's so angry all the time.'

'I remember the time when there was this Danish chap here. He looked Japanese on account of his father being from Japan. Any-way, he was too polite and went out for the afternoon tour. Dunbar came back an hour later saying how extraordinary it was that this chap should lose his footing and fall in the lake. Later Douglas, one of the brothers who looks after the grounds, you haven't met him yet. Anyway, Douglas tells me he saw it all. The Danish chap just flung himself in the lake when Dunbar had his back turned. Said he had to change his clothes because he was soaked and hid after that. Mark my words, hide and it will all be forgotten. He won't stop until he can't find you.'

'Did he sign the papers?' Mum asked.

'Yes, let's hide,' Dad conceded.

'Brilliant,' said Hector.

'Time to practise those evasion skills,' said Andrè, 'And just to make it more interesting if anyone is discovered in the first hour I will intervene and suggest the tour continues just for him or her.'

'Can I have a gun?' Hector asked, 'In case Lord Rothwell finds me.'

'Are you going to shoot him or yourself?' Kate asked.

'Not sure,' said Hector.

'Why isn't Lord Rothwell a headmaster any more?' asked Hector, keen to find out more while Nana was so willing to divulge information.

'Well, as I said, he was locked out of the school by teachers and pupils,' Nana began, 'But that was just the end if it all. He was appointed headmaster with excellent references from his previous school. He rose quickly in his profession, but that was because he always got excellent references and letters of recommendation. Every school he worked at was desperate to get rid of him, so they always gave him super references.'

'Dunbar instituted Friday lectures as soon as he took over as headmaster, where he spoke to the whole school all Friday afternoon. Well, you've just had a taste of what they're like; a mixture of maddening boredom and Dunbar Hellstone self promotion.'

'Then he sacked two of the staff he thought were plotting against him. The pupils started making snoring noises during his lectures. Then someone painted his car pink during the night. Not just the car panels, the windows and everything ended up pick. Except for the wheels, they were purple. Dunbar said it was a sign;

a careful part of the seditious conspiracy. I think they just ran out of pink paint.'

'Next he replaced the head of English with his own wife and managed to drive off several of the best teachers. I think the pinnacle of his achievements came when Dunbar hired private detectives to follow some of the staff. He wanted to see if they were meeting up after school where they might be planning to overthrow him. He confronted all of the staff at a big meeting and told them all he knew where they had been.'

'So Dunbar became very paranoid,' Dad confirmed.

'Strictly speaking no,' said Nana, 'Paranoia is the delusion that everyone is talking about you and plotting against you. It wasn't a delusion. By this point everyone was plotting against Dunbar.'

'Oddly enough, the plots came to nothing. A student prank to lock the gates and doors while Dunbar was off visiting took hold. Everyone joined in and Dunbar was simply locked out of the school. He sent messages sacking staff, but they were ignored. He called the police, who had no idea what to do and said it was a civil matter. Dunbar decided to go to court, but no one knew who to sue. Funny thing was even his wife sided with the students locking him out; they divorced shortly afterwards.'

'I wish I'd known all of this earlier,' said Dad, after which there was a pause.

'I think you'd better be off if you want to hide,' said Nana, leading to a remarkable collective movement, where all fears of being bored beyond endurance suddenly came to the fore.

Kate disappeared up to their room. She decided to hide in the wardrobe with a book. Oddly enough, Andrè approved. He said it was appropriate for the threat. It also greatly reduced the chance that she would be caught while looking out from her hiding place.

Mum and Dad raced towards the cars and Hector followed. To his disappointment they had disappeared in Dad's Jaguar by the time Hector got there. So much for family.

Hector decided to be inventive. Hiding in the woods would work, but it would mean a long wait in the rough damp of the trees. Andrè had explained that the best hiding places were unexpected and provided comfort. He had also explained that most people are caught when they move or look out from their hiding position.

Lord Rothwell's black Range Rover drew Hector's eye. If it was open it would be comfortable. Nana had said that lots of people in the country did not lock their cars. Hector ran forward and tried the rear door. It was open and he clambered in. The drawback of the Range Rover as a hiding place became immediately apparent. The windows in the Hall looked straight down, through the car windows. He would be easily spotted.

Hector glanced around. He was distracted by the plush cream interior of the vehicle. It was an older model, but it was spotlessly clean. He looked to the rear. The willow tree behind would have given him perfect cover if the Range Rover had just been parked five metres further back.

Hector could not start the Range Rover and move it backwards. He did not have the keys and in any event was not sure he could drive. Nevertheless, the ground sloped away to the rear. All he had to do was let the hand brake off and it would roll backwards.

Hector clambered into the front, moved the automatic gear selector from Park to Neutral, and released the hand brake. It took all of his strength to lift the handbrake arm, press the button and let it fall away. The Range Rover moved just a few centimetres slightly downhill, but then stopped. Hector felt frustrated, and he rocked back and forth in the seat to try to get it to move.

As he got out of the Range Rover he was reminded just how large it was. It seemed impossible that he could move it. On the other hand, it was on a slope. Hector gave it a small push, resting his hands on the front bumper. Nothing happened. He got lower, dug his toes into the ground and pushed with all of his might. It moved a little, and then began to move slowly without his help.

Hector was delighted. He had moved the giant Range Rover all by himself. It was rolling very slowly, like some giant spacecraft moving into position ready for launch. Hector walked alongside, aware that it was moving a little faster. He grasped the open door and pulled to bring the Range Rover to a halt. Nothing happened, the Range Rover kept moving.

The Range Rover was now exactly where Hector wanted it to be, but was gathering speed. Hector pulled hard, but found himself pulled along with it. In a flash he could see all that was about to unfold. The Range Rover was heading for the lake; Hector had to get into the car and pull the handbrake on.

Hector raced around the door, but every time he went to jump into the high Range Rover he was aware of the nearest front wheel, spinning, waiting to crush his legs if he failed. It was gathering speed and Hector was running faster. Defeat, defeat, defeat. Hector knew he could not jump, it was just getting too fast.

He ran out from the door's path and watched Lord Rothwell's Range Rover race towards the lake, backwards. It did not seem so fast when watched from a distance. Hector felt helpless as he reflected that he was in so much trouble.

The smart polished black Range Rover slowed as it hit the water. A bow wave developed and ripples spread out across the lake. The car continued at a slower rate, as if being reversed on purpose by a thoroughly aquatic driver. As it disappeared into the lake large bubbles rose up.

Hector ran down to the edge of the water, the feeling of dread lifting slightly. The Range Rover had completely disappeared. 'Brilliant' Hector thought. All he had to do was cover his tracks, quite literally.

Only the mud near the edge of the lake showed tyre tracks, and Hector trod on it and squished it around with his trainer to obscure the tread marks. Then he ran back the way the Range Rover had come and trod on the odd tyre mark here and there.

Once he had finished he returned to the lake. He was not sure why he did this. He felt like a criminal returning to the scene of his crime. He looked into the water and realised that in the gloom he could see the Range Rover's headlights staring sadly and reproachfully back out at him.

Hector thought about the Range Rover. It was very plush and posh. Despite having Lord Rothwell as a driver, it had been well cared for. It had many happy years motoring to look forward to, at least until Hector Trogg rolled it into a lake.

'Ahh, the only one. Good, good,' said Lord Rothwell. Hector jumped, and then turned around, trying not to look guilty. Then he realised the Range Rover's demise had not been seen, but he was not going to get away with it completely. The tour was going to be his punishment.

'I thought we could start this afternoon looking over the outbuildings. There are several additions over the years, and one or two are tantalising in their historical relevance.'

Hector had no idea what this meant, but he could see an afternoon of sheer tedium ahead of him. He did the only sensible thing; while Lord Rothwell's back was turned he made a short run and flung himself into the lake.

CHAPTER TWELVE

Gardens

'I think it was foxes,' Nana lied.

Hector and Kate had woken to cries and sobbing on a still and quiet morning. Lord Rothwell was by the lake. From their window they did not have a very good view of Marmaduke's empty grave.

'He's gone Dunbar. We have to let go,' said Nana, in a comforting voice.

'I have let go!' yelled Lord Rothwell, 'I just didn't think he would be dug up!'

'He had a good life,' Nana added.

'Even the foxes are cruel to me,' Rothwell sobbed.

'Foxes, yes, cruel beasts foxes,' said Nana.

'It could have been that horrible dog,' said Lord Rothwell, suddenly shrewd and suspicious.

'I don't think Bandit's the sort,' Nana lied.

'Yes he is! He is! He's a thieving, grave robber of a dog!' Rothwell declared.

'This isn't doing any good Dunbar,' said Nana, as kindly as she could.

'Grave robber! Grave robber! You horrible, vile, stinking dog!'

'Does he ever stop?' Hector muttered, as he, Kate and Bandit watched from the window.

While Kate and Hector looked on in wonder at the desperately unhinged Lord Rothwell, Bandit was desperate to be out there. Maybe he could excavate a bit more of the grave in case any more parrots were hiding. If not, he could always wee on Lord Rothwell. That chap was a screamer and a chaser. Bandit found him exciting.

Over breakfast there were more screams. Lord Rothwell seemed to have discovered that his Range Rover was missing. Ms Rogerson was running around in a flap, as if the Range Rover might have been left in a cupboard or drawer and all she had to do was find it. Eventually, she called the police.

'Maybe the foxes took the Range Rover as well as Marmaduke,' said Hector.

'You're a wicked child,' said Nana with a grin.

'Yes, I think he might be,' said Andrè, who was just finishing a very English breakfast. Andrè fixed Hector with a stare. Hector was speared with a pang of doubt and fear; maybe Andrè knew his guilty secret.

The previous evening, as Hector and Kate had chatted before bedtime, Hector had been tempted to confess. He knew, however, that as soon as he upset Kate in a major way she would broadcast his secret. Now, Hector was thinking about what Mum and Dad would say if they knew he had destroyed Lord Rothwell's Range Rover. Did Andrè know? Would he tell them? Was it serious enough for him to go to jail?

Shortly after breakfast Hector got his answer. Andrè announced that Hector's woeful evasion meant more work and had dragged him off to the barns and stables for practice.

'Why did you sink the Range Rover?' Andrè asked.

'I didn't,' said Hector, instinctively.

'Hector, there is hidden CCTV everywhere and I have a record of your movements.'

Hector said nothing as he desperately searched for a lie that would get him out of trouble. Nothing occurred to him.

'Hector, I am here to protect you. I am not your moral guardian. I will not tell your mother and father, but I do want to know what you did and why you did it.'

Hector decided that a complete confession was the best option. As he explained what had happened Andrè laughed, and Hector went on to explain about covering the tyre tracks and then being caught by Lord Rothwell in time for the tour.

'Hector, I am very unhappy about you pushing that car. You could have easily killed yourself. You would not have been the first child crushed by a car they had started to push.'

'Are you going to tell Lord Rothwell?' Hector asked, fearing the worst.

'There are times when an open and honest approach is by far the best Hector, but this isn't one of them,' said Andrè, 'Lord Rothwell is a confused and difficult character. It's bad enough that your dog dug up his parrot. If he discovered this happened on the same day that you launched his Range Rover into his own lake I cannot imagine what he might attempt. This can be our secret.'

'Thanks,' said Hector, genuinely relieved.

'You better not move any more cars,' Andrè cautioned.

As Andrè and Hector began walking back to the Hall there was a scream from the kitchen. Bandit fled past, towards the woods with something in his mouth. With luck, Hector thought, Bandit might overshadow him. There could be no doubt; Bandit was intent on a major food-focussed crime spree.

Over the coming days Bandit adapted wonderfully, crafting a routine that perfectly suited his environment. Nana began letting him out of Hector and Kate's room very early in the morning so that he would not wake them with his whining.

First thing was the dawn hunt. He would race through the woods after rabbits and anything else that would run, including anyone called Dawn. When he heard his name being called the hunt stopped immediately, because his breakfast would be ready.

After breakfast he would try to steal the cat's food. Following the incident when he first arrived, he could no longer get to either Otto's dish or Otto's supply of food in the low cupboard, but there was a principle involved, and there were often rewards for perseverance.

Next on Bandit's itinerary was a duck hunt. He would dive into the lake and swim towards the ducks barking. They would swim or fly away, but it was still tremendous fun, plus Bandit suspected there was always a chance one of them might surrender. The added entertainment of the duck hunt was Lord Rothwell, who would appear and shout at him. This always happened when the ducks had all fled, and so Bandit would get out, shake himself all over Lord Rothwell, dodging out of the way if Rothwell aimed a kick at him.

For the first couple of days Bandit got to race around Lord Rothwell and in through the open door to his study and rooms. He could hurtle around and across the chairs, settees and loungers, while Lord Rothwell pursued him screaming with fury. When Lord Rothwell was out of breath he would encourage him further by rubbing and drying himself on the expensive rugs.

On the third day Lord Rothwell had the sense to shut the door, which was a huge disappointment. Things improved, however, when Bandit went racing around the building looking for a way in;

a desperate and breathless Lord Rothwell in pursuit. Once he found a door open, he was in, with the screaming Rothwell just behind.

Over the following days Lord Rothwell would tear around the building shutting the doors once Bandit was in the lake, but Kate or Hector would always open one. Bandit learnt to run more slowly. He cantered from the lake around the building, because this way Lord Rothwell could keep up and that made it much more exciting.

Hector and Kate adored Bandit. He liked cuddles; he was sweet; he provided endless entertainment, but best of all he was part of their gang. Otto both liked and admired Bandit some of the time, and hated him a bit on other occasions. Mum, Dad and Andrè were less keen.

Bandit had Lord Rothwell wound up to fever pitch. All were agreed that Dunbar Hellstone, the Eleventh Earl of Rothwell was a difficult and unstable character who needed careful management. Bandit offered nothing but trouble.

The police were still looking for Lord Rothwell's Range Rover. Every so often Hector would stand by the lake and peer into its depths until he could make out the vehicle's headlights staring back.

Lord Rothwell was not the only one with car troubles. Dad's new Jaguar was always flashing up warning messages for tyre pressure failures that had not occurred. Kate noticed other lights that would appear and make Dad sigh or get angry. Ms Rogerson, in her new role helping the Trogg family, took up the cause with the Jaguar dealers, but to no avail.

Eventually, Dad got a letter from the Jaguar Car Company informing him that the water in the rear lights was a characteristic rather than a fault. Andrè thought he should buy fish to swim in them. Andrè began to tease Dad, suggesting that he should take Mrs Warp everywhere with him, because she was strong enough to push it.

Hector and Kate thoroughly enjoyed Dad's attempts to use the speech recognition system, with its multiple confirmations, mistakes and constant worry that just a touch of the brake would cancel the whole process. It drove Dad into a fury. No one liked the Jaguar XJ's bumpy ride, and everyone preferred the more comfortable Toyota Hilux, which was supposed to be a rough and ready off-road monster.

After a while only Dad went out in the Jaguar XJ. Kate felt sad about it, as Dad had always dreamed of owning a Jaguar. Ms Rogerson kept assuring Dad that something was about to be fixed, but nothing happened.

'Why does he persist with that useless car?' Mum asked in exasperation one wet lunchtime, 'It bumps along, its electronics are hopeless, the SatNav is a confusing whirl of red dots at every roundabout, there's water in the rear lights, and it just feels unsafe.'

'He could have got a Citroen, they are very good now,' said Andrè.

'And that useless woman. She is supposed to sort things out, but nothing happens,' Mum continued.

'Dad's car repairs are like war; he thinks it will all be over by Christmas,' Kate chipped in.

'Now, now, he's had a hard time,' Nana said. 'Allow him his little fancies. He's not the first man to waste money on loose cars and slow women.'

'Don't you mean fast cars and loose women?' Mum corrected.

'Err, no, not in this case,' said Nana.

'I'm fed up with Mrs Personal Assistant,' declared Hector, 'I'm fed up with her bossiness, and her messing everything up, and I'm fed up with her squeaky voice. I want to shrink her and introduce her to Otto.'

'I think we need to sort out some education for you two,' said Mum. While this was clearly a sign of bad temper, Kate and Hector worried that she might be serious. They had missed weeks of school and they were enjoying themselves. The threat of education to Kate and Hector was as welcome as a bucket of warm soapy water was to Bandit.

'I'm also wondering whether some obedience training might help Bandit,' Mum ventured.

'I doubt it,' said Nana, 'He's got rogue stamped right through him. You'll get some temporary good behaviour, but all of the really naughty stuff will still be there.'

Kate suspected that Nana liked Bandit exactly as he was. Mum might be reviewing Bandit's position, but Nana had no problems with a bit of thievery providing the dog had a kind nature.

Otto was also reviewing Bandit's position. There had to be some doubt as to whether he could be considered a friend. When Otto caught a mouse, and settled down to play with it, Bandit often turned up. His arrival always coincided with a gulping sound and the disappearance of the mouse.

In Otto's alphabetical set of relationships F for friend was only one step away from E for enemy. F for friend was only two steps away from D for dead. Otto had moved several friends from F to D, but Bandit was too large and too healthy. Additional complications were that he was too confident and too happy.

In truth, it was the happiness that bothered Otto the most. There was no doubt that Otto was happy, but that did not mean that he liked to see anyone else in a state resembling happiness. He liked to see uncertainty, self-loathing and doubt. Nagging fear was exactly what he wanted in others.

Bandit did experience fear. The problem was that the box labelled 'fear' sat right next to the box called 'wild excitement'. Bandit liked fear in the same way that someone who enjoys terrifying roller-coasters does not believe they are truly in danger.

Bandit had such vast reserves of self-belief and confidence that he could not be a friend to Otto. On the other hand Bandit was useful, and in Otto's world only useful friends were worth having.

These contradictions did not bother Otto too much. For a cat he had a brilliant mind. Yet, Otto had gone to considerable trouble to see that his brilliant mind was not troubled too much.

Hector and Kate had both met the two gardeners, Douglas and Gary Hepstall. They were identical twins. They were short, balding men in their fifties, with a good deal of grey hair sprouting from their necks and ears. Only Nana seemed to be able to tell them apart. Other than 'Hello,' and sometimes only a nod, they did not appear to communicate at all.

The French soldier called Henry was staying with Douglas and Gary. The brothers were unlikely to welcome anyone, but Henry was apparently very unpopular. Andrè had spoken to them, but they had not replied. Nana had to negotiate, but achieved nothing.

'Douglas and Gary are refusing to talk to Henry. I think they are making life as difficult as possible,' said Nana to Andrè, just as Kate and Hector bounced in looking for a snack.

'He probably will not notice,' said Andrè, 'He is very odd.'

'They've started calling him names,' said Nana.

'I know. They call him unpleasant things back in France; it will not upset him,' said Andrè.

Henry greatly annoyed Lord Rothwell, who had tried to insist that he displayed some deference, as Douglas and Gary did. Henry was supposed to blend in and work as a gardener. Unfortunately, he looked like a purple alien in a green landscape. He had a mass of black, curly hair, a large bulbous nose that matched his large onion-shaped head. His eyebrows appeared too dark for such pale skin, and beneath them were two black eyes that seemed to stare, unblinking at whatever had taken his attention.

Andrè was unflinchingly unkind about Henry. He explained that Henry was given this assignment partly because everyone wanted him out of the camp in France. Andrè warned everyone that Henry was there for when the fighting started; he was not someone they should entirely trust.

'He has a very cruel streak,' said Andrè, when talking to Dad one day.

'Does he torture people?' Hector asked, displaying his usual directness.

Andrè looked at Hector and then shrugged his shoulders. He was not going to answer. Clearly, Henry had done some things that left other soldiers feeling uncomfortable.

Henry's contribution in the garden was a problem. Instead of doing as he was told, or simply doing nothing, he played a surprisingly energetic part. He moved large shrubs, replanting them, leaving most of their roots behind.

Douglas or Gary, it was impossible to know which one for sure, had been seen complaining to Lord Rothwell. These complaints quickly made their way back to Dad.

'I'm sure he is doing his best,' said Rothwell at an impromptu meeting, 'but according to my gardeners he's killing anything he moves.'

'Oh,' said Dad, turning to Andrè and Henry. Andrè spoke in French and then translated the slow reply.

'He says that they will grow back next year.'

'Without any roots?' Rothwell questioned, as he stepped towards one, lifting it easily out of the ground.

Henry said something and Andrè translated.

'He says it was fine until you just killed it,' said Andrè.

'I lifted it clean out of the ground,' complained Lord Rothwell, 'It had no connection to its roots. That's why it was leaning to one side,' Rothwell gestured across the grounds where a number of shrubs were leaning in the same way.

'Look at them,' said Rothwell, 'They all lean.'

Again, Henry spoke slowly.

'He says they are resting, but they will all grow next spring,' Andrè translated.

'Then why did some of them roll away in the wind this morning?'

Henry looked confused and Andrè translated for him. As Andrè reported Henry's view that the shrubs were too round and should have been more of a square shape to stop them rolling, Dad intervened concluding that Henry must not touch any more plants, and in future must restrict his work to fences, gates, mending machinery or whatever else Douglas or Gary told him to do.

Rather than looking offended Henry agreed, disappearing with the strange mechanistic walk he had. Lord Rothwell had been surprisingly calm throughout. When Dad suggested that Gary and Douglas pick out some new plants for the gardens and Dad would pay, Lord Rothwell simply said that was very kind.

Rothwell's laid back approach to Henry's damage in the garden lasted exactly two hours. There were shouts and screams from the stables. Hector and Kate arrived just after Dad to find Lord Rothwell shouting at Henry.

'That wooden wheelbarrow is Victorian,' Rothwell yelled into Henry's face, 'It is meant for show. It is kept dry. It is used for flower displays, not for moving heavy loads of earth you imbecile!'

The wooden axel of the wheelbarrow was broken. Earth was piled high, straining its attractively painted wooden structure. Henry just stood, staring back at Lord Rothwell. Andrè arrived panting.

'He can repair it,' said Andrè, 'He is very talented with wood.'

'I'm not surprised. I suspect his brain's made of the stuff.' Rothwell angrily shouted.

Rothwell then stalked off. Andrè began to remonstrate with Henry. Dad looked at Kate and Hector, shrugging his shoulders.

Later, Andrè wanted a talk with Dad, alone. They decided to walk around the gardens, which were still littered with some of the bushes Henry had dug up. It looked, at a glance, like a very green scene from a cowboy film, with large shrubs as the tumbleweed.

'We need to start attracting attention,' said Andrè, 'It will be a slow process and we need to start soon.'

'I'm quite happy hiding,' said Dad, and Andrè smiled.

'It is always easier to sit in the trench and wait for a little bit longer,' Andrè said.

They walked in silence for a while.

'Why the rush?' Dad asked.

'Two reasons,' Andrè replied, 'First, attracting attention will take time. We want him to think we have slipped up. If he suspects information is being fed to him he will be better prepared. Second, we are tracking him using his mobile phones. I think he will dump them soon, contact the people he needs to talk to using new phones, and we will have lost our best way of keeping him in our sights.'

Dad sighed. He accepted the logic, but was unhappy with the conclusion.

'In the past, dealing with someone as deranged as Rothwell, or your tame idiot Henry, would have caused me such worry. Now, it seems trivial.'

'I think both of them are capable of causing some real trouble,' said Andrè.

'What do you want me to do?' Dad asked, 'Anything specific? Talk to the local press about the attack at the zoo in France?'

'No, no, he would know immediately that he was being lured here,' said Andrè, 'I want you to get rid of your Jaguar and buy two much flashier cars.'

'Oh. Not a Citroen!'

'No, I suggest a Rolls or Bentley and an Aston Martin. They are very English cars.'

'Bentleys are finished at the old Rolls Royce Crewe works I think, but they are really Volkswagons underneath,' said Dad.

'Get a Continental Speed. Four wheel drive. Very good if you are in a difficult spot,' suggested Andrè.

'Have you been in one?' Dad asked.

'Just once. Luxurious, but very, very fast. Probably the best getaway car in the world,' said Andrè, leaving Dad wondering just what sort of operations Andrè had been involved in.

'The Astons were Ford owned. They are independent now, and very good by all accounts,' said Dad, betraying a knowledge somewhat beyond that of a disinterested motorist.

'I think you will know what to get. Just make sure it attracts attention,' said Andrè.

Dad was initially against the idea. Yet, the more him pictured himself in a Bentley Continental Speed and an Aston Martin Rapide, the more willing he was to accept the idea as an essential part of the plan.

As Andrè and Dad continued to talk about cars, Henry appeared and spoke in his slow, low accent.

'He says he has now fixed the wheelbarrow, and the wheels will no longer come off,' Andrè translated.

Andrè and Dad continued their walk until they rounded a corner to the stables and reached the wheelbarrow. A number of huge, bent nails were sticking out of it, with several in each wheel.

'Well, the wheels will not come off again,' sighed Andrè.

'No,' replied Dad, 'and they won't go round either.'

Dad walked back to the Hall on his own. There was a lot of shouting in French in the distance. It seemed as though Andrè had finally had enough. He was fed up with Henry being difficult. From the ferocity of the shouting he guessed that Andrè would get his way.

As Trevor Trogg reached the Hall Lord Rothwell's voice boomed out. It was rising in pitch, working towards its soprano scream. Hector had been getting Lord Rothwell's name wrong again.

'It's not Brothmell, it's not Frothimere, it's not Drothdroid, it's Rothwell, Lord Rothwell,' he screamed.

In the past Dad would have intervened. He would have been angry about anyone shouting at his son. Now, however, he was taking a more laid-back approach. He would intervene if Hector was at risk. However unreasonable Rothwell was in shouting at a child, Hector had undoubtedly started the whole thing. Trevor Trogg could see a bit of Hector's face and the synthetic innocence told him that Hector was not too bothered. In such circumstances, Hector should be left to his own devices Dad concluded.

Just fifteen minutes later and Rothwell had calmed down and was in the kitchen explaining the special delivery of 'exceptional food' as he described it. Lord Rothwell had his own kitchen in his rooms. He used the communal kitchen as a temporary dumping area while he sorted out his purchases into their carefully planned places.

There were cheeses, cured meats, specially prepared fish, and even sausages laid out in an attractive display. All were in special boxes; some cardboard and some wooden. All had clear glass or cellophane windows through which you could view the foods.

Lord Rothwell began to explain each of the very expensive foods he had ordered, picking up their boxes and describing them. Hector thought Lord Rothwell would have liked to give the same speech to starving workhouse inmates.

Rothwell began waving two of the boxes around, before opening the box containing the display of sausages. Strangely, the sausages were all of different types, but they seemed to be connected in a single string.

Hector thought this was probably revenge for Hector getting his name wrong. Rothwell was boasting about all of the food he had. He was showing off and Hector knew he should not be annoyed. Nevertheless, he was irritated.

'Now, does anyone have any questions?' asked Lord Rothwell, with the condescending air of a second-rate public school head-master having just explained to some poor children how stupid they really were.

Bandit lunged, appearing from nowhere, the force knocking Lord Rothwell back. The sausages fell from their display box, and almost seemed to hover in the air, until a set of teeth clamped down with all of the force of a car crusher.

In one movement Bandit turned and fled. As he accelerated past Dad he looked back, with a wild mixture of fear and excitement. Lord Rothwell yelled, screamed and then ran after Bandit. Kate and Hector took up the pursuit, followed by Mum, and then even Nana.

Andrè arrived just as the sausages rounded the corner of the lake. In just a few seconds Bandit had put more than one hundred and fifty metres between the sausages and their rightful owner. Only Otto could match that sort of speed, and not for long.

Otto was looking on with interest. He really liked Bandit; he caused such a lot of trouble. Bandit would be told off. Bandit would look briefly guilty. Bandit would get all of the blame and draw everyone's attention. Otto sauntered towards the box with the fish.

CHAPTER THIRTEEN

Golf

Lord Rothwell was genuinely pleased when Henry presented both the repaired wheelbarrow together with a replica he had created. Henry had even copied the faded painting on the original wheelbarrow, although the replica looked fresh and new. Rothwell's initial pleasure was short-lived, although there seemed to be no particular reason for this swing in mood. Henry's reward was to be told off again by Rothwell, who went over the issue of overloading wheelbarrows in minute and excruciating detail.

'Dunbar can't say thank you and always thinks the worst of everyone,' said Nana, 'If he dropped twenty pounds and you picked it up and returned it, Dunbar would assume he'd dropped forty and that you'd stolen the rest. I tried with that boy, I really did, but he just cannot think or say a good thing about anyone.'

Nana was serving Kate and Hector with breakfast. Another consignment of 'very special' food had arrived for Lord Rothwell, while Mum, Dad and Andrè had gone off to a driving course. The idea of Mum driving fast had been the cause of a great deal of amusement for Kate and Hector. Kate wondered whether the definition of fast might be Mum overtaking an old cyclist, or a wheelchair being pushed up a steep incline.

Hector had been beside himself with jealousy when he discovered that the first day involved racing go-karts and then racing cars around a proper racing circuit. His repeated requests to be included were refused. He nagged and complained that Kate had driven the armoured car around the zoo in a crisis and hence he should be included. Andrè concluded the argument.

'The central problem Hector, leaving aside the legal issues, is that your legs cannot reach the pedals,' said Andrè, 'Now, even I am fed up with you moaning about this. Please shut up!'

Hector accepted his exclusion by thinking of the days when Mum, Dad and Andrè were away as days of freedom. Mrs Warp was out of her cupboard. Hector and Kate had been given buttons they could use to summon Mrs Warp in an emergency. Unfortunately, these buttons did not include the override facility Hector and Kate had abused at the zoo.

Mrs Warp's presence put Nana on edge. She kept offering Mrs Warp cups of tea, that were always refused, and then making waspish comments about Mrs Warp disappearing to plug herself in. Nana eventually realised that Mrs Warp was impossible to offend, and so Nana really got stuck in, asking Mrs Warp about whether she needed to borrow a travel adaptor for the British electric sockets, and whether there were more advanced models that included refrigerators for picnics. Mrs Warp just smiled.

Kate and Hector had plans to sail to the larger island. They had agreed to take Bandit with them, to keep him out of trouble. Kate was less than keen on this. She had a clear memory of the chaos Bandit caused last time they had taken him sailing. Hector was pleased. Bandit was always fun, and he had already pictured himself yelling 'dog overboard'.

'Excellent!' said Lord Rothwell, appearing in the doorway, 'I was hoping to catch you Kate.'

Kate said nothing. She stared back at Rothwell's beaming face. Hector stared as well. Lord Rothwell looking happy and pleased was as disconcerting as it was unusual.

'Your father said you would help out with the swimming pool. Today's the day. The swimming pool will be open at 10.30am. Looks like you're already dressed for it. See you at the pool in ten minutes,' Rothwell concluded.

As Lord Rothwell disappeared, back towards his own rooms, Nana looked after him.

'I'm afraid some of this is my fault,' said Nana, 'I should have warned your father. He'll want you to clean, or take the money off the children when they arrive. I knew your father had agreed to something. Trust Dunbar to want his pound of flesh when your parents are off for the day.'

'I've never seen him so happy,' said Hector, displaying his puzzled face.

'I'm surprised given his car problems,' said Nana.

'Still not found his Range Rover?' Hector asked, guilt and fear flaring inside him like a roman candle at a fireworks display.

'It's not that,' said Nana, in the tone she used when she was about to divulge secrets, 'He got his old Volvo out. It had failed it's MOT a couple of years ago. Needed some welding underneath. There was actually a hole on the passenger side. You could see the road if you lent forwards.'

'You're not allowed on the road with a car without an MOT certificate, according to Dad,' said Kate.

'And he's quite right,' said Nana, 'Dunbar should have taken it to a good garage, but he wanted to save some money so he got a couple of people he knew in Laceby to sort it out. Now, you know when you weld metal, well they were going to add a bit more to replace the bits that had rusted away. Welding metal is sort of melting it a bit. It gets hot, and you have to remove the car's carpet, otherwise it might catch fire.'

'Dunbar starts complaining that they're taking longer than they should. He wanted me to give him a lift down there to pick it up. When we get there the car sort of looks alright. The problem is they've given him new seat covers and a carpet free of charge. Dunbar was puzzled, but rude as ever and said he liked the old seats, thank you very much. He whips the covers off and the seats are all burned down to their springs. Oh, the smell!' Nana laughed.

'It had a mixture of horrible, plastic burnt out smell, and buckets of air freshener. Then I can see the inside of the windows are blackened, but scrubbed partly clean. It must have been well alight. Dunbar went bonkers, said he wasn't going to pay. They wouldn't give him the keys. Oh, they were yelling, Dunbar was screaming.'

Nana stopped, heaving with laughter. It was clearly something she had thoroughly enjoyed.

'Eventually, I said why don't you call it quits. The car's been wrecked. I said they should give it back. I also said that in return Dunbar shouldn't demand compensation. They all agreed, and Dunbar paid them forty pounds for the MOT certificate.'

'So Lord Rothwell is driving a burnt out car?' Hector asked, a grin as wide as a cheshire cat stretched from one side of his face to the other.

'It's worst than that that,' said Nana, tears in the corners of her eyes, 'It didn't occur to me, but they melted all of the wires in the fire. When Dunbar put the lights on as we were driving away, the brake lights went on. When he braked the reversing light came on. When he signalled left the right indicator flashed, and when he signalled right everything flashed on an off like a christmas tree.'

'How angry was he?' Hector asked.

'Not much at first,' said Nana, 'as he didn't know what was going on. But people kept pulling out in front of him. It was lucky the brakes weren't broken. I worked it out about half way back. When he braked the reversing light came on, and it also flashed the head-lights. Well, a lot of people flash the headlights to invite people to pull out. All Dunbar had to do was touch the brake pedal and the headlights would flash. No wonder all those people pulled out in front of him.'

'Do you think he'll crash?' Hector asked, with far more enthusi-asm than was decent.

'No, it smells so bad he can hardly bear to drive it,' said Nana.

'Why doesn't he buy a new car? I don't know how much money Dad has paid him, but it's loads more than a new car costs,' said Kate.

'Dunbar has debts,' said Nana, suddenly looking serious.

'Gambling debts?' Hector asked, 'Where someone comes round and breaks your toes for not paying.'

'No, Dunbar's not a gambler. But where the debts came from I cannot say,' said Nana.

There was a pause, as everyone gathered themselves. Hector thought about the island. He could not get there without Kate. Nana appeared to read his thoughts.

'I think it might be better if you put off your jaunt to the island,' she suggested, 'I think Kate ought to look in at the swimming pool. And you Hector, you might want to go up to Dunbar's little golf course. You could mess about with sand castles in the bunkers and entertain that nuisance of a dog of yours. And by the way, the pan-try is strictly out of bounds. I really mean that. There's sensors on it and a camera that records everyone who has even looked in. You are not to even open the pantry door, or else you'll have me to an-swer to.'

Hector was not in the slightest bit puzzled by the warnings about the pantry. He suspected that he was not entirely trusted near food.

This did not bother him, it just made him feel he had more in common with Bandit.

What did puzzle Hector was the ice house. It was locked. He wanted to go inside and explore. There were other buildings he could get into, but not the ice house.

Nana had explained to him that in the days before refrigerators, large houses had an underground store that was filled with ice. It was used to keep food cold throughout the summer. Insulated by the earth, the ice would slowly melt. It was replaced in the winter, often with a delivery from somewhere colder.

Hector had stopped on his way to the golf course to gaze again at the ice house. It was a door in a hill. The house itself was underground. Nana had said it was locked because it was not safe. This made Hector even more curious. He resolved to find the key to the lock so he could have a look around.

Lord Rothwell's five-hole golf course was as hideous as it was bizarre. One hole extended to a huge distance, stretching across the top of a hill, so that the golfer could not see the green until she or he was almost upon it. Another hole crossed a small stream, and Lord Rothwell had added various features, such as a miniature windmill, a fake grotto or cave and several tiny colourful houses complete with gnomes. Hector suspected that only someone who really enjoyed dressing dolls would approve of the additions.

After settling down with a bucket in one of the bunkers, Hector noticed there were other strange additions. One fairway had a single point through which all players must pass. Hector had seen a number of golf courses when playing computer games. Digging through a small hill, leaving a passageway for the fairway seemed more like crazy golf than the full-sized game. Hector suspected that Lord Rothwell's greatest sporting achievement had been on Cleethorpes sea front crazy golf course, probably when aged six.

The sand was perfect; slightly damp, but not wet. Hector was soon crafting a deep moat, confident that a large and impressive castle would soon dominate the bunker. Bandit was also digging. He was in the next bunker. Every so often he would look over the lip of the bunker to check Hector's progress.

Hector was clearly an amateur in Bandit's view. All Hector had managed was a small ring of digging. Bandit was right through the sand and into the soft earth below. Hector's behaviour puzzled Bandit. If there were creatures hiding underground, possibly even parrots, how could Hector hope to unearth them if he did not dig down further than a few inches.

More puzzling still was Hector's refusal to accept help. Whenever Bandit tried to help Hector start a decent hole, Hector told him to go back to his own bunker. Probably a possession thing or pride.

What Hector did not know was that Bandit had already been around the golf course on his own. He had even watched Lord Rothwell play a round of golf. On that day, Bandit had the sense to stay still and watch. The sand was an attraction and he had plans to excavate all of the bunkers.

Bandit liked digging. He was good at it. The deeper he got, and the more earth was thrown behind him, the greater his sense of achievement. Best of all was the sudden movement; the flurry and panic as a rabbit or some other creature fled. Two of the bunkers had rabbit holes and these were wildly exciting. Bandit was not welcome in Hector's bunker, but he did not want to leave for the bunkers on another hole. Bandit was a pack animal. He liked being with Kate and Hector.

The hole in the middle of the green had captured his interest on that day when he had watched Lord Rothwell hit a white ball around with a stick. Bandit was intrigued by it. Defensive mounds of earth surrounded it, and behind these were dips or bunkers filled with sand. The immediate area surrounding the hole comprised neatly cut grass. Someone had tried to spear the animal hiding in the hole using a pole with a flag on the end. Maybe the pole marked the place where the particularly dangerous or valuable animal hid.

Bandit had seen Lord Rothwell feeding the creature using a small white ball. Rothwell would knock the ball into the hole, before retrieving it, presumably after the creature had quickly emptied the innards.

Lord Rothwell might be afraid of the creature, or even worship it. He might feed it special food and have defensive sand bunkers around it, but Bandit was not afraid. He liked danger. What he needed now was a life and death struggle with the monster under the golf green.

Hector had completely lost the plot. Instead of digging he had created a mound of sand. Hector was absorbed by it. Bandit would just have to tackle the monster under the golf green by himself. The hole seemed to be protected by a plastic cup, and this cup supported the flag. A spot right next to the hole seemed best. Bandit began to dig.

Kate arrived at the pool. The door was open. Inside the pool looked uncared for, just as it had the first day they arrived. The difference from that day, Kate discovered, was that both the water and air heaters had been turned on.

Lord Rothwell appeared and ushered her down to the plant room. As she walked past the pool she noticed that the fun inflatable was now pumped up, with a number of bicycle puncture repair patches over the wounds left by Bandit.

The plant room was lower than the pool. It was damp and dark. There were two huge metal cylinders. Lord Rothwell explained that these were the sand filters. The electric pumps drove the water into the top of the filters. It was cleaned and returned to the pool.

The problem, as Lord Rothwell explained, was that dirt collected in the filters. To remove it a pump had to be turned off, all of the valves had to be set to their alternative positions, the pump then had to be run for three minutes and then stopped. The valves then had to be turned back again and the pump restarted.

'It's called a backwash,' Lord Rothwell explained, 'All of the dirt left by those unwashed, hideous children is washed down the drain. You will need to do this to both pumps at the end of the session. The pool will drop in level by about two inches during a backwash, and so you will need to leave the hose pipe on, refilling it overnight.'

'Why do I need to do it?' Kate asked.

'Because you're the life guard,' said Rothwell, 'Today's one of the days I open the pool to all of the children from around these parts.'

'What will you do?' Kate asked.

'Collect the money,' said Rothwell, as if Kate's was the most foolish question imaginable.

'I can't be a lifeguard,' said Kate, feeling thoroughly flustered.

'Kate, Kate, you'll have to be the life guard,' barked Lord Rothwell.

'I can't do that,' said Kate, 'I'm not old enough.'

'Kate, you're a brave, sensible teenager, and a very strong swimmer,' said Rothwell in a much kinder voice. 'It will be good experience for you.'

'But, I'm only thirteen.'

'Really, that's amazing,' said Lord Rothwell, 'you swim so quickly. I've never seen such an impressive stroke.'

Rothwell paused while Kate stuttered, and looked at her, as if making a decision. Kate was trying to think of any time when Lord Rothwell had seen her swim. She was sure he had not.

'Kate, some of the children who come to the swimming pool need someone like you. Someone they can admire. Someone to look out for them. I think you're perfect,' Rothwell beamed.

Kate was completely taken aback, and in truth rather flattered. She rarely received compliments, and despite the fact that Rothwell's change of manner was disconcerting, she could not help but feel pleased.

'All the children are at school, aren't they?' Kate asked.

'No, no. Today's a training day. All the parents are annoyed as usual, and so it is always a good time to…' Lord Rothwell trailed off.

'Make money,' Kate finished the sentence for him.

'No, provide a valuable community service,' said Lord Rothwell.

Kate stared at the pool.

'How long is it open?' Kate asked.

'All day, until four. Right, don't go in the water, you have to sit in the high chair and watch everyone. If you need the toilet be quick in case anyone starts drowning' said Lord Rothwell in his usual brisk way.

'What do I do if anyone starts drowning?' Kate asked, suddenly flabbergasted at what she had just agreed to do.

'Just prod them with that pole until they take a hold and then drag them out,' Rothwell said, 'Oh, and don't press the emergency alarm button.'

'Why not?'

'Because it doesn't work, and you'd just be wasting time. I had it disconnected because it made too much noise, but it looks good so I left the button there.'

Lord Rothwell began to walk off towards the entrance.

'You've sacked the life guard to save money haven't you?' Kate blurted out.

'He was a thief; he had to go,' said Rothwell in a could-not-care-less tone of voice.

Rothwell marched out leaving Kate as the first children entered the pool. Kate bristled with anger, annoyed as much as anything with the casual way in which Lord Rothwell was willing to brand the sacked life guard a thief. Of course, it could be true, but Kate suspected he had simply made it up.

Kate found a whistle on the life guard's chair, and was surprised at herself when she told off a boy for running. What was more surprising was the way the boy obeyed.

Just ten minutes after the session had started forty children were splashing and screaming around the pool. There appeared to be no adults at all.

After a while she was rather pleased with her new powers, but decided to speak to the boy who liked running after she had told him off for the third time.

Kate explained to the boy and his friends that he could run as much as he wanted as long as he could promise not to leave any blood, bits of skull or brains if he slipped over and really hit his head hard. As expected, the boy promised, and so Kate then asked him for two hundred pounds to cover the cleaning costs in advance.

The boy looked surly, and so Kate suggested a game of sharks. In this way, Kate discovered the wonders of diversion. In order to control the boys it was better to suggest what they could do, rather than list everything they could not. Kate mentally made a list of things she could suggest once sharks had run its course, and came up with swimming underwater, handstands and tumbling competitions.

After forty minutes the heat and humidity was taking a toll on Kate. A girl who had been threatening to punch a smaller boy had agreed to stand for ten minutes in the corner rather than leave altogether. Two boys had left crying, but she had no idea what had happened. Another smaller boy was causing her great anxiety. He seemed to have no fear, but also no ability in the water. She had rescued him twice with the pole. Kate was frightened that he might easily drown if she was distracted and failed to spot him. Kate was discovering a surprising sympathy for some of her teachers at school.

After an hour Kate had found how easy it was to drift into a daydream and see nothing of the flailing swimmers in front of her. Kate was just marvelling at the ferocity of the pretend great white shark bites the boys were delivering to each other, when she saw Lord Rothwell open the door at the end of the pool and stride along the side.

'Kate, this is splendid,' said Rothwell, sounding genuinely pleased and surprised, 'and you've managed to control the Hill brothers. They usually get thrown out after the first five minutes. I should really just take their money and make them leave before they get undressed.'

Kate reflected that Dunbar Hellstone, the Eleventh Earl of Rothwell, would do exactly this to all the children in the pool if he could get away with it.

'Are you going to take over now?' Kate asked.

'No, no, I just take the money and leave you to it. You've another six hours to go,' said Rothwell.

'Do I get paid?' Kate demanded.

'Yes, yes, after your shift. I'll get Nana to bring some sandwiches down for you.'

After two hours Kate was hot, irritable and three more children were stood in corners waiting for their punishment to end. Some of the children had left. They were cold. Lord Rothwell might have turned the heaters on, but he was never going to warm the pool up to the point where it was a pleasure. Unfortunately, other children had arrived.

'Kate, this is an outrage,' said Nana, surprising Kate and making her jump, 'I thought he'd get you to help. I bet he's sacked Simon.'

'Lord Rothwell didn't give me a choice,' said Kate, 'But he said I'd be paid.'

Nana muttered something and gave Kate her sandwiches.

'Could Mrs Warp do this instead of you?' Nana asked.

'She's not good with water,' said Kate.

'No, no, I bet she isn't,' said Nana, 'Do you want me to get Andrè or your Mum or Dad.

'No, they'll think it's an emergency,' said Kate, 'but actually Mrs Warp stood in the corner might be a help. I had to push one boy out into the changing rooms, and she'd be good at that.'

Fifteen minutes later Mrs Warp had not appeared, but Lord Rothwell had with Nana behind him. He closed the pool, ordering everyone out. He seemed furious. From the little Kate could hear Nana had threatened to call the police.

She had got used to being a life guard, and was resigned to doing it for the rest of the day. Kate had hoped Hector would turn up, but there had been no sign of him.

As the children disappeared into the changing rooms, the disagreement between Nana and Lord Rothwell ignited. He screamed at her and she shouted back. It was the first time she had see Nana really angry.

'You don't give a damn, do you Dunbar?' Nana shouted, 'What about Kate and her conscience if one of them drowns? What about the children? Who does she call for help when one of them slips? She hasn't even got a phone! She's thirteen! She's working alone!'

Lord Rothwell suddenly stopped shouting and screaming back. He looked at Kate; there was venom in his stare, as if it was all her fault.

'Finish the shift!' he shouted at Kate, 'Clean the filters!'

Kate got down off her high chair and went to the plant room. She felt tearful, but also angry. She turned both pumps off, reversed all of the valves and then turned the pumps on.

Kate could hear shouting in the distance. Clearly the argument between Nana and Lord Rothwell had reignited. She tried to listen, but could make nothing out. The only thing that was clear was their anger with each other.

The pumps whirred and Kate felt drained. She had completed her job, and so she left the plant room by the back door to avoid the pool. She walked up on the grass as some of the children were spilling out, calling parents on their mobile phones. She longed for a rest on her bed.

The pumps pumped, although the filters were clean. The backwash was still in progress. Thirty-three minutes later the pumps turned themselves off when the water pressure dropped below the minimum. The pool was completely empty.

The sun spilled through the clouds as Hector walked down to the Hall. As he climbed over a fence he looked at the large island on the lake and reflected that he could look forward to visiting it tomorrow.

Hector had done his best to fill in the hole Bandit had dug in the golf green. It had been hard work, partly because Bandit had dug such a big hole, and also because Bandit had been trying to start another hole. Hector had to frequently pause to tell Bandit to stop.

Hector's attempt to fill in the hole had initially not gone well. For one thing, there was too much earth. It ended up as a mound. Hector had no idea where Bandit got the extra earth from. The other problem was the lack of grass. Either something had eaten the grass Bandit had dug up, or Bandit had shredded it.

As Hector had stood back to admire his repairs, all hopes that the former hole would be almost impossible to identify were dashed. It was so noticeable that he suspected it could be seen from space.

His Plan B was much better. He dug the hole out a little, widened it, and then sprinkled it with sand. Now the green had a new bunker, right in the middle. The flag had fallen over and the hole for the flag had disappeared in Bandit's excavations. Hector had planted the flag in the middle of his new bunker.

As he stood to look at his work he had been pleased. The new bunker was a little ragged, but it almost looked as though it might fit with the other bunkers. In any event, the eye would be drawn by the impressive castle rising out of the bunker on the left of the green.

Now Hector's thoughts were for his stomach. He was happy but hungry. Bandit was very happy. Bandit felt he and Hector had worked well as a team.

As Hector reached the kitchen there were complaints and shouts. Lord Rothwell was shouting at Nana and walking backwards and forwards.

'You!' said Lord Rothwell, pointing at Hector, 'You can look for it as well.'

'He's lost his contact lens,' said Nana.

'Come on! Apply yourself!' Rothwell yelled.

Hector began looking on the floor of the kitchen, just as Lord Rothwell began to retrace his steps outside. Hector felt a flare of anger. Rothwell was so unpleasant, demanding and rude. Then he remembered Kate's words, 'revenge, served cold'.

Hector stopped. There was something shining on the floor. Now he was about to please Lord Rothwell, and that did not please Hector at all. He decided that he would opt for revenge served hot, but could not bring himself to stamp on the delicate glass lens.

'I've got your contact lens,' Hector yelled from the kitchen window, waving his hand in the air.

'Don't keep it in your hand, rubbing dirt and grit into it,' Lord Rothwell yelled ungratefully, 'Clean it. Get the dirt off.'

Hector disappeared from the window and Lord Rothwell marched inside.

'Give it here! Give it here!' Lord Rothwell demanded, before inserting it back into his eye in a process that reminded Hector of Mrs Shoesmith, the mad sports teacher removing her glass eye.

Lord Rothwell turned to leave without saying thank you, and then paused and turned back.

'You didn't lick it to clean it, did you? Very unhygienic. Well?' he demanded in his overly loud voice.

'No, no,' stuttered Hector, as ever caught out by Rothwell's shocking rudeness, 'Kate told me all about the horrible eye infections you can get if you lick contact lenses, because we've all got lots of bacteria in our mouths.'

'Yes, well,' paused Lord Rothwell, who seemed now on the verge of astonishing Hector and Nana with a word of thanks. 'Yes, mouths do have lots of bacteria, and you shouldn't lick contact lenses.'

'I think,' said Nana firmly, 'that Dunbar Hellstone means to say thank you.'

'Oh, errm, yes. Thank you for finding the lens and washing it under the tap,' said Lord Rothwell in a much quieter voice.

'You're not supposed to wash them under the tap either,' said Hector.

'Yes, you are! What do you know?' said Lord Rothwell dismissively, returning to his usual volume, before realising that there might be a problem, 'and what did you use?'

'I let Bandit lick it,' explained Hector in his cheery voice, 'he'll lick anything, even the stamps that are supposed to stick without licking.'

'What! You did what, you stupid boy?' yelled Rothwell, turning that familiar red colour.

'He was licking your butter yesterday,' Hector added, for good measure.

Oddly enough, Hector was more comfortable with Lord Rothwell yelling at him for doing something wrong. The unexpected demands when he had anticipated a quick thank you rocked him back on his heals, but the full-frontal yelling Rothwell was much more familiar. The key was firmly in Rothwell's back and he was definitely going to give it a few turns.

'Sorry,' said Hector, in his cheery voice that meant he was not sorry at all, 'but I mustn't lick it, and I couldn't use tap water, and you said I should clean it and so Bandit helped me.'

'Oh my god!' yelled Lord Rothwell, quickly yanking his head around dramatically as he took the lens out again.

'It's ruined. You can damn well pay for that. What if I lose my eye? Well? What about my eye? Pay me for the lens!' shouted Rothwell, as he approached top scream.

'That's not fair,' Hector said, in a slightly hurt tone, 'you can still use the contact lens.'

'How the hell can I use a lens impregnated with your dog's vile bacteria?' he bellowed and then squeaked as he reached top scream.

'Well, all the food you put on our kitchen table after you've been shopping, you know, before you take it through to your very, very nice kitchen, well that's all been licked by Bandit, and you still eat it,' said Hector.

'What!' came the scream.

'Bandit even nibbled some of the chicken, and he had to be chased when he got your fillet steak and began killing it. We had to put sticky tape on it and everything so you wouldn't go off like a Banshee on a bad night,' said Hector cheerfully, rather pleased that he'd remembered the Banshee comment he had overheard his mother use.

Lord Rothwell ran screaming to his kitchen. There was the sound of a window being opened wide, and then food was thrown into the flower bed. It seemed as though Lord Rothwell was emptying his fridge and cupboards.

Bandit rocketed towards the flower beds. He had every intention of eating the lot. He needed to get as much down before Hector, Kate or Otto got there. Hector and Kate might be top notch partners in crime, but when it came to food it was every dog for himself. If he scoffed quickly, he might even stop Kate or Hector hoovering up any crumbs or bits that got scattered in the frenzy.

Rothwell clattered, ran, screamed, issued threats, shouted, cried, stamped and threw yet more food. He sometimes stopped to phone someone so he could shout at them, but always lost patience before the call was answered and returned to finding every edible thing and throwing it out as dramatically as possible. The bangs became more pronounced, the screams more shrill, and the threats more deadly. Bandit simply concentrated on eating himself into oblivion.

Fifteen minutes later all was quiet. Lord Rothwell seemed to have disappeared off somewhere, probably to find someone to complain to. In his temper he had flung all of the doors to his rooms open wide, which Bandit appreciated, as it allowed him to creep inside and snuggle down on one of the fluffy sheepskin rugs.

Labrador dogs can eat extraordinary amounts of food. Even slim ones can become almost spherical in just a few minutes. Very few Labradors, however, can keep such large amounts of food down. Bandit was no exception. No matter how comfortable the expensive carpets and lush rugs were, he soon reached a tipping point, where the full stomach needle in his head passed straight through the amber and red danger signs to hit the full stop marked 'Explode'.

A short time later, after he'd finished the unpleasant bit, Bandit surveyed the gigantic pool of vomit with relief. It had spread a long way, in parts like a river, lapping the shores of expensive white rugs and hand crafted wooden and leather furniture.

Bandit felt ill, but this was quickly passing, to be replaced by feelings of regret. He felt disappointed that he had failed to keep all of the food down. Bit by bit, however, his feelings returned to their usual optimism. It was a big pool of sick, but he was sure he could eat most of it.

CHAPTER 14

Edward

'Andrè ordered me to bed,' Hector complained at breakfast.

Dad just raised his eyebrows. It was unclear as to whether he simply did not believe Hector, or he did not care.

'Now, I like Andrè,' said Nana, 'He's the sort of man you could trust with your soul. You could lay it in his hands and be sure it would be safe. I think he's done some things that shouldn't have been done. But fundamentally, he's a safer bet that some parish priests.'

'Yes, I think we can all trust Andrè,' said Dad, keen to head Nana off before she got onto the subject of parish priests.

'Now, parrots, I wouldn't trust parrots,' said Nana, as everyone tried to think of any reason on earth why trusting parrots might be a pressing issue.

'I think parrots are like politicians,' said Nana, 'or puddings.'

'Why does Lord Rothwell breed parrots?' Hector asked.

'I don't know,' said Nana, 'Safer than polar bears I expect.'

'I think this morning was all about words beginning with P,' said Kate, in hushed tones to her mother.

Both Kate and Hector had noticed that some mornings Nana just meandered on about nothing in particular. It seemed to be her way of getting conversation going.

'Next time Andrè orders me to bed, can I say no?' asked Hector.

'Hector,' Dad began, 'when we arrived home yesterday, was it peaceful?'

'Can't remember,' said Hector untruthfully.

'We left you in charge of Bandit,' said Dad, 'When we returned Lord Rothwell's rooms were swimming in dog vomit.'

'That wasn't my fault,' said Hector.

'Lord Rothwell was also furious that the swimming pool was empty,' Dad added.

'Kate's fault,' said Hector.

'Did Kate start a small mineshaft in the second green of Lord Rothwell's golf course?' Dad pointed out.

'That was Bandit,' said Hector.

'You were in charge of Bandit,' said Dad.

'I only turned my back for a minute,' said Hector in exasperation, 'I'd just finished my castle. I looked up and there's Bandit's waggly tail instead of the flag for the hole. I did my best. I tried to put it all back, but it was lumpy and there was no grass. I thought he might not notice an extra sand bunker.'

'How could he miss that?' asked Dad in exasperation, 'It was right in the middle of the green. It's only a small green. Your new bunker covers most of it.'

There was a pause as Hector wondered what he might say to improve things. Nothing occurred to him.

'Things would be more difficult if Lord Rothwell hadn't so flagrantly broken the law,' said Dad.

'I still don't see why I was sent to bed,' Hector moaned.

'I think you got off lightly,' said Dad, 'I had no idea yesterday morning that I would be returning to a swimming pool calamity, a giant hole in the golf course, and another Bandit disaster.'

'Dunbar will be fully occupied today,' said Nana, changing the subject for Hector's benefit, 'He's got a video company in to film him.'

'Really,' said Mum, 'What's the film about?'

'What might any film funded by Dunbar be about; it's about Dunbar,' said Nana, 'Or at least it's about his art company.'

'Crowded house then,' said Dad, 'Some people are coming to build the safe room. They will be here for the next few days.'

'Aren't you off to change your car?' Nana asked.

'Almost, I get rid of the Jaguar and the new cars arrive.'

There was a cheer. The end of the Jaguar was a popular decision. Mum did not look too happy about the new cars, but Dad would not tell either Kate or Hector what the replacements were.

'Are you going to collect them?' Hector asked.

'I cannot collect two cars. The cars are being delivered in a lorry,' said Dad, looking over to Andrè, 'And they are not completely what you suggested.'

Andrè raised his eyebrows, but said nothing. Hector was bouncing with excitement. He glanced at Kate. She was trying to look disinterested, but he knew she was desperately curious.

Thirty minutes later Kate, Hector and Bandit were in the boat. Kate had objected to Bandit on the grounds that he was profoundly unstable on water. Dad and Mum were insistent. As far as they were concerned Bandit could not dig, tunnel, chase or steal when he was trapped on a boat.

Hector was not entirely pleased that Kate seemed to be in the clear for emptying the swimming pool. Mum and Dad saw her as the victim, and yet he was blamed for Bandit's digging. On the other hand, he had been promised first ride in the new cars.

Hector had Bandit firmly held between his legs. He left the sailing to Kate. Andrè had given both Hector and Kate small but powerful binoculars when they first arrived at the Hall. Hector used his to survey the shoreline. He was captain and he had to be sure there were no submarines, enemy ships or pirates.

As they neared the island Bandit became restless. It was not long before the inevitable happened and Bandit fell in. Captain Hector ordered Kate to leave Bandit to his watery grave, mainly because they were only five metres from the island shore.

The island had a small sandy beach, as well as a stone jetty. Kate tied the boat up to the jetty and they all went to explore. Bandit charged ahead, causing several shrieks as startled birds flew up. It was difficult to walk as everything was overgrown. There were no real paths. Hector wished he had a machete to hack his way through; yet another weapon he was not allowed.

Kate thought the island was roughly forty metres long and about twenty-five metres wide. The rocks and mud that surrounded it contrasted with the small sandy beach, and Kate suspected that the sand was not natural, but had been added, probably at the same time as the stone jetty.

Tall scots pine trees towered over them. Two of the largest on the island had been blown over. Judging by the way their roots were overgrown they had fallen down some time ago.

In the middle of the island there was the makings of a clearing. There was a very small stone hut together with a ring of stones. Hector spotted the blackening on the stones and immediately suggested they start a fire. The fact that he had no means of lighting the fire did not trouble him. He set to work collecting dry wood and then spent a good twenty minutes hitting stones together in an attempt to light it.

While Hector was busy with his fire, Kate battled through the undergrowth with Bandit. He had chased anything that could fly off and was now convinced that Kate knew of some other creature they were going to tackle. Kate found nothing of interest. Bandit found a hole and decided to dig down.

Some time later Kate and Hector were sat on the jetty, dangling their feet over the edge. Bandit was still in the island digging. If the island were a ship Bandit would have bored through the bottom and sunk it. Fortunately, Bandit was struggling against some very hard rock and was about to give up.

'I could live the rest of my life here, on an island with a sailing boat, and Bandit,' said Kate.

'I'd send you food parcels, from my castle in the mountains,' said Hector.

'Anything edible?'

'Probably not. Just parcels.'

'What should we do?' asked Kate, as she shielded her eyes against the sun, while marvelling at the shades of colour created by a hillside of beech and ash trees. The beech were turning a darker green, while the ash were just coming into leaf.

'Now? Later? When Sludge turns up?' Hector enquired.

'All of them,' said Kate.

'I think we're safe with Andrè. He really wants to get Sludge. Even Dad and Mum look pretty mean on the firing range. Andrè's skills plus Dad's temper have got to be bad news for Sludge.'

'I suppose so,' said Kate, happy to seek comfort from anything she could grasp.

'When we get back, I want to have a look at the safe room,' said Hector.

'Shall we sail back?' Kate asked, half hoping that Hector would suggest they stay longer in the sun on their own tiny beach.

'Sort of,' said Hector, 'Do you want a race?'

'How can we race?' asked Kate, for a moment wondering whether Hector was planning on swimming back.

'Why don't you sail me and Bandit to the side of the lake furthest from the Hall. Then we'll run and you can race us in your boat.'

On the sail to the shore Kate had to endure Hector boasting about how fast he could run cross country. Just as Hector was speculating about how many olympic gold medals he would win when he was older, Bandit lurched to one side, almost capsizing them.

While Bandit swam ashore, Kate landed Hector in a particularly boggy area. She felt this was slightly unfair, but reflected that Hector would quite happily dump her in quicksand if it meant winning a race.

As Hector struggled through the bog, with Bandit plunging unhelpfully ahead of him, Kate noticed the wind had turned. She would have to tack at least once, probably twice. She glanced back and saw Hector struggling to get over a fence. Odds on she would win.

Kate sailed as close to the wind as she dare, leaning out as far as possible to balance the boat. Only after she had gone about could she steal a glance at Hector. He was in open parkland now, keeping a steady pace behind Bandit. Even from a distance she could see he was coated in mud. In truth, this was Hector's natural state; it would not slow him down.

As Kate reached the small jetty by the boathouse she jumped, slipping on the greasy timbers. It was the fastest knot she had ever tied. Then she took off. She still had to reach the first step in front of the main door to win. Hector was sprinting. It was going to be close.

Kate drove with her arms, bringing her knees up to increase her speed. She could hear Hector pounding just behind her. He was faster than she expected, but he was tired. Kate drove her arms harder. She was going to make it.

Bandit's brainless decision to run immediately in front of both Hector and Kate failed to topple either of them. Kate sprang onto the first step just before Hector.

'What on earth do you think you two are doing?' shouted Lord Rothwell, clearly angry.

'Racing,' panted Kate, as Hector could not utter a word.

'And what about everyone else? Ehh?' shouted Rothwell, 'Not worried if you knock some poor old person over are you! So long as you have your fun!'

'There isn't anyone else here, except you,' said Kate indignantly, 'are you old and infirm?'

'Don't you take that tone with me!' shouted Lord Rothwell, his pitch rising.

'We're very, very sorry,' Hector finally managed to gasp. Rothwell stared aggressively, obviously surprised by the apology.

'Hector?' Kate exclaimed, questioning his decision.

'It was wrong and selfish of us,' said Hector, 'It won't happen again Lord Brothmell'.

'What?' screamed Rothwell, 'It's Rothwell, Rothwell, not Brothmell!'

'Hotbroth?' Hector half-asked.

'How stupid is he? He's a moron!' Rothwell screamed, 'Rothwell, It's Rothwell, Rothwell, ahhhhhhhhhhh!'

The last prolonged scream was accompanied by Rothwell jumping backwards. Bandit had, once again, used Lord Rothwell as a lamp post, and then shot behind Hector and pretended to sniff something.

'I think we're ready for another take sir,' said a man who appeared at the door with a clipboard.

'What? What? Right. OK. In a minute.'

Kate and Hector walked back round to the kitchen. They took their time. Kate was caught between admiration at the way Hector had managed to wind Rothwell up on one hand, and a sisterly need to say nothing positive to her brother on the other.

Hector's mind had turned to other things. Sometimes secrets are needed. Yet, secrets are obstacles. They need to be kept, and that creates the problem. They can be undone or revealed by careless words. There must be nothing careless if secrecy is to be maintained. Secrets are like doors keeping people apart. Even Hector appreciated that these were complex thoughts. It was as if the thinking had happened without words, and now the words floated on top as pretend explanation and justification.

'Can we walk to the lake?' Hector asked, and changed direction.

It is hard to be spontaneous and have fun with someone if secrets have to be kept. Hector wondered why this had now become something he thought about. He sighed as he realised that somewhere, a small part of him was whispering the idea that he might not live; it might not all turn out alright, with Hector unscathed.

Hector had moments in the past when doubts had surfaced. The attack on the plane when he could not fire the gun. The moment when Sludge almost reached him at the zoo. At these times he doubted his own immortality, but his belief always returned. He would be fine. He would survive. It would be a great adventure; a gripping story. Everything would turn out as he hoped.

Now, for the first time, Hector doubted this. He was still optimistic. He was still very sure everyone would come through it all. What had changed was faith. His unquestioning faith that he would survive everything and live had slipped away.

'Look into the lake,' said Hector. Kate looked, but saw only darkness.

'Can you see a pair of eyes looking back?' Hector asked.

Kate peered into the gloom but could see nothing.

'Hector, if you tell me there's a monster…It's not going to work. I will still go sailing.'

'No, look, really. Look hard.'

After a short period Kate muttered an 'Oh'.

'You can see them?' Hector asked.

'Yes. Maybe they're just rocks.'

'Kate, it's a secret. They're headlights. It's Lord Rothwell's Range Rover.'

Kate looked at Hector in surprise, and then back at the lake. It took a moment or two, but then events clicked into place for Kate.

'So, it was you,' said Kate.

'It was an accident. I was looking for somewhere to hide and it was open. It was in the wrong position so I let the hand brake off, moved it into neutral and pushed it back, but it kept rolling. I didn't mean to do it. Don't tell Mum or Dad.'

'They already suspect you did something,' said Kate, a grin spreading across her face, 'They just didn't think you could have driven it away. It didn't occur to them that you'd dumped it in the lake.'

'Andrè knows. Why didn't Dad question me?' asked Hector, puzzled as to why he did not receive the usual full interrogation.

'Well maybe Dad and Mum didn't want Lord Rothwell to find out that his beloved Range Rover had been used as a submarine by Roger the Wrecker,' said Kate, the laughter beginning to spill from her voice.

'I didn't mean to,' said Hector.

Maybe it was the background worry of Sludge. Maybe it was another encounter with the horrible Rothwell that had united them more closely. Possibly it was a sense that somewhere in the chaos of events was a form of rough justice. Kate and Hector gazed at the forlorn eyes of the Range Rover looking reproachfully from the depths of the lake and cried with laughter.

As Kate and Hector walked back to the kitchen Otto strolled out to meet them. He allowed Kate to pick him up. Otto closed his eyes as he was stroked and cuddled. The three of them continued on their way and came across two men from the video team sat looking at the lake.

'Your father didn't sound too pleased with you,' said one of the men. He had a close cropped beard and narrow, close eyes set in a thin face.

'He's not our father,' said Hector quickly, 'Lord Broth-Hell is nothing to do with us.'

'He always shouts,' explained Kate.

'Yes, we've noticed,' said a smaller blond man, who also had a close-cropped beard.

'What did you do wrong?' asked Kate.

'We didn't do anything wrong,' said the first man to have spoken, 'It was that horrible cat there.'

'Otto is really nice,' said Kate, stroking Otto as he purred in her arms.

'Not if you're a rat who doesn't want his innards sent hurtling through the air,' said the man. They all began to laugh.

'Oh yeah,' said Hector, 'He usually chews the head off and flings that in.'

'Yes, that's right,' said the blond man, 'we've even got it on camera, sailing across in front of Lord Rothwell's face.'

'The thing is,' said the first man laughing, 'It was his best take. He'd almost finished, and he was ignoring the small splats as bits of rat hit the window, and then this rat head flies in and almost hits him.'

'Brilliant,' said Hector, 'Otto's a good boy.'

'No, that wasn't his finest moment,' said the blond man, 'We filmed Lord Rothwell talking about some of his art exhibits. We were all praying it was the last take. Only when we looked at the clip afterwards did we notice the cat in the background, sat on Lord Rothwell's desk, licking its bottom.'

'I bet old Dun Duns went bonkers,' said Hector.

Kate turned towards the kitchen feeling cheered as they said goodbye to the two men. Lord Rothwell's video was going badly, which was deserved, and Hector had sunk Lord Rothwell's Range Rover, which was funny.

After a brief period looking at the safe room that was being installed, Kate and Hector went for lunch. Nana had made a shepherd's pie and a vegetarian pizza. She seemed to have a knack of appearing with food ready just as Hector and Kate arrived.

'I need your help in a while,' said Nana, 'and I'd also appreciate a bit of discretion.'

There was a pause as both Kate and Hector began to eat. Nana looked at both of them and then turned her attention to Hector. He looked like a boy who had landed in a pig pen. As far as she could see, Hector could get dirty without moving, and if he did move this just made the grime and muck he acquired even more spectacular.

'There is someone I want you to meet,' said Nana, 'but it has to be hush hush.'

'What do you mean?' asked Hector, revealing an unattractive mouthful of shepherd's pie.

'I mean it's a secret. So you're not to tell anyone.'

Kate and Hector looked at each other.

'As I see it,' said Nana, 'Andrè's a fantastic chap, but you might need a bit of extra help. I've asked a friend down and I'd like you to tell him what you know. Also, I want him to meet you. If he likes you and he's willing to help he'd be quite an ally.'

A short while later Kate and Hector were introduced to Edward Grantham. He looked slightly older than Nana, with grey thinning hair, tweed clothes and a gait that suggested slightly too many well-cooked meals. Two fingers from his left hand were missing, and his right eye had a milky quality, suggesting blindness.

Nana had been conspiratorial in the way she checked the windows and doors to ensure no one could hear them. Kate and Hector told Mr Grantham their story. He listened attentively, asking questions here and there. As the conversation progressed Kate and Hector both warmed to Mr Edward Grantham.

'I have a little test for you Hector,' said Mr Grantham, in a very similar accent to Nana, after listening and questioning them for half an hour.

'What is it?' Hector asked, now quite relaxed.

'Why did you destroy the Range Rover?'

'Erm, well, I,' stuttered Hector.

'Hector isn't a vandal. He's not a criminal. He's really kind,' said Kate, suddenly very defensive, 'He doesn't even drop litter.'

'Really?' said Edward Grantham in a questioning tone, 'I think the CCTV footage of Hector pushing the car into the lake makes him look like a criminal. Kind of Kath here to destroy the video, but the evidence was there.'

'He's not! He's not a criminal!' shouted Kate, 'He was just trying to move it backwards so he could use it as a hiding place. It's not his fault it went wrong!'

'And you smashed in the head of an old lady who was trying to help you?' Mr Grantham asked.

'She wasn't an old lady, she was mechanical and she had gone wrong and we thought she was going to kill us,' Kate snarled.

There was silence as Kate glared at Mr Grantham. Hector was annoying, tedious, horribly competitive and mean to Kate, but no one was going to call her brother a criminal. Edward Grantham looked down to a piece of card he had just extracted from his pocket.

'Edward?' Nana asked, as if seeking an answer to a question that had yet to be asked.

'Spirit, loyalty, adventure. Of course I'll help,' said Edward Grantham, starting to laugh.

'Now Kate,' said Mr Grantham, 'I admire your loyalty, I really do. I wanted to see what you'd say. I will not help criminals. I have enough of them stealing from my farm, but I don't think you're criminals.'

'What can you do Mr Grantham?' asked Hector, 'I thought Andrè had everything sorted out.'

'Call me Edward,' said Mr Grantham, 'and I am sure that Andrè does have everything sorted out. I don't know much about him, but the little I do know suggests that he's a bit more than a soldier. I suspect he's rather special.'

'A wise general prepares for his defeat,' said Nana.

'We don't want defeat,' said Hector, unimpressed.

'What Kath means is that you should always prepare for things going wrong,' said Edward, 'You have intelligence problems, traitors and a very frightening enemy. It's good to have a plan B, a plan C and something else besides.'

'As I see it,' Edward continued, 'they will know you have some support. They'll send in some cannon fodder to flush out the defences and they will be prepared for some of the things Andrè will have ready for them. Soldiers like Andrè are good at killing people, but that also means they have to be careful not to kill their own. They won't be expecting some of our more rural defences. We're a bit less discriminate.'

Now Kate and Hector were interested. Nana checked that the coast was clear, and they all went for a walk to the stables.

As they toured Lord Rothwell's property Edward explained that he had spent a lifetime dealing with people trying to steal things from his farms. It became clear that Edward's methods were slightly unusual, and they all revolved around explosives. Edward was fascinated with guns and bombs.

'The key thing,' said Edward as they entered one of the older stables, 'is not to kill or really injure anyone. You don't know who you are injuring. It could be one of your own family or a worker. It could be someone who is lost. Even if it is a thief then the penalty isn't death or dismemberment. Also, you don't want to end up in lots of trouble with the police.'

'What do you do then?' asked Kate.

'Well, it depends. On some of my buildings I have booby traps that set off loud explosions. That's usually enough to send them running. On other buildings I have movement detectors, and I get a phone message and pictures. If it's someone I don't recognise I can set off the explosives with my phone. Just enough to give them a good fright.'

Edward stopped to survey the square in the middle of the stables. Nana shook her head.

'I see what you mean now,' said Nana, obviously referring to an earlier conversation.

'What is it?' Hector asked.

'Well, this is exactly where anyone who attacks the Hall will gather,' said Edward, 'It has cover, and it's slightly higher than the Hall. Now special forces wouldn't touch the place, as it's got killing field written all over it. I would guess that André and his chap will do exactly that. If they do it's up to them. However, they might fail if there is a traitor about. We might need a plan B.'

'They're not going to run away if there are a couple of bangs,' said Hector.

'Aren't they?' Edward responded, 'Well some will if he's using a rabble. Anyway, I think we'll make these bangs slightly bigger. The sort that leave you feeling sick and completely deaf for two days.'

'We're going to leave them some food as well,' said Nana, 'with some poison in so they are really sick.'

'Vomiting soldiers don't attack well,' said Edward, 'and most of these will not be soldiers. We'll leave it in a picnic hamper.'

'I'll put fresh sandwiches in every few days, and there will be chocolate bars and other things,' said Nana, 'but you mustn't eat any. Also, you mustn't open anything otherwise Otto or Bandit will get in.'

'I've heard about your dog,' said Edward, 'Now he is a criminal!'

'Yes, but he likes cuddles and he's sweet,' said Kate.

'Got you wrapped round his little finger has he?' Edward laughed.

'Dogs don't have fingers,' said Hector, 'They have paws and claws.'

'Oddly enough, Bandit did have some fingers,' said Nana, 'Just yesterday Captain Smash and Grab got Dunbar's chocolate fingers.'

'Once the trouble is started you mustn't come into this courtyard, otherwise you might get caught in the blasts,' said Edward.

'We'll be in the safe room,' said Hector.

'You think you will,' said Edward, 'There's many a slip between cup and lip.'

Edward then took them to his rather sleek Mercedes. He showed them a firework rocket he had in the boot.

'I'm going to give Kath a few of these,' said Edward, 'They go very high and they are very loud. Send up at least two. You can use these to alert me and I can call in help. I know Andrè will have it all sorted, but just in case, this approach is difficult to jam or cover up.'

'Thank you Edward,' said Kath, and she kissed him on the cheek.

As Edward Grantham left Kate was overtaken with curiosity. She wanted to know more about Edward.

'I know what you're going to ask,' said Nana, 'and yes he comes from Devon. We were sweethearts many years ago. Then we got married, and then we got divorced, and now we get on quite well.'

'He must think a lot of you to help us when it's so dangerous,' said Kate.

'Partly, I think he does. Partly, he just loves a fight. Good against evil. Romantic after a fashion, but in an explosive and gunfire sort of way. Edward had a farm in Devon when I met him, inherited from his father. He sold it to a property developer as it was right on the coast. Bought two much bigger farms up here and that's how he and I ended up in Lincolnshire.'

Just five minutes after Nana, Hector and Kate had retreated to the kitchen for a cup of tea, orange juice and apple juice, Kate noticed a large removals van pull up. The cars had arrived. Hector bounced with excitement, while Kate tried to appear more reserved. Only Nana was not interested.

Hector arrived outside eating, and was promptly ordered back inside the wipe around his mouth. He reappeared moments after he had disappeared. A quick glance at his sleeves told Kate exactly where the excess food had gone.

The Bentley was a metallic grey colour on the outside, with cream leather coating almost every surface of the interior. Kate thought it looked as though the whole car had been carved from a giant tree, while Hector thought it was not unlike the car in the last Batman film he had seen. Hector's only doubt was the large amount of wood in the dashboard; it looked as though the car had collided with an ornate wooden desk at some point.

The man who brought the Bentley gave Dad a detailed introduction to the car. Hector lost interest as details of self-closing doors, digital television, hidden refrigerators and suspension settings droned forth. His interest only resumed when he heard about the top speed of two hundred and three miles an hour.

With Hector now asking questions, the man explained that this was the official top speed, and that a German had reached two hundred and eleven miles an hour in exactly this model of car. The six-litre, twin turbo charged engine could propel the almost three tonne monster from standstill to sixty miles an hour in under four seconds.

'Can we go over two hundred?' begged Hector, 'Please, please can we, please, please!'

'Not a chance,' said Dad, 'I want to live. In any event, I cannot see why I would want to let the grub monster anywhere near the beautiful cream leather interior. I will take you if you have a shower and change your clothes.'

Hector was about to protest, but felt Nana's hand on his shoulder. He knew this was not something he could negotiate. He had to give in if he wanted a ride. At least Kate accompanied him to their bedroom and so he did not feel that she was getting a special treat he was missing.

'I wonder what the other car will be like?' Kate mused.

'No idea. Don't care!' Hector exclaimed, 'The Bentley is fantastic and I don't care about the other car. Dad can dump it in the lake as far as I'm concerned.'

'I thought that was your job,' said Kate.

'What do you mean?' Hector asked.

'Dumping cars in the lake,' Kate replied.

'Oh yeah,' said Hector, completely unabashed, 'I'll dump his other car in the lake and then we'll get taken around in the Bentley all of the time.'

Hector raced out of the bedroom with his trousers only half up. By the time Kate had made it to the stairs Hector had slid all the way down the banister. His crimes on the banister were now well known, and in the last week he had been caught three times in one day. Only Lord Rothwell did not appear to mind. Hector suspected this was because Rothwell hoped Hector would fall to his death.

'Wow! Woooooowww!' was all Kate could hear for the last flight of stairs.

Beyond the doors was a deep red open top sports car. It had a huge grill and curves and gleam.

'Kate, Kate, it's a Maserati,' yelled Hector.

Kate had no idea of what this meant, but she liked the look of it. A quick glance around told her that Nana and Andrè liked it as well, but Mum definitely had her disapproval face set to level ten.

'I like it,' said Andrè, 'It will certainly attract attention.'

Once the man with the van had departed with the unwanted Jaguar, Dad tried the cars on the drive. The Bentley had a low rumble, like distant thunder. The Maserati, on the other hand, sounded like a slightly subdued version of a Formula One racing car. The good thing, from Hector's point of view, was that neither was silent.

An hour later everyone had enjoyed a ride, with the notable exception of Bandit, despite leaping clean into the Maserati at one point. Nana had rung a nearby farmer she knew so that they could use part of the old wartime aerodrome that was spread across several of his fields. Kate and Hector had been delighted to discover that the Maserati became much louder when Dad pressed the Sport button. Both cars had exceeded one hundred miles an hour, although in the Bentley it felt like sixty miles per hour.

The Maserati was thrilling, while the Bentley was either wonderfully relaxing or so deceptively fast it was frightening. Dad seemed to believe he had just arrived in heaven. Hector was slightly disappointed that Dad would not try for two hundred miles an hour.

Once they were back in the Hall a happy chatter flowed from the kitchen. When Kate returned from the toilet she caught sight of Nana's face. She seemed happy, very happy, but more than this she appeared deeply content. For the first time Kate felt sorry for Nana, as this was what she seemed to long for but could not have. She clearly loved having a family stay. She was always sorting things out for everyone. Mum could do very little when they had first arrived because of her injuries. Nana had done everything Mum would have done, but also seemed to have lifted a little of the weight and worry. Kate decided that she was going to talk Hector into doing something for Nana.

Although Dad had planned to park both cars in one of the outbuildings, he left them sitting on the gravel for the first night. Kate thought it was so he could gaze at them. She noticed that anyone on their feet would steal a glance at the Bentley and the Maserati.

As both Hector and Kate stood up ready to go to bed, Dad looked out of the window and groaned. The last warm glow of the day spread across the parkland around the hall. The sun was setting, casting great waves of orange and gold across the underside of the clouds, and silhouetted against the sunset was Otto, on top of the beautiful Maserati, trapping and squashing flies onto its spotless windscreen.

CHAPTER FIFTEEN

Plans

Hector woke with Kate shaking him.

'What, what?' he asked angrily.

'Shhhh, be quiet,' said Kate, 'I've found something.'

Kate led Hector into the bedroom on the other side of the landing. There was a large cupboard in one corner that sank into the wall next to a window. At the back of the cupboard was a bolted door, but it was swinging open. Beyond that was darkness.

'What is it?' Hector asked, rather hoping it was Narnia.

'I think it is an entrance to the hollow walls.'

'What? What hollow…ohhh,' said Hector as realisation dawned, 'We could explore around the house. There's bound to be secret passageways.'

'I don't think so,' Kate replied, 'I think it is just that the walls are hollow so they can run all of the wires and pipes and things.'

A short while later Hector was caught yet again sliding down the banister en route to the kitchen to borrow a torch.

'I don't mind the last stretch Hector, but it is a huge fall from higher up,' Dad lectured, 'Everyone is tired of telling you about this. One more time and there will be no rides in the nice cars for a week.'

Hector inwardly groaned. Dad had found something he cared about, and unlike the threat to send him to a boarding school or prison, this was a threat he knew Dad would carry out.

Both Hector and Kate were frustrated to be forced to stop for breakfast. Hector explained that he wanted to get going soon because there was a very dark part of the woods he found interesting, hence the need for a torch. Kate thought this was a terrible excuse and suspected that Nana had already guessed their intentions.

'Well, wherever you go be careful,' Nana said, 'There are some surprising drops in dark places,' She gave them a knowing look.

'What are you planning to do?' Dad asked.

'Nothing, just a trip to the darker woods,' said Hector, keen to shut Dad up and get going.

'Oh, I've just remembered,' said Hector, 'I've got a question.'

'What is it?' said Dad, with a slightly weary tone of resignation, as Hector's questions were usually deliberately idiotic.

'Why did you decide to grow hair on your body?' Hector asked.

'Sorry,' said Dad, unsure he had heard the question properly.

'Well,' said Hector, very happy to explain his interest, 'You know it used to be the fashion in Victorian times to grow very large beards or moustaches. Obviously, no one does that now as it looks weird. The thing is some men, like you, have masses of body hair, and I just wondered why you decided to grow it when it's so grotesque and old fashioned.'

Nana was laughing silently, muttering about not knowing where the boy got his ideas about from. Dad was thinking that Hector's vocabulary was expanding. It was the first time Hector had described anything as grotesque.

'Excellent,' said Andrè, appearing at the door. He was looking at Hector and Kate.

'What's the matter?' Hector asked, worried that one of his previous crimes might have been unearthed. It even flashed across his mind that Lord Rothwell had spotted his Range Rover in its watery grave.

'This morning we are going to have an exercise on evasion,' said Andrè, 'and we will follow it up with some night time exercises.'

The good news was that Andrè had some presents for them. It included a kit bag, with a communicator, a night sight, a torch, camouflaged clothing, a small amount of food and even a small box that Andrè said would expand into a sleeping bag if opened. The bad news was they were now expected to keep these with them at all times.

The morning was taken up with some theory and a lot of practice. They were shown how to smear the camouflage paint on their faces and hands. They were allowed to practice with the night sight in a darkened barn.

Both Kate and Hector began to appreciate how useful evasion could be. Andrè explained again that most people were spotted when they moved or looked up from their position. He had gone through this with them in the past, but there was a certain urgency in his manner that made them pay more attention. Andrè also demonstrated how the eyes would show up if a torch was flashed across a dark area.

'What if we need to move and hide during the day?' Kate asked after a lot of practice in a dark barn.

'You stay still and sleep during the day and move at night, unless it is desperate, or unless they have dogs,' Andrè said as he looked at them with a very sombre face.

'You've very serious,' Hector pointed out.

'Oui, it matters. Your life will probably depend upon it,' said Andrè.

'I thought we were going to hide in the safe room?' Hector pointed out.

'Possibly, but if you get a chance to hide I want you to disappear into the woods and keep going away from here for several days. I want you to contact no one.'

'Which direction?' Kate asked.

'Any, just don't tell me,' was Andrè's surprising answer, 'Just stay in the countryside out of sight until you get a message on the communicator.'

'Can we use a mobile phone?' Hector asked.

'No, your position can be monitored by the security services and there might be a leak there. Also, mobile phones stay in touch with the mobile masts. They emit a signal that can be tracked easily.'

'If there has been an attack we might not know what has happened to Mum or Dad or you or Nana,' Kate said, a certain fear and sadness creeping into her voice.

'That is correct,' said Andrè, and the hint of a kind smile formed across his lips, 'You may be separated and not know whether the other is alive. But I want you to hide. I do not want to know where you are because hiding is the hardest thing for your enemy to deal with. It is your best chance of survival.'

'What if we find a farmhouse?' Hector enquired.

'Exactly where they would look,' said Andrè, 'They will check roads and buildings. You sleep in dry ditches, and make sure you use the thermal blanket over your whole body, especially your head, to hide your thermal outline.'

'What's a thermal outline?' Hector asked, before realising that he knew exactly what Andrè was talking about.

'They will use thermal imaging equipment. They will look for you,' said Andrè, 'Try to pick areas with sheep or cattle as they will confuse a thermal scan.'

'Is this what special forces soldiers do?' Hector asked.

'Oui, yes, some of the time,' Andrè replied, 'You must only answer to the communicator. Other than me, Bertrand is the only one who can contact you. If you have to hide do not trust messages from me, or your parents or anyone else. It might not be us. And don't tell us where you are thinking of going. I want you both to have an idea of where you will go together, and where you will go separately. You must not tell each other where you plan to go on your own if you are separated. You must not tell me or your parents where you plan to go.'

The day seemed very dark and dismal, despite the sunshine powering through the cracks in the barn door. Both Kate and Hector understood why they were not to tell their mother, father, Nana or Andrè about where they intended to go if they had to hide. The idea of spending several days and nights hiding, with no idea of what had happened to each other, made them feel homeless and abandoned, cut off from what they had left.

'There is another thing,' said Andrè, waking them from their thoughts, 'There is a British guy arriving. Do not tell him I have taught you these things. Your mother and father know, but I cannot be sure who we can trust. He's probably very good and honest, but there is no need to tell him anything.'

'Andrè,' Hector began, 'Nana and Edward Grantham have a plan.'

Hector was not sure why he betrayed Nana. He felt guilty the moment he started, and yet Andrè's apparent willingness to put Kate and Hector before himself seemed to change everything, in that dark in the barn.

'What is their plan?' Andrè asked, without emotion.

Hector explained everything, and was surprised Kate had not objected. As Hector finished his regrets rose. He felt that he had done everything Nana had asked him not to do, but worse than that he had caused trouble and disagreement between Andrè and Nana, both of whom he realised he liked very much. Both of whom cared for him. Hector had set them against each other.

'I think Edward Grantham's plans are not a problem,' said Andrè, to Hector and Kate's surprise, 'He has already been checked out. He is not someone I am worried about. But thanks for the tip off about the poisoned food, I wouldn't want to eat any of it.'

Hector immediately cheered up, and spent much of lunchtime very unkindly miming choking and dying as a result of eating Nana's food. This amused Andrè, but alarmed Kate, as she was afraid that Nana would see him and assume that he objected to her excellent cooking.

Just after lunch Mike Jennings from the British security services arrived. He was very pleasant, and Andrè left to show him around. Kate raced out to the Bentley, ready for a shopping trip with Mum and Dad.

Hector was to be left with Nana, who was a trusting sort. Andrè was too busy with Mike Jennings to pay him attention at the moment, and Lord Rothwell would never trouble himself with anyone as insignificant as Hector. Close to perfect, as only Bandit and Otto would see what he did, and when it came to secret plans they were good mates. Best of all, should the need arise, they could be easily distracted with small bits of food.

As far as Hector was concerned, the logic was simple. If Andrè was constructing defences with the help of Dad, and Nana was making preparations with her friend Edward, then Hector should do his bit. It was disappointing that he was not allowed explosives or guns, but he would just have to make do.

Hector had heard Dad's views on, 'Hector's unhealthy interest in radical oxidisation,' and after a bit of research Hector discovered that oxidisation, where oxygen atoms combine with other atoms, usually carbon atoms, was the main chemical process behind fire and some explosives. Dad had been quite clear about the range of substances that should be denied to Hector, and unfortunately Andrè appeared to agree.

Hector had spent quite a lot of time listening in to Andrè's and Dad's conversations, while pretending to be totally absorbed by whatever lego weapon he was constructing. Somehow they thought that by speaking in hushed tones Hector would not be able to understand. As is so often the case, the quieter voice was usually the cue that told him to pay attention.

Hector heard many things, including the plans for fake booby-traps around the garden. Andrè had explained that real traps were too dangerous, but that fake ones would confuse, distract and delay any attackers. Hector was surprised when Andrè repeatedly encouraged both Dad and Mum to practise with the guns.

Yet, it was Andrè's appraisal of him and Kate that gave him greatest reason to stop and think about himself. The report was neither cruel, careless nor kind, and for this reason seemed imbued with a granite authenticity. Andrè explained that Colonel Bertrand and some others had examined both Hector's and Kate's behaviour as part of their planning.

Kate was described as pleasant and normal for her age, given to worrying, and apparently easily flustered, but clever, resourceful and brave in a crisis. Hector was described as normal and likeable, very energetic, but prone to speaking and acting without thinking.

Andrè said that most children were nothing in a fight other than an encumbrance to whomever they belonged. Kate and Hector were different. Kate was likely to be very dangerous if she or Hector were threatened. In short, while most children and adults would not really pull the trigger as the assassin approached their family, Kate would.

Hector, on the other hand, was a game-changer. He could act so unexpectedly that he could completely transform a situation. He had stalled a large plane and crashed it into a pursuing fighter. He had burnt down the château. Hector might not know what he was doing, but he could have a radical effect on events.

Most children are like a weight, Andrè had explained, but Kate and Hector are dangerous to both sides. Hector could turn victory into defeat, and certain death into glorious escape, as he had when flying the old bomber. Kate, on the other hand, might kick Hector when she thought no one was looking, but was quite capable of killing anyone heading at speed towards her brother if she had the means, and this could include someone on her own side if she was confused.

On that particular day Hector had constructed a very strange lego object as he pretended to be oblivious to the whispered conversation. Yet, this was not the information that had so motivated him today. He had overheard Andrè saying that, because of the layout of the house, any attack would inevitably lead to the large, three-story circular hall. Andrè's plan was for Hector, Kate, Mum and Dad to retreat to a safe room in the cellar, but then use the hollow walls to move higher up the building. The attackers would spend their time breaking into a safe room that no longer contained their targets.

Hector thought that he should make the grand circular hallway more of a problem. He was denied explosives, but Hector had no-

ticed during the incident in Colonel Bertrand's office that water
and electricity did not mix well. Hector formulated a plan. When
the attackers got in, he would turn on a pump that would flood the
hall with water. It would reach the level of the electricity sockets
and the attackers would all go blue and shaky. It was a simple
plan, but Andrè had said that simple plans were often the best.

Hector's aim was not to save himself and his family. That was
implicit; assumed, and simply not worthy of thought. Hector
wanted to be a hero. He kept the medal he had been given in
France after crash-landing the plane. It was in a box with his most
treasured things, even though he had since noticed that it was a
sporting medal for rugby. Presumably, the local French officials
had experienced some difficulties coming up with a medal at short
notice.

Hector craved the praise and even respect he sensed when some
of the adults spoke about how he had behaved in the different cri-
ses. He may have played a central part in destroying a French safe
house, and in Mrs Warp twice, a key piece of French technology,
but Andrè clearly respected both Hector and Kate for fighting back
and surviving, even if they had misunderstood their situation.

While Hector was normally allergic to the effort involved in
tasks such as cleaning and tidying up, he had no objection to hard
work for a good cause, providing he defined what was and what
was not a worthy endeavour. Now he had a chance to make a contribution. Hector had a plan.

Hector spent his first ten minutes of absolute freedom practising
going shaky and turning blue in front of the mirror, just so he
could imagine what the attackers would look like. The turning
blue bit was hard to do, but the shaky part looked excellent, especially when he dropped his Nerf gun.

Next, Hector made for the shed where he knew Andrè had some tools. Bandit was immediately at his side, ready for adventure. The escapade with the parrot had been top notch, and he had high hopes for this one. Bandit had even postponed his afternoon duck hunt just to make space in his crowded diary. Bandit lived in a world of his very own, but in Bandit's opinion it was a great place to be.

The Pump House was an ornate stone building in a courtyard behind the Hall. This courtyard was a hidden private place. While the grand facade of the front of the Hall shone down upon the great parklands it overlooked, the courtyard was the place where things were done but nothing was seen. In the past it was where servants would have gone about their business and done every-thing that was needed to make the Hall tick. Now, it was full of damp and moss and still air and small echoes. Now it was silent and empty. That suited Hector perfectly.

The Pump House was large, with a metal chimney suggesting that it once housed a steam engine. It had a roof tiled in stone, and a great doorway that had been filled in using brick rather than matching stone. From the Hall it appeared as though there was no way into the Pump House, as the small wooden door was on the other side, next to the lake.

The small entrance had a lock and a very strong padlock, but the wood in the door was rotten and Hector quickly prised the hasp from the flaking timbers. In fact, it was so easy Hector suspected someone else had already done it, before pushing the hasp and screws back into the wood.

Once inside the Pump House Hector shut the door, enclosing both himself and Bandit inside its musty, dim interior. He could see four stone blocks that would have originally supported some huge engine, but now held only an electric pump.

Hector knew that the switch for the pump was in the house, because Lord Rothwell had turned the fountain on during his tour. To his relief, he spotted another electrical isolator, and he switched it to the off position, just to make sure that the pump could not be turned on while he was working on it. Strangely, this idea made him feel great. He was an engineer, almost a medical surgeon, about to perform a life-saving operation, taking the first obvious steps, before embarking on the more complex procedure.

It was at this point that Hector's plan began to falter. The second step was to loosen and remove the pipe from the pump to the lake, but the band supporting the huge hose was far too tight. He had just the right adjustable spanner. He had taken the largest one he could find, and it was the best choice, because it only just fitted. Yet, when he put the spanner on the nut, he simply could not make it turn. He had neither the strength nor the weight required. This struck Hector as odd, as he had spent a lot of time posing in front of a mirror and he was perfectly sure he had a superhero physique.

Ten minutes later and Hector was frustrated, while Bandit was bored. In fact, if Hector had not shut them both in the Pump House, Bandit would already have returned to his itinerary, and an afternoon duck hunt and provoking Lord Rothwell were right at the top of his to-do list.

Hector sat and looked at the pump and connectors. There had to be a way. Andrè might have his plans, Nana and Edward might have theirs, but it would probably be Hector who saved the day with this brilliant electrocution surprise.

As Bandit began to whine to be let out, Hector decided to think more widely about his problem. He considered cutting the canvas hose from the pump, but when he took it in his hands it felt very tough. The other problem was how to attach anything to the hose once he cut it. He wondered about using drain pipe as a sort of canal, but then remember that water had to be in a tube and under

pressure to go uphill. He needed the water through the top window of the house for his plan to work.

Hector pulled at the hose where it dipped into a hole in the floor
on its way into the lake. He felt it give a little. Hector pulled again,
and the hose moved slightly. Hector then got low to the floor,
wedged his feet against the wall and pulled with all of his might.
The hose moved about half a metre, causing Hector to partly fall
backwards. He tried again, and then felt the hose suddenly lurch
towards him as Bandit seized it and pulled as well.

Bandit liked this. He had been bored, but Hector had discovered
some sort of giant sleeping snake and they were both going to pull
it out of its hole, have a big fight, kill it and hopefully eat it.

Two minutes later and everything had come to a full stop. As far
as Bandit was concerned the snake had woken up and was rather
unsportingly clinging on to something. Hector had no idea what
was stopping the hose from moving. Each time he and Bandit tried
to move the hose it stuck. Frustrated and a little angry that they
were getting nowhere after several metres of the hose had already
come out, Hector pulled again and shouted encouragement to
Bandit. Suddenly, the hose moved, just as a there was a clang and a
splash from outside.

Hector tentatively opened the door to the pump house and
peered out towards the lake. Bandit stood by him. Everything
looked the same, except for ripples spreading out from the centre
of the lake. This excited Bandit, as the snake was obviously getting
desperate, but it was definitely a snake, and it was struggling.

Hector's view of things was different. He was anxious that
someone was about. He did not want to be disturbed. Hector
looked for a person around the lake, and then into the waters for a
large fish that might have made the splash. After a minute of look-

ing and thinking he realised that whoever it had been was now gone.

With that problem solved, Hector returned to the task of hauling in the hose. Bandit abandoned all thought of a duck hunt and joined him, ready for a final heroic dog verses snake death match.

By the time Hector and Bandit had pulled all of the hose out of the hole Hector was aching all over, and wondering whether he really had caused just too much trouble this time. At the end of the hose was Rothwell's ancestor; the gruesome head from the centre of the lake. The clang and the ripples were now explained. Hector had just ruined the greatly-prized Rothwell fountain.

Bandit was equally disappointed. He had no problems with the snake having the head of a man. Mythology was not one of his strong points, but men with snakes' bodies were quite acceptable in his world. The real let down was the lack of a fight. As the head clanged into view Bandit had growled and leapt forwards, but all that had happened was that Hector let out a moan as the nose and left ear of the ugly head were broken away by the fall.

Hector opted to sit outside the pump house for a while in the sun wondering how on earth he was going to reattach the nose and the ear to the metal head. The only consoling thought was that the Rothwell's screams when he discovered what had happened would probably be so high they would be beyond human hearing.

Bandit decided to take himself off to the aviary. The snake had obviously died while being pulled out, and he needed something else to do. He would just have to chalk the snake up as an easy victory. Bandit had failed to break into the aviary so far, but Bandit was well aware than persistence has its rewards.

Hector considered cutting the hose just beneath the fountain head, but decided instead to keep it attached. He reasoned that he could use it to direct the spray, and that could be useful. The damage was done. Maybe once he had saved everyone the damage to the Rothwell head would be forgiven.

The next hour saw Hector haul the fountain head and hose across the small courtyard, and then hoist it up to the top window using a rope. Next, he returned to the courtyard with a spade, dug a small trench in the semi-loose stones, and buried the hose. Although the hose was wider that Hector's thigh, he was pleased to see that as the water drained the hose became flatter and easier to hide.

The hose emerged from the loose stones of the courtyard in a dark corner. It stretched up the building, hung beside an old, rusting drainpipe. It was easily lost in the grey back of the Hall. Hector had considered painting it to make it blend in, but as he stood back he quickly realised that the ageing, grey hose looked as though it had hung in that forgotten corner for the past one hundred years.

After he had turned the pump isolator back to the on position, and carefully pressed the hasp back into the pump room door, making it appear just as locked and secure as it had before, Hector returned to the fountain head on the top floor. He secured this with a rope to the metal banister. The small, circular top floor was right above the central hall, but was rarely used and dimly lit. Originally intended for servant's bedrooms, the two grimy rooms from the top floor were just used for storage; all part of the Rothwell decay.

It was a job well done. Definitely one of Hector's best ever plans. The destruction of the Rothwell fountain was clearly a minus point, but the plus point was huge. All he had to do when the assassins arrived was to turn on the fountain and wait for them to go blue and die as the water met the electricity sockets in the central hallway.

Hector had just popped into the kitchen to beg a sandwich from Nana, when there was a scream from the garden. Lord Rothwell was in full operatic shriek, and a cold shiver ran down Hector's back as he realised that he had probably just been discovered. There was almost certainly some sort of ghostly ancestral link between the Rothwell and the ugly head in the middle of the lake. Once removed the Rothwell would open its eyes and trudge with arms outstretched while screaming in pursuit of the perpetrator.

As it happened, Lord Rothwell was going berserk near the aviary, first screaming and then trying to get hold of a brown wagging tail protruding from a hole under the wooden hut the parrots slept in. Unperturbed by the noise, Bandit was still digging, and would sometimes partly reverse out so that he could fling more soil out of the hole using both front legs at once.

'I'm going to shoot it, I'm going to damn well shoot it!' Lord Rothwell was screaming, just as more soil was hurled at his neatly-pressed trousers.

Fortunately, Andrè arrived. He lay down to get a hold of Bandit and dragged him from the hole. Bandit immediately sat down and looked very sad, almost as if he had come across the hole and had been guarding it. He was now hurt and upset that anyone might think he had dug it.

After Andrè had said a few sharp words to Bandit in French, which Hector assumed meant 'Bad Dog,' Bandit was released, and immediately returned to his jaunty trot with a waggly tail look. Lord Rothwell turned and stalked back to the Hall, unaware that Bandit was following, intent once again, upon using Lord Rothwell as a lamppost.

CHAPTER SIXTEEN

Chase

Hector was relieved the following morning to find that no one had discovered his handiwork with the pump house and the fountain. He half expected to be woken at midnight by a furious Lord Rothwell foaming at the mouth.

As it happened Lord Rothwell was foaming at the mouth. He was furiously angry with Otto. Hector and Kate caught some shouting as they made their way downstairs. Lord Rothwell swore and Dad's voice punched through the air with an immediate demand that Lord Rothwell control himself. Kate reflected that Dad had changed. He was calmer, but also firmer and more in control.

Lord Rothwell retreated to his rooms just as Nana produced both Hector and Kate's breakfasts with her usual magical timing. There was silence, which Hector assumed was to allow Lord Rothwell to disappear a good distance into his sumptuous lounge.

'What's Otto done?' Hector enquired.

'Nothing much,' said Mum.

'I tried to train him,' said Nana, 'but it didn't work.'

'There's a shock,' thought Kate sarcastically.

'I read in this magazine that you could train cats to use toilets,' said Nana, 'so I thought I would keep Otto in when Dunbar has guests and he could behave like a civilised being and use the toilet rather than any of my pot plants.'

'Civilised?' Hector exclaimed, 'His favourite hobby is dismembering rats and throwing their bits through windows.'

'Which is why I thought keeping him out of sight might be a good idea,' Nana explained.

'Is Lord Rothwell angry that Otto can't be trained?' Kate asked.

'No, Otto understood perfectly I suspect,' said Nana, 'The little so-and-so never used the toilet when I wanted him to. However, rather than go in the bushes he jumps through the window into Lord Rothwell's rooms at night and uses his toilet.'

Hector and Kate began to laugh. Hector resolved to steal a small portion of fish from the fridge later for Otto as a reward.

'I don't want to upset you,' said Nana, with a huge grin spread across her face, 'but it's worse than you know. Part of it's Dunbar's problem.'

'Well, he shouldn't leave his window open,' said Kate, forever on the side of Nana and Otto.

'No, no, not that,' said Nana, 'Dunbar has always been terrible for not flushing the toilet. On top of that, I think he must have eaten something that disagreed with him.'

By now Kate and Hector were totally focussed on Nana. They simply could not work out what could have happened.

'I think Otto had jumped in during the night to use the toilet,' said Nana, 'Unfortunately, Otto doesn't flush either. Worse than that, he fell in. Of course, he left a great big trail of toilet stuff all over the white rugs and carpets. When I went in there I thought Dunbar had been attacked by a skunk.'

'What I did not see coming,' said Nana, 'was the strange route Otto takes through Lord Rothwell's rooms: all through his kitchen and in the dining room. It looked like Otto had been used as a giant, smelly mop to clean the place backwards.'

'Unfortunately, I had to clean the place forwards,' said Nana, 'And Dunbar shouted at Otto. Not clever. There'll be a few extra rat's heads thrown in for that misjudgement. Otto's not the forgiving sort. He doesn't forgive the guilty.'

Kate reflected that Otto was not the sort to forgive the innocent either.

After breakfast Dad was going to the shops in Caistor. He intended to use the Maserati. Hector immediately volunteered to go along. The idea of shopping had put him off, but he knew Caistor was a small place with small shops. He had been tempted by the prospect of sailing to the large island again with Kate, but the Maserati definitely came first.

By the time Hector had rushed downstairs after cleaning his teeth, the roof of the Maserati was down, the engine was ticking over with just a hint of racing menace, and Mrs Warp was installed in the rear seat. He was disappointed to have her along, but he remembered that she had the strength to fight Sludge; she was essential security. As he got into the front passenger seat and Dad pulled away, Hector was pleased the hood was down; there was always a chance that Mrs Warp's wig would blow off.

Hector thought that a Maserati Gran Cabrio Sport had to be every boy's dream. It certainly brought out the boy in Dad, who looked to be about eleven years old as he took the racing line along the drive up the hill. The engine had the most fantastic suppressed racing roar. The sun broke out from behind a cloud just as Dad unleashed the monster, the engine shouted a threat to the heavens, the wheels briefly spun, and they were pushed back in their seats as they were thrust forwards along the road as if the devil himself were pulling them into Hell.

Hector was smiling, although he did not really know why. If asked, he could not possibly have explained the bolt of joy that had coursed through him. When he looked Dad was smiling as well.

Dad did not really drive that fast; he stuck to the speed limits. He seemed to prefer slowing down and then accelerating. Hector accused Dad of being addicted to the noise. Dad just laughed.

As they entered Caistor Dad slowed down. Hector was surprised by how many people looked at them. He realised they were really looking at the car. The Maserati was low and wide and had a huge grill, with wide-set lights for eyes. It had curved arches over the front wheels, and the whole car stretched back in curves and waves. Hector was sure that if he ever got married it would be to a Maserati. After all, who on earth would want to marry a girl.

By the time they parked the car in the market place in Caistor, Hector was quite sure the Maserati was having exactly the effect Andrè had wanted. The car was an attention magnet. Hordes of invading deadly space creatures could be sneaking up on the market place while almost everyone looked at the spectacular Maserati, oblivious to their fate.

It took Dad and Hector several minutes to get to the Co-op shop, even though it was only a few metres away. Several people announced that the car was 'beautiful' or 'fantastic' and went on to ask Dad all about it. By the time they were inside the shop Hector noticed that three people were gathered around the car. Dad had left the hood down. He had also left Mrs Warp in the back seat and she looked utterly peculiar.

As Dad worked his way through things to buy, Hector kept stealing glances out of the window. Mrs Warp was speaking to some of the people. On one hand, he was very keen to know what she was saying. On the other, he was fairly sure it was her small talk. She would be blabbering on about this or that. Hector was just looking at the elegant shape of the deep red car, with its beautiful curves and black wheels, when he walked into a post card display and the whole thing toppled over with a crash.

Hector moved on to filling his own basket. He decided that a balanced selection of foods was likely to be most acceptable to Dad. After just two minutes concentrated snatching he had amassed one apple, five chocolate party packs, four giant bars of fruit and nut chocolate, several bags of wine gums together with a small fudge bar for Kate. Hector carefully balanced the apple on top of the mountain of chocolate.

'Dad, I've selected a few things for me and Kate.'

'Hector, you've selected an apple,' said Dad, in his sarcastic tone.

'Yes,' said Hector, his voice still hopeful, 'I've chosen a range of nutritious foods.' Hector noticed that even the lady at the till had raised an eyebrow.

'Hector, it's too much,' said Dad.

'I could put the apple back,' Hector offered.

'Hector, it looks like a diabetes starter pack,' said Dad, 'There's no way I am going to buy you all of that chocolate.'

'What's diabetes?' Hector asked, hoping he would be able to distract Dad, frustrate him and ultimately argue for some of his chocolate mountain.

'Well type two diabetes can be triggered by living on chocolate, so the answer is a definite no.' Hector had failed, and had to return his items to the shelves before trailing after Dad back to the car.

As Dad stowed the shopping in the Maserati's tiny boot, another person approached him to ask about the car. Hector was growing bored of the talking, but reflected that Andrè would be very pleased. Hector knew that force was measured in newtons, and weight in kilograms. He had no idea what the agreed measure for attracting attention might be, but he suspected that when it came to the Maserati it might be buckets.

In the distance Hector saw someone with a camera and tele-scopic lens taking photographs of them. He was almost certain it was someone photographing the car, but it left him feeling uneasy. He pointed it out to Dad who shrugged. Mrs Warp had seen them as well. She had even taken a photograph of the person and re-layed it back to France, although Hector and Dad were quite oblivious of this.

As the car roared into life Hector looked forwards. There were so many people looking at them. Even Hector was slightly embar-rassed. Although a lot of people had been friendly, and a few had spoken, he suspected that some would think they were showing off. Of course, they were showing off, and usually Hector had few problems with this. As the engine's hum echoed off the surround-ing buildings, Hector decided to sit back and enjoy it. Too much thinking was not always a good thing.

They pulled out of the square and Hector suggested turning the Sport on, so the engine noise would rattle from building to build-ing. His feelings of embarrassment had been very short lived. Dad drove carefully, and while the car was always louder than other cars, he would not allow it to roar.

'Hector, I'm not going to behave like one of those yobs in a little hatchback car,' said Dad.

'You had Sport on before we got here,' Hector countered.

'That was in the countryside, away from any houses,' said Dad, his eyes straying to the rear view mirror. Hector looked in the wing mirror rather than be conspicuous and turn around altogether.

'Is that the person you saw photographing us?' Dad asked.

'I don't know,' replied Hector, 'but they seem to be following.'

The black BMW behind them kept its distance, but after a couple of turns both Hector and Dad thought it was following. Dad signalled to turn right, and the BMW behind signalled to turn right as well. Dad turned left, and the BMW also turned left. Both Dad and Hector briefly looked at each other.

'Any suggestions Mrs Warp?' Dad asked.

'If they have guns I can only defend against one of them,' she said, in a very matter of fact manner, 'I suggest you outrun them. Do not return home.'

This struck Hector as odd. They had no intention of returning home to their old house. Then Hector realised that Mrs Warp was suggesting that they do not return to the Hall.

Dad was already on the road back towards Rothwell. As they rounded a corner out of sight he accelerated, braked sharply and performed a quick u-turn in a field entrance. As the BMW drove down the hill to Rothwell, Dad, Hector and Mrs Warp roared past in the opposite direction. Hector felt a frightening thrill run through him as he saw the BMW perform a dusty hand-brake turn. Now the chase was on!

The rear end of the car had juddered slightly as the wheels spun. Then the car gripped and they were thrust up the hill. As they roared away Hector laughed. He could not help himself. There was something about the sound and acceleration that left him happy for no reason at all. Dad glanced at Hector and rolled his eyes.

Dad braked late on the corner, accelerating as soon as he was turning. Once on the main road to Tealby, Horncastle and beyond, Dad opted to use both sides of the road where he could see.

One hundred and ten, one hundred and twenty, one hundred and thirty. The speed kept climbing and climbing. Then suddenly there was crushing braking and squealing tyres as Dad turned down towards Stainton-le-Vale. There was more screeching from tyres on every bend. Hector was impressed; Dad was dangerously fast.

The road was not the best, but this did not stop Dad flooring the accelerator. The countryside was rocketing past at a frightening speed as Hector was thrown from one side of the car to another with each and every bend.

He looked around. The BMW had lost some ground, but was still rocketing after them. It looked more out of control than they did. It was clearly closer to coming off the road than the Maserati. Hector was thrown this way and that, while Mrs Warp rattled like an old shop-window mannequin in an earthquake; she just did not know how to ride out the jolts.

'Hector, look at the sat-nav map,' shouted Dad, 'Choose some turnings. I don't want single-track lanes and I don't want anything too big and fast. I want wide but twisty lanes, then I can lose them.'

Hector focussed on the map and used the dial to zoom in. He was amazed by how fast it was. He shouted to go left at the next junction, and then turned right round in his seat to look at the pursuing BMW.

They sped down a hill and Hector saw another car parked near an entrance to a field. His jolt of fear quickly passed as he realised it was a farmer's pickup truck, not another assassin. The farmer was moving a flock of sheep across the road to another field.

'Ahhhh,' Dad exclaimed as the tyres shrieked and squealed with the effort of slowing the Maserati before it hit the sheep in the road.

'Left, left!' shouted Hector, 'Go left into the field!'

Dad turned in to the grass field the sheep had just left.

'Follow the hedge,' Hector shouted, 'There's another entrance near the truck.'

The car skidded along on the dry grass, dust flying behind them. An old sheepdog jumped down from the track and ran towards them barking. Dad turned back onto the road, just as the BMW sped past. They were too soon; the BMW driver had seen them. Just a moment longer and he might have assumed they were in front of the sheep.

Dad shot through onto the road and the Maserati roared back up the lane. Hector glanced behind to see the BMW reverse into the gap in the hedge and turn to pursue them. Mrs Warp was also looking backwards, but Hector noticed she had not turned her shoulders. Her head had simply rotated one hundred and eighty degrees. It was unpleasant to look at.

Hector laughed again. He simply loved the sound of the car as it raced.

'I cannot believe you're laughing,' said Dad, his voice slightly constrained as he concentrated on driving, 'Oh, no, no, no, no!' he went on to exclaim as he saw the road blocked by huge straw-laden tractor and trailer.

'Left, left,' shouted Hector, 'There's a farmyard. We can hide.'

Dad gunned the car round the corner into a large farmyard. Beyond several farm buildings was a large, ivy-covered farmhouse. Dad stopped the car behind one of the barns and turned the engine off.

'I've got a plan,' said Hector quietly.

'I thought we were going to hide,' hissed Dad, just as they heard the BMW enter the farmyard.

'Mrs Warp could get out, take the wheel off the BMW and we could drive off and leave her,' Hector suggested, reflecting again on how useful it was to have someone who did not matter; someone who could be abandoned without thought.

'Can you do that?' Dad asked of Mrs Warp.

'Yes,' said Mrs Warp, climbing from the car after Hector had shot out and opened the door for her as quietly as he could.

'Where is it?' Dad asked, 'I can't hear it.'

'It's there, there,' Hector whispered as he lay on the ground, looking through a gap in the barn, 'They're hiding in the barn waiting for us to come out.'

Mrs Warp walked calmly around to the front of the barn. Hector continued to look, despite Dad's hissed instructions for him to return to the car.

'She's entering the barn,' whispered Hector, 'They'll be confused to see a sweet old lady.'

There was a very loud metallic crunching and tearing noise.

'She's pulling the front wheel off; I meant the steering wheel,' said Hector very loudly, over the din.

'Yes, yes, I can tell. Get in the car Hector!' Dad insisted.

There was more crunching. It sounded as though Mrs Warp was rocking the car, trying the rip all of the steering gear and suspension around the wheel off. The car alarm went off with a loud whooping noise.

'The car's alarm has gone off,' shouted Hector.

'Yes. I know. I can hear it. Get in the car! Get in!' yelled Dad.

Mrs Warp rounded the corner, carrying a car wheel.

'We don't need the wheel!' yelled Dad, aware that Hector's plan was careering badly out of control.

Mrs Warp plonked the dirty wheel in the back of the Maserati and got in. Hector jumped in, and Dad started the engine just as Hector asked about the colour of the BMW.

'It was black,' said Dad loudly.

'I think the farmer has a dark blue BMW,' said Hector, as they left the farmyard and the black BMW that was waiting in the lane resumed its pursuit.

'What?' Dad shouted, as he looked at the BMW in his rear view mirror and roared up the lane.

'Well, the barn was dark,' said Hector, 'Simple mistake. Could have happened to anyone.'

'So we didn't disable the car, we just ripped the wheel from some farmer's car,' said Dad in a constricted voice as he concentrated on his driving.

'Yes, but I have another plan,' said Hector.

'What is it?' Dad shouted.

'Mrs Warp, throw the wheel at them,' Hector instructed.

Mrs Warp hurled the wheel out of the car. It was supposed to slide on the road, into the path of the BMW, which was then supposed to slip off into a hedge. The wheel bounced and crashed into the windscreen, before flying off into a ditch.

Hector was looking back at the dented and crazed windscreen. The driver had his head out of the window and was shouting something. He seemed very angry. It occurred to Hector that the driver and his companion might not be assassins, but could just be local idiots who wanted to race a Maserati. Nevertheless, thought Hector, better safe than sorry.

When they returned to the main road Dad took a chance and opted for the racing line, pulling wide onto the other side of the road. They were lucky; there were no other cars. The Maserati roared up the road until Dad braked heavily and turned right onto a slightly smaller road.

Dad was concentrating now. The BMW seemed even more out of control, but it was slipping back, disappearing from view. Dad and the Maserati were too fast on the curving roads. Then Hector saw something fly up.

'I think they're off the road,' said Hector.

Dad slowed down and dialled Andrè with their position so that Andrè could anonymously call the Fire service to report the accident. He briefly considered going back to check, but decided against it, just in case they were assassins and they had weapons.

By the time they got back to the Hall, Andrè, Mum, Kate and Nana were waiting for them. Mum hugged them all, even Mrs Warp, and Nana hugged Hector. Kate looked at her brother with dismay. Hector had never been in more danger of dying of happiness. He had just finished a glorious car chase in a Maserati. As far as Hector was concerned, life could not get any better.

As they all retreated to the kitchen, there was shouting from the utility room. Lord Rothwell was dressed only in boxer shorts. It looked as though he had gone to retrieve a pair of trousers from the tumble drier. Bandit had the trousers on the floor and was trying to kill them.

Lord Rothwell seemed annoyed, but nowhere near as angry as usual. He then stood in the kitchen and delivered a small lecture about honesty and theft, before accusing Kate and Hector of stealing some chocolates.

'Dunbar,' said Nana reproachfully, 'I do hope you have some evidence. Did you see them?'

'All of them were unwrapped neatly,' said Lord Rothwell, 'So it couldn't be your vile dog.'

'That just proves it was a human,' said Nana, 'It could have been you when you were drunk.'

'I do not get drunk,' said Lord Rothwell, 'and the chocolate box was left on the floor. They were my favourite orange chocolates. I never eat those quickly.'

'Dunbar,' said Mum, 'I will happily pay for the chocolates, if only to please you, but do not accuse my children without some very good evidence!'

The sentence had a finality to it that brought the matter to a very certain end.

A short while later Hector bounded towards the stairs, en route to change his clothes. Kate was with him and spotted something under the stairs.

It was brown, in a heap. It smelled of dog vomit and chocolate.

'How did it happen?' asked Will Thatcher, as he stared in the gloom of the barn.

'First,' said Adrian Jenkins, 'I was in the field and there was this car crash. I heard this very loud car and this other one racing. One of them crashed, and a wheel came flying into the field as I was there with my agronomist looking at the barley.'

'Me and Kevin Peterson, my agronomist, we looked for the car that had crashed, but couldn't see anything. Well, we couldn't work it out. How could a car lose a wheel and carry on? Then I said the wheel was the same as the one off my BMW. Fancy that. Fancy a car crashing with the same wheels as my car, but there being no car left.'

'How did your car crash?' asked Will Thatcher, waving his hand at the ruined BMW in the barn, 'It doesn't make sense. There's no scratches or anything. It's really, really smart, except for the wheel being ripped out, and half the front suspension, and all of the steering gear, and all this brake fluid and coolant everywhere and stuff. Other than that's it's like new.'

'Why would anyone rip the wheel off my car and throw it in my field?' And how could they do it?' asked Adrian Jenkins, 'They couldn't get any machinery in here to do that, and they'd need something to clamp the car?'

'Maybe they crashed your car and then dragged it back?' Will Thatcher suggested.

'How? How on earth could they do that?' asked Adrian Jenkins in a loud voice that betrayed his growing anger, 'How could you crash a car and get it back into this barn?'

'Strange times,' said Will Thatcher.

'Yes, you're right,' Adrian Jenkins agreed, 'Lord Rothwell came to see me a couple of days ago and asked me to sort out messages for him. Said the phones don't work and you can't trust the Post Office now. I'm wondering what'll happen next.'

CHAPTER SEVENTEEN

Turducken

The day did not start well. Hector was caught by Dad and Andrè sliding down the banister. Andrè seemed almost as cross as Dad. He made Hector stand in the corner with his arms outstretched until they really ached. Hector had protested to Dad that this was inhumane treatment. Dad just said that it was more humane than allowing him to kill himself in a fall from the top of the stairs.

Added to this there was a lot of shouting from Lord Rothwell. Today was the day when there would be a gathering at the Hall to launch the new season for his art gallery. There was to be a meal cooked by a well-known chef. He had proudly announced that only the top people from the art world were invited; the ones who mattered. Everything had to go as planned. Lord Rothwell would not accept a hair out of place.

'Unfortunately, Dunbar, you have rented the Hall to us,' said Mum as she surveyed him in the main hall, 'You seem to be double-booked.'

'Madam,' replied Lord Rothwell, 'This is my home. I own this great Hall and its lands.'

'No,' said Mum, 'Your family trust owns this Hall and the lands. You rented it to us, and so you cannot just start demanding that we get out of the way because you have a big launch party you only told us about the day before yesterday.'

Hector and Kate had been expecting this. Lord Rothwell was always rather dismissive of Mum, apparently believing her to be weak and quiet. In fact, Dunbar Hellstone believed that quiet was weak; that someone who was not constantly forthright and outspoken must be fragile and easily dominated. Hector and Kate knew that Mum was very polite and almost always held her tongue so that she could reflect upon things. Once pushed too far, however, Mum had few problems in turning the tables.

'You cannot prevent my launch!' shouted Lord Rothwell, his face angry and contorted.

'Yes we can,' replied Mum firmly, 'You were supposed to let us know the names of anyone visiting at least seven days in advance so they can be checked. We have a need for security, and this is why we are paying you such a large rent.'

'I will have my launch,' Lord Rothwell yelled.

'Not unless you can wind back time seven days, provide the names and get our permission for the event,' said Mum calmly, 'You signed up to this Lord Rothwell. You were very happy when you were accepting the money.'

'You stupid, stupid woman,' Lord Rothwell screamed, before stalking back to his rooms and slamming the door.

'I'll put the kettle on,' said Nana, who had been listening from the kitchen.

Twenty minutes later breakfast was underway when Lord Rothwell appeared again. He had a piece of paper. Kate glanced at it and saw a list of names.

Lord Rothwell apologised for his 'outburst'. He went on to explain how much he appreciated the money he had been paid, how much he valued the Trogg family despite their occasional differences, and how much the launch meant to his gallery. He begged and pleaded, and at one point seemed close to tears.

Mum took the list from Lord Rothwell and told him she needed ten minutes to find out if all of the names could be checked in time. Fifteen minutes later the launch was back on. Then came Lord Rothwell's most surprising confession.

'I think the easiest way to deal with this is to be frank,' Lord Rothwell began, 'It would be difficult for me to admit that I have rented the Hall out and so I have told some of the guests that I have some new servants.'

'You mean us?' asked Mum, incredulous.

'Yes,' Lord Rothwell replied, 'and I would be very grateful if you could wait on.'

'You're kidding?' said Mum, half laughing.

'What does that mean?' Hector asked.

'He wants your Mum and Dad to be waiters and serve the drinks,' Nana explained, a grin from ear to ear.

'I'll do it,' Hector blurted out, 'I've always wanted to be a waiter. Kate, Kate, you could do it. Kate, come on, it'll be fun.'

Lord Rothwell looked unhappy with this, but as he glanced at Mum and Dad it became apparent there was no prospect that they would act as waiters.

'I'll go along with your plan Dunbar,' said Dad, 'but I will not wait on your guests. Nor will I lie if I am asked directly by anyone.'

'I understand,' said Lord Rothwell, although anger was clearly brimming, ready to spill over. Kate reflected that Lord Rothwell was capable of controlling himself when he chose to.

'Can we be waiters?' Hector asked, 'Please, please, please!'.

Lord Rothwell, Mum and Dad agreed, although all clearly had a wide variety of concerns. Kate thought it could be either boring or quite fun. Hector was really looking forward to it.

After breakfast Mum appeared with a surprise gift for each of them. Clearly, this was to keep them occupied and out of the way. Kate had a small, inflatable pool. Hector had a bow and arrow.

Kate set up her pool on the grass behind the stables. She inflated the single ring at the top, rigged a hose pipe, and left it to fill. She returned to the kitchen to see if she could help Nana.

Hector decided to use the lawns between the Hall and the lake for his first experiments with the bow and arrow. He took the rubber ends off the arrows and fired all six. He then walked to pick them up. The bow was very pleasing, but the arrows less impressive. Hector was also unhappy that he had so few arrows. It would be better if he had thirty or forty arrows. After a few minutes his first impression was confirmed, and Hector reflected that he seemed to spend all of his time walking to pick up his six arrows.

Hector remembered the shed with the small tools. It had several crates of canes for supporting small plants, all about seventy centimetres long. As expected it was unlocked. The canes were in cases, but they opened more easily than he first expected.

Hector took one and fitted it to the bow. The cane had no notch into which the string could slot, but when he aimed, pulled back and released the cane flew much better than his arrows, despite the lack of feathers.

At first, Hector shot the canes at random around the lawn. Then he started using the first canes he had fired as targets. Best of all, he did not have to walk. There seemed to be thousands of canes in the shed.

An hour and a half later and Hector was growing bored. It was fun, but there was only so long you could spend on your own as Robin Hood or one of King Arthur's archers before it became tedious. The lawn was a sea of arrows. Hector collected twenty canes and returned them to the hut. There seemed to be thousands and thousands; far too many to collect.

Hector sat down just as Bandit appeared. As ever, Bandit had mud underneath him. As Hector put his hand out to stroke the muddy hound, Bandit lurched forwards, delivering a disgusting kiss. Hector shot backwards and wiped his mouth.

Bandit had very recently started attacking people like this. He would look like he was moving towards the person sniffing affectionately, and then dart his tongue into the victim's mouth as he checked for food. It was quick and utterly revolting, like being attacked by a vacuum cleaner with a tongue.

Hector decided to leave the canes and clean his teeth. Just the excuse he needed. He would collect the canes later. If he was lucky there was always a chance someone else might pick them up.

As Hector reached the door to the main hall he heard Lord Rothwell. He seemed to be speaking to Mike Jennings, the man from the British security services. Hector decided to wait and listen.

'Well you and I are cut from the same cloth,' said Rothwell, 'but this lot.'

'They seem quite pleasant,' said Mike Jennings.

'Yes, on the surface,' Lord Rothwell replied, 'but since they've arrived the shrubs have been cut down in the garden, I've had chocolates stolen, my Range Rover has been stolen. Suddenly, I find I'm mixing with the wrong sort.'

'Oh,' said Jennings, 'I'll bear it in mind.'

'As for that vile dog of theirs, it uses people as toilets, it steals food, it vomited all over my apartments, and it killed my favourite parrot.'

'I suppose dogs can be a nuisance,' replied Jennings, 'but he's not aggressive I think.'

'He is if you're a parrot,' said Lord Rothwell crossly.

'OK,' said Mike Jennings, clearly trying to bring the conversation to a close.

'And the boy's as bad,' said Rothwell, 'Dim, annoying, can't remember anything. Gets names wrong all of the time. I gave him a tour of the grounds and he fell in the lake.'

'Well, I suppose we have to make allowances,' said Jennings.

'Waste of public money trying to educate him,' Rothwell continued, apparently unaware of Mike Jennings' disinterest, 'The whole family are a grubby example of the worst that is produced by state-funded education and welfare.'

Hector decided that this was the point at which to appear.

'Hello Lord Brothmell,' he said cheerily.

'It's Rothwell, Rothwell!' shouted Dunbar Hellstone after a brief pause.

'Oh, I'm very sorry,' said Hector, 'I'm looking forward to being a waiter.'

Hector managed to skip as he made his way to the kitchen. He had noticed that the happier he appeared the angrier Lord Rothwell became.

'Hector, there you are,' said Nana, 'Just in time for a sandwich.'

Hector sat down next to Kate. They were crammed into a corner of the table, as the rest was being used by the chef, who appeared flustered.

'I still can't believe you wanted to be a waiter,' said Nana, 'but I'm sure you'll enjoy yourself.'

'You think I'll be OK?' Hector asked, 'I'll be good at it?'

'No, no,' replied Nana, 'I never said that. I said I was sure you would enjoy yourself.'

The chef looked over at Hector. He seemed angry. Both Hector and Kate were quite sure he did not approve of the choice of waiting staff.

'Even after all these years Dunbar surprises me,' said Nana, 'Ha, the cheek of the devil asking your Mum and Dad to be waiters. I'm going to enjoy telling that to everyone.'

Lord Rothwell's voice loomed out of the Hall. He was speaking with Ms Rogerson about the arrangements for the day.

'Ahh, good,' said Lord Rothwell, 'You are here together. We can go through the arrangements.'

Hector looked at Lord Rothwell as he was speaking and reflected that he was the only person he knew who could call Mum 'stupid' and twenty minutes later be begging her to act as a waitress as a special favour. He had the cheek of the devil.

What puzzled Hector was why the devil was so feared. If the devil was number 666, then what happened to the previous six hundred and sixty-five? Maybe the previous things were angels, and 666 was the bad one. The problem with this is that it made six an important number, and Hector remembered it was the seventh son of a seventh son who became a sorcerer. It should really be the sixth son of a sixth son. On the other hand, why not a daughter? In Hector's experience girls could be pretty mean.

These thoughts occupied Hector, which was unfortunate. He missed all of the instructions Lord Rothwell and Ms Rogerson provided. As they stopped speaking he realised he had no idea what he was supposed to do.

'Right then, off you go upstairs for a shower and a change into clean clothes,' said Ms Rogerson.

'Can I just finish please,' said Kate, pointing to her sandwich.

Lord Rothwell turned angrily and stalked off. Ms Rogerson followed.

'He seems extra touchy,' said Kate, with an unusual bluntness.

'I think he's anxious about the launch today,' said Nana, 'He has managed to get journalists and buyers from the modern art world here, so I suppose he doesn't want anything to go wrong.'

'I see,' said Kate, as resentment clearly rose within her, 'And we're not supposed to do anything to further dislodge the delicate imbalance of his mind.'

Nana laughed and even the chef smiled. Hector suspected that Kate had been reading bigger books; the ones he only used when he needed something to stand on.

An hour later Kate and Hector were being shown around the exhibits laid out in Lord Rothwell's rooms. They were dressed in the clothes Nana had selected for them. Mum came as well. She had at first seemed angry, but a short talk with Nana improved her mood. Nana had told her to relax and enjoy it, whatever happens.

The paintings were either colourful abstract shapes, or comprised dark cloudy depressed figures. The sculptures were strange, with one made up of metal bottle tops. Lord Rothwell started practising his speech on them and Hector quickly became bored.

Rothwell was mainly speaking to Mum and Ms Rogerson, and so Hector entertained himself playing with one of Lord Rothwell's executive toys. It consisted of a marble block with lots of metal pieces sticking up. The metal could be bent into all sorts of shapes.

'Thank you Dunbar,' said Mum suddenly, 'It is interesting, but I'm probably not the best one to listen to this.'

Lord Rothwell seemed annoyed and nodded curtly.

'I am going to help in the kitchen,' announced Mum, 'Trevor will help with anything that comes up.'

'Where's Andrè?' asked Hector, suddenly curious.

'He has things to do,' said Mum, while giving Hector a look, 'He is about.'

Hector understood that he was not to ask, at least not in front of Ms Rogerson or Lord Rothwell.

As the guests arrived it began to rain. It was not driving rain, but a gentle soaking half-mist. Soon the end of the lake could not be seen. Only the shadows of the huge trees broke the endless damp.

Mrs Warp emerged from her cupboard to take coats and hang them up. All of this was impressive, and Lord Rothwell was clearly pleased. He was less happy when several of the guests saw Mrs Warp close herself into the small cupboard. One of the guests had asked if she was alright. Lord Rothwell assured her that Mrs Warp was quite senile and enjoyed standing in a small cupboard with coats.

'If I could just have your attention,' said Lord Rothwell, 'This will be my virtual gallery's second summer season. I'm hoping it will be even more successful that our first summer season, three years ago.'

'I am so very excited by some of the pieces I have assembled. I'm sure you will be as well.'

'What's for lunch?' shouted a tall, willowy man dressed in a dark blue blazer. Everyone laughed.

'Marshall, Marshall. As ever the joker,' said Lord Rothwell, 'Ladies and gentlemen, I'm sure you all know Marshall Braithwell. His own gallery is still not virtual, but nevertheless worth a visit.'

'For lunch,' Lord Rothwell continued, 'I have hired in none other than Elan Greetespaun, the famed chef I know you will all be familiar with. He has prepared a variety of treats, as well as his world-renowned turducken.'

Hector and Kate were puzzled. Mum lent down and explained that it was a chicken, inside a duck, inside a turkey.

'Sounds like a bad road accident,' Kate muttered, who was never keen on meat, even when it had not been compressed into something unmentionable.

A short while later Kate and Hector were wandering around with drinks. They each had a tray filled with champagne glasses. Kate just seemed to do it well. Hector struggled. People would move when he did not expect them to, and as a result he almost tipped the tray over twice.

He decided to try balancing the whole tray on just one hand because he had see waiters on television carry trays of drinks like this. Ms Rogerson caught him just in time and made him carry the tray in two hands. Yet, Hector knew this would not work. Someone was going to bump into him and then it would be his fault that the drinks were all over the floor.

Kate was just starting to relax. The people were very kind. Although everyone was chattering about people they knew or about the art exhibits, everyone took time to thank her, and several people asked her about herself. Then Hector's voice boomed from the other side of the room.

'Coming through, coming through! Beep, beep. Come on, budge over.'

'How novel,' commented Marshall Braithwell, the man who had asked about lunch earlier.

'Well, I've got to,' said Hector, 'No one can see me and I've almost dropped the tray twice when some of you have stepped backwards. It would be easier if you all had lights and beepers like lorries when they are reversing.'

'I think that's a super idea,' said Marshall as the chatter of small-talk returned to the room.

'Do you think I could have a double gin and tonic with ice and a lime?' asked Marshall.

Hector thought about it.

'No chance,' he said shaking his head, 'by the time I get back to the kitchen I'll of forgotten the lot.'

'Oh,' said Marshall in rather a dramatic way, while folding his arms.

'Could you write it down?' Hector asked.

'I could come to the kitchen and tell them what I want,' Marshall suggested.

'Great idea,' Hector replied cheerily, 'This way.'

Ten minutes on Marshall had his gin and tonic. Hector had served more drinks, but was now speaking to quite a few of the guests. He was very happy to discuss the exhibits, and had even sent two guests back to the kitchen to get more drinks because he was heavily engaged in discussing art. Marshall was growing more interested in Hector's opinions.

'Do you know anything about this Hector?' Marshall asked, joining the group Hector was talking to.

'Oh, that's not an exhibit,' said Hector, 'It's an executive toy. Look, you can bend all of the bits of metal into all sorts of things, like planes or animals. There are three of them.'

Soon Hector had several people bending the metal wires into different shapes. The guests kept disappearing to get trays of champagne and Hector was thoroughly enjoying himself.

'Don't worry about any bits that break off,' Hector announced, 'Just leave them on the floor by the toy and we'll superglue them back on later.'

Lord Rothwell arrived just as Nana appeared.

'What are you doing?' Rothwell half-demanded and then choked back.

'Playing with your toys Dunbar,' said one of the guests, suddenly realising that they were, in reality, art exhibits and not toys.

Nana watched it all. As far as she was concerned Hector, Kate and everyone else seemed happy, with Dunbar being the expected exception. Nevertheless, it took her only moments to recognise that from Lord Rothwell's point of view, Hector's overconfidence was dangerously in play.

'Hector,' said Lord Rothwell slightly too loudly to be polite, 'I think it's time you served some of the hors d'oeuvre.'

Kate had been serving food for a few minutes, and passed Hector in the main hall with another full tray. Hector was immediately determined to get more food on his tray than Kate had managed.

The chef was busy with a dessert as Hector piled everything he could onto the largest tray he could find. Hector grabbed several small pots or dips, unaware that some of them were supposed to be added to food before cooking. The ginger, in particular, tasted horrible if eaten raw.

Hector staggered out of the kitchen, barely able to carry the tray. It tottered dangerously and Hector set it down on the main hall floor with a thump. Even Hector recognised that the tray was badly overloaded. He set some of the pots that had fallen over back the right way, and then began to push the tray across the floor of the hall.

As he reached the rooms where the guests were now listening to Lord Rothwell talk about the exhibits, Hector began to ask people to 'budge over,' and 'move along'.

'Is there something you wanted to say Hector?' asked Lord Rothwell, clearly angry to have been interrupted.

'Oh, sorry, yes. Grub's up! Well down actually, on the floor. I overloaded the tray. But don't worry, I guarded it all of the way and the dog and cat didn't get anywhere near it.'

Several guests laughed, while Marshall picked up the tray and set it on a table. Lord Rothwell was about to resume his speech, but Marshall got their first.

'Hector, you intrigued me with your opinions of the pieces earlier. It's so refreshing to have a new eye on these things.'

'I'm not sure Hector will have a useful opinion on anything here,' interrupted Lord Rothwell.

'Oh, come on Dunbar,' said Marshall, 'This is part of the excitement of modern art. It's the reactions it provokes, not just in us old fuddy-duddies, but also in the young, untrained eye.'

Lord Rothwell started to object, but Hector was well away with his opinions on the first piece.

'I'm not sure I like this one. It's just white with four dots. It's a bit boring. Also, they haven't been very careful because the artist has left hand prints and smudges on it.'

Kate looked again at the picture. She had seen it earlier, and it had been clean, pristine even. Now, however, Hector was correct. There were Hector-sized hand prints, only Hector had not appreciated they were his. No one had time to spot this however, as Hector had moved on to the next piece.

It seemed as though the damage Hector could accomplish with his hands was nothing compared to the destruction he could bring about with his opinions. Once started he was difficult to stop. The problem was not that he said deliberately unkind or critical things about the exhibits. Hector tried to pretend he liked them, but inevitably compared each one to something he had seen in school during art. As the seconds ticked by, and each exhibit was examined and discussed by Hector, the value of the painting or sculpture in the buyers' eyes diminished. Hector managed to make them all sound as if they had been created by young children during a wet playtime.

The only difficult moment for Hector was when he gave a glowing appraisal of a piece in the corner. It was mostly white, but with a blue translucent top containing water. He described it as clean, refreshing and exciting. Hector's laughter when it was pointed out that it was a water cooler, not an exhibit, merely added to the happy mood.

During all of Hector's in-depth analysis, Marshall Braithwell had remained mischievously curious and encouraging. Lord Rothwell looked white and hardly seemed to be breathing.

The shouting from the kitchen first alerted Trevor Trogg to the problem. When he arrived, the cat was on the table licking the cream from the top of a splendid gateau. This, however, was not the major problem. Otto's was merely a small crime of opportunity.

Bandit had his front feet on the kitchen table and was taking the meat from some sandwiches. The chef was clearly afraid of dogs, and quite unaware that all he had to do was grab Bandit by the scruff of the neck. Instead, he was trying to push Bandit with a brush. He was not pushing very hard and so Bandit thought it was a game he was winning easily.

Dad lunged, but Bandit ducked and scrabbled away. Otto was playing as well, there was food involved, it was a rough thrilling game. Bandit was wildly excited. He shot towards the chef who yelled and fell backwards. Bandit jumped clean onto the kitchen side behind the chef and seized the turducken; the turkey stuffed with a duck that had been stuffed with a chicken.

Dad slipped on the floor as he tried to grab the fleeing Bandit. The dog moved like lightening, scrambling to make the corner in the Hall. Bandit could not put the full power down on a slippery surface, but he could still outrun anything on two legs in a sprint.

Trevor Trogg raced out of the Hall, grabbing a dog lead from a table top on the way. There were two chauffeurs, but fortunately their backs were turned. They saw a man running, they did not see the dog. Bandit was hurtling towards the stables, but dropped the hot, heavy turkey. Dad advanced, but Bandit picked it up and made off again.

Bandit could run forever. Trevor Trogg did not really think he could possibly catch Bandit. As the chase continued, however, Bandit's weakness became obvious. The turkey was too hot to hold for long. All Bandit could do was sprint for a while and drop it.

As Bandit made his way past the stables, into the trees, and then back in a circle, the turkey was repeatedly grabbed, carried at high speed and then dropped, so that it rolled in the mud and bounced off trees. Trevor Trogg was out of breath and about to give up. The problem was that Bandit was heading back to the Hall. There was every possibility that he would parade his prize and try to invite more of a chase.

Bandit began to run across the lawn, in full view of the windows filled with Lord Rothwell's guests. What impeded him were all of the canes sticking out of the lawn. He turned sharply as he saw Dad loom into view. He dropped the turkey again and it rolled, hitting the wall of the Hall with a splat.

Bandit dashed for the turkey, but Trevor Trogg was going for it as well. It was a misjudgement. Bandit did not realise that Dad was not really aiming for the turkey, he was really aiming for Bandit. Dad had decided to go for the place where Bandit was shortly going to arrive, rather than head straight for Bandit.

There was a horrifying moment for Bandit as he braked desperately to avoid the outstretched hand aiming for the scruff of his neck. The problem was that his brakes had never really matched his acceleration. It was an area of physical performance that had never much bothered him. He braked late and sometimes he hit things. That was how Bandit moved. Now, however, it had all gone wrong. He would have to deploy the big, sad brown eyes.

Trevor Trogg rested against the wall of the Hall, just under one of the windows to Lord Rothwell's rooms, where so many of the guests were eating and discussing the art exhibits. Bandit had returned to his happy look, despite now being on a lead. He liked games of tug, and while he was disappointed to lose the giant roast bird thing, he had hopes Trevor Trogg might throw it for him.

The turkey was still hot. It steamed; even the bits covered in mud. Dad inspected it, hoping it could be cleaned up. The mud and dog saliva might wipe off, but the obviously dog-sized bite marks everywhere were impossible to disguise. The turkey had been too hot for Bandit to hold for long, so he had repeatedly dropped it and picked it up again. When it was dropped he was usually travelling at speed, and so it had bumped into trees, shrubs and walls. The more he looked at it, the more convinced he became that it could not be salvaged. He needed to hide it in the bin.

Yet, both ways around the Hall to the bins were blocked by people. Several people were stood, drinking and chatting under large umbrellas, on the steps to the entrance overlooking the lake. If he went the other way there were at least a couple of chauffeurs, but also quite possibly some of Lord Rothwell's guests.

Trevor Trogg closed his eyes and wished he had never set eyes on Bandit. He would have to go across the lawn to the trees and then wedge it up a tree so that Bandit could not drag it back in again. He did think about throwing it in the lake, but Bandit would probably swim out to it. He also thought about attaching Bandit's lead to a tree, but Bandit would bark and might escape. To add to his problems, the path across the lawn was impeded by vast numbers of small plant canes. He was still puzzled as to how they got there.

As the guests moved about, Dad stole glances up into the room. He was trying to work out when the best time would be for him to make his move. The training was working, however, as he was not going to scurry or skulk. He intended to walk quickly, but purposefully, as if he had every right to be walking across a cane-filled lawn looking for a tree in which he could hide someone else's lunch.

'And what would be your valuation of these exhibits Hector?' Marshall Braithwell asked.

'Hard to say,' said Hector, 'They're all very good, but it would have been better if more of them were made of wood, that way you'd have something to pop on the fire at Christmas once you'd finished with them.'

Hector had clearly not appreciated that the exhibits were pieces of art, intended to last forever, or at least many years. He had assumed they were kept until shortly after the Christmas Fair.

'I think my valuation,' said Hector loudly, completely undaunted by the look of horror and waving hands from the suddenly animated Lord Rothwell who was stood behind everyone, 'would be nothing. Nothing at all. My old class at school would happily knock you up a load of bits like this for free in just a couple of art lessons.'

'Well, what an informative and original analysis,' Marshall Braithwell began, before being interrupted by Hector.

'Ohh look, there's my Dad,' said Hector pointing through the window at his father on the lawn, 'What's he doing?'

Everyone looked as Trevor Trogg walked quickly across the lawn, stepping from side to side to avoid the hundreds of small canes. He seemed to be carrying something heavy. Bandit jumped up, lunging playfully for the giant turkey, causing it to roll to the ground.

Hector saw Dad pull Bandit back on the lead and then bend down to pick the turkey up. Bandit dashed forwards, grabbing the turkey, ready for another fight. Dad fell over just as Bandit made a run with the turkey. Dad's arm seemed to be half yanked from its socket as Bandit reached the end of the lead.

Kate guessed immediately that Dad was trying to dispose of the turkey without being seen. There was still hope. The guests might not realise that the giant, heavy, flesh-coloured ball was their lunch. She racked her brains trying to think of some way of distracting everyone into looking at the art exhibits. The problem was that Hector had already ruined everyone's interest in the art, and now Dad and Bandit were ruining lunch.

Kate turned to point to one of the exhibits, determined to ask about the artist. Her eyes scanned the room. Everyone was transfixed. There was no chance that they would turn away and stop watching. The only hope was that they might not realise what Dad and Bandit were trying to wrestle from one another.

'Gosh, that looks like a battle,' said Marshall Braithwell, 'I wonder what they're fighting over.'

'It's a turducken,' said Hector, 'It's a turkey, stuffed with a duck, and the duck was stuffed with a chicken. I think it was your lunch.'

Dad had got to his feet and pulled Bandit to him on the lead. Each time he tried to lean down to get to the turkey Bandit lurched forwards. In desperation Dad kicked the turkey towards the trees, and then followed it closely so he could kick it again. Bandit was on a tight lead.

The whole room watched as Dad repeatedly kicked lunch. Bits began to fall off, and Bandit lurched towards them, determined that Otto would not get anything. The turkey had already been battered in the chase with Bandit, and its structural integrity was never going to be good enough for a dog versus human game of rugby. Bandit then started to lick Dad's right foot, which had a few bits of turkey spread across the shoe. Dad fell over and Bandit tried to escape again.

'Is that really our lunch?' asked an older woman in a blue dress with matching ear-rings.

'It was your lunch,' said Hector in a matter-of-fact tone, 'I'm not sure I'd want to eat it. Our dog has had his teeth all over it, and our dog eats cat poo.'

Inside Kate was screaming. She wanted to cover her eyes and yet she could not look away. Most of all she wanted Hector to fall silent.

Hector on the other hand was relaxed. He liked giving his opinion on the art. He liked Marshall Braithwell. He was enjoying himself. In addition, he was fairly sure he had done nothing wrong. It might be a total disaster, Bandit would probably be tied to a stake and shot at dawn, but Hector was in the clear.

Dad had fallen over again. He was becoming rather muddy, and was trying to gather bits of the disintegrating turkey in his arms. Bandit was trying to grab bits and eat them. Dad then tried holding Bandit down with a leg, but Bandit circled him, wrapping the dog lead around.

'I know he doesn't look very dignified at the moment,' said Hector, 'but Dad's really nice most of the time.'

'Why is he taking our turkey into the woods?' the woman asked.

'Don't know,' replied Hector, 'He had a good breakfast. I don't think he's hungry.'

'Do you think there might be sandwiches?' the woman asked hopefully.

'Not in the woods,' said Hector.

'I'm sure Nana will be able to make some sandwiches,' said Kate, trying to rescue things.

'But you'll have to get them before the cat does,' Hector added.

'Oh, thank you for that bit of advice,' said the woman, who glanced around at Marshall Braithwell and grinned.

Kate glanced at Lord Rothwell. He was white. He seemed to be in a strange state between anger and despair. She had expected shouting.

Trevor Trogg reached the woods. He and Bandit both had hold of the turkey. It looked like a joint effort, but there was really no co-operation. Bandit had been distracted by the fact that it had cooled on the outside and tasted nice. Dad was just pleased to get the turkey and Bandit out of sight. He was praying he had not been seen.

Once the turkey was finally wedged in a tree out of reach, Trevor Trogg sat down in the rain. Bandit sat down beside him, but looked up at the turkey. How had it come to this? At breakfast he could not possibly have guessed that he would be mud wrestling a labrador for a turkey. The problem, he reflected, was that despite his size and strength he was badly outclassed. Bandit was a natural mud wrestler.

The various guests were milling in the main hall. Marshall Braith-well approached Kate, Hector and Mum.

'I would just like to say that I have never been to such a marvel-lous launch,' he said with a grin, 'The art's dreadful, I suspect the food disappeared into that dog, but I haven't had such an enjoy-able time for quite a while now. Thank you so very much for a truly memorable day.'

Hector beamed. It might be the end of Lord Rothwell's art gal-lery, but Hector had enjoyed himself. Marshall Braithwell had been very kind to him. All in all, a top day.

By the evening Lord Rothwell was upset, shouting and drunk. He kept staggering around and calling for Bandit.

'Come on Bandit, come to death, Lord Rothwell's going to shoot you,' he yelled.

'He'll have to wait his turn in the queue,' said Dad, while sat at the kitchen table playing whist with Nana and Mum, 'I want first go.'

'As for you Hector Trogg, Hector Trogg, Hector Trogg, Hector Troll, troll, troll! I'm going to drown you!'

As Lord Rothwell became more threatening Andrè and Mike Jennings disappeared outside to check that Rothwell had nothing sharp or dangerous. Dad had wanted Lord Rothwell's gun cabinet emptied just in case he found a way of breaking the lock off. Andrè confessed that the gun cabinet had been empty for some time; he had taken the liberty of removing the guns just after Lord Rothwell had agreed to it being locked.

Kate was slightly worried by Lord Rothwell. He shouted and threatened. Andrè, Mike Jennings and Dad were all reassuring. When she thought about it, Nana and Mum were quite capable of sorting Lord Rothwell out. Nevertheless, it was unsettling.

'Would it help if I said I was sorry?' Hector asked, just before bedtime.

'No!' everyone answered in unison.

Kate and Hector laid in bed. On the whole, Kate had enjoyed the day. The people to whom she had served drinks had been very pleasant; fun even. Hector had provided some shocking moments, but now she looked back at the calamities and thought they were funny. Lord Rothwell deserved his bad luck.

There was a yell and a scream of rage from the grounds. Hector and Kate ran to their window to look. There was the sound of people running. It looked like Dad, Andrè and Mike Jennings. Lord Rothwell was screaming and dripping, slipping and splashing. He had fallen into Kate's inflatable pool.

CHAPTER EIGHTEEN

Spirits

The first part of the morning was a grubby affair. Hector and Kate both rose early and went to explore the Hall's hollow walls. This had been planned for some time, but they had needed an opportunity to be in the house and yet remain unwatched. Kate had the idea of exploring before breakfast. They used the entrance in the bedroom opposite their own.

The space between the walls was rough; the width varied. The Hall did not look as robust and well made from the inside of the wall. There were scaffolding plank walkways connected with wooden ladders. There were pipes, wires and dust everywhere. There was mortar, like frozen stone dripping from the cracks between bricks.

As Kate and Hector walked along the plank paths they would meet blocks in their way. They would have to climb a ladder up or down to go further. Sometimes blocks were close to other blocks above and they could only make progress by crawling. It was as if someone had built the inner and outer walls of the Hall and then pushed large brick blocks into the wall.

'Oh,' said Kate, 'I've just realised. They're windows. The blocks are windows and outside doors.'

'They're hard to climb over,' Hector complained. He had already scraped himself in several places.

For some time they explored. Kate was becoming slightly worried that they were lost. After a while, however, the shape of the

Hall became obvious to both her and Hector. They understood which rooms they were next to. Hector noticed other small doors and realised there were several ways into the hollow walls.

Hector was starting to become bored. It was all bricks, pipes, dust and wires. There was nothing to see. He had been intrigued when they were in the wall beside Lord Rothwell's rooms. Nevertheless, the dust, wires, pipes, bricks, planks and ladders were just the same as the other places.

Kate motioned to another door. Beside it were packages wrapped in black plastic bags. These were less dusty. Immediately, Hector and Kate were intrigued. As if on cue music drifted through the wall. Kate and Hector looked at each other. Both recognised it as the dreadful modern music Lord Rothwell liked to play. It was all the confirmation they needed.

'Let's be rats,' said Hector, as he burrowed his fingers into the plastic wrapping, making a hole. Kate was unsure. She was never as quick to make a decision as Hector. Hector saw himself as bold. Kate thought he was reckless.

They both shone their torches. The thing inside was all yellow. It looked like a painting.

'What should we do?' Kate asked.

'Tell Andrè,' said Hector, quite certain.

'Then we'll be in trouble.'

'No, Andrè said he wouldn't tell as long as we didn't put ourselves in danger.'

'What will we tell him?' Kate asked.

Hector had to think about this. It was odd, but he could not work out why he thought their find was peculiar.

'I don't know,' said Hector, after a few moments.

Once Kate and Hector were back in their room they both had a shower. Hector had objected at first. Kate had not argued, but just pointed to the mirror. Hector found himself looking at a chimney sweep. It was him, but it looked as though he had been taken on a face down whirlwind tour of a vegetable patch by Bandit.

As they arrived in the kitchen Nana produced breakfast. Kate was beginning to suspect that she had magical powers; her timing was perfect.

'Queer kind of morning. Sort of morning for spies and quislings of all sorts,' said Nana.

'Yes, I suppose,' said Mum, trying to look interested.

'I've been thinking,' Nana continued, 'What sort of queer, curious mess are we in? It's all questions, questions, questions.'

'What do you mean?' Mum asked.

'All this danger, all this trouble, and the art fiasco. Quintessentially, Dunbar's a fool.'

'I told you,' whispered Kate, 'P the other day and Q today. She's very attached to the alphabet.'

Hector had to reluctantly concede. Nana was lovely, but she was fundamentally potty.

'Oh dear, oh dear, oh dear,' said Nana, 'If the place is going to be attacked then Dunbar really ought to be leading the defence.'

'Is he any good?' Hector asked immediately.

'No, not really,' Nana replied, turning away from the sink to face them all, 'but I reckon it would be dangerous. I think conflicted souls like Dunbar should die in battle.'

Hector suppressed a smile while Kate looked at Mum. Unfortunately, she seemed to have been surprised by this and could think of nothing to say.

Hector appreciated that Nana meant that Lord Rothwell should die in any sort of battle, even one involving a large set of clothes in an overloaded tumble dryer.

Fortunately, Andrè appeared. Unfortunately, he had a question for Dad about encryption. Dad had been explaining the mathematics of hiding messages. In particular, he was keen on repeatedly encrypting messages because this meant that the early stages of breaking an encryption did not have a recognisable goal state. Everyone was bored.

Hector and Kate got up to leave, but Andrè said they should stay as he needed a word. Once Dad had finished his explanation and Andrè made sure he understood it all, Andrè turned to his more pressing matter.

'As you all know the new safe room is accessed using a thumb print. I have an access list here,' said Andrè, producing several sides of A4 paper.

'Trevor and Sarah, you have accessed the room twice each. I have been in there fourteen times. Kate you have entered five times. So thank you all for making sure you can get in.'

'Hector,' Andrè continued, 'You have entered the room one hundred and forty three times.'

'I wanted to be really sure it works,' said Hector brightly.

'Also, I found this bag of sweets in the corner of the room,' Andrè continued, producing a scruffy paper bag. 'Hector, it is not your private sweet storage area.'

'OK,' said Hector, still unabashed, 'I'll do my best.'

'Hector,' said Andrè, 'Stop playing with the fingerprint reader.'

'And just one more question Hector,' said Andrè, 'Mrs Warp reports someone repeatedly calling her name, but when she checks no one is there.'

'Can't say I've heard anything,' Hector replied, looking earnest.

'Mrs Warp has played the message to me, and it is your voice. I think you have been calling her and disappearing into the safe room.'

'Hector,' said Dad, 'You've been warned about playing with Mrs Warp.'

'Sorry,' said Hector. Of course, Hector was only sorry that he had been caught.

As Andrè left Hector followed him out and indicated that he had something private to discuss.

'Andrè,' said Hector in the tone used by children all over the world who are about to either ask for something they are not permitted or confess to a crime, 'I've done something I don't want Dad to know about.'

Andrè looked at him. Andrè's shoulders sagged as a wealth of possible disasters crossed his mind.

'Have you dug a tunnel and undermined the Hall?' Andrè asked, 'Have you constructed a bomb using the compost heap?'

'No, no,' said Hector relieved and suddenly laughing.

'Is Lord Rothwell on fire? Have you managed to drain the lake?' Andrè continued.

'No, but they're good ideas,' said Hector, 'I've found something.'

Ten minutes later Andrè was inside the hollow walls with Hector, opening all of the parcels. He photographed each piece of art and then repackaged it. Hector was struck by how calm and purposeful Andrè was. Hector had to hold a plastic bag for the old packaging. If Lord Rothwell had appeared at his small door they would have been caught, but this did not seem to bother Andrè too much.

'What do you think they are?' Hector asked as they ascended through the hollow wall after completing their task.

'They may just be works he wishes to hide in case there is a break in,' said Andrè, 'Or they could be stolen. I will assume they are legitimate, but I will get our people to check them. We already know that Rothwell is heavily in debt. If he has connections with the criminal world this could be a problem.'

'Will you arrest him?' Hector asked, completely failing to disguise his feelings of hope and glee.

'No, I am afraid not. I will have to tell your father though.'

'Oops,' said Hector.

'I will tell him I was checking around. I won't mention you,' said Andrè.

'Oh, thanks,' said Hector.

'Hector, please, please think before you act,' said Andrè, 'If you had fallen who knew where you were?'

'Kate was with me.'

'Still, if you had both fallen you could have died. I would have assumed you had been kidnapped.'

'But we have the locators,' Hector argued, 'You can track us.'

'Yes,' said Andrè, 'But still. There is no point in me protecting you from Sludge if you manage to kill yourself. And do not say anything about the locators aloud. I do not want Mike Jennings, Rothwell or anyone else to know.'

By the time Hector had emerged from yet another shower it was almost time for lunch. Hector had argued about the shower, but Andrè was adamant; he did not want anyone to know he and Hector had been inside the Hall's walls.

As Hector made his way down the stairs he noticed the kitchen was strangely dark. There were hushed mutterings, and at times an almost tuneful half-chant or hum. The door was pulled to; the curtains were drawn; a single flickering candle illuminated the room. As ever, sensitive to the situation, Hector barged in and asked about lunch.

'My friend here is just looking into your future,' said Nana, in a slightly disapproving tone Hector completely missed.

'Great,' said Hector, 'Does it include a chocolate cake?'

'You're disturbing the astral plane,' said a woman on the opposite side of the table to Nana.

The woman had long hair. She had a scarf over her head. Her earrings glittered in the candlelight. She was looking at him, but Hector could not see her eyes. He began to look around the shaded corners of the kitchen.

'You cannot see the spirits,' said the woman, in a very posh, ghostly voice.

'I'm looking for Astrid Plane,' Hector explained, suddenly suspecting that the strange woman might be called Astrid.

'This is my friend Wendy,' Nana began, 'She's a medium. She's going to summon her spirit guide and see what's in our futures.'

'Would you like to join the circle?' Wendy asked in her mystic voice.

'OK,' said Hector, sitting between Mum and Kate. Wendy, Kate, Nana and Mum were already touching hands.

Over the next few minutes Wendy led them in a series of deep breathing exercises. Everyone except Hector had their eyes closed. Fortunately, Kate was not much bothered about touching Hector's hand, and so he took advantage of the dark to eat each of the small cakes on a large plate next to him. He realised he had been rather lucky, it was the only plate on the table. It had occurred to him to offer them around, but they were very tasty and he did not want to disturb the mysterious but apparently absent Astrid Plane.

As Hector was the only one who did not have his eyes closed he studied the others. Mum looked her usual worried self and wore a slight frown. Kate had her head back and seemed to be almost smiling. Nana lent forward slightly. Wendy was bolt upright. Mum, Kate, Nana and Wendy breathed deeply; Hector munched cakes as quietly as possible.

After a while Hector was growing restless. There had been a lot of cakes, but Hector had worked his way doggedly through all of them. Now, he was bored.

'What happens next?' Hector asked, affecting a loud stage whisper.

'I summon my spirit guide,' said Wendy, in her mystic but now slightly tetchy voice.

'She has to meet her spirit guide on the astral plane and ask him to join us,' said Nana, 'Wendy's guide is an American Indian called Little Hop.'

Wendy sighed in a slightly irritated way, but this did not stop Nana adding a further thought.

'These spirit guides, they always seem to be native Americans, never recently deceased lavatory attendants or odd job men.'

'We need to relax our bodies and open our minds to the spirit world,' said Wendy, trying to quell Nana.

'Plumbers are good at opening things up,' Nana continued, 'You should see the mess they can make when they unblock things.'

'Please Kath,' said Wendy sharply, now with a touch of a Yorkshire accent, 'we need to let our minds go blank. We need to be calm and comfortable. We need to be in touch with our senses.'

After several more minutes of silence Wendy reminded them all that the circle should not be broken. Hector decided that it was better not to mention that he and Kate had not touched hands. In any event, Nana had just sneaked off to turn the flame under a pan down. Unaware of this, Wendy led them all in a chant.

'Our beloved Little Hop, we ask that you commune with us and move among us. Our beloved Little Hop, we ask that you commune with us and move among us.'

This chant went on for around three minutes, before Wendy said quite dramatically, 'Are you with us Little Hop? Knock once for yes and twice for no.'

Hector did as he was told and knocked once.

'Oh, that was quick,' whispered Nana.

No one else had knocked and Hector realised it was the spirit that was supposed to knock, not him. He was then temped to knock twice to correct his mistake, but could see that if the spirit was not present it would be difficult for it to knock twice for no.

'Welcome Little Hop,' said Wendy, 'And thank you for entering our world.'

'Ohh yes,' Nana added, 'Hello Little Hop.'

'At the table today is a troubled family; a mother and her two beloved children, Kate and the boy,' Wendy continued, evidently unaware of Hector's name.

'Hello Little Legs,' said the boy, 'My name's Hector.'

'Please knock once Little Hop,' said Wendy, emphasising the name in the hope that Hector would not call her guide Little Legs again, 'if you can help guide this troubled family?'

Nothing happened, so Hector knocked once under the table.

'Little Hop,' Wendy continued, 'Please accept this plate of cakes as a small token of our love and appreciation.'

Hector was pleased everyone had their eyes shut. He had not realised the cakes were for the spirit. He speculated on how many knocks it would take to say, 'Don't worry about it, I'm not hungry, maybe Hector could eat them for me,' He could have used morse code, as Andrè had made he and Kate practice it until they could both send and receive messages accurately. The problem was that the message would involve a lot of knocking and only Kate had any chance of understanding the answer.

'Beloved Little Hop,' said Wendy, 'do you wish to take possession of my body so you can speak through me?'

There was silence.

'Knock once for yes and twice for no,' Wendy added.

Hector knocked twice.

'Hmm, right,' said Wendy, clearly ruffled by this refusal, 'Sarah, is there a question you want to ask?'

Mum's face creased with doubt. She hesitated.

'Will we all live through the attack?' Mum asked, in a faltering voice.

In his haste to knock once for yes, Hector knocked twice, and then in panic added a third, louder knock. There was a sharp intake of breath from Mum.

'These questions are difficult ones,' said Wendy, 'Maybe if you entered my body you could explain using my voice.'

Hector knocked once.

'Does this mean you want to enter and commune?' Wendy asked.

Hector knocked again, just one knock.

Wendy threw her head back, exhaled all of the air in her body, and then breathed deeply. After a pause of several seconds she spoke in a deeper voice.

'I am Little Hop. I can see your future.'

'What is our future?' Mum asked in a small voice after a pause.

'There are several possible paths,' continued the voice of Little Hop, 'but two shine brightly.'

Everyone waited for Little Hop to continue. After a while Hector spoke.

'Could you tell us about the two paths please.'

'In the first path one of your family will be lost when he who has no soul arrives,' said Little Hop.

'I suppose that must be Sludge,' said Hector brightly, 'and how many of us die on the other path?'

'If the soul of the family dies then all will perish,' said Little Hop, 'A terrible end is carried to my nostrils by the breezes of fate and destiny.'

'That's the cat,' said Hector, 'I think he's just burnt his tail on the fire again.'

'You seem unconcerned for your family's fate young warrior,' said Little Hop, 'Do you have a question for me?'

'Yes,' Hector replied, 'How do submarines work?'

'Hector!' said Mum, just as Otto jumped on the table.

'And Otto wants to know when he'll be fed,' Hector continued.

'Hector is a child and his rudeness is of no consequence,' said Little Hop. 'The cat knows his future well enough. He can see me as well as hear me.'

'Is there a path where none of us dies?' asked Mum hopefully.

'Yes,' replied Little Hop, 'and it is the one where Hector meets his true love.'

'I don't want to meet my true love,' declared Hector indignantly.

'You already have,' said Kate, 'Just look in the mirror.'

'Well, well, well,' said Nana, interrupting them all, 'That's been very informative Little Hop. Thank you very much, but it's time for you to leave. We have to break the circle because I've got to get lunch on.'

Nana stood up, scraping her chair much more than was necessary. Kate realised it was to let Wendy know that the circle had been broken. Hector noticed this as well, and was very tempted to point out that the circle had never been made.

'Oh my,' said Wendy with a start, 'Have I missed anything?'

'No, I don't think you have,' Nana replied.

As Nana busied herself around the kitchen, Mum and Wendy chatted about Little Hop, the spectral plane and life as a medium. Hector kept giving his sister knowing looks. He was desperate to tell her that he had been the one knocking under the table. Kate had already worked this out.

Soon Hector and Kate were setting the table, and Mum had the job of seeing Wendy out. There was a brief scream when Wendy went to retrieve her coat and discovered Mrs Warp stood in the hall cupboard, but Wendy was soon in her Fiat Panda grinding up the drive and out of the way.

'How long have you been interested in mediums and holding a séance?' Kate asked Nana.

'Ever since Wendy took it up,' said Nana, 'Always a bit of fun, but I don't take it seriously. Complete tosh really.'

'Of course, at first Wendy was very convincing,' Nana continued, 'Then I noticed that all of the predictions were pretty much the same stuff. Nothing you could pin down.'

'Now, she did once tell me that Dunbar would die when he was thirty five in an accident with a bee hive. Gave me false hope for quite a while that one, not to mention a painful hobby.'

'What hobby?' asked Hector.

'I started keeping bees,' said Nana, 'Thought I ought to try and tweak the odds.'

After lunch Kate noticed that Henry had appeared. The strange French soldier had been lodging with the two gardeners, Douglas and Gary Hepstall. He had cut down a good number of the larger shrubs in the garden, much to Lord Rothwell's annoyance. Henry was not a popular character. Now he was waiting outside.

Mike Jennings and Andrè joined Henry. Andrè glanced through the window and caught Kate's gaze. He gave her a reassuring nod. Kate felt a knot tighten in her stomach. A belief, a feeling like cast-iron certainty settled upon her. It was the end game.

Dad went outside to invite Mike Jennings in. Once Mike had a cup of tea, Hector lost no time telling Mike all about the séance, and Kate revealed that it had been Hector knocking. Mum seemed outraged, but Nana thought it was very funny. Mike was kind enough to explain how submarines work. He revealed that he had served on two submarines, and even escaped from a submarine hatch in an exercise.

Kate, however, found it difficult to be part of the conversation. She felt that trouble was looming. She guessed that Andrè was briefing Henry. These were the instructions for the final phase. Sludge and his band of thugs were on their way.

To everyone's surprise Edward Grantham appeared. The kitchen seemed rather full. Nana greeted him warmly, and it was apparent from Mum and Dad's reaction that they knew him rather better than Kate might have expected.

'I'll do this,' said Edward to Dad.

Kate and Hector looked up. Kate was anticipating bad news. Hector was expecting to be allowed to drive a tractor.

'I reckon you've got some trouble coming. When Bandit runs into harms way, are you going to protect him?'

'Yes,' said Hector and Kate together.

'And is he an obedient dog?'

'No,' both said together.

'So, when he runs out into danger he might drag you into it with him, don't you think?' Edward Grantham asked.

'No, no,' said Kate, realising what was being proposed before Hector truly appreciated the question. Both suddenly saw that Bandit was with Edward, on a lead.

'Bandit, is a thief, a marauder, a digger, an escaper, and the less said about the exhumation of that damn parrot the better,' Edward continued, 'But, he is a lovely dog. He's affectionate, he's fun, there's no malice in him, and I think you two love him, as you should.'

'He's our dog,' Kate declared, tears in her eyes.

'He is,' said Edward, 'But he's also a weakness. I don't want to hear about some criminal putting a bullet in him, and so until this is over your dog is going to stay with me.'

'Dad!' Hector exclaimed, appealing for help.

'I'm sorry,' said Dad, 'Edward is completely right.'

'I'll look after him, don't you worry,' said Edward.

'Even if we don't survive?' Kate asked. The room stopped, as if time had been held and the ice had formed all around them. Edward seemed trapped, unable to speak. Nana broke the spell.

'Well, first, if we all do as André tells us we will survive,' she said, 'and second Edward is a good man and would look after Bandit even if something terrible happened, which it won't.'

'Yes,' said Edward, 'Now, is my word good enough for you?'

Both Hector and Kate agreed, aware that they had agreed to
Bandit's exile as they accepted Edward's promise.

After Bandit and Edward had left the mood was sombre. Kate had
cried and Hector hid his face. It was as if a light had been removed
from the Hall. Bandit was a source of utter joy and mayhem. There
was definitely something liberating about the innocent, four-
legged pirate.

Kate left for the bedroom, but was caught by Andrè. He persuaded her to sit half-way up the stairs with him.

'I'm sorry Kate,' said Andrè, 'this was my idea.'

'Whenever anything was wrong I could always hug Bandit,'
said Kate.

'Even when he'd been in the mud?'

'He made me smell,' Kate replied, laughing a little through the
tears.

'How would you feel if you never saw him again?' Andrè asked,
'When they come they will shoot him or use him to kill you and
Hector.'

'This is all Irvine Deed's and Sludge's fault,' said Kate bitterly.

'When we lost Pierre I was consumed with hate,' said Andrè,
'We haven't lost Bandit. He's been sent somewhere safe; just another brown labrador they will never come across, until we can
bring him back.'

'You must really miss Pierre,' said Kate, 'I wish he was here.'

'So do I,' said Andrè, 'He was a great friend, but I only really
missed him when I stopped hating Sludge.'

They sat is silence for a few seconds, before Andrè got out his
notebook and showed Kate a poem he had written out..

'I wrote this down. I wanted to practice my English, and I needed to get it out of my system.'

When my wave of vengeance has passed

And I can look upon my enemy and understand him

And I can offer my hand, and not care how many times I am turned away

Then I will have conquered his towering shadow

And all that will be left of him is the small lost boy

'It's very good,' said Kate, unsure as to what it really was, 'Although, I'm not sure I can see Sludge as a small boy.'

'He was once,' Andrè replied.

'You're not really going to offer to shake hands with him are you?'

'No, I'm going to kill him, but the poem made me feel better.'

An hour later they were all gathered around the kitchen table. Andrè was uncharacteristically blunt.

'Lord Rothwell has some stolen art hidden in the hollow walls of the Hall,' said Andrè, 'He will be in touch with some criminal intermediaries and we should assume that he has the potential to betray our efforts. I do not want him alerted. I am going to feed him some false information.'

'Sludge is aware of our location,' Andrè continued, 'He is hiring some local thugs and will attack next Saturday according to our intelligence. Until then we will practice.'

'Why next Saturday?' Nana asked.

'Probably because the police will be stretched on a Saturday night. They respond best between nine and five I believe,' Andrè explained.

'Two other assassins were hired a month ago, but both have been killed by Sludge, who lured them to a meeting to agree on cooperating. We think that other family members hired them. It looks like Irvine Deeds was not the family's only skunk. In some ways this is good. Once we have taken care of Sludge you will be too risky a target to attack. I think that is it,' Andrè finished.

'Mrs Warp,' Dad prompted.

'Oh yes,' said Andrè, 'Because he is so dangerous, Mrs Warp has been programmed to attack Sludge and kill rather than just re-strain him. If she goes wrong stay out of her way.'

'I'll put the kettle on then,' said Nana, getting to her feet.

'I miss Bandit,' said Hector.

'We all do,' said Nana.

It all looked very serious. Bandit had gone and there was a week left before Sludge arrived.

CHAPTER NINETEEN

Lincolnshire Moon

Hector woke up early. Kate slept in. He and Dad drove down to Caistor in the Bentley before breakfast. Andrè was convinced there would be spotters in Caistor watching the shops. He wanted Dad to be photographed. The aim was to appear relaxed, as if they believed themselves safe; confident there would be no attack.

Dad required little excuse to go for a drive in the Bentley. Hector needed no excuse to go along.

The Bentley Continental Speed was Hector's dream car. The Maserati was fantastic; a car full of noise and drama. Yet, in Hector's world it fell short when it came to top speed. The Maserati Gran Cabrio Sport had a top speed of 177 miles per hour, while the Bentley had a blistering top speed of 203 miles per hour. Hector had discovered that this was only the official top speed. Someone in Germany had achieved a top speed of 211 on an unrestricted autobahn.

One evening Dad, Andrè, Mike Jennings and Hector had spent an enjoyable half hour arguing about top speed. Hector believed it was the most important thing about a car. Dad, Andrè and Mike all believed that top speeds over 150 miles per hour were irrelevant. Only an idiot would drive at 200 miles per hour.

'What you have to understand Hector,' said Mike Jennings, 'is that if you crash at two hundred you'll have no need for an air bag; they can just pick bits of you out of the trees afterwards. The forces are colossal.'

Hector was wholly unconvinced. He viewed two hundred miles per hour as a reasonable cruising speed.

As sun spilled through the trees in the morning, Hector relaxed in the Bentley's quiet, leather-clad cocoon of comfort. It weighed almost three tonnes, and yet with its six-litre twin-turbo-charged engine, electronics and four-wheel drive, it could reach sixty miles per hour in under four seconds. If Dad had just kept the pedal down it would have kept accelerating at roughly the same insane pace. Yet, in Hector's opinion, Dad was annoyingly slow. He kept to the speed limit and was irritatingly calm and considerate, allowing other cars to pull out in front of him.

Hector wanted to change two things. First, he wanted some sort of large metal battering ram welded to the front of the car. Second, he wanted a different driver, preferably himself.

Mrs Warp was positioned in the back of the car. This time she was to be let out, so she appeared more normal. Her brief was to look into the shop windows as if she was interested.

In the main store Hector tried his previous trick of assembling a chocolate and sugar mountain of breath-taking proportions and then hiding it under a selection of fruit. He sidled up to Dad at the checkout with his basket, only for the woman on the till to recognise him.

'Well, you've used more fruit this time,' she laughed.

'Hector,' said Dad, 'Not a chance.'

To Hector's disappointment all of the chocolates and sweets were left at the till. Only the fruit was bought.

Hector was also disappointed that the Bentley attracted less attention than the Maserati. He felt justice demanded that faster cars got more looks.

Hector called Mrs Warp as they returned to the car. He and Dad realised that she had spent all of the time in the market place staring into an off licence at the various beers, wines and spirits. If anyone had seen her they would have been convinced that she had a major drink problem. Dad reflected that this was probably better than being suspected a robot capable of defending against hired killers.

By the time Hector and Dad returned and had reached the kitchen, Nana had a full cooked breakfast waiting. Hector was beginning to suspect that she was either a witch or a brilliant spy who had been tracking their movements.

Lord Rothwell had the doors to his rooms open, so that the excess heat spilled out into the main hall.

'That's what Dunbar does,' said Nana, 'heats the Hall on the hot days of the summer and then keeps it all to himself when it's cold. He'll be shouting in a moment. He usually makes telephone calls about now.'

As if on cue Lord Rothwell's angry voice drifted out. Ms Rogerson could be heard twittering nearby.

'I think Dunbar's lost his edge,' Nana continued, 'In the past he could reach extraordinary volumes, often over the smallest thing. I remember when he called up Tom Beasily, he's got some land to the north. Well he called up Tom to complain that his house was too bright and clean and it distracted him while driving.'

'Of course, Tom pointed out that he lived down a lane, and you couldn't see his house from the road. Dunbar had got the wrong house, but Dunbar just started shouting insults. Now, Tom's not the kindest person, but he is six-foot-six and roughly square in shape. A bit touchy if you ask me. Anyway, he sees Dunbar's Range Rover parked outside the Blacksmiths Arms down in the village next night. He waits outside until Dunbar emerges and then confronts him.'

'Of course, Dunbar starts yelling and shouting. Tom was trying to reason with him by all accounts, but Dunbar was having none of it. Tom picks up Dunbar, carries him over to those wheelie bins, opens the lid, and puts Dunbar in upside down.'

'Well, the noise. You'd have thought the Luftwaffe were overhead. Dunbar was drunk, angry and frightened. Mary Collins, who lives up the road and likes horror movies tells me it was just like a sound from one of those. Dunbar in a wheelie bin, what a haunting sound.'

Unfortunately, from Hector's point of view, Lord Rothwell seemed happy. It turned out that he had heard about Bandit's departure and his only regret was that he had missed the chance to shoot the dog in front of his owners.

The other reason he was happy was that his new Range Rover had arrived. It gleamed and shone. Hector did steal a glance at it. Unfortunately, Andrè caught Hector looking.

'This one better not end up in the lake!' said Andrè.

'I don't know what you mean,' Hector replied in a mock injured tone.

After breakfast Kate and Hector went sailing, despite little wind. As usual, Kate did all of the work while Hector barked orders. It was fun, but Bandit was sorely missed. However disruptive and annoying Bandit might be, his wild enthusiasm and cheerfulness filled the day with excitement, fun and sometimes fear. Bandit was never dull.

'I miss him,' said Hector, as Kate guided the boat next to the jetty on the island. Kate said nothing.

'I wish we hadn't inherited the money,' Hector added.

'Then we wouldn't have found Bandit,' said Kate.

'True,' said Hector, 'But Irvine Deeds was horrible. I'm glad he's dead.'

'Mum says you shouldn't wish anyone dead,' Kate said.

'What about Lord Brothmell?' Hector asked.

'I think I'd wish him to be stuck upside down in a wheelie bin,' said Kate in a thoughtful tone, before adding, 'I wish I'd been there to see it.'

'I wish I'd been there to nail the lid down,' said Hector.

'If it wasn't for Irvine Deeds we would never have met Bandit,' Kate pointed out again. Hector pulled a face.

'I've written a poem about Irvine Deeds,' said Hector, 'Irvine Deeds was a horrible man. I wish I'd run him over and squashed him with a van.'

Kate thought back to her English lessons. There were some great modern poets, but Hector seemed unlikely to join their ranks.

After some more chatter about this and that, Kate and Hector slipped into wondering what the world would be like if they just lived on the island. Once this had been just Kate's dream, but now it was Hector's dream as well. As fear and threat had crept closer the idea of escape and isolation seemed more attractive.

Both of them speculated on the type of house they would build on the tiny island. Kate preferred something small, next to the water. She wanted to be able to step from her living room, through large glass doors to a wooden jetty, and then straight onto her boat.

Hector was planning something larger. He saw it as a building to rival King Arthur's Camelot. He described spires, turrets, courtyards, stables, rocket pads, swimming pools and his own go-kart track. Any problems with space were to be dealt with by the castle growing wider as it rose from the island. Hector viewed it as a utopia; Kate thought it sounded like an evil, dark tower of unimaginable proportions.

Hector had just moved on to the problem of how to keep snow on his castle's ski slope all through the summer, when the spy-comms device they both carried buzzed. Andrè had shown them each how to use it some weeks ago, but now they were expected to carry the small satellite communications devices everywhere.

Hector and Kate both had something that looked like a small, square mobile phone. It had a display and a number pad. It never made a sound, but would vibrate silently if a message was received. To look at a message they each had to type a long password into the numbered pad. Kate had chosen 'buttercupmeadows,' while Hector had selected 'toiletexplosion'. If they entered the wrong password three times it would destroy itself. If captured they were to give a long number as the pass code, with at least three number ones in it, as the number one was the enter key.

Kate and Hector raced each other to enter the code. Kate was concerned as they had never received a real message on it until today; only practice messages had been sent and received. Hector was, as ever, hopeful there would be some excitement.

The message simply said that they should return for lunch. Hector had been hoping for trouble, he had been planning to unpack the flash grenades he had taken from the safe room and hidden in his backpack. As they sailed back to the boathouse and the Hall, Hector speculated about the things he could do with the grenades.

'I don't think you should have taken them Hector,' said Kate.

Hector was defiant. 'They only make a really loud bang and a flash. Andrè said you could only get small burns from them if you were very close.'

'I know what they do,' Kate retorted, 'They leave people disorientated and temporarily deaf. But, we'll be in trouble if they're found.'

'Why don't we try several on Lord Rothwell,' Hector suggested.

'Well, that would be funny,' said Kate, relenting slightly as an image of a deafened and stunned Lord Rothwell came to mind.

'Let's let one off underwater,' said Hector, suddenly producing one, pulling the pin, and dropping it from the boat.

'Hector, no!' Kate yelled, too late to stop him.

There was a muffled bang, a bright light under the water, and they were both coated in a great plume of lake water.

'You idiot,' shouted Kate angrily, 'Now were both soaked.'

A short while later Kate was laughing as they arrived back at the boathouse. Just two minutes later, the whole thing seemed rather funny. Yet, Andrè was waiting to meet them behind the boathouse door, and it was clear that he was utterly furious.

'How could you do that, you stupid, stupid boy?' Andrè yelled, 'I guessed you had taken them, but to let one off. In plain view. We may well be watched, and now they will know we have flash grenades. The family is not just hiding, it has professional help. This is our biggest advantage, but you thought you'd throw it all away. I am not risking my life, and Pierre did not give his life, so that you can lead your family to their deaths!'

Andrè shocked Hector with his anger. He surprised Hector by not asking for the other grenades. He stared at Hector in a long horrible silence. Kate felt close to tears, and so did Hector.

'Sorry, really, really sorry' Hector finally managed to say.

'I don't care about the flash grenades, but you cannot keep that gun,' said Andrè, holding his hand out.

'I haven't taken a gun,' Hector replied, 'I can't get into the arms locker.'

'I assumed you'd worked out the pass code,' said Andrè.

'No, I only took some grenades when there were all those boxes being delivered.'

'OK, go up to the house,' Andrè instructed, 'I do not want to be seen walking with you in case we are being watched. Tell anyone that asks that you both fell in.'

Mum, Dad and Nana were all quite prepared to believe Kate's account of Hector falling off the jetty on the island and dragging her with him. Hector was slightly annoyed that he had not thought of blaming Kate first.

Once changed Kate opted to stay with Nana, have a spot of lunch, and help with some baking. Hector chose to go with Mum and Dad to the Kings Head in Tealby for lunch. Hector had been to the old, thatched public house before. The food was good, but best of all he might be allowed chips. His real reason, however, was that Dad would be taking the Maserati, and with the sun shining he was bound to have the top down and the engine roaring.

After lunch, and an hour or so of mixing and preparing, the cakes were in the oven, Nana had a cup of tea, and Kate was snuggled in the corner chair with a book.

'Ahh, Kate,' said Andrè as he entered the kitchen, 'Could you give me a minute alone with Kath please?'

'No, no, Kate's fine,' said Nana, magically producing a cup of coffee for Andrè, 'I expect you want to ask about the missing gun.'

'Yes,' said Andrè, clearly taken aback, 'How do you know?'

'Kate told me about you asking Hector about it,' Nana explained, before adding, 'And I didn't really believe the story about falling in either. People who fall in get wet through to their under-wear. Kate and Hector's socks were mostly dry.'

Andrè looked at Nana with a strange look on his face, then he laughed.

'Are you sure you didn't work for MI6?' Andrè asked.

'Ha,' Nana laughed, 'Good lord no.'

'I believe you,' said Andrè, 'MI6 are good, but not as good as you.'

'Now, I know you're missing several crates of flash grenades, because your colleagues brought too many and then some disap-peared before they could be returned' said Nana, confirming her super-spy status.

'How do you know that?' asked Andrè.

'Because I took them. I have them stashed about the place. I like the idea of flash grenades; unpleasant but not deadly.'

'But you didn't take the gun?' Andrè asked, with a smile.

'No, that would be daft. Guns are dangerous things. Besides, Edward sorted these out for me.'

As Nana finished speaking, she pulled up a chair, stood on it to reach a higher set of wooden shelves filled with paper and books, and pushed it to one side. They slid easily, revealing two rifles, three shotguns, two hand guns, and a quantity of what appeared to be ammunition in thin cardboard boxes.

'Now this is my favourite,' said Nana, lifting down something that looked like a short shotgun. 'I like it because it's clean and shiny and hasn't got any of that silly engraving on it. Edward said it would be very effective at short range because you don't have to be very accurate. All the shot spreads out because of the short bar-rel.'

Andrè was looking at Nana with his mouth open. This was in part because of what she held, but also because she had broken a golden law of gun handling, and was pointing it at Andrè.

'May I see it?' asked Andrè, taking it from her.

'Of course,' said Nana, 'And I was pointing it at you. That was very rude of me. I'm really sorry Andrè. Don't forget your coffee.'

'It's loaded,' said Andrè, in a slightly constricted voice.

'Yes, well you can't be too careful. If there was a surprise, I don't want to be fumbling in a cardboard box when I should be removing the middle part of Sludge's body.'

Nana took a sip of her tea, and looked with interest at Andrè, clearly eager to see if his opinion of the weapon matched Edward Grantham's assessment.

'Well, this would remove the middle part of his body,' said Andrè as he unloaded the gun, 'It is a sawn-off shotgun. The type used in armed robberies. It's highly illegal.'

'Oh, only slightly illegal, and I don't think it's been used in robberies,' said Nana, 'Edward shortened it himself just for me. It was his rabbiting gun.'

'OK,' said Andrè, 'But please keep it unloaded. I assume Lord Rothwell doesn't know.'

'Dear me no,' said Nana, 'Dunbar and guns are not something that should ever be combined. I'm glad you've removed his.'

'Yes,' said Andrè, clearly still taken aback that their apparently innocent housekeeper was armed to the teeth.

Hector had enjoyed lunch. They had sat outside in the sunshine, on one of the tables on the lawn. He had been allowed to go into the Kings Head and order lunch for everyone. Consequently, he ordered a large plate of chips for Mrs Warp.

'Hector,' you know she can't eat anything,' Mum complained.

'It's OK,' explained Hector, 'I'll tip them on to my plate once I've made some room.'

Hector had ordered a strange combination he had invented from the menu, that included pork and duck, chips, slices of chicken, but no salad or vegetables whatsoever. Dad made a mental note never to trust Hector to order food again.

By the time Hector had porked his way through the ridiculous meal he had no space for the giant pile of extra chips.

'How many people did you say the chips were for Hector?' Mum asked.

'Five,' said Hector, completely unabashed.

A large woolly dog had made its way to Hector. Its owners appeared engrossed in conversation and had failed to notice the escape.

'Can we give your dog a chip?' Hector asked loudly, as several tables full of people turned to look.

'You naughty dog,' said the owner, before addressing Hector, 'Errm, yes, please feel free to give him a chip.'

Hector picked up the plate, and to the dog's delight, tipped all of the chips over the dog and grass. The owner stopped and partly closed his eyes, as if annoyed. Then he darted forward and dragged his dog away before it ate enough to make itself ill.

Hector was so full he did not even protest when Dad refused to allow him a pudding. He did not want to admit to feeling ill, but he had undoubtedly eaten far too much.

As the Maserati pulled out of the Kings Head car park, four teenage boys rode past on small, loud motor cycles.

'Not as cool as a nice car,' said Mum.

'I think they were the four riders of the alcopops,' Dad quipped.

At times Hector thought that motorbikes were cool. Last year Dad had shown him a map of road accidents in Lincolnshire in an effort to get Hector to understand how many deaths involved motorcycle riders. The problem was that Hector thought himself immortal; incapable of dying or being seriously injured.

The motorbikes made their ponderous way up the hill out of Tealby. As the Maserati followed, Hector reflected that they sounded and smelled exactly the same as Dad's petrol lawn mower just before it broke down for the final time.

Dad thankfully turned left at the crossroads, leaving the four riders of the alcopops to go on to whatever grisly fate awaited them. Judging by their direction and the road signs, it was Grimsby.

As they drove back Dad slipped the car into Sport and the engine roared. Mum tutted and Hector relaxed. Other than being in the rear seat instead of the front, Hector did not think life could get better than this.

Once back at the Hall, Hector spotted Otto playing with something near a window. Music was drifting from Lord Rothwell's rooms; the sort he always played when he had visitors. Hector assumed that Otto had caught a rat and was trying to fling bits of it through the window. As Mum and Dad made their way to the kitchen, Hector settled down on a bench to watch the fun and wait for the screams.

What had started as an almost still and bright day was changing. The wind had picked up to a strong breeze; large clouds were arriving from the west. Lord Rothwell had started shouting out of the window at Otto. Hector looked around. It took him just a moment to realise that he was looking for Bandit. Suddenly, Otto's rat seemed less amusing. Hector felt a sadness, only slightly improved when he looked towards the lake and thought of the Range Rover in its depths.

An evening meal was planned. Nana was promising special dishes. Hector and Kate had to agree. They did not want to upset Nana, although neither of them found the idea of a more formal evening meal, with adult chit chat, in any way appealing.

The compensation was a chance to go sailing again. After a small tea to 'keep you going,' Kate was once again master of her yacht, and Hector was its demanding captain. Neither Kate nor Hector would have admitted that the real interest was in escape on the island. Both claimed the stronger winds made sailing more exciting.

They had to return by six o'clock. They had to be clean and dressed in smart clothes ready for the meal by seven o'clock. They had to be on their best behaviour. They had to be nice to Lord Rothwell.

'Hold tight to the wind, or I'll have you keel-hauled,' Hector yelled in threat to Kate.

'If we tack against the wind we'll go in the wrong direction dumbo,' came Kate's mutinous reply.

'Right, how do I keel-haul you?'

The discussion of what keel-hauling was and the best ways of achieving it in a small boat were interrupted by their arrival on the island. Captain Hector Blackbeard decided to let Midshipman Kate off with a reprimand.

'Let's find the hole Bandit was digging,' Kate suggested.

It was a small island and finding the hole was relatively easy. Both Kate and Hector could see the rock that had prevented Bandit digging further. They soon had the idea of setting up camp and not returning for the evening meal.

Hector and Kate emptied their backpacks. They had some rations, a small bottle of water, a night sight each, binoculars, thermal blankets, maps, a compass, not to mention a number of flash grenades that had been illicitly acquired. Hector was even working out the sort of wildlife they could kill and eat.

Almost two hours later they were both growing tired. The game had been fun. They had worked out cunning traps for anyone entering the island. Kate had climbed the highest tree, and discovered that you could remain hidden and yet see a long way. Nevertheless, the game had run its course. It was time to gather their things and make their way across the lake back to the Hall.

'They're nagging already,' said Hector, seeing a message listed on his spycomms box.

'Maybe Nana isn't a witch and the food really does have to be ready for a particular time,' suggested Kate.

'When this is over,' said Hector, 'I hope Nana stays with us. I really like her, and Mum likes her and she makes Mum's life really easy.'

'Do you think we'll miss Lord Rothwell?' Kate asked.

'What!' exclaimed Hector, 'How could you miss Screaming Lord Rothwell?'

'I know, but he is entertaining,' countered Kate.

'He still hasn't forgiven me for his art gallery launch,' said Hector, 'I did my best, and I made friends with several of the weird people he invited.'

'Hector, you ruined it,' said Kate, laughing, 'You've sunk his Range Rover in the lake, you've dug up his golf course, you keep getting his name wrong to annoy him, and you ruined his art exhibition by saying that all of the exhibits were no better than things you've seen produced in a school art lesson.'

'Oh,' said Hector, laughing, 'I didn't really mean to. Also, he doesn't know about the Range Rover.'

'And you pointed out that Dad and Bandit were in the grounds murdering his precious turducken meal,' said Kate.

'But I wasn't involved,' said Hector.

'Plus, you've been sneaking into his rooms and squashing those orange chocolates he really likes.'

'No I haven't,' Hector protested, before adding, 'How do you know?'

'Because I saw you sneak in like the cat, and repeatedly thump the top of his sideboard. I didn't see the chocolates, but I guessed that was what you were doing.'

'I've also been removing all the toilet paper from his lavatory,' Hector confessed, 'So he goes for a big poo and has nothing to wipe his bottom on.'

Kate was laughing, while typing in the password to her spy-comms box. Her smile vanished.

'It says we should stay here. Something is wrong. We have to de mast the boat and hide it under the wooden part of the jetty without being seen.

Hector entered his password and saw a slightly different message.

'It's from Dad. I thought only Andrè had one,' said Hector, 'He says no lights. Don't be seen.'

Kate sent a short message back which read, 'Both messages received. Understood.'

'Boat first,' said Kate.

'No, clothes,' Hector objected.

Immediately they both looked each other over for bright clothes or objects. Hector removed his white top and put on a dark grey one from his backpack. Kate took off her hairband and rubbed mud into her white trainers.

Ten minutes later they were both wearing camouflage. Kate applied Hector's paint and Hector helped Kate. The aim was to disrupt the shape of the face. They even had some in their hair. Andrè had said that brown hair was better than blond, but Kate and Hector were stuck with blond. Finally, they put on their night glasses. These provided some protection against unseen brambles and thorns, but also prevented the eyeballs from reflecting light shone at the face. It was still light, but for some odd reason the glasses made them feel slightly less visible.

Kate was anxious as they crept towards the boat. Hector was excited. His tiredness had disappeared. He felt as though huge bolts of electricity were coursing through him.

They waited close to the ground, observing the lake shoreline opposite. Two to three minutes were needed. The boat and its sail might be spotted, but it was better to stay still and hope the boat was missed rather than draw an enemy's eye to the island with movement.

After seeing no one in the parkland surrounding the Hall, Kate crept along the jetty and into the boat. Hector remained, watching the shoreline. His job was to signal Kate if he saw anything, so she could remain still until the danger passed.

It took Kate several minutes to de rig the boat. De masting her was a lot of effort, and the boat swayed as Kate struggled to lower the mast. She reflected that they were lucky the mast was hinged. One that had to be lifted would have been beyond her.

Kate then got back on the jetty and pushed the boat under the wooden part. She managed to push the boat along and then grip the front and tie it. The boat was now wedged against one of the supports holding the wooden portion of the jetty above the water.

Hector and Kate retreated to the centre of the island with the same caution they had used while approaching the jetty. Once back at their camp, Hector sent a message.

'Boat de rigged and de masted. Hidden under jetty. Both in camouflage. Standing by.'

Hector had not the slightest idea what 'standing by' meant, but he had heard it said in action films. It sounded wonderful to his ears.

The minutes ticked by like hours. Both spoke in whispers, as André had taught them. Voices can carry on the wind, whispers generally do not.

'I think it's a false alarm,' said Kate, who had just returned from the edge of the island where she had been observing the lake shoreline.

'Maybe all those sensors they set up have been triggered by something,' Hector suggested.

'What should we do?' Kate asked, 'We were supposed to head away and hide, but we're on an island next to the Hall.'

'We could stay here, but they could easily check it and then we've got no chance,' said Hector.

'Like sitting ducks,' Kate added.

'Yes,' said Hector, 'Sitting ducks on a duck island.'

'Let's wait until it's dark and then go to the nearest shore and head east,' suggested Kate.

'Maybe we should go to the Hall to check first,' said Hector.

'Are you kidding?' Kate exclaimed in a whisper, 'They will be waiting. That's what André said we mustn't do if we were outside when trouble started. Even if we were in the Hall we were supposed to escape. We are to leave Andrè, Dad and the Henry to do the fighting.'

A plan was agreed. They would paddle the boat to the nearest shore and go east. They would not even send a message on the spycomms to confirm this. Dad, Andrè and Mum had drilled it into them that they must trust nothing and no one. They should hide.

Thicker clouds rolled in as the light fell. Kate and Hector both felt this was helpful, as the moon was due to be full and would illuminate them almost as well as a searchlight. They speculated on what would be happening at the Hall.

'I think Henry will have tied Lord Rothwell to a chair,' suggested Hector.

'I think Mum will be in our bedroom,' said Kate.

'Why?'

'Because she's the best shot and our bedroom has a balcony with a wall she can hide behind,' Kate announced, rather pleased that she knew something Hector did not, 'and Andrè has been training her with a sniper's rifle.'

'I don't think Mum could shoot anyone. Why wasn't I trained with a sniper's rifle?' Hector complained.

'I think she will be shooting them in the legs,' said Kate, as she also had doubts that Mum would be able to bring herself to do anyone else real harm.

As they continued to discuss what might be happening, Hector and Kate concluded that it was probably nothing. Kate suspected it might be a drill or exercise.

'I bet the only person watching us is Andrè,' she ventured, 'He might even have a video so he can show us what we did wrong.'

'Yeah,' said Hector, suddenly feeling tired and rather hungry, 'Let's go back and get tea. Nana will know we're coming; she'll have asked Little Hop to leave Astrid Plane and have a look at exactly when we are going to turn up for tea.'

'It's the astral plane,' Kate corrected, 'Astrid Plane sounds like a person.'

'What is the astral plane?' Hector asked, for once unconcerned at being corrected by his sister.

'No idea,' Kate replied, 'Just rubbish.'

'I think it's all true,' said Hector with a grin, 'I heard the knocking.'

'Yes Hector,' said Kate, 'and I felt your arm move exactly in time with the knocking.'

'How dare you!' Hector exclaimed in a stage whisper while shaking with mock rage, 'You idiot, you idiot, idiot!'

'You're impression of Lord Brothmell is getting better,' Kate laughed.

Kate and Hector had completely relaxed. It was time for tea. Mum had ordered a DVD copy of the film Stormbreaker. Hector had read all of the Alex Rider novels. Kate and Hector had previously seen the film at a friend's house and thought it was brilliant. They were both looking forward to seeing it again.

As they walked back towards the jetty they could see light seeping through cracks in the billowing clouds. Despite the absence of any real light, they could see the trees swaying in the strong breeze.

'Stay down,' hissed Kate, 'Andrè will be watching. We better do it properly.'

They crept closer to the jetty as the clouds parted to reveal a full moon, just above the hills. The moon was huge, amplified as it is when it first rises. Light spilled across the trees.

'A Lincolnshire moon,' said Kate, 'Nana says it's something special. She says a Lincolnshire moon brings magic into the night.'

Both of them stared at the beautiful giant globe, hovering above the trees. It glittered on the choppy waters of the lake. It was lost in the folds in the earth, and cast shadows behind the great beech and willow trees that stood alone, closer to the water. It shone a great arc of light on the elegant Hall and the stable buildings beyond.

Yet, all of its beauty was lost on Kate and Hector. Instead, they were transfixed by the way the Lincolnshire moon illuminated the groups of armed men making their careful way towards Mum, Dad, Nana and Andrè.

CHAPTER TWENTY

Island

As Hector viewed the men, some with guns in silhouette, he felt a surge of adrenalin. All the tiredness and hunger slipped away. Kate realised that she had stopped breathing.

'Right,' Kate whispered, taking control of the situation, 'We both have to count the men we can see. Then we'll compare numbers and send Andrè and Dad a report.'

Hector liked this idea, although he found counting the men harder than he first imagined. They kept slipping in and out of view. In addition, he was trying to be as quick as possible. If the moon was covered he would not be able to see the shoreline let alone the armed attackers. Their night sights were just not good enough at this distance.

Kate thought she could see twenty three men. Hector had counted twenty five.

'Let's tell Andrè both of our counts,' suggested Hector, 'He will know it's difficult. He can decide.'

'OK,' said Kate, 'Let's see if there are any on the other bank.'

Hector and Kate were now employing all of the tricks Andrè had shown them. They moved in the shadows. They were careful not to push branches aside, but slipped under them instead. It was a slow method of moving, but it made them invisible to the men on the shores of the lake.

Kate counted thirty one men on the north side of the lake. Hector counted thirty. They retreated closer to the centre of the island

and Kate opened her spycomms box. Hector had already covered
Kate's head with his thermal blanket to make sure that no light
emerged from the communicator's illuminated display.

'South of lake: 23 or 25 armed men advancing. North: 31 or 30
men advancing.'

Five minutes later there was a reply.

'Weapons?'

Kate replied immediately.

'Only saw guns, no tubes or launchers.'

'Stay where you are,' came a reply just a minute later.

Hector and Kate waited by their camp in the middle of the island.
The minutes ticked by. Hector wanted to send a message asking
what was happening. Kate thought they should stay still and wait.
The uncertainty was terrible.

The wind rocked the trees. Clouds scuttled by overhead. The
world was lit by the giant moon.

Hector was just suggesting again that they should ask what was
happening when there was a sound of an explosion and then gunfire. It had come from the direction of the Hall. Kate and Hector
instinctively moved to see what was happening. Yet, they had gone
only a few paces when both of their spycomms boxes vibrated
with a new message.

'We have a traitor. Communications and surveillance sabotaged.
Assume they know about you and where you are. Check hidden
compartment in bottom of backpack, code 4933. You're on your
own. Good luck.'

Both of them scrambled to find out what was hidden at the bottom of their backpacks. Hector got there first, primarily by throwing everything out as carelessly as possible. Once the false bottom

was pulled away from the velcro he could feel something solid. He preyed it was a gun.

Afraid that any light might be seen, he gripped his small torch, pushed his head into the backpack and turned the torch on. There was a plastic, waterproof box with a numbered lock. Hector entered the number and opened it. There was some money, a GPS map device, chocolate, but no gun. There were some small black pebbles. Hector hoped they were bombs, but then recognised them as decoys. They could be set to go off after a certain amount of time, and then thrown or left. They would make a small noise that could distract someone who was looking for them. They were not bombs.

Kate was worried. She knew this meant things were desperate. They would not have been told they were on their own unless it was very serious. She knew why Andrè had kept the bottom of the backpack secret; Hector would have played with the GPS until its batteries were flat, and eaten all of the chocolate, and spent the money in Caistor.

Hector expressed his disappointment at the absence of a gun or bombs. Kate was afraid, and she found herself with the same feelings as Hector.

The gunfire grew more intense. Windows were being shattered in the Hall. It was frightening, but not as loud as Kate expected. Then came three huge aerial blasts. They echoed off the hills and seemed to stay ringing in Kate and Hector's ears.

'Nana's rockets,' said Kate, 'She said she had some to alert Edward Grantham. Isn't it odd. They're no longer married, and yet when she's frightened she calls for him.'

'Yeah,' replied Hector, with a certain disinterest in the girly analysis, 'but with explosives. There's not a lot that's romantic about removing your ex-husband's false teeth with an explosive shockwave.'

Both Kate and Hector were shaken from their thoughts by the noise of an engine. It sounded like an outboard motor. Frantically, they began repacking their backpacks. Kate had to help Hector, as he had been less careful and flung the contents about. The things they were looking for on the ground could be seen in the moon-light, but it was hard to distinguish between something from the backpack, and a darker fold or clump of grass. Both of them knew they could not risk a light.

As Andrè had taught them, they headed for a darker area with trees. They positioned themselves about ten yards apart. Now Kate appreciated why he had explained how a gun should be kept trained on the person searching. If firing started, the people doing the searching would be attacked from two sides at once. He had even explained the protocol. The person most likely to be discovered fires first. Always two shots per searcher. The problem was they did not have a gun.

They could hear the boat being dragged up the beach just as they were settling in. They had pulled undergrowth, grass and anything they could find over themselves. They both had their night glasses on to prevent their eyeballs reflecting light shone at them from a torch.

From the voices Kate thought there were three men. They spoke loudly and swore often. She was pleased. This meant they were not well trained. They would most probably be hired thugs Sludge had picked up locally or in Scotland.

As the minutes passed it was easy to track their searchers' progress. They were rarely silent, and seemed incapable of speaking without swearing. She bit her lip when one of them noticed the jetty, but was relieved that they did not appear to have discovered the boat.

As the attackers approached the place where her and Hector were hidden her heart beat thumped in her ears. She was sure they would hear it. She was convinced they would hear her panicked breathing. Only the noise of the wind and distant gunfire brought her comfort, together with the hope that they would mask her shallow breathing.

One of the attackers was framed against the moon. He had a shaven head, a large nose and protruding ears. It was the machine gun slung at his side that drew most of Kate's attention. Judging by the way he handled the gun, he had only just been given it. Even in her fear Kate suspected the man was very pleased to have the weapon and was keen to try it out.

The men spoke in loud, corse tones. One had a Geordie accent, while the other two sounded as though they were from Liverpool or Manchester. Kate could not be sure and she reflected that it did not matter. What did matter was how close they were to Hector.

Kate wished she had a gun trained on one of them. She wished Hector had a gun. She was ready. She had the first attacker in her sights. She only had to slip the safety catch off and squeeze the trigger. She had only to wait for Hector to fire first.

The man trod closer to where Hector was hiding. Surely, he had seen Hector. Kate's finger closed on her imaginary gun. Then she remembered. She pulled out one of the decoy pebbles. She had pocketed two as she repacked her backpack. She knew she had to press hard until she felt it give. Then, she had to count seconds and press again. The time between the two presses was how long she would have until it made a noise.

Kate looked around as well as she could without moving her head too much. The first man was now almost standing on Hector.

She needed somewhere to throw the decoy, but there were branches all above and around her. It would just bounce back. Kate felt her mouth start to open. They could not find Hector. She was going to yell. Her fear had been overwhelmed with anger.

The man turned and looked straight at her. She could not see his eyes, but she believed she could feel his stare. She had made a noise, she was sure of it. She had given them away.

'Reckon we could shoot any rabbits if we see 'em,' said the man.

'Machine gun a rabbit,' said the second man laughing, 'That's well sick.'

The men moved on, just by the spot where Hector was hiding. Kate could not understand how they had both been missed. She felt relief, but also anger with Hector. She did not know why she was angry with him, as she knew he had just hidden and done nothing wrong. It was as if he had a magical cloak but he had kept it secret, just for himself. Kate wanted to ask Hector if he was alright, but Andrè's training had its effect. She remained silent.

'They're going,' said Hector, startling Kate as he was stood behind her.

'How did they miss you?' Kate asked, still confused as to how Hector had moved without her noticing.

'I've not been there for a while,' whispered Hector, 'As it's windy, I thought I'd try the moving trick, so I went behind them, but then I thought about their boat, so I've fixed it.'

'What?' Kate exclaimed, as well as she could in a whisper.

'That boat is the fibreglass one with the crack. So I made the crack wider with my pen knife and jammed that hook thing from the boat in it, and just levered it wider until I could get some of the rope in.'

'Why?' was all Kate managed just as she heard the boat's engine start.

'So it sinks,' said Hector in triumph, 'It will let in loads of water. The crack's really big now, and the engine will stop in a minute.'

Kate followed Hector to the edge of the trees to watch the small craft make its way back to the boat house. Judging by the way one of the men was stood up and shouting, Hector had succeeded in widening the crack in the hull.

'Shut up and sit down,' one of the men yelled, 'We'll get to shore before it sinks.'

The arguing could be easily heard above the noise of the small outboard motor. The boat bobbed as if on a huge sea, but this was because a second man was on his feet, keen not to get his trousers wet. Then the motor stopped and the arguing could be heard even more clearly.

'How did you break the motor?' Kate asked.

'Well, I wanted to mix lake water into the petrol, but I couldn't keep any in my hands when I scooped it up. But it's got a really small tank and so I used it as a toilet and filled it with wee instead,' Hector finished, in a slightly embarrassed tone.

Kate had to admit that it was quick thinking. Disgusting, but effective.

'What if they swim back to the island?' Kate asked.

'Hadn't thought of that,' Hector admitted.

'If they returned to Sludge and said the island was empty we could have stayed here,' Kate went on.

'They might have come back to the island in the boat,' Hector replied, 'and now they can't.'

Kate had to admit this was true, but she was sure there was a old wooden rowing boat somewhere near the boat house that could still be used to reach the island.

The stricken craft was now low in the water. One of the men was shouting that he was not a good swimmer, and another that the lake water was cold. They were all trying to take their clothes off, and evidently struggling with the laces from their boots or shoes.

It was fun to watch, but Kate reflected that Hector was strong on small, quick plans, but not very good when it came to thinking more broadly about their predicament. The men who searched the island might be too dim to realise what had really happened, but someone with intelligence above that of a local thug might be suspicious about an island that boats can reach but cannot return from. She was sure the island would be searched again, and that next time it would be done properly.

Hector and Kate had watched the firefight at the Hall for some time. A lot of shots went into the Hall, but few came out. There had been two attempts to storm the Hall, but with each attempt men fell screaming as they were shot in the legs. Neither Hector nor Kate knew who had shot them, but Mum and Andrè had to be top of the list of suspects. Hector thought the speed at which several of the second group had been shot suggested it was Andrè rather than Mum.

Kate thought that Andrè was trying not to kill anyone. A mass slaughter involving members of French special forces in England would not go down well. Hector had a more cynical view. He said wounded people needed help, and that absorbed the attackers' time and effort. It also worried the remaining attackers, as wounded friends describing their pain would discourage them.

Kate was sure it was about numbers. Hector thought that the police would not really care too much about people who had set out to kill and armed themselves with automatic weapons. He even suggested it would be described as a fight between rival drugs gangs. Kate thought this had to be a possibility, but there was a little bit of her that hoped that Mum, Dad, Nana and Andrè had shot attackers in the lower legs because they simply did not want to kill, even when their own lives were threatened.

There were two huge blasts from the stables. Kate and Hector both agreed that they were probably Edward Grantham's explosives. He would be trying to deafen and disorientate the attackers. They had to hope that he had been correct when he assumed they would use the stables as a base.

Hector spotted the drenched men from the lake walking towards the stable block. He and Kate watched them through binoculars. They had previously watched their slow progress to the lake shore after the boat sank. As it happened, the boat did not completely sink, but remained close to the surface, with just the prow poking up through the waves.

Now the men had completed their walk around the lake. They were reporting back to whoever was in charge. They were probably arguing. Kate and Hector agreed it was time to move.

Hector kept a watch on the lake shore while Kate retrieved the boat from under the wooden section of the jetty. Soon they were both aboard, paddling to the north shore with the aid of the wind. They kept the mast and sail down. It was too easy to spot.

Kate had wanted to raise the mast as it would have made their journey very quick. Hector had pointed out that it would make the boat noticeable, and they would have to de mast it again to hide it in the reeds. Kate surprised Hector by agreeing. They had decided to raise the mast and sails only if they were spotted, when speed would be more important.

Their journey across the lake was helped by the wind in two ways. It pushed them on their way, but it also created waves, breaking up the surface of the lake, and making a boat paddled by two children less of a feature. Nevertheless, it was nerve-wracking. They both kept looking up and down the lake. Each expected the beam of a spotlight to rest upon them at any moment. Kate and Hector were also worried there might be someone waiting. Someone with the sense to keep their head down and wait for the prey to come to the predator.

Once into the reeds progress became slower, but Kate and Hector felt less exposed. The pressure to move quickly out of view had passed. Kate was now relieved that she did not have to de mast the boat again. She was not entirely sure she could get the mast up again in any event.

Inevitably, the boat came to a halt. No matter how hard they paddled or pulled on reeds to the front, the boat would not move. There was nothing else they could do, but step down into the water. Kate was just about to lower herself over the side when Hector stopped her.

'Look over there,' whispered Hector, 'There's an old wooden jetty. I bet no one has stood on that for years.'

Kate looked and tried to work out whether it was worth going back a little and then across to reach the jetty. It had a gate at its end, but that would not present a problem. Her other worry was that it was old and looked unsafe. She agreed with Hector that no one could have stood on it for years.

Neither of them had any idea that it was a place where Otto would sometimes sit, and occasionally sunbathe. Neither of them knew that it was the same jetty used by Bandit to chase a cat. Neither Kate nor Hector suspected that Sludge had stood at the very end of the jetty just an hour earlier counting out the time until he could kill the whole family.

It was some time before they could get the boat out of the reeds and across to the jetty. The old timbers were dark and slippery, but both Kate and Hector were pleased for once to avoid a swim in the lake. Without a warm shower, towels and clean clothes to look forward to, it was hard to view a dip in the lake as anything other than unwelcome.

Kate and Hector did not hurry or scamper, as such movement attracts the eye. They walked purposefully, as if they had nothing to fear. Once they could huddle nearer the reeds they looked around. The sporadic gunfire inevitably drew their attention.

'It doesn't look like much of an attack,' whispered Hector.

'They're not soldiers, just hired thugs,' Kate replied, 'They think Mum and Dad are not well prepared and so they will keep sending the thugs in until Mum and Dad have no more ammunition. Then Sludge will walk in.'

'I think Andrè wants Sludge to get frustrated and lead the attack himself,' Hector suggested, to Kate's nods, 'I can't imagine Andrè aiming for the legs if Sludge appears.'

Kate realised that she and Hector were staring at the Hall. They had stopped paying attention to their surroundings. She looked up to see the southerly wind driving the clouds ever north. The moon was smaller but brighter now, casting light and shadow across the lake, the grounds and the Hall. She caught a whiff of cigarette smoke. It must have come from the other side of the lake. Hector glanced at her. He had caught the scent as well. It was time to move.

Hector and Kate both removed their night sights from their backpacks. They pressed them tight to their eyes before turning them on to ensure than the small amount of light they emitted did

not spill out and alert anyone to their position. After several minutes they could see no one. Hector had switched to infrared mode
and could see nothing.

Again, they walked with purpose, following the line of a hedge
up the hill to the north east. They really wanted to go due north,
but the hedge disguised their shapes. If they headed directly north
they would have to move from giant tree to tree, and in the open
spaces between they would be obvious to anyone who was looking. Instead, they would take a longer route to the woods.

Hector was struck by how well he and Kate were getting along.
Andrè's training had worked, as they walked in silence. When he
and Kate had first tried to move from one place to another, while
Andrè trained them, they bickered throughout. Andrè had complained that he could have tracked them in a blindfold because
they were so noisy.

Hector was less worried now the attack had started. While he
and Kate had agreed on a plan to flee north then east and hide for
several days, Hector half hoped it would not work out. He hoped
they would be caught, but that he would turn the tables using the
stun grenades he had in his backpack.

He had to admit to being disappointed that Andrè had not
trusted him with a gun or some small bombs. In fact, just one
medium-sized bomb on its own would have been acceptable;
something large enough to wipe out a medium-sized settlement of
twenty or thirty houses would have been sufficient.

As they approached the woods Hector reached for the stun grenade he had in his pocket. Kate had one too, and he noticed that
she had it in her hands. If anyone was there they would plead ignorance. Kate would cry and they would run screaming, while
dropping their stun grenades just in front of them so they could
not be seen, and running past in apparent terror. They would then

roll on the ground and cover their ears and eyes. It was not a great plan, but it was the only one they could think of.

Once in the woods, and confident there was no one waiting for them, Kate and Hector breathed again. They checked for anyone watching from a distance. They first used their eyes and then their night sights. It was almost becoming second nature.

The silent trudge uphill through the wood was lit by a full Lincolnshire moon illuminating gaps and glades. Until that night Kate and Hector had no idea that moonlight could bathe a night landscape, and turn a darkest ink-black scene into a subtle, shaded and half-seen day.

In places the woods were damp and muddy. Both of them made more noise than they would wish, slipping and squelching in the dank, shallow pools. The wind caught the trees overhead, creating an ever-present rush of noise. Between the trees it was quieter, even eerie.

Hector tapped Kate on the shoulder, and was about to speak in a whisper, when he caught the smell of cigarettes. Kate and Hector turned around to see torchlight in the woods below them. There were at least two torches, but there appeared to be three or four people judging by the voices.

Kate stopped. Hector whispered in her ear that they should crouch down and watch. The people below were not moving upwards, towards Hector and Kate, but transversing the hillside, walking from east to west. For several minutes Hector and Kate watched. They could hear corse talk and foul words. They were sure they were some of Sludge's thugs.

The torchlights below moved further west. Kate and Hector stood up to carry on their journey. Relieved, they resumed their trudge up the hill. Hector considered consulting his GPS device, but decided that getting away was more important than the exact direction.

Bit by bit Hector's belief that everything would ultimately turn out right returned. He felt excited and pleased. Being hunted by a gang of thugs in the employ of an assassin with an international reputation for savagery was probably the way his life was meant to be. He always escaped and he always would. He felt surprisingly elated and awake. He wanted to laugh out loud.

There was a shout from above and then lights. A beam swept the trees. Hector stepped behind Kate just in time. She was already behind a large tree. There were the same corse voices, together with the rustle and push of people crashing down a hill in pursuit. Someone knew they were there. The thugs were almost upon them.

CHAPTER TWENTY ONE

Attack

'No, no, no, no. Stop, stop!' Lord Rothwell yelled.

There was gunfire from the grounds accompanied by thumps and bangs as the bullets hit the walls inside the Hall. Lord Rothwell was sheltering, crouched down in the kitchen. Nana was stood up making a cup of tea.

'You don't have to hide there Dunbar. They're not shooting through this window.'

'All the damage,' Lord Rothwell moaned.

'I'm sure it will all be put right,' Nana continued, while allowing the tea to brew in the pot for a while, 'Just a few holes. Nothing a bit of filler and paint won't put right.'

As Nana spoke there was a blast from the dining room. Bits of chair, lights, sideboard and painting were blown through the door into the main hall.

'Why is Mike Jennings tied up?' asked Lord Rothwell, suddenly indignant instead of whining.

'Turns out he's not on our side,' said Nana, in a matter of fact tone, 'He damaged a lot of equipment that Andrè needed for this and that.'

'I cannot believe that's true,' said Lord Rothwell, 'He's just the sort we need in a tight spot. We should release him.'

'He blamed all of the damage on you,' Nana added conversationally, as several more shots thumped in through the drawing room door into the main hall. 'If you release him there's always a chance Mike Jennings will kill you by way of saying thank you.'

'I didn't damage any equipment,' Lord Rothwell blurted, suddenly afraid that he might be tied up as well.

'Of course you didn't,' said Nana reassuringly, 'Andrè said it was a very professional job. Made to look amateurish, but cleverly leaving every bit of kit beyond repair. Andrè knew immediately you weren't capable of that.'

'My telephone line's been cut. I can't send an email. I've tried to call the police,' said Lord Rothwell, returning to his worried schoolboy voice.

'That was why Andrè said it was so professional,' Nana said, putting a cup of tea on the table for Lord Rothwell before disappearing with a tray, en route to finding everyone else.

As Nana entered the Hall Andrè appeared. He accepted the cup of tea and gestured for Nana to be quicker, and to keep herself out of the lines of fire. Lord Rothwell followed just behind Nana.

'I didn't damage any of the equipment,' said Lord Rothwell as soon as he saw Andrè.

'It's alright Dunbar,' said Nana, as another shot thumped into the dinning room, 'We know. As I said before, it was apparently really professionally done. It looked like your work at first, but Andrè said that closer examination showed that whoever did it really knew what they were doing.'

'You are completely in the clear,' said Andrè in a tone that suggested he had not the slightest interest as to whether Lord Rothwell kept himself in or out of the lines of fire.

'And what about all of this damage?' Lord Rothwell yelled as he saw Dad, who was crouching behind a window, half-obscured by a line of sand bags.

'It will all be paid for,' said Dad.

'You've boarded up most of the windows,' shouted Rothwell.

'Yes, and if they try to get the boards off we shoot them,' Andrè explained.

'Those windows are hundreds of years old. They're priceless!' Rothwell yelled.

'Dunbar,' said Nana patiently, 'How can the windows be hundreds of years old. The Hall burnt to the ground just eighty years ago. Those windows are only copies of the windows that used to be there.'

'What if I'm killed? What then?' Lord Rothwell demanded, changing tack.

'I suppose we'll give you a very good funeral,' said Nana. As ever, her patience with Dunbar Hellstone was running out.

'Yes,' said Andrè, 'We'll sort out a really heavy tomb so Bandit can't dig you up.'

Lord Rothwell glared at Andrè and then stalked towards his rooms.

'I cannot believe it,' said Andrè, 'He is in real danger. His life could end today, and he is still trying to lie and cheat to get more money.'

'Oh, you should have heard some of the arguments we had about his pocket money,' said Nana, 'He'd swear black was white.'

Nana found Mum in Kate and Hector's bedroom, exactly as Kate had predicted to Hector. She was armed with a high-powered air rifle. Her aim had been to cause pain and fear, not serious injury. So far she had shot three attackers in the lower legs, and two in the bottom. Nana noticed that Mum also had a snipers rifle.

'Andrè tells me you've been doing well,' Nana said to Mum.

'I think so,' Mum replied, 'although I can't say I like it. I just think about those thugs shooting at Trevor or the children and that makes it easier to squeeze the trigger.'

'That's right,' said Nana reassuringly, 'They get a lot of pain, but a scar no bigger than a pimple. Horrible people. You keep shooting.'

Mum turned away from the window and sat on the floor cradling her cup.

'I suppose using this monster might be more of a problem,' said Nana gesturing to the rifle.

'Yes,' said Mum, looking slightly glum.

'Is it as powerful as it looks?'

'Yes,' said Mum, 'It has smallish bullets, but they travel faster and that causes more damage. If you shot someone in the leg with this they would lose it, assuming they didn't bleed to death. Anywhere in the middle of the body and they die. I didn't mind shooting at targets, but I'm not sure I could aim it at a person.'

Nana sat down and picked up the rifle, careful to first check the safety catch.

'Thing is, when Sludge is in view you've got to use this,' said Nana, 'He would kill Kate and Hector in an instant. If you get Sludge then who knows how many you will have saved.'

Nana and Mum sat in silence. They were both pondering the outcome. Soldiers like Andrè had training and experience, but to Mum it all seemed like the worst of nightmares.

'I reckon they're going to know there's someone up here soon,' said Nana.

'It's OK. Andrè has put dummies in a number of places. They've already been firing at one of them on the floor below.'

'Mmm,' replied Nana, 'resourceful chap our Andrè. That Henry, however, I think he's part man part fish.'

'I know,' said Mum, taking another sip of her tea, 'Not the kindest sort.'

'Now, would you mind if I borrowed this for a minute or two,' said Nana, standing up with the rifle.

'I suppose not,' Mum replied, very surprised.

'It's just that our unwelcome visitors have parked up several trucks and I'd like them to go wrong.'

Nana carefully opened the bedroom window in the room opposite Kate and Hector's room. She knelt on the floor and rested the rifle on the windowsill. In her sights were four vehicles. One was an old Astra car, while the other three were four-wheel drive trucks.

Nana aimed for the truck at the back. She had the cross-hairs on the rear tyre. She squeezed gently. There was a thud as the gun went off and recoiled into her shoulder. The tyre appeared undamaged. Nana tried again, but hit only the centre of the wheel.

'Bother, bother, bother,' said Nana, getting to her feet and leaving the rifle by the window.

'Everything OK?' Mum asked as Nana stomped in.

'No. I keep missing. I think you need to do it.'

'What do I aim for?' Mum asked.

'I was going to shoot out each tyre and then try and put a couple in the back seat, where the petrol tank should be,' Nana explained.

'I'll give it a go,' said Mum, getting to her feet.

'I'll see if I can hit any of those thugs if they turn up,' said Nana, taking Mum's place.

A short while later Mum was busy shooting out the tyres. She worked her way methodically down the row of vehicles. Once she had shot all of the tyres in view, Nana surprised her.

'Doesn't seem to be anyone attacking so I thought I'd see how you were getting on,' said Nana, 'I wish Edward was here. He'd love to put a row of holes in a criminal's car.'

'Hector would give his right arm to do this,' said Mum, 'I quite like it.'

Mum then spent some time shooting into where she believed the petrol tank might be. It was only when she shot the old Astra that a fire started. It quickly spread to the diesel leaked by the trucks. A minute later fire engulfed all four vehicles.

Jordan Rogers was watching the burning trucks from the stable block. He felt uneasy. This was supposed to be well paid and easy. He had been told that the four-wheel drive trucks would let them get away on the roads or across fields. Now they were on fire.

Jordan had earlier seen a senile old lady leaning out of the window with a gun and thought little of it. As far as he could see the mad old bat would have trouble hitting a barn from ten metres. Somehow, while he was looking elsewhere, she had been lucky.

He was sure it was the same demented old lady that had lowered a tray with buns and tea earlier. She said she did not want to get involved, and that he and his friends should take it as a peace offering. Two of the lads had raced to get the buns first. That was when she dropped the stun grenades. He was sure he could still see the flash, burned into his retinas. The two idiots racing for the buns were now deaf and disorientated.

The mad old woman had just yelled 'Sorry boys, I must of got the cake mix wrong.' She had even whipped the tray back up.

Jordan had seen his solicitor just before he came on this job. Alistair Stevens was a fat weasel of a man who was good at getting him acquitted at court. He had assured Alistair that he would stay out of trouble for a couple of weeks, when his last suspended sentence finally ran out. He made this jaunt an exception because he had been told how simple it would be, and how amazingly well paid.

Jordan was not worried about what Alistair might say if he ended up in police custody. Alistair did not care what he had done. He had even helped him plan some of his criminal activities, and advised him on what to say if he was caught red-handed. His solicitor had simply given him good tactical advice, which he had ignored because of the money on offer. Jordan was worried because this simple, well-paid job was getting more complicated.

The other lads were less concerned. They did not appreciate the way things were not working out. Jordan Rogers knew he was the bright one amongst the assembled pond life, and this was why he alone felt uneasy. He did not mind if some of his brothers in arms were killed; after all, a number were rivals, and a couple almost enemies. Jordan's fear was that they would be caught and mention his name to the Police. This concern, however, was eclipsed by his top worry; he feared he would be shot, either on purpose or by accident.

Jordan had been appointed leader for his group of ten. They were sat in the stables scoffing food they had found. Two other groups were there, bringing the total to thirty. There were also bottles of vodka with the food, and these were being shared around. Jordan was a career criminal with a reckless past that led him to be admired by some. He had even rammed a stolen car into a police van once and remained to set the car alight to destroy DNA evidence. He was used to taking risks.

Yet, a room full of thirty thugs, many of whom shared past quarrels, all of whom had been given automatic weapons, most of whom were drinking quickly and heavily, seemed to him more dangerous than a crocodile pen at the zoo. He was contemplating leaving and forgetting the money on offer. The problem was Sludge, the terrifying Australian who had threatened anyone who ran away with the most prolonged and painful death he could think of. Usually in the criminal world such threats were idle bombast. In this case, however, Jordan believed Sludge, as did everyone else. Sludge had taken photographs of them all. He also had their names and addresses.

Jordan checked his watch. Once again, he refused a swig from a vodka bottle that was being passed around. He then turned down another offer of food. Jordan was very particular about his diet. He ate only crisps, burgers and chips.

The lads who had been shot were more drunk than most. One or two had been shot with air rifles or pistols in the past. It was a cause for cheer and celebration that the people in the big Hall were firing back with nothing more than an air rifle. Yet, to Jordan's mind this was wrong. How could they only have air rifles, and yet also have stun grenades and something capable of destroying four cars from a distance of about two hundred metres. He knew something was not right. He knew he should flee. He also knew he did not want to meet Sludge tomorrow in a possibly prolonged and painful period just before the afterlife.

Jordan checked his watch again, and then started to move the heavy box to the stable yard. His job was to let off some of the biggest fireworks he had ever seen. He admired Sludge's reasoning; if people heard bangs and cracks from the Hall, but then saw spectacular fireworks, they would assume it was a celebration, not an attack. Anyone who heard the bangs would not call the police. Even if they did, an explanation that included fireworks would undoubtedly lead the call to be put firmly at the bottom of the police list of things to look into.

Jordan lit the first firework exactly five seconds before the hour. He was keen to be on time. Just ten minutes more and the mass attack would start. They were all to charge the Hall. Only Jordan had misgivings. Nevertheless, even Jordan Rogers could not see what chance the people inside might have. His ten men plus the other twenty were not the only ones this sad, bereft family had against them. Sludge had apparently employed some specialists, although Jordan had no idea what they specialised in. Sludge's attractive female friend had mentioned them, and that they had been at the Hall for the past two weeks.

There was a silence in the house. Dad, Henry, Lord Rothwell and Nana on the ground floor could not work out why there had been a spectacular firework display. They expected something to worry or depress them. Something to move them closer to surrendering. Possibly something to kill them more quickly. A firework display, however, was the last thing they anticipated.

Andrè appeared in the main hall.

'Everyone OK?' Andrè asked.

'Yes, Oui, Fine,' said Dad, Henry and Nana, while a muffled, 'I'm OK' from Mum came through on the encrypted walkie-talkies they all carried.

Andrè opened Mrs Warp's cupboard and invited her to join them.

'I think this is the first real attack,' said Andrè, 'But I've no idea why they've let off fireworks.'

'I do,' said Nana, just as the answer also dawned on Dad and Andrè.

'Clever distraction,' said Dad, 'No chance of the armed police turning up if we're having a firework display rather than a gun battle.'

'OK,' said Andrè, 'Positions everyone.'

'What should I do?' asked Lord Rothwell.

'I think you should hide,' said Andrè as kindly as possible.

Andrè joined Mum in Hector and Kate's room. He had several remote control devices with him, together with some pull cords. Again, he explained what had to happen just in case he was hit. The remote controls would spring the trap. If the remote controls were jammed the cords would also complete the job.

'You must put down the air gun and pick up the rifle,' said Andrè to Mum. It was not a command, but was gentle, full of regret. Andrè held Mum's hand and then took the air gun from her.

'I don't want to kill,' said Mum as Andrè handed her the sniper's rifle.

'Then don't kill. Save Trevor. Save Hector and Kate.'

'You only put me up here because I couldn't shoot someone coming through the window,' said Mum, suddenly feeling angry with Andrè.

'Partly,' said Andrè, 'but you are also the best shot. Trevor is fast and he's pretty good now physically. He will beat these thugs if it comes to hand to hand combat. He will not beat Sludge. That's your job.'

'You want me to be a killer.'

'I want you to be a mother. I want you to stop a killer,' Andrè replied.

'I'm sorry,' said Mum, as tears welled up in her eyes.

'If you didn't have doubts you would be like Henry,' said Andrè.

'He is very odd and creepy,' said Mum, surprised that she was laughing.

'Are you OK?' Andrè asked.

'OK,' Mum replied, 'I'm as ready as I'll ever be.'

'Right,' said Andrè, 'Sludge will be at the back of any attacking group if he appears. I want you to think of it like an exercise. Clear your thoughts, it is just us practising in the woods. Aim and squeeze. You are more likely to miss by pulling the gun. Track him and squeeze. Think of Hector and Kate if you have problems.'

'I will take out anyone who looks like they are more than the average hooligan.'

Sludge was unhappy. He had arrived at the stables pleased that the fireworks were on time. It took him just moments to appreciate that not everything had gone to plan. Thirty very drunk men, armed to the teeth with automatic weapons, was as far from a disciplined force as could be imagined.

'Who brought the booze?' He demanded, to laughter and whistles. The alcohol seemed to have dulled their fear of him.

Sludge took out a pump action shotgun and racked it. There was brief silence, and then someone laughed. Sludge turned in an instant and shot just above the man's head. He slumped to the floor in shock and fear. The man next to him got to his feet just as Sludge racked the gun again.

'Is he a good friend? A brother?' Sludge asked, while aiming the gun at the standing man.

'No, no. I only just met him' said the man quickly, but with slurred speech.

'The good news is that there might be more money to share around if I decide to kill any of you,' said Sludge, with a lopsided smile.

The attractive woman beside Sludge stepped forwards, resting her hand on Sludge's shoulder.

'He's quick to anger, my brother,' she said, but with an eastern european accent while producing a short machine gun, 'On the other hand, I might be a slightly better shot, but he can break arms, legs and necks really easily. It takes me some effort. Would you like to follow the plan and be paid, or die here?'

Shooting Sludge from behind had definitely popped into the minds of one or two of those present. Sludge's bizarre sister had just dispelled that as an option.

'Put the drink down,' said Sludge. Only the sound of breathing, the wind outside, and the clink of bottles making contact with the stone slabs on the floor could be heard.

Sludge then explained the plan. Two groups were to attack the broken windows, while the other group was to try to get through the boarded windows. It was essential that they all attacked together. He made it clear that he expected the men who had been shot with an air rifle to join the attack.

Nana watched from a first floor window. It was the room where Mike Jennings was tied up. He was watching her.

'I really am getting desperate,' said Jennings.

'Oh dear,' said Nana.

'Please, please can I go to the toilet?' he implored.

'Well, that's a reasonable request Mr Jennings. I can untie you so you can go to the little boys room and then I'll tie you up again. But, you'll have to give me your word of honour that you won't try to escape.'

'I will, I will,' said Jennings.

'OK,' said Nana, approaching him, before she stopped. 'Hang on, I've just remembered. You're a traitorous, lying stoat. I think you'll just have to use your pants as a toilet.'

Jennings muttered something rude about Nana before lapsing into a thoughtful silence.

'You can't beat this attack off you know,' said Jennings after a few minutes. He was moving on. He was trying to wear Nana down.

'I agree,' said Nana, 'I think we're done for.'

'Let me go and I'll make sure you get away safely,' said Jennings.

'That's very kind Mr Jennings, but I've got a rather nasty end in mind for you. I really wouldn't want to miss it.'

Jennings stared at her. He suspected she was bluffing; repaying his attempt to wear her down by creating fear in him.

'Of course, there is a chance I won't get to you in time,' said Nana, as Jennings started to feel suddenly confident that her threat was bogus, 'Henry likes dealing with prisoners such a lot I reckon he'll be up here like a rocket as soon as things start to fall apart.'

Jennings slumped back. Henry was not a bogus threat. Henry was real and worrying. Andrè had told him some of the things Henry had done. Andrè had also lied and told him they were the reasons he was dishonourably discharged from the French Army. Andrè had forgotten to mention his own service with the French special forces.

'Now if you could tell me something useful,' said Nana, getting to her point, 'I could tell Andrè and he could give Henry some extra warnings about behaving like a human rather than a reptile with a tasty meal.'

Jennings stared at her, wondering what he should say as Nana continued.

'Henry's not a nice character. Can't say I like him,' Nana continued.

'They've known where you are for two weeks. There has been a team here preparing something, but I don't know what,' Jennings said.

'What have you told them?' Nana asked.

'The wrong things. I thought Andrè was an amateur security guy who had nothing other than flash grenades. Andrè lied to me. I realised that when I found some of the surveillance kit.'

'So, Sludge thinks we've got one security guard who's out of his depth, and one ex-soldier?' Nana asked in confirmation.

'Almost. That's what I told them. I didn't even know about Henry then. I just said there were three useless gardeners,' Jennings said with the bitter tone of someone who had been out manoeuvred, 'Now keep your side of the bargain and get Andrè to call Henry off.'

Nana picked up her walkie talkie and told Andrè what Mike Jennings had just said.

'Not enough,' said Andrè so that Jennings could hear.

'No, no!' Jennings shouted, 'That's it. That's all. They think you're a civilian!'

Nana turned to look at Jennings just as Andrè's voice came over the walkie talkie to say it was starting. Nana was supposed to be on the floor above.

Jordan was surprised when his group charged toward the boarded up windows in comparative silence. The drunken roars from the other two groups attacking the open windows were expected. He had spent some time trying to convince his group that they should remain silent. Sludge's glowering presence no doubt had some effect. Nevertheless, he had expected something noisier.

Jordan directed them to attack three of the boarded windows. They had iron bars to lever the wood away. Yet, they all stopped in shock at the colossal barrage of explosions from the other side of the house. There were shouts, some gunfire and then comparative silence.

'Get on with it,' came a threatening hiss from the stables. Sludge was watching. All thought of retreat had vanished.

As the twenty drunken men at the front of the Hall attacked, Andrè had pressed his remote control. Fifty stun grenades had been shot towards the group. The effect was stunning. The men were stopped dead by the bright flashes, the colossal noise, the disorientation and the surprising deafness. Several men let off their weapons, others dropped their guns.

At the rear of the house, Nana was prepared. She was waiting just out of view at a second floor window. The men in Jordan's group had paused, but then ran on to the windows. As quickly as she could Nana opened the middle window and threw flash grenade after flash grenade. Suddenly they began to explode.

The percussion was stunning. Even Nana found it hard to take, and she was some distance from them. There had been twice as many explosions as Nana expected. Andrè had been throwing grenades from the tiny windows in the floor above Nana. Worse than this, he had thrown his upwards, so that they exploded in the air on the way down, increasing the effect.

Jordan and his men were in disarray. They were shocked, deafened and disoriented. They were in the same state as the men at the front of the Hall. Several were sick. A number had been feeling ill for a few minutes. The poisoned food and alcohol had its effect. The explosions had provided the final trigger. It was as if someone had taken each attacker's head, locked it in a box and let off fireworks.

Sludge fumed. He watched the men vomit and stagger about. He knew they were just local criminals, but he had hoped for better. He was also furious with the security man the family had hired. An amateur would normally be expected to give up in the face of such a large assault. This one had achieved a great deal armed only with stun grenades and an air rifle. He would show the man respect, offer to let him go, and then kill him in a painful way.

Now Sludge had a problem. The attack was supposed to overwhelm the defenders. It was also supposed to show him if they had shotguns or any other deadly weapons. His only fears prior to the attack had been that the police might be called and turn up with reinforcements, or that the criminals would kill the family in the assault.

Sludge's main concerns now were that they would use the same defence on him, and that they may yet have a shotgun or two. He had to get this group to attack again. Given that they were ill, drunk and deaf this could be a problem.

CHAPTER TWENTY TWO

Return

As the thugs crashed down through the undergrowth towards them, Kate and Hector held their breath. Kate had ducked down, and was a heap on the floor behind a tree. Hector was just behind her. Yet, it was the wrong tree. It was not a tree with brambles and undergrowth. The tree had flat grass around it. Hector knew that he and Kate would look like discarded bags of clothes. They would still stand out.

'We've got 'em, got 'em,' a voice shouted.

'Where?' came an incredulous cry from above.

The men were almost there. Stay still, stay still! Andrè's words were screaming inside Hector's head. There was nothing he could do against two full-grown men. It was a lost cause, but he had to stay still. Running was futile. Moving was suicidal. Yet, they were bound to be seen. The men would run past, and then turn to check the bundles on the ground. He and Kate would be caught.

It happened almost without conscious thought. Hector was fighting to stay still, but everything told him their cause was lost. Hector was not really sure that he meant to do it. It was a stupid, stupid thing to do. He did not intend to move at all. It was as if it simply happened.

Hector dived into the path of the first running man, shoulder first. A foot hit him hard in the arm as the man went hurtling over. The second man was just behind. He tried to swerve, but Hector stuck a leg out. The man half-collided with a tree and then fell, hitting his head hard on another tree.

'Grenade lose,' came Kate's hissed warning. Hector could not believe she had acted so quickly. He expected criticism. Instead, Kate just went with it.

The first man was just struggling to his feet when the stun grenade exploded. Hector and Kate were curled up on the floor covering their eyes and ears. Immediately they were both racing towards the thugs. Both recovered short machine guns from the disoriented and wholly deaf men.

Kate dived behind a tree, flicked the safety catch off and fired a burst into the ground, just short of the men stood watching above.

'The next volley kills,' she hissed loudly, just as Andrè had taught her and Hector. A hiss is unexpected, and children's voices are more difficult to identify if there is just sibilance, and no tone.

Hector darted forwards to another tree, further up the hill towards the men. Andrè had also taught them this. If the situation is hopeless and you cannot escape then consider an attack. It will surprise and confuse your enemy.

Kate moved to the next tree and hissed again that the men should throw their weapons down the hill and kneel. Hector reached the next tree just as the men above were starting to raise their weapons. The whole incident had been too fast for them, but they were recovering.

Hector fired a short volley into the ground in front of the men just as Kate darted forwards. The pursuit, the fall of their colleagues, the stun grenades, the sudden attack, the expert soldiers advancing on them. It was all too much. The two men threw their weapons forward, down the hill.

'Kneel. Hold your hands high,' Hector hissed.

The men did as they were told. They thought they were going to die. They trembled as the soldiers advanced.

'What are you going to do with us?' one of the men blurted out.

'Tie you up and move on if you cooperate,' Kate hissed, 'Or kill you if you do not do exactly as we tell you.'

'We've got some cable ties,' the man said quickly.

'Put them in front of you,' Kate hissed.

Once the men had laid down on the floor, Hector left his gun with Kate and used the cable ties to secure their hands behind their backs, and then tie their feet. Next, he attached each one to a tree using cables ties and bits of backpack, so they could not crawl towards each other and cut the cable ties.

Hector and Kate then turned their attention to the men Hector had tripped. They were still confused and deaf. Kate motioned to them to kneel while Hector used some of the cable ties he had obtained from the first men he had tied up.

In moments, Hector was back to feeling euphoric. Four grown, armed men, and yet he and Kate had triumphed. He felt there was nothing he could not achieve. Most of all he wanted to see Andrè and Dad so he could tell them just what had happened.

Hector looked at the confused men. It was apparent even in the darkness that they had no idea what was happening. Consequently, he marched up the slope to the men at the top.

'Hello,' he said, in his best cheery tone, 'My name's Hector. I'm eleven years old. Thanks for being my first prisoners.'

The men swore, and one of them promised to kill Hector if he ever met him again.

'Don't worry about that,' said Kate, stung by their threat to her brother, 'Sludge will probably get you first.'

As she walked away she fumed. It was perfectly acceptable for her to do almost anything to Hector. No one was going to harm Hector Trogg, unless it was his sister, armed with whatever she found to hand.

Yet, a few paces later she felt better. They had overcome the thugs, despite the terrible situation and Hector's recklessness. Better than that, she had made the men fear Sludge. Fear was like any form of bullying; effective, but not as good as loyalty and bravery. Given a chance, they might betray Sludge, even kill him. She and Hector, on the other hand, had humiliated and hurt these men; but spared their lives. It was reason to dislike her and Hector, but not enough to seek any ultimate revenge. Andrè had explained that most of the worst thugs had a conscience of some sort. They also had fears. Kate had played on both.

Feelings of relief and even exhilaration quickly faded. There were more thugs coming. The explosion and gunfire had attracted them.

'Sorry,' Hector whispered, 'I should have stayed still. I just thought it was a rotten hiding place.'

'Yes,' Kate agreed, 'we've really told them where we are, but it was a rotten hiding place, I thought we'd be found.'

'What now?' Hector asked.

'We could hide, but they will be after us,' Kate reasoned, 'They will find us and tell the other men which way we were going.'

'Let's change direction,' Hector suggested, before realising the problem.

'They only direction they will not expect is back to the Hall,' whispered Kate.

'You decide,' said Hector, 'Chance an escape through their lines, stay still and hide, or head towards the Hall.'

Kate was amazed that Hector was being so reasonable. She probably would have disagreed with whatever he had suggested, and yet here he was behaving as though he was eighteen and really responsible. It could not be further from the Hector she knew; they boy whose record of recklessness and destruction would rival that of a small invading army.

'Let's head towards the Hall, and then see what we think,' whispered Kate, before adding, 'We could break off then and head away.'

There was a burst of fireworks from the Hall that lit up the surrounding countryside. Hector marvelled at the rockets, the colours, the noise and the excitement fireworks brought. Kate used the extra illumination to look around. Any patrolling thugs would be unlikely to disguise their position. Kate could see no one.

'Why fireworks,' Hector asked.

'I think it's Nana, signalling to Edward Grantham.'

'I thought she had already done that with those very loud ones that were not very pretty.'

'Yes,' Kate agreed, 'I still think it's romantic.'

'Why? Why would it be romantic?' Hector asked, 'If female humans want to attract a mate and coloured lights do the trick, lots of women would be walking around with very loud, explosive bottoms, all of them illuminated with christmas tree lights.'

'It's Nana calling for him,' Kate explained, although it was wholly wasted on Hector, who had moved on to the subject of illuminated behinds.

Kate and Hector walked through the trees towards the wood, while Hector explained why most people should have well-lit bottoms. Kate reminded him to whisper a couple of times, but it was comforting to have her brother go off on one of his wild sidelines. It distracted her.

'What annoys me,' Hector went on, 'is the way ladies in shops just stop suddenly to look at something. If they were fitted with braking lights it would give me a bit of warning.'

'Hector, ladies who shop do not have brakes, just legs.'

'But they use their legs to brake. All they would need would be some sort of accelerometer to detect a change in velocity. Actually, indicators would be a good thing too. If they turned their heads, and also there was a leg movement that suggested turning, then a right or left indicator would flash.'

Kate was laughing. She was thinking about Hector explaining his ideas to shoppers.

'No one is going to wear all that equipment,' said Kate.

'We could make them,' Hector countered, 'especially very large people, the ones that fill up a pavement all by themselves. At the very least they should be forced to have reversing lights and make a beeping noise like a lorry.'

Kate and Hector stopped for a while near the edge of the trees. They could see torches behind them, approximately in the place where they had tied up the four thugs. The two of them now described it as an ambush, and this made them feel rather proud. As far as they could tell, there were torches further up the hill, as well as down the hill, nearer the lake. Fortunately, there did not seem to be anyone coming their way.

'I still can't believe we managed it,' said Kate, 'those thugs…'

She never finished the sentence. They were distracted by the shouting coming from the Hall. It sounded like an attack. There was gunfire followed by the most terrific volley of explosions. Kate

and Hector simply watched, awestruck as there were more yells
and one or two shots.

'I think the big explosions were our stun grenades,' said Kate,
'Lots of them.'

'I hope so,' said Hector.

After a minute Hector was quite convinced that it was an attack
that had failed. His usual jaunty mood returned. Even Kate felt
buoyed by it. Hector suggested that they use the guns they had
taken and murder Lord Rothwell. Then he suggested that they shot
lots of holes in Lord Rothwell's Ranger Rover.

'You're not just going to push it into the lake then?' Kate asked,
laughing.

'No, certainly not,' Hector replied in a mock tone of indignation,
'it might crash into the first one that's still down there.'

Despite the happy mood, a decision had been made. It was unspoken, but they were going to return to the Hall. Both of them
knew this was not what Andrè would have wanted. He would
have expected them to turn to the hills, put several miles of walking in, and then hide for several nights and days. Yet, in a crisis
they wanted to be sure that Mum, Dad, Nana and even Andrè
were safe. They knew it was the wrong decision, but it was made
by both of them, quite privately.

They decided to stay close to a hedge to decrease the chance that
they might be seen. It was Hector's idea to walk confidently, and
carry their guns openly. By trying to look like a couple of thugs
brandishing their weapons they hoped to be overlooked if they
were spotted.

Hector was about to return to his topic of making people wear
indicator, brake and reversing lights. Kate suggested they walk in

silence, despite the enjoyable distraction Hector's more lunatic ideas provided.

When they reached the stables they were surprised to find them quiet. They had expected a number of thugs, and so had moved up the hill and approached through the trees. The clouds scudded overhead in the moonlight, the wind rocked the trees, but the stables were evidently deserted. This struck both Hector and Kate as odd. Andrè had assured them that any attackers would make it a base.

Kate and Hector walked into the courtyard, and to their horror the open side of one of the barns was full of men. There had to be at least twenty-five thugs. They both gawped, incredulous at their own carelessness. Instinctively, Hector raised his weapon.

One man looked at Kate and Hector and asked them, in coarse terms, what they were looking at. He told them to go away using as many swear words as he could fit into a sentence. It dawned on both Hector and Kate that their glasses and clothing had disguised them. They had been mistaken for thugs. The disorientated man had not looked carefully. If he had he would have noticed that they were too short.

Kate and Hector stayed still for a while. The men were vomiting. They were not speaking to each other. It occurred to Kate and Hector that most of them were temporarily deaf.

The two of them slunk around the other side of the huge stables square. They were more careful now. It was apparent that the attack had failed, because there were so many ill and apparently deaf men. As they slowly rounded a corner they saw more thugs in the distance. These were smoking and talking. They were more of a danger. They had hearing and they were not vomiting.

'In here,' whispered Kate, beckoning Hector to join her in a shed attached to the main wall of the stable. Hector looked at the brick built shed and wondered why he had never noticed it before, and then why anyone had built a shed when there was so much space already available in the stables and barns.

The shed was a good choice. It had a number of dusty, small windows. This made it easy for Kate and Hector to observe outside, although probably difficult for anyone to see in, unless they were silly enough to shine a light.

Nevertheless, it was imperative that they remain silent. The door did not fit well. It allowed every rustle, scrape or clink to find its way into the shed. Presumably, sound found its way out just as easily.

After a few minutes Kate and Hector had formulated a plan. They had seen that most windows in the Hall were boarded up. The windows facing the lake were destroyed. All they had to do was go up to the open windows, announce themselves so they did not get shot, and then jump through. Simple, at least in Hector's mind.

After forty minutes they both had less conviction. Three of the men who could walk, smoke, talk and carry guns, were still outside, watching the house with apparent confidence. Their only options were to remain still and silent, or burst out and machine gun the men to death. Even Hector was not in favour of this.

Kate let out a large sigh, just as there was a sound like a window opening.

'Hello there,' came Nana's voice. Hector and Kate almost fell over each other as they jumped to their feet so they could see out of the window.

Nana was on the top floor, lowering a tray on a rope, with a steaming pot of tea.

'I know we've got our differences, but that's no reason to be un-civilised. So, I thought you might want a cake each and a cup of tea. If you win I shall expect the same courtesy from you.'

Hector and Kate could not believe their ears. The men seemed surprised. They laughed, and went to catch the tray as it de-scended. Unaware that Nana had done this once before, the men waited.

Suddenly, the tray was on its way up again and the men were confused. There were two objects falling from the window. This time Nana had delayed her throw, and they both exploded in mid air with crushing percussive effect, just a metre above the men.

Even through the walls and windows of the shed, Kate and Hec-tor were affected by the blast. They slumped down on the floor. They could not see each other clearly in the dark shed, despite the moonlight. Nevertheless, they both had an idea of the others facial expression.

'Nana doesn't fight fair,' said Kate.

'I think she's poisoned most of those men we saw in the barn,' Hector added.

'Fancy having to fight your way past Nana, only to face Andrè,' Kate laughed.

Kate's good humour was savagely cut short, when a rough Aus-tralian voice appeared outside, raining down insults on the cower-ing, confused and deafened men. It was Sludge, and he could not be more than two metres away. Hector was closest to the door and he instinctively took the safety catch off his gun.

Hector was in turmoil. Sludge was there, looking towards the Hall. Hector could just burst out and gun him down. This was his chance. If he did not act, if he failed, Sludge might get Andrè and Dad and Nana and Mum. But what if his gun jammed? How much ammunition was in it? He did not know. To dive out and fail would be like jumping in front of a train; a large, cruel Australian train. He would probably condemn Kate to death as well.

Hector felt Kate's hand on his arm. She had the same thoughts. The same fears. The same desire to finish Sludge and release them all from his pursuit. What had made her mind up was an image of Andrè. She imagined telling him that she was going to remain hidden, and also that she was going to jump out and attempt to kill Sludge. She immediately knew what he expected of her.

Although Nana was well on the way to destroying most of the attacking force all by herself, she was thinking about what she could do next. She had poisoned at least half of them and deafened a good few more. She rather fancied firing through the stable roof to see if she could hit anyone. The problem with this is that it went against two of Andrè's rules.

Andrè had explained that the first death in a battle is a line. Once crossed there will be more. Try not to be the first to cross the line. We must not kill first if we can help it. Clearly, Andrè saw Sludge as an exception, together with anyone else that appeared to be expert.

The second rule was that they must give the impression that they were poorly prepared and poorly armed for as long as possible. Nana liked and respected Andrè and did not want to break his rules. The damage to all of the telecommunications and surveillance equipment had obviously been a blow. The number of men involved in the first attack had been a shock.

Nevertheless, the poison, alcohol and stun grenades had taken a heavy toll. Nana was clearly in Andrè's good books. He believed the alcohol and poisoning was a work of genius. Debilitating but not fatal. His fear had been that copious amounts of vodka would lead to a wild attack, and deaths would follow. However, coupled with the stun grenades and the poison, it had turned a group of

fired-up and probably slightly fearful thugs into a nauseous nothing; a group almost useless to Sludge.

Nana reflected that it was the boredom and waiting that were
worse than the fighting. Andrè had said she would not get away
with the tea and stun grenades trick twice, but she had, and thoroughly enjoyable it proved to be. Now, there was waiting. This
bothered her. Something was wrong.

'Andrè,' Nana said as Andrè was walking in to check on her,
'Why are they waiting? The police or whatever could be on their
way. Time isn't on their side. Why wait?'

'Two reasons,' Andrè replied, 'First, Sludge suspects there is
someone in here who is a good shot. It might only be someone who
is good at paint-balling, but a good shot is a good shot. He hasn't
survived this long without being cautious some of the time. Plus,
he does not have a way through a barrage of stun grenades. Second, I think they have something else up their sleeve, but I don't
know what it is. Sorry, but sometimes waiting is most of what is
involved.'

'I'll need to pop downstairs in a while,' said Nana, 'Dunbar will
need some paper.'

'Why?'

'Well, when he's worried he goes to the toilet. I should think he
will have been there all of this time. I better give him a bit more
toilet roll. Not that it's going anywhere. By now, Dunbar's toilet
will be bunged solid. Always does it does Dunbar. Then he will
move on to the other toilets and block those.'

There was silence before Nana continued.

'I know he's annoying, but he's mine. He's the one I failed. Of
course, I know it's him, but it's how I feel. That's why I never left. I
couldn't have children and they became my children, and Dunbar

was always wrong, and angry and sad and I could never make it right.'

Andrè listened and nodded. He was not surprised. When death was close at hand some people had a habit of saying things they would never dream of divulging.

'Cut him loose. He was a child who made the wrong decisions. He has had more opportunity than so many other children, and yet his choices have been stupid. Enjoy your life and tell Dunbar Hellstone to go to hell or do the same.'

'I think you're a good man Andrè,' said Nana, as she peered out of the window, 'I'll have to cook you something special after this is finished.'

'That would be good,' said Andrè as he took a bun from the tray with the tea.

'No, no, not that one,' said Nana, taking it from Andrè's hand.

Andrè laughed, and Nana told him that there was ready-to-eat food in the main fridge if he was hungry. Andrè turned, and headed for the kitchen.

'Andrè!' said Nana sharply, beckoning him to return.

Andrè walked quickly to her side, and looked down, following her gaze. She was staring at the corner of the stable block.

'There were eyes in that shed window. I think it's Kate.'

Andrè did not speculate about whether Nana had imagined the eyes. Instead, he took a chair and moved it to the middle of the room. He took a small torch from his pocket, stood on the chair, and began signalling in morse code to the shed. By standing further back in the room Andrè ensured that his signals could only be seen from the shed, or at least very close to it.

There was no reply for thirty seconds. Nana let out a sigh. She was about to apologise for wasting time and effort. Andrè anticipated her.

'It does not matter if you are wrong,' said Andrè, 'I want you to tell me something like this again, even if you are wrong again. You might be right a second or third time.'

'I think they would have signalled by now if they were there,' said Nana.

'Let's give them more time,' said Andrè, sending the signal again, 'They may not see the signal at first, and they may be struggling to find a torch in the darkness.'

After two minutes Nana had given up. Andrè had timed himself and already decided to allow another five minutes for a reply. Even then he might return and try again, just in case it was Kate and Hector.

Then it came. A series of flashes. Andrè watched intently. Nana only appreciated what had happened when she realised that Andrè had stiffened slightly.

'What was the message? What did they say?' asked Nana, partly in excitement, but also in fear that they were out with the thugs, unable to protect themselves.

'Just one word,' said Andrè, 'Bandits.'

'And what does that mean?' asked Nana.

'It is plural, so they are both there, and Bandit is the code that tells me they are not injured.'

'What are we going to do?' Nana asked.

'I am going to create a distraction on the other side of the Hall. You are going to cover them when they run. You shoot to kill if anyone levels a gun at them. I need to tell them to run into the door once they hear explosions on the other side of the Hall. I need to get Henry to open and then guard that door.'

Yet, events and circumstance were not kind. Bandit had been removed because of the great danger he posed. Now an equal problem emerged.

'Here kitty. Come on kitty. Come on,' said a voice from below.

A man with a machine gun was sheltering right next to the shed where Kate and Hector were hidden. Otto was in the space between the stables and the Hall. He was carrying a rat that was too limp to be alive.

'Just shoot it,' said another man behind, 'I 'ate cats. Scum they are.'

The man who wanted to shoot Otto stepped out with his gun and stared.

'That's just because you keep pigeons,' said the first man, 'This one in't going to get any of your pigeons.'

'Don't care, he's still a scum cat,' said the man levelling his gun and firing a shot.

The shot missed, but Otto jumped and dropped his rat. Only Lord Rothwell had ever shot at him, and Otto had haunted him with dead rats ever since. Otto looked carefully at the face so he would remember upon whom he should take revenge.

The man aimed the gun for a second shot, just as the first was objecting. Then several things happened at once.

'You shoot at my cat again and I'll put a right load of holes in you,' said Nana, appearing in the top window with her sawn-off shotgun, 'Go on punk, I'll make it pay,' she added.

Hector heard it all. He was sure the line was 'Go on punk, make my day,' He was also fairly sure it was from a Dirty Harry film. These thoughts vanished, as Kate burst from the shed door, right into the first man who had been trying to tempt Otto over. The man fell over with a yell.

The thug aiming at Otto spun around to see a figure in glasses with a machine gun, but no discernible face hissing at him.

'Drop your weapon. Drop your weapon,' Kate hissed, as she dropped to one knee.

The man was so shocked he let the gun fall to the ground, just as Hector, caught out by Kate's sudden action, bundled out of the shed, tripped over the fallen man's feet, and trod right on the fallen man's private parts. The man screamed, as Hector completed his fall, jamming his elbow painfully into the man's eye.

'Sorry,' said Hector, instinctively.

'You're those kids,' said the man who had let his weapon fall. It was apparent that he suddenly believed Kate would not pull the trigger.

'I have a present for you,' said a voice from the Hall.

It was Andrè, in full flight towards the man. He had an angry Otto under one arm. Kate and Hector could not work out why Andrè would run towards the man to give him Otto.

As the man bent down to pick up his gun, Andrè was only a few metres away, but he was not going to be quick enough. Kate had to shoot or Andrè would die.

'No, no, no,' Kate muttered.

As the gun lifted from the ground and Kate's finger tightened on the trigger of her gun, Andrè threw something. The half-disemboweled rat hit the man full in the face.

'Rat. Rat. It's a rat,' Andrè shouted, creating panic and revulsion in the thug, who dropped his gun again.

Kate and Hector were up and running. Hector ran to one side. He did not want to be in the way of Kate shooting. He released the catch from his own gun. Andrè pulled an automatic pistol from his pocket as he ran back towards the Hall, but it tumbled to the ground as he failed to hold it as Otto scrabbled to break free.

Both thugs were now on their feet, and there was a cry of rage from the man who had the rat thrown at him. Kate let off a short burst above the men's heads.

'Drop your weapons. Drop! Drop!'

The men did not stop. There was a panic; a desperation. Kate's threat had not worked. She was going to have to shoot them.

'I've got a clear shot,' said Hector, who was stopped and kneeling. His voice was amazingly calm.

'Take it! Take it!' shouted Andrè, but the men were already lowering their guns. There was something clinical in Hector's voice; something that confirmed an absolute certainty that he would shoot to kill.

Andrè left Hector standing guard, threw Otto inside the house, and took Kate's gun from her as she went through the door.

Now there was just Hector and Andrè, but Andrè was armed as well.

'Hector, fall back but keep your weapon levelled,' said Andrè, unsure as to whether the gun he had taken from Kate still had any ammunition. He need not have worried. The two thugs were already beaten.

CHAPTER TWENTY THREE

Fire

Otto was not in the least bit grateful for his rescue. As far as he was concerned, it had been noisy and he had lost his rat. He had been thinking of the rug in front of the fire in Lord Rothwell's rooms. He had plans for that rat. He was going to play with it in front of the fire and then splat it around the room. Otto believed that he always slept better after making a really big mess.

Yet, Andrè had stolen his rat and threw it at someone. This angered Otto, who was moving through his usual alphabetical stages and concluding that Andrè was too large to kill. There was nothing for it, he would have to find another rat.

Henry had secured the door. He spoke to Andrè in his leaden tones. Andrè clearly disagreed with Henry's suggestion.

'He thinks we should shoot the two thugs outside so they will not report Kate and Hector's position to Sludge.'

'Oh, I think I can fix that,' said Nana, who had been cuddling a restless Otto. She disappeared upstairs.

'You two,' Nana shouted to the thugs still waiting at the corner of the stables.

One of the men drew his gun round to aim it at Nana. In return, the sawn-off shotgun was aimed back at the man.

'You'll have to be very lucky to hit me, but I'm almost guaranteed to get you with this,' said Nana, 'Now, point it at the ground.'

It was just like being told off by teacher. The man obeyed, but remained sullen.

'I don't want you to tell the Australian chap about the two children,' said Nana.

'Oh yeah,' said the man who had aimed a shot at Otto, 'Yeah, yeah, yeah, we're going to do what you tell us.'

'Well I think you should,' said Nana, 'I don't want him to know, but the more important thing is what he'll do to you if he finds out you missed them.'

'He doesn't frighten me,' said the man.

'Really,' Nana replied, 'I'll take it the executions haven't started then. He usually has a round of executions. That's why he can afford to pay you so much, because by the time he's finished there's not so many to pay.'

The men were quiet, but looking at each other. Nana got out one of the cigars she believed no one knew about. She slowly lit the cigar.

'I tell you what,' she said between puffs, 'I'll fill you in. You probably know that his favourite approach is breaking someone's neck just using his hands. Those two children were there in France when he shot a man and threw him to some lions. The man was one of his own, on the payroll, just like you.'

'You're making this up,' said the man Hector had trodden on.

'Well I could be,' said Nana, 'but I reckon you have already worked out that I'm right. You want to get paid, not killed, so keep it to yourself. Just say you surprised someone and there were a couple of shots, that's all. I tell you what. How about I throw four of these cigars down and we have a deal. That way we all win.'

'OK,' both of the men said together, moving closer to the Hall to catch the cigars.

Nana drew four cigars from her pocket, but then fumbled, dropping them before the men could catch them.

'Oh, I am sorry,' she said, as the men lunged to catch them and then stooped to pick them up.

Nana managed to get four stun grenades into the air before she slammed the window and crouched down. For the two thugs, the world erupted into a kaleidoscope of light and shocking percussion. As the men reeled from the blasts, confused and deaf, Nana trotted back downstairs. She skipped a little on her way, and although she would never have admitted it, she cackled.

Mum and Dad had rushed to hug Kate the moment she appeared. All of her past bravery vanished as she dissolved into sobs. Once Hector was inside he rushed to join them, only to be stopped by Andrè who first removed his gun.

'You fools,' said Dad after a minute or so, 'You were supposed to go and hide.'

'Forgive me,' said Andrè interrupting, 'What is done is done. I want to know what happened and what you saw.'

For the next ten minutes Kate and Hector described their adventure. Andrè praised their evasion, was quiet and cool about Hector's sabotage of the boat, but clearly impressed by how they had both dealt with the men they had tied up.

'You have done well,' said Andrè, 'but damaging the boat was an unnecessary risk. The way you tackled the four men was very, very good. Your decision to come back here was your biggest mistake. And Kate, attacking to save a cat was not clever.'

Kate was outraged by this, whereas Hector took the judgement as it was intended; a guide for the future, assuming there was one.

Nana put the kettle on. It was something she did almost instinctively. It also felt British. When under attack, make a cup of tea.

A short while later it seemed as though the gunfire, explosions, yelling and danger had never happened. Kate had discovered than most of the toilets were blocked, and Hector was working his way through a pile of cakes. Only the guns and the boarded up window seemed different to a normal evening.

Andrè explained that Sludge was not attacking because he feared another stun grenade shower. However huge, frightening, strong and skilled Sludge might be, he was not immune to the effects of deafening explosions. Andrè also feared that something else was planned.

Henry appeared with a suitcase. Once opened everyone could see it contained gas masks.

'I do not believe that they will use gas, but I think you should carry them with you just in case,' said Andrè.

'I believe the best course now is to use the safe room,' Andrè continued, 'We will weather the attack and hopefully get Sludge. The numbers involved have been a surprise, but I think most are drunk, vomiting and defeated.'

Everyone looked at Nana.

'It's just my cooking,' she said, 'You're all immune to it.'

'Kate and Hector, I am afraid you are going to have to wait in the safe room,' said Andrè, 'I think another attack will probably come soon, but it could be several hours. It will undoubtedly be within the next eight hours. They cannot wait any longer.'

'Jolly good thing too,' said Lord Rothwell as he entered the kitchen, 'best to pack the tots off to bed where it's safe.'

'Hello Dunbar,' said Dad, 'Actually, Kate and Hector have been rather brave. They have done very well indeed in the main.'

'That's what they've told you is it?' said Lord Rothwell, 'Of course, I remember my time in cadets at school. Lots of tall stories. I expect they were fighting giants and protecting you from trolls.'

While Hector was normally ready to wind Lord Rothwell up, this time he was angry. He had no respect for Lord Rothwell and did not feel that his status as an adult or his title gave him any special protection.

'Well Kate and I have been hiding from people hunting us, sabotaging boats so they sink, tackling four men with machine guns and tying them up. What have you done, except for hide and block up the toilets?'

Lord Rothwell looked furious. Hector had no doubt that he would have been hit if it was not for his father and Andrè being there. If Rothwell had a gun Hector would be dead.

'How dare you? How dare you? I have not blocked the toilets, I just had a minor bowel problem' screamed Lord Rothwell, before turning to Dad, 'It was rude. Unbelievably rude.'

'Yes,' said Dad, 'it was rude, but factual. Now is not the time for your pride Dunbar. All of our lives are at risk. We need to pull together.'

'If we were together you would let me have a gun,' Rothwell retorted, 'Come to think of it, you would let me have one of my guns.'

Dad was stuck. His argument had reached an impasse. He wanted Lord Rothwell to be as helpful as possible, but neither he, Andrè, Mum or Nana would ever agree to Dunbar Hellstone being given a gun.

Something in Andrè's pocket buzzed. Henry also had the same receiver.

'They are on the move,' said Andrè, 'Positions everyone. Kate, Hector, I want you in the safe room.'

'A or B?' Dad asked.

'Could you check everything is set and then join Kate and Hector?' Andrè asked.

'If you are sure?'

'Yes, yes. Quite sure,' said Andrè as he strode from the room.

Kate pressed her thumb onto the reader to open the door to the cellar and safe room. The entry was into a room that had frosted glass windows between it and the main hall. There were then a set of steps down to a cellar that had been turned into a safe room.

'Let's wait here,' suggested Hector, stopping in the outer room with the old desk and broken chair, 'If the baddies come we can always rocket down into the safe room. They've got to get through the door first. Let's wait for Mum and Dad.'

The breathless seconds stretched into minutes. Neither Kate nor Hector wanted to say anything, but where were Mum and Dad? There was some distant gunfire and explosions. After a minute the gunfire was closer. Between the odd gunshot and explosion there was absolute silence.

There were footsteps, growing closer. Then Lord Rothwell's voice.

'Wait here for the parents.'

A shadowy man moved into the alcove by the door. He was short and stayed quite still. Only his outline could be made out through the frosted glass.

'Hector, what are we going to do?' Kate whispered urgently.

Hector had disappeared down the steps into the safe room. He had already guessed Mum's code for the gun cabinet. He emerged from the safe room seconds later with a pump-action shotgun and several cartridges.

'Hector, you can't use that,' hissed Kate.

'Why not? He's here to ambush Mum and Dad. Rothwell must be a traitor.'

Hector sat down on the floor. It took him some time to work out that the gun was already loaded, and the cartridges he had taken from the box were not needed.

'Hector, don't! Hector, killing someone deliberately is a big step,' Kate pleaded.

'But, he's waiting to kill Mum and Dad, who matters most?'

'I don't know Hector, but it's not right. Please Hector, please.'

Kate could not believe they had been in the kitchen minutes earlier enjoying cakes and tea. It seemed like another brightly coloured world. Suddenly, they were back in the dark land of life and death.

The shadowy figure beyond the frosted glass stayed still, not moving a muscle, as only someone would if they were waiting to ambush the innocent and unwary. Hector, raised the gun to his small shoulder so that it pointed at the head of the grey figure in the gloom.

Kate was sobbing now, muttering the word 'please' again and again quietly. Hector pushed the butt of the shotgun into his shoulder as Andrè had taught him. He pushed the safety catch to red, held his aim and began to squeeze the trigger.

The figure remained completely still, waiting with the patience of a cruel spider. Hector squeezed and squeezed, but never quite enough to fire the gun. The firearm was heavy, his arm was aching despite his elbow resting on his right knee, and Kate was sobbing. However hard he tried he could not pull the trigger. He could not shoot someone in cold blood. But the man waiting; the man stood like a statue would kill; he would shoot Mum and Dad. Hector squeezed a little harder.

The bang and the blast were shocking in the small room. The glass in the door shattered. The person stood beyond seemed to sway and slump.

Almost as shocking as the blast was the silence that followed.

'Hector! Hector!' said Kate after a while. She could not believe he had done it.

'He was going to kill Mum and Dad. He'd been told to wait for them.'

Kate rushed to the smashed window, as if there might be something she could do to call back time and undo Hector's violence. Hector sprang to his feet, leaving the gun on the floor.

Neither Kate nor Hector could quite believe their eyes. The figure Hector had shot was still standing, but missing most of a head. The cardigan, the stockings, the brown shoes; Hector had shot Mrs Warp.

'It was Mrs Warp,' said Kate, as if Hector might not know, despite the wires and small bits of machinery protruding from her neck.

'Oh no,' Hector groaned after a pause, 'That's three we've ruined.'

'We? We? It was you this time,' said Kate, 'I didn't do anything. You better not say I was involved.'

'Let's just say she got shot by Sludge,' Hector suggested.

'What happened to open and honest Hector?' said Kate, but her serious face was slipping, and the giggles rising within her.

'Hector, Hector, what have you done?' Kate struggled to say, as both of them clutched each other and they collapsed into gales of laughter.

'Hector, Hector, that's number three,' Kate cried and laughed.

'Maybe we can blame it on Henry,' said Hector, 'Anyway, her head has only lost the machinery for expressions and eye movement. She probably still works.'

'Yes dear, I do,' said Mrs Warp, in her normal voice, but it now emerged from her throat. It stopped Kate and Hector dead.

'Oh, look, we're really sorry,' said Kate, 'Can you see? Can you hear?'

'Yes, I am fully functional, but I believe much of my head is gone.'

'Can you ride a horse?' Hector asked, prompting both he and Kate to burst into laughter again as they imagined Mrs Warp as the headless horse woman.

There was a bang from the safe room, and then a man's voice. Kate and Hector recovered in moments.

'A tunnel!' Kate hissed, 'A tunnel! They must have been tunnelling for ages,' As she spoke she turned towards the safe room, removing a stun grenade from her rucksack at the same time. She sprang down the steps and threw it in, pushing the heavy door shut just before the grenade went off.

Hector could never work out his sister. Sobbing, soppy and weak one moment, and yet frighteningly accomplished and deadly the next.

As the bang shook the room, Kate did not hesitate to open the door and shine a torch into the darkness, although she was careful to hold the torch to her side, in case someone shot at it. Hector had already picked up and racked the shotgun.

There was a hole at the end of the room, with rubble on the floor. Three men were on the floor in amongst the bricks and dust. One was on his knees. Kate told them to lie on their front with their hands behind their backs. She used the hiss Andrè had told her to use.

Two of the men did as they were told, but the one on his knees who had obviously been the last out of the tunnel tried to struggle up. Hector fired into the ceiling and then racked the gun again. The third man quickly complied with Kate's instructions.

Kate sprang down the steps and went straight to the gun cabinet Hector had carelessly left open. There were pairs of large cable-ties already looped. In less than twenty seconds all of the men had their hands secured. She told each of them to move to different positions in the wall using a shouted whisper. Then she tied their feet together, and tied each of them to the rings in the wall.

Through all of this Kate had shone the torch on the men. They could not see her face. Then one of them guessed.

'It's the girl,' he said groggily.

'Well done,' said Kate, in a normal, sarcastic tone she usually reserved for Hector.

'My brother has just blown someone's head off,' Kate shouted, assuming these thugs were as slow and deaf as the ones in the stable block.

'Big deal,' said the man who spoke first, suddenly growing in confidence.

'Well yes, it was,' shouted Kate, 'and I want you to tell me where Sludge is, and what your orders were.'

'Forget it darling.'

Hector tried to rack the gun again, but it was already primed. Nevertheless, he was silhouetted in the doorway and his movements could be clearly seen. There was nervousness amongst the men now. These were the children who had survived several assassination attempts. However, Sludge was someone you only betrayed once. In the silent seconds Kate worked this out.

'Strangely, the woman Hector shot is still alive,' shouted Kate.

'What? You've shot her head off but she's alive?' laughed one of the men, in a tone that partly exuded disbelief and partly his confused state.

'Mrs Warp, could you come through please?' Kate said loudly.

Kate shone the torch on her, careful to only flick the torch briefly onto her neck so that no one noticed the protruding wires.

'Mrs Warp, please pick up that man by the trousers, but use only one finger.'

The small lady with no head walked quite normally down the steps into the safe room, put her index finger into the top of the first man's trousers and lifted him half a metre off the ground. Kate shone the torch on the man and Mrs Warp as it happened, as one of the other men began to scream.

'Calm down!' said Kate in a very loud voice, 'Tell me what you know and I'll call her off.'

A few minutes later Kate had discovered that these three had just been released from prison days earlier, and had been paid in cash just that morning. They knew who Sludge was, and they believed there were roughly sixty people involved in the assault. The tunnel had been dug by someone else, who had left as the attack started.

Kate reopened the gun cabinet and took two MP5 machine guns, two small handguns and several clips. Her and Hector put a handgun and the clips into each of their rucksacks. Kate then locked the cabinet, but not before helping herself to several more stun grenades.

Hector was confused on two counts. First, it was plainly wrong to feel anything like admiration for your sister, but this was definitely the emotion he was currently experiencing. Second, he could not fathom how she could go from sobbing wreck one moment, to in-charge, lock and load, gun-toting interrogator the next. He suspected it was something to do with her reaction to immediate threat; either that or her weird breakfast cereal.

Once in the outer room Kate tucked the wires protruding from Mrs Warp's neck back down what should have been her throat. She had hopes of using the headless trick again, but the wires were a distraction and she might not be so lucky with the light.

'What are we going to do?' Hector asked, returning to a whisper.

'Find Andrè, Mum and Dad, tell them about the tunnel, and give them these guns,' Kate replied in a matter of fact tone.

They opened the door to the main hall and checked around. There was gunfire and some distant shouting. Kate edged out first, machine gun in hand, her finger ever-ready to flick the safety catch off. Kate marvelled at how much Andrè had managed to teach them. She remembered his warning about how easy it was to shoot your own side, and how safety catches should be on unless there was a very high chance of meeting an enemy and being ambushed.

Kate ran to beneath the stairs, glanced around and shouted that everything was clear. Hector followed just as it occurred to Kate that she should have sent Mrs Warp out first. Hector also had his gun ready, safety catch on, with his finger ready to flick it off in an instant. The door to Lord Rothwell's rooms opened and both Kate and Hector immediately aimed their guns.

'You've got guns,' exclaimed Lord Rothwell, 'You've got guns and I haven't. Why not? It's not fair!'

'We could give you the code to the gun cabinet in the safe room if you like,' said Hector.

'No,' said Kate.

'Yes. I think that would be the best thing to do,' said Lord Roth-well, his child-like whinging tone falling away.

'The only trouble is that there are three armed men down there,' said Hector, 'but don't worry, Kate tied them up.'

'I don't believe you! Don't start playing games with me!' Lord Rothwell shouted.

'Mrs Warp had her head blown off, but she's still alive,' said Kate.

'I don't have time for these childish games,' yelled Rothwell, 'Tell me the code for the gun room or you will regret these lies.'

'Mrs Warp,' sang Hector, in the voice he normally used to taunt Kate during hide and seek, 'Mrs Warp. Come out please.'

Mrs Warp walked into the open. Rothwell stared at her, failing to notice that Hector was whispering instructions.

'What has happened,' Rothwell gasped, 'She should be dead.'

Mrs Warp turned slowly towards Lord Rothwell, almost as if she was on a turntable rather than legs. Her arms then began to rise very slowly. In total raising the arms took about six seconds, after which Mrs Warp had achieved the classic zombie or egyptian mummy effect, of two straight, dead arms held out in front.

Mrs Warp began to walk towards Lord Rothwell. As she did she started to make a strange, unearthly noise. Lord Rothwell stayed still, his eyes opening wide in fear. Then, when Mrs Warp was half-way across the hall, Rothwell let out a loud, shrill scream and rocketed back into his rooms, slamming the door behind him.

The scream attracted Nana, who appeared at the top of the stairs to see what was going on. Only when Nana spoke did Kate turn her gaze away from the place Rothwell had been standing. To her shock there was a man standing behind Hector in the shadows. Instinctively, she spun her gun around.

'Hang on, hang on,' said Andrè, who moved from the shadows.

'Oh,' said Kate, pointing her gun down and reapplying the safely catch.

'I think Mrs Warp has gone wrong because she went after Lord Rothwell,' said Kate.

'Kate, I was here when Hector was whispering instructions to Mrs Warp, explaining that Rothwell might try to grab the guns and this was a risk, so I know this is not true,' said Andrè sharply, 'Why have you got those weapons?'

Kate quickly explained the men in the cellar. Andrè checked and then sealed the men into the safe room once he had checked the gun cabinet was secure.

'The next attack is imminent and we have lost the safe room,' said Andrè to Nana, 'It's time for your plan.'

As Nana advanced down the stairs she explained what they had to do.

'There's an old tunnel from the kitchen to an ice house about forty yards from the Hall. About the only thing that survived the fire all those years ago. We can escape that way. I'm afraid Andrè was the only one I told about it. That's why I was so fierce about the pantry being out of bounds.'

Hector and Kate handed over their weapons to Andrè. He left them with stun grenades and one last piece of cruel advice.

'Use your evasion skills. Walk some distance from Nana. She is more likely to get caught. Do not attempt to protect or save her, even if they are about to shoot her. Do you understand?'

Andrè had never looked more forbidding. Hector felt shaken, and Kate found tears welling up in her eyes. Andrè grabbed Kate by her jacket and shook her.

'Do you understand?'

'Yes' Kate managed to stutter. Hector nodded. All of the amusement of seeing Lord Rothwell panic and flee had evaporated.

Nana walked quickly towards the kitchen with Kate and Hector following just behind. She moved to the pantry door, opened it and beckoned Kate and Hector in.

The wood nailed to the kitchen window shook as someone started wrenching it free. Kate ran forward, but Hector paused. There was a bang as part of the wood was broken away, and then the sound of glass breaking as something was thrown into the room.

Kate dived for the pantry door as Hector dived back towards the Hall. There was an relatively small explosion but a brilliant light. A whoomphing noise rattled the room as the incendiary device ignited the kitchen. Bright fire burst everywhere.

Andrè ran forwards and yelled. Kate and Nana confirmed they were unhurt and Andrè told them Hector was also unharmed.

'If we wait a moment there's a sprinkler system,' shouted Nana, 'It will put the fire out.'

'No, you must avoid the smoke. Go! Go!' Andrè shouted as he slammed the kitchen door shut to keep the flames and smoke at bay.

'What now?' Hector asked, unhappy at his separation from Kate.

'You need to hide in the walls,' said Andrè, 'Do you still have your torch?'

CHAPTER TWENTY FOUR

Kate

Gunfire rattled the Hall, a strange combination of almost distant crack and unnerving thuds as bullets flew through the broken windows into the rooms.

Andrè and Hector raced upstairs. They had to unleash some more stun grenades to prevent the boarded windows being breached. Hector knew he would be expected to hide in the gap between the walls. In the meantime, however, he hoped to throw as many explosive devices as possible.

Hector picked up several grenades from an open box outside the bedroom he and Kate shared. Andrè had gone to the balcony over-looking the lake, and so Hector opted for the disused bedroom from which Nana had spotted Kate hiding in the shed next to the stable block.

Hector did not need to look. He could hear voices. He stole a single, fleeting glance to check the position of any men, and then threw four grenades through the window in quick succession. He did this while crouching, throwing them upwards so that they would explode in the air on the way down. It also meant there was almost no opportunity for the men below to catch the grenades and throw them back.

Hector counted four explosions and then glanced out of the window. One man was sat on the floor. Two others were laid down. Yet, the fourth man was aiming his gun at Hector's window. Hector ducked down and ran back for more grenades. This time he did not look out, just in case the man had his gun aimed ready to shoot him. He simply threw four grenades out of the window, one after the other.

Hector looked out using a mirror on a stick that had been left by the window. In fact, Andrè had left mirrors like these by all of the windows. Hector could see, but could not be shot. They could only shoot the mirror.

All of the men were now on the ground. They seemed to be disorientated. Hector felt pleased.

Hector was about to turn to report what had happened to Andrè, but two more figures appeared. They were on the edge of the woods. It took Hector only moments to realise it was Nana and Kate.

They crouched down and seemed to be in discussion. As it was dark and they were some distance away it was difficult for Hector to judge.

'Get out. Get going,' Hector hissed.

'My thoughts exactly,' said Andrè from behind him, making Hector jump.

'I got four of them with stun grenades,' said Hector, pointing to the figures below.

'Well done,' said Andrè quietly, although his thoughts were clearly not on the deafened men on the ground, 'Do not shout out to Kate or Nana, whatever happens.'

Hector and Andrè watched for another minute or so. Kate and Nana moved along the line of the trees to two parked cars.

'No! No!' Andrè hissed.

The lights on one of the cars flashed as Nana unlocked it. Kate quickly got in the passenger seat. The car started and moved forwards slowly, before stalling and then starting again.

'It's a mistake, isn't it?' Hector asked.

Andrè did not reply, but groaned as he saw the car lights come on. The car moved forwards again, but then seemed to come to a halt. There appeared to be a man standing in front of the car. He had a gun. Hector and Andrè's view of the car went black as the moon disappeared behind a cloud.

'Hector, get the sniper's rifle from the other room,' said Andrè quickly, as he drew his pistol and aimed it at the distant figure.

Hector raced into his bedroom and grabbed the rifle Mum was supposed to use. He grabbed some ammunition, checked the safety catch, and then ran back to Andrè.

Andrè accepted the gun and took aim at the man. Hector looked out at the distant scene, which was difficult to make out in the gloom of moonlight filtered through trees. There were brief moonless periods where nothing could be seen at all. The driver's door was now open and the man seemed to be speaking to Nana. Hector assumed he was threatening her, about to take Nana and Kate hostage.

Hector glanced back at Andrè. He was resting the gun on the window frame and was completely still. Hector could see that Andrè's finger was not touching the trigger. He turned his attention back to the darkened scene.

Hector found guns exciting, but now felt that he did not really want to see anyone shot. Although he had shot Mrs Warp believing her to be an assassin, he rather regretted it. Now, as he watched an expert preparing to kill, he could hear his own breathing. Andrè was very still, so very like Otto as he watched his prey. Yet, Otto was a cat; he was wired to hunt and kill. Watching Andrè made Hector look upon the gun as something evil. However much he liked and admired Andrè, he could only see the gun as dark, contaminating and wrong.

For the first time Hector wondered what the time might be. He guessed it was around one o'clock in the morning. It seemed strange that he should have this thought with his sister and Nana in mortal danger, and with Andrè preparing to kill the thug who had stopped Nana's car.

Hector then noticed Andrè's finger had moved further away from the trigger. The man had closed the passenger door and was now behind the car pushing it. Maybe Kate and Nana were going to be able to just drive away. Most of the attackers were either ill or engaged in attacking Mum, Henry and Dad at the front windows. Kate and Nana would probably escape easily. Maybe the thug was ready to give up himself.

The car began to move, slowly at first. The man who was pushing stepped back and disappeared into the woods, just as shouting erupted. The shouting became louder. Someone was yelling at the car to stop. The shouting continued, and echoed around, clearly heard, despite the gunfire from the front of the Hall.

Then there was a volley of shots above the car and more shouting. The car continued, but seemed to be heading out of sight, towards the lake. Then came a crescendo of shooting, as several guns were fired at once into the car. Hector was transfixed, willing Kate to appear and run from the disintegrating vehicle. He could see bits flying off the car as it disappeared from view. Then there was a flash of orange light as the car's petrol exploded and it caught light.

'Kate! Kate!' Hector yelled, unaware that he had been yelling for some time. He was still staring at the space where the car had been, watching in horror as the flames he could not see illuminated the woods with a flickering orange light.

'Did she get out?' he asked Andrè as tears flooded his eyes, 'Did you see her?'

Andrè turned to Hector but seemed unable to speak. Hector could not see it through his clouded vision, but Andrè had tears in his eyes. Andrè took a deep breath and allowed his feelings to fall back into a cold, determined but settled fury.

'Hector, I need you to hide in the walls now. I have to help your Mum and Dad.'

Hector screamed at Andrè. He did not care about anything else. It was pure rage at the world and the men who had just killed his sister.

Andrè put out a hand and took Hector by the shoulder, but Hector was already turning to run. Andrè took off after him, but Hector had a good start.

'Hector, Hector, stop. Please,' Andrè implored as they raced towards the stairs.

Hector vaulted onto the banister and rocketed down the stairs at twice the pace Andrè could run. He reached the bottom too fast, and fell, rolling on the tiled surface of the main hall.

Immediately, Hector was on his feet, running towards the open windows. Henry was just getting to his feet. Without thinking Hector slipped into a rugby run, low down and running at an angle to one side of Henry. At the last minute he took a step back into Henry, hitting him hard with his shoulder.

Henry fell, and Hector scooped up Henry's machine gun. Bullets were flying through the window now, but Hector was sprinting towards them, his fear eclipsed by rage. Dad dived across the room, realising too late where Hector as going.

Hector dived headlong through the glassless window, landing in some shrubs. He had no idea if he had been hurt, but got to his feet and charged. There were two groups of men, one hidden behind the stable block corner, and the other by a dip in the land. Hector headed for the ones in the dip.

He fired the machine gun as he ran. Screaming that he hated them. Screaming that he would kill them. Several shots flew past Hector, but the men were getting up to run. Someone running and firing without a care for their own safety was bound to kill, and they were ready to flee.

As Hector reached the top of the rise one shot rang out from the stable block and narrowly missed his head. Several of the men from the dip were running, but three were cowering, their hands in front of their faces, as if flesh hands could stop metal bullets.

'I hate you! I hate you!' Hector screamed as he aimed the gun and squeezed the trigger.

Hector rose several inches from the ground, as if an avenging angel had lifted him. He looked down upon the terrified men, and then struggled as a hand wrenched the gun from his hands. He gasped as he was crushed by the arm holding him, and as he tried to turn around to see if it was Andrè, he was thrown to the ground, and he slid partly down the slope.

Hector looked up at Sludge. The huge assassin grinned and immediately became everything Hector raged against. Without any fear, Hector flung himself at Sludge. He aimed his fists at the giant Australian's stomach, and then lower. He found himself pushed to the ground again, and then dragged down the slope by a hand on his neck.

Kate and Nana crouched in the woods as Nana fumed about her burning car. Kate had suspected that driving away in a car was not the best idea. She had been shocked when they were stopped by an armed man, but then relieved when it turned out to be Edward Grantham. Edward had ordered her and Nana out of the car before pushing it down the slope towards the lake.

Edward's 'told you so' attitude when the car was shot at and then destroyed did not help Nana's mood. Kate reflected that it might be one of the reasons they ended up divorced. Nana was muttering about what a good car it had been, and how she had liked the colour.

'Even the inside was something special,' she managed to whisper angrily, 'Several people were sick in it and it always cleaned up perfect.'

'I think we would have been killed,' whispered Kate.

'I'd have driven faster and dodged the bullets,' Nana replied, 'Edward always did think he knew best.'

'I'm sure Dad will pay for a new one,' said Kate, pretty sure that Nana's flaming car and the cost of a replacement was the least of her father's worries.

Edward appeared at their side.

'I hope you're going to replace my car,' said Nana, only for this to be ignored by Edward.

'Hector's gone on a jaunt of his own. Sludge has him. I think your parents are about to surrender Kate.'

Kate immediately got to her feet and was surprised to find Nana's strong grip on her arm.

'Sit down and think,' said Nana.

Kate reluctantly crouched down again. She felt tearful and worried. This was not what was supposed to happen.

'Could we attack from behind?' Nana asked, all thoughts of her car gone.

'Not enough of us,' said Edward, 'Plus they will just defend the house, and they'll have hostages.'

'We could go back in,' Kate suggested, 'through the ice house tunnel. The sprinklers will have put the fire out and we can go up to the top floor through the walls.'

'I reckon that's a plan,' said Edward, 'but I think I should stay out here. I've been catching them and tying them up. If you have them from inside they won't be watching the window.'

'Yes,' said Nana, 'attack from two sides. Just be careful Edward.'

'I'm always careful,' he replied, 'Oh they have a password. It's Andromeda. Stupid password because most of them are too thick to remember it. I've heard andromeana, arrowmedia and acroman-chulia. I just ask 'em the password and while they're trying to think of it I wrench their gun off them.'

'Have you got any of those grenades I could borrow?' Nana asked, 'I think it's time to be less pleasant.'

'I have, but no, stick to stun grenades,' said Edward, 'That way if you make a mistake you'll only deafen Kate's parents, not kill 'em.'

Hector felt forlorn and beaten. He sobbed, but then felt rage. He hit Sludge again, but it had no effect.

'Your little boy's with me,' shouted Sludge to the silence in the Hall.

'You can surrender now,' Sludge continued, 'or you can listen to him scream as I snap bits off. You can give in now, or give in when he's screaming.'

'What do you want us to do?' came Dad's voice, 'Do you want us to throw the guns out?'

Sludge laughed. There was silence for a minute. It was as if no one was breathing.

'Stand in the middle of the room with your hands on your head,' Sludge shouted, 'Don't bother throwing any guns out, you'll have plenty in there, there's no point.'

Sludge stood up with Hector in front of him. Behind Sludge, waving at everyone in the Hall, was Sludge's sister.

'I'm the insurance against a head shot,' she shouted in her strange eastern european accent, somewhat gleefully, 'If we do this right everyone lives.'

The walk to the Hall seemed like a bad dream for Hector. Sludge held on, effortlessly dragging him. Hector felt quite certain that once Sludge had what he wanted everyone would be killed.

When they reached the window Sludge's sister trained a gun on Mum, Dad, Henry and Andrè while Sludge climbed in, dragging Hector up like a rag doll behind. Sludge's sister followed, and once she had climbed in, she tied up Henry and Andrè in the main hall. Then she moved all of the guns to a corner, away from Mum and Dad. Finally, Mum and Dad were ushered into the main hall, followed by Sludge dragging Hector.

There was a bang as the door to the cupboard opened. A headless Mrs Warp lurched out, towards Sludge. Hope flared in Hector, and just as quickly died. Sludge calmly pulled out a taser from his pocket and electrocuted Mrs Warp. To make sure Sludge took out another taser and electrocuted her again. Mrs Warp slumped down, dead and useless. There was a smell of burning electronics. Sludge had come prepared.

'Where's Jennings?' Sludge asked.

'Your spy?' Andrè replied from the floor, 'He's tied up in one of the bedrooms. Unless he caught a stray bullet he should be OK.'

'I only asked where he was,' Sludge replied, 'I'm not his mum.'

Sludge gestured to his sister who disappeared to search the hall. She bounded up the stairs, gun at the ready. It was apparent that her approach was to move fast to make herself a difficult target.

Then there was silence. No one said anything for at least five minutes. It was as if they were all waiting for a train that was about to arrive in the room at any moment. Eventually, Dad spoke.

'What is it you want?' Dad asked.

'Nothing,' Sludge replied, first looking at Dad and then looking away again.

The silence wore on, until Sludge's sister came running down the steps. She explained that only Mike Jennings was upstairs, and that he had confirmed the numbers to her. There was just one person missing.

A short while later a terrified Lord Rothwell had joined them in the main hall. He seemed unsure as to whether he should plead and whimper, or shout and demand. Consequently, he managed a bit of both. Sludge said nothing in reply, only glancing up at him once Rothwell became irritating. Lord Rothwell immediately fell silent.

In the following minutes there was silence. All that could be heard was the wind outside, breathing and the occasional sigh.

'What's your name?' Mum asked of Sludge's sister, hoping to establish some rapport.

'Marina,' she replied, 'but it will not do you any good. Once we have what we need I'm not the sort who tends to write and keep in touch.'

Dad and Andrè both had the same thought. They believed that Marina was her real name. It made them think the plan was to murder them all and set the Hall on fire. Sludge would have guessed that there were cameras recording each room, but he and his sister made no attempt to hide their faces. The only thing Dad could do now was to play for time and pray that armed police arrived.

There was a knock on the door closest to the lake. Marina left to open it, which took some time.

'Gentlemen and lady,' came an American voice, 'Sorry to have kept you waiting. My name is Irvine Deeds.'

CHAPTER TWENTY FIVE

Money

Nana was grumbling. She and Kate had managed to return through the ice house tunnel, and were now struggling through the gap in the walls. Kate was more active than Nana, smaller, and more accustomed to squeezing through tight spaces. Nana grumbled about the narrow openings, the dust, the ladders and the obstacles created by the windows.

As they made their way up the floors, Nana and Kate discussed the possibility of releasing Mike Jennings. He had the special forces skills and training they needed. He could kill Sludge and whoever was with him provided he had the element of surprise.

Andrè had told them Mike Jennings had a reputation for being good at what he did. The problem was that Nana and Kate now suspected this had been more of a warning than a compliment. Nana felt they had little choice but to trust Mike Jennings. Kate disagreed as she believed that she and Nana would also have the element of surprise.

Nana and Kate struggled out into the bedroom on the top floor. Both armed themselves with stun grenades. Nana considered taking the sniper's rifle, but Kate thought it was too long and heavy. Instead Nana took her sawn-off shotgun and a handgun. Kate also took a shotgun, together with a short machine gun.

Kate wanted to return downstairs using the passageways through the walls. Nana disagreed. As a compromise they crept down the stairs to the floor below and then entered the gap in the outer walls. Nana might have had some trouble moving through the passages, but she knew all of the entrances.

The arrival of Irvine Deeds confirmed Dad and Andrè's worst fears. Someone who had gone to such trouble to ensure the authorities in several countries believed him dead was not about to leave witnesses alive. All they could do was to play for time. Yet, Deeds was surprisingly relaxed. He did not seem to be in a hurry.

'First, I would like to apologise for all of this,' said Irvine Deeds, 'It's the rougher end of business, and business is business, but that doesn't mean I like it. I'm sorry. You deserve better.'

'What is it you want?' Mum asked, noticing for the first time that Deeds had a brief case.

'I want my money.'

'Then why leave it to Hector and Kate?'

'Only if I am dead. As you can see, I am not dead. All I'm trying to do is rectify an administrative error. I am sorry you've been caught up in this,' said Deeds, sounding both sorry and reasonable.

'You faked your own death. You have murdered. There are several people dead because of you,' Mum seemed utterly unafraid for herself. She was not angry, but collected. Trevor Trogg had thought that he would have to negotiate and delay things, but decided to remain silent instead.

'I'm not going to deny it,' said Deeds, setting down his brief case, 'but that's the real world. That's business. Anyone who runs a big company has ordered killings. All the politicians do it, anyone who is successful has to operate in the real world, not the one you read about in the newspapers or see on the television.'

'Rubbish,' said Mum.

'Hey, business is tough. This is the real world, not a cosy office or factory with nice shifts and comfy seats. I'm no different to any other business leader or politician who wants to get things done.'

'Utter rubbish!' Mum declared, 'A few bad apples and you condemn everyone and pretend they're as bad as you. I know some people who run big companies. They even agonise about sacking someone who has done something wrong. They would never kill. You are a thief and a killer.'

Deeds was clearly stung by this. Hector suspected that Deeds usually killed anyone who spoke to him in this way. He had a pleasant manner that disguised poor self-control.

Deeds and Mum began to bicker. Dad was pleased because it was delaying the point where they would receive an ultimatum. Hector found it allowed him to recover as well. He remembered the pump house. Above them was strapped the Hellstone fountain head, next to the small rooms on the tiny floor above his own bedroom. All he had to do was escape from Sludge, switch on the pump and hope that Mum, Dad and Andrè survived the electrocution better than Deeds or Sludge. It was a rotten plan, but it was the best he had.

'Hey, hey,' said Deeds, trying to shut Mum up, 'The difference between the good guys and the bad guys, is that the good guys only kill when they have to.'

'Rubbish,' Mum replied, but she was cut off by Irvine Deeds.

'Now quieten down and listen,' said Deeds.

'My wife will speak as she wishes,' said Dad, keen to maintain the bickering.

'Sludge,' said Deeds, turning to his henchman.

Sludge stamped down on Andrè's right arm breaking it. There was a cry of pain from Andrè and gasps or horror and surprise from Mum and Dad. Hector was not as affected. He knew that if he had not been so reckless Irvine Deeds, Sludge and his sister would not be standing before them. Hector was determined to set things right.

'Now look,' said Deeds, 'We are not going to be friends. We are not going to be best buddies or swap jokes on email. That doesn't mean I'm evil, and that doesn't mean I'm not going to be reasonable.'

Mum and Dad stared back at him in silence.

'All I want here is to undo the administrative error. Give me back my money and I'll even leave you with five million of your British pounds. It's my money. I'm being generous.'

Deeds spread his arms wide.

'How reasonable is that?' Deeds asked.

'You look like a game show host, except you're bald and fatter,' said Hector.

Dad winced, but said nothing. Mum had argued from a moral perspective, whereas Hector simply opted to say the most insulting thing he could think of. Dad had in no way accepted Kate's death, whereas Hector had, and was keen to injure Deeds and Sludge in any way he could. Fortunately, Deeds did not get Sludge to turn his attention to Hector.

'I have a computer here. I have a satellite connection so we can get onto the internet. All you have to do is wire the money into the account I tell you and this will all be over. We can say goodbye.'

'Don't do it,' said Andrè from his face-down position on the ground, 'You will be killed the moment you've transferred the money.'

Sludge kicked Andrè hard in the face. Andrè made no noise, but turned to look up at Sludge, blood trickling from the corner of his eye.

'I agree with you on this Mr Deeds,' said Dad, 'but unfortunately, the money is in a trust. I don't have the powers to do as you ask.'

'Rubbish,' said Deeds, imitating Mum's earlier use of the word with a bad English accent.

'After all of the trouble they had, you've been given full access,' said Deeds, 'You can do as you want. I arranged it. My spies have done their job.'

'It's in several accounts. I don't remember the details,' said Dad.

'Fortunately, I do,' said Deeds with a smile, 'What I do not have are the passwords for the accounts. As you know, you have to enter two passwords for each account. One error at this time of night and there is a delay of at least an hour until the account is unfrozen. So I can't afford to guess the passwords.'

'I could guess the passwords,' Lord Rothwell suddenly offered, 'I bet Kate and Hector will be part of each one.'

'Hey, sure,' said Deeds, 'I like that. And if you get it wrong and I don't get my money, Sludge here will pull you to bits until there's no more blood in you.'

'Oh, right, OK,' said Lord Rothwell, 'Have you thought of breaking into the bank?'

'If you don't shut up I'm going to let Marina here use you for target practice. She hasn't killed in two weeks and she's a girl that gets agitated when's she's gone that long without any fun.'

'If Trevor transfers the money you will kill us,' said Mum plainly.

'Well, it's about trust. You've got to trust me. I don't kill whole families,' said Deeds.

There was silence as Deeds gave Dad and Mum time to think. He was a seasoned criminal. He tried to avoid explicit threats if they could remain unspoken.

'I'm not going to get Sludge to kill Hector,' said Deeds, once he was tired of waiting.

'Good,' said Mum.

'I'm going to ask him to shoot Hector in the foot. Such a complicated arrangement of bones. Hector will just have to go through life walking rather than running. No soccer or baseball for Hector here.'

'You would shoot a child?' asked Mum, in a tone that exuded disgust.

'You've lost your little girl. There's no need to lose your son as well.'

This was Deeds' modus operandi; kill one and let the rest realise that nothing else was worth the loss. 'Destroy hope and you've destroyed the person, their dreams, their will, everything that matters to them,' This was one of Deeds' favourite sayings.

'Monster,' Mum shouted, while Dad looked away, tears in his eyes. Until that point they had hopes that Kate might have survived.

'I haven't got forever,' said Deeds, 'At least you've got your son. Do you want him whole or in bits? Of course, if I don't get what I want you can have a double funeral for both children.'

Hector dropped to his knees, out of Sludge's reach. He scrabbled for the kitchen, crashing into the door and turning the handle. Once inside he wrenched open the cupboard and threw the switch for the fountain in the lake. As he did his feet left the ground. Sludge had him by the neck. Mum was screaming.

'What did he do?' Deeds asked urgently, trying to crane his neck round to get a better view.

'Tried to turn some lights on,' replied Sludge, dragging Hector back to the centre of the main hall.

Hector suddenly felt weak. He had seen a spirit. In the corner of the kitchen had been the ghost of Nana, stood stock still, but with her finger raised to her lips. He briefly felt hope. Nana might rescue them, and yet she had died in a hail of bullets and the fireball that had engulfed her car. Even if Nana was alive, there was nothing she could do against Sludge and Marina.

Hector looked up. The pump should be working now. Water should be gushing in. All he had to do was to shout to Mum and Dad before they were electrocuted. Maybe he could drag André away by his uninjured arm. Yet, nothing was happening. There was no water, not even a drip. It had not worked. His plan had failed.

Outside two thugs stood guard. They were watching the ground in the moonlight. It was odd, but it looked as though a snake was crawling under the gravel. It seemed to have come from a building next to the lake, and was making its way to the Hall. They looked at each other and both took a step back. Then they heard a voice behind them.

'I've a gun at your back. Drop your weapons, take one step forwards, and then lie face-down on the ground,' Edward Grantham was fairly sure these were the last two. His only disappointment was that he had not fired a shot.

In the Hall, everyone was looking up. They had all followed Hector's gaze, but could see nothing but the balconies and the glass dome high above. Then came a few drips of water, and then a spray. Hector dropped to his knees, squirmed free from Sludge's grip for a second time and darted forward to his parents.

'You're going to be electrocuted. Run!' Hector cried, just as there was a splintering sound from above.

Sludge stepped forwards to grab Hector, but paused as he glimpsed something falling in the rain from above. Hector turned to look and collided with his father. It was as if everything was happening in slow motion. Sludge drove a foot into the ground in a desperate attempt to change direction and avoid the falling object.

As Sludge slipped, the Hellstone fountain head and part of the balcony railing it was strapped to, came crashing down, hitting Sludge with immense force on his left shoulder. Sludge was struck to the ground by the falling metal head. He crumpled without a shout or cry. The only sound was water, and the clang as the fountain head bounced away, dragging the broken balcony with it. Even a monster like Sludge could not recover from a blow that broke his arm, shoulder and ribs. It was all so unexpected no one reacted.

Water cascaded around them. Sludge then let out a groan. He seemed to be unconscious. Hector noticed movement and turned to see Marina aiming a gun at him, but at her side was Nana, reaching behind Marina.

'There you go,' said Nana, almost conversationally, 'There's a grenade in your pants.'

Marina scrabbled for her underwear, suddenly fearful that she might have moments left to live. She could not defend. All her efforts were focussed on the grenade and on her own survival. Irvine Deeds had drawn a handgun while retreating from the inevitable explosion. He was trying to get a shot at Nana, but his aim was blocked by Marina's frantic efforts. Nana took advantage of Marina's total focus on her pants and hit her hard around the ear with her sawn-off shotgun. As she hit her a second time, and Marina crumpled, Nana lost grip on her shotgun just as a bullet whizzed past her head.

'Don't worry,' Nana said, 'I didn't pull the pin out.'

'That's the Hellstone head, from the fountain,' Lord Rothwell screeched as his eyes settled on the metal head that should have been adorning the smaller island in the middle of the lake, 'It's you, isn't it, you stupid boy! You did this!'

Hector did not reply at first. Sludge and Marina were unconscious. Nana was alive. Plus, if Nana was alive then maybe Kate got out as well. The Hellstone head was going to be a small telling off at worst given events. All of a sudden, Hector knew everything would turn out right. He felt his Bandit-like confidence returning.

'Sorry,' said Hector to Lord Rothwell, while not feeling in the slightest bit sorry about any of it.

'Hey, hey,' said Deeds, 'Pay attention. I'm the one with the gun.'

'That! That!' screamed Rothwell, 'That is a symbol of my family's heritage and bravery.'

'You haven't looked very brave,' Hector replied, expecting to be told off at any minute for being rude.

'How dare you! How dare you!' Rothwell raved, while Deeds rolled his eyes in exasperation. 'My ancestor charged artillery. He practically led the Charge of the Light Brigade.'

'Was he in charge of the compass?' asked Hector, all confidence restored and in full working order.

'You stupid, stupid boy,' Rothwell screamed.

'Hey, hey,' shouted Deeds, 'Let's focus people.'

'Sorry Lord Brothmell,' said Hector.

Rothwell screamed incoherently. There might have been words involved, Hector could not be sure.

There was a shot and a yell. Deeds had shot Henry in the leg.

'As I said,' Deeds shouted, 'I'm the one with the gun, and if I don't get some passwords into this machine right this minute, Hugo the fountain destroyer here is going to lose feet, hands and anything else I want to shoot.'

'I'm called Hector, not Hugo,' said Hector.

Deeds turned the gun on Hector, aimed for his foot and shot. Hector moved just in time. Deeds aimed the gun for Hector's middle. Now Hector knew he had gone too far. Deeds had lost what little control he had. Hector was going to be shot. He was probably going to die.

'Down! Down!' came a hiss from Lord Rothwell's rooms.

Deeds turned to see Kate, laid on the ground, with just her head and a shotgun showing around the door.

'Get the butt into your shoulder Kate,' Andrè gasped, 'There's a big recoil.'

'Put the gun down,' Kate hissed again, 'Down! Now!'

'You haven't got the…' said Irvine Deeds, who never quite made it to the word 'guts'. He dodged to his left as the shotgun discharged exactly where his head had just been.

Kate scurried around in an instant and reappeared with a machine gun. Deeds saw Kate reappear and knew the game was up. His dive, roll and run coincided with Kate removing the safety catch. He ran headlong for a window that was boarded up on the other side and dived, expecting to smash through it. He crashed down, having broken only a few panes, as bullets exploded into the wall and window.

'Don't worry Andrè,' shouted Kate, 'I've remembered. Short bursts.'

Deeds staggered to his feet, thinking that window frames were tougher than they appeared in the films. He ran for the door, just as another burst of automatic fire ripped into the wall beside him.

Deeds fell again as he collided painfully with the doorway, leaving a smear of blood where he had been hit by shrapnel. He swore as he scrambled into the night on hands and feet, bullets flying over his head.

'Damn!' Edward Grantham exclaimed as he walked through the door a minute or so after Deeds had fled, 'If there was someone I wanted to shoot it was Sludge, but someone's already bagged him.'

'Hector got him with the top of a fountain,' said Kate, noting that Edward saw the battle as a giant shoot where the aim was to bag the top prize.

'Well done Hector,' said Edward, 'I daren't come in before because of all of the bullets flying out of the windows. I was thinking of shooting the chap who ran out, but I wasn't sure who he was.'

'The man who paid for Sludge,' Kate answered, providing Edward with all of the information he needed.

'Right. I like a hunt!' Edward exclaimed as he turned back to go out.

Henry was having pressure applied to his wound by Dad. Mum had untied Andrè and helped him to his feet. Andrè's mood was nothing like as cheerful as Edward's. His face was ashen, possibly from the pain of his broken arm, but more probably from barely concealed rage.

Andrè walked over to the gun Deeds had dropped, picked it up with his good arm and turned to face the now conscious Sludge. As Andrè aimed the gun Kate shouted.

'No, no Andrè. Please no!'

'How many have you killed?' Andrè asked him.

'How many have you killed?' came Sludge's reply, as blood continued to trickle down his forehead.

'I only killed when I had to in defence. I don't murder.'

'Please Andrè. I don't want to see anyone murdered,' said Kate, 'He's vile, but unarmed and injured.'

Kate's pleadings had no effect.

'Any last words?' asked Andrè, 'Or should I kill your sister first so you can watch her die? That's your style isn't it?'

Andrè could not hide his disgust for Sludge.

'Andrè no, please no,' said Kate, as Hector, Nana, Mum and Dad looked on.

'If I let him go he will escape again,' said Andrè, showing the first signs of reason.

'They have prisons people cannot escape from,' said Kate, 'Pierre would not have wanted you to be a murderer, certainly not on his account.'

'How do you know this?' Andrè asked, 'You don't know what Pierre and I have done. You did not know him as well as I did.'

'Pierre was a good man, like you Andrè. We all love you. Please, please don't.'

'Andrè,' Dad called quietly, 'You remember we spoke about a test. Maybe this is your test.'

Andrè looked at Kate and tears welled in his eyes. He removed the clip of ammunition from the gun and then threw the gun into Sludge's face.

'Trevor,' said Andrè with a sigh of someone who has been awake for a year, 'Please tie Sludge's arms to his belt at the back. I don't care if it hurts him. He's still dangerous. Use three cable ties.

CHAPTER TWENTY SIX

Rothwell

PC David Western was struggling. He had been trained to take statements from children. PC Somerscales was looking on wondering how they could deal with Hector Trogg.

Annette Somerscales had enjoyed seeing various well known local criminals paraded off into prison vans because they had run out of space in the police vans. Yet, Rothwell was a sleepy place, and an incident with automatic weapons was a major surprise. She had been one of the first on the scene at three in the morning.

PC Somerscales had used a number of bricks and plastic bin liners to protect the various weapons from the weather. She had hopes that the DNA on them would land the collection of local vomiting thugs in prison for a long time. Quite how they had come to be involved in a mass armed attack was a puzzle. It seemed a bit out of their league.

It was now eight in the morning and PC Somerscales was tired. There were supposed to be two police officers interviewing a boy. His parents were nearby. Officially, Hector was a vulnerable child who had been through a terrible ordeal. He had survived several attempts on his life. PC Somerscales was supposed to ensure that the interview did not distress Hector. As far as she could tell, quite a few of the ordeals had been started by Hector, and distress was generally something Hector caused rather than suffered.

Annette Somerscales felt quite superfluous. Hector looked tired, but getting him to talk really was no problem at all. The complication was PC Western, who in her view lacked common sense, and was just as happy to arrest a victim as the perpetrator.

Added to this, PC Western was on very good terms with Lord Rothwell, and it was apparent that Rothwell did not like Hector. She suspected that Lord Rothwell and PC Western belonged to the same club, or shared some other common interest.

Kate had already been interviewed at length. Now they were checking her story against Hector's account.

'Hector,' PC Western said, 'You've told me quite a bit about things in general. I'd just like to check a few specific events with you.'

'Do you understand Hector?' Annette Somerscales chipped in.

'Yes,' said Hector rather indignantly, 'I'm not dim. I only pretended to be stupid with Lord Rothwell because it annoyed him so much.'

'Is it the saw-off shotgun?' Hector went on, 'Only I realise they are illegal so I'd just like to say that Nana found it, because one of the attackers dropped it. It wasn't a shotgun that Edward Grantham shortened for her.'

'No Hector, it wasn't the sawn-off shotgun,' said David Western, holding up his hands to try and stop Hector speaking.

'Hector, when you were on the island, did anyone turn up to find you?'

'No, no, we were on our own. Andrè, Mum and Dad were in the Hall.'

'So no one came to the island looking for you?'

'No,' said Hector firmly.

'The island wasn't searched by three men in a motor launch?'

'Oh that,' Hector replied, 'Yes, we hid from them. They had machine guns.'

PC Western pointed to the lake, where the mostly-submerged boat could still be seen.

'Is that the boat they used Hector?'

'Yes.'

'Do you know why the boat sank Hector?'

'Because I made holes in it.'

'Did you think that sabotaging a boat, in the dark, was irresponsible?' PC Western went on.

'A bit. I could have been caught,' Hector mused, 'but it was also really hard work. Making holes without making noise is difficult.'

'When you made the holes in the boat Hector did you realise that the boat might sink?'

'Yes, but only slowly. The holes were quite small.'

'Why was that Hector?' PC Western asked.

'Because I couldn't make them any bigger,' said Hector, incredulous that the police officer should ask such a stupid question.

'So you made small holes and you hoped the men would make it back to shore?'

'Oh no,' Hector replied, 'I didn't want them to make it. That's why I used their petrol tank as a toilet.'

'I don't understand?' said PC Western.

'I did a wee wee in the petrol tank so the outboard motor would break down.'

'So you believed that by using their petrol tank as a toilet it would make their boat's engine break down?'

Hector was getting fed up. He had decided this police officer was terminally dim.

'Yes,' said Hector, 'and it worked. I did my business in the petrol tank so their boat would break down on the way back. Turns out that my wee wee isn't very combustible; that means it cannot catch fire by the way.'

'Did you worry about the men drowning if the boat sank?'

'No. My main worry was that they wouldn't drown, and that they'd swim back to the island. But I was planning to throw rocks at them while they were swimming if they did. I'm quite a good shot.'

'Hector,' PC Somerscales chipped in, 'did you feel threatened? Were you afraid?'

'Oh yes, but on the plus side that helped me produce a lot of wee.'

'How did you feel when they were searching for you and your sister?' asked PC Somerscales.

'Frightened. I wanted to bite them,' Hector replied.

'Have you bitten anyone before?' PC Western asked.

'No, my teeth are too small, but one of my friends at school told me about this programme on telly where you can grow giant teeth so you can maul lions and tigers.'

PC Western wrote more notes. Hector was growing bored. He got the feeling PC Western was not on his side. He reflected that although he was over the age of criminal responsibility, there was really no chance he would be prosecuted. He was contemplating confessing to a huge imaginary crime.

'Hector, to turn to another matter, we have an allegation that you stole and damaged a very valuable fountain head,' said PC Western.

'I didn't steal it. I just moved it to the top floor of the Hall.'

'Why did you do that Hector?'

'So it would spray down water. The water would get to the electricity sockets, and then Sludge would be electrocuted.'

'So you intended to kill the person we know as Sludge?'

'Yep!'

'But instead, the fountain head fell on him.'

'Yes. Quite lucky really.'

'The gentleman who was hit by the fountain head has sustained very serious injuries…'

'Not serious enough,' Hector interjected.

'And in the past you have tried to kill this man we know as Sludge by crushing him with an armoured car?'

'No, that was my sister Kate, I was just egging her on. I couldn't reach the pedals. Could I ask a question?'

'Yes, of course,' PC Western replied.

'Did you do a law degree before joining the police?'

Hector noticed that PC Somerscales had turned away.

'Hector, people have been hurt. We need to find out what happened,' PC Western said.

'Sludge is an assassin. He tried to kill me in France. I was there when he killed Pierre,' said Hector, as he found his temper rising.

'Who's Pierre?'

'He was a French special forces soldier. Andrè is special forces.'

'Did he teach you to use weapons?'

'Yes, but he told us that killing crosses a line. He told us we had to run away and hide. He taught us evasion. We were supposed to hide for several days until it was safe.'

'While we waste thousands of pounds trying to find you?'

Hector's temper was at it's limit. Worse than that he saw Lord Rothwell in the background listening in. Hector took a wild guess that Rothwell knew PC Western.

'When did Andrè tell you he was a special forces soldier?'

Hector had to think. He had never been told this.

'Hector,' PC Western went on, 'did you ever think that Andrè might have made this up?'

'I was there when Pierre was gunned down by Sludge. Andrè was there as well,' said Hector, defiantly. PC Western said nothing, but returned to his notes. Hector suspected he was enjoying himself. He also suspected he was being unpleasant to please Lord Rothwell.

Hector struggled to control his fury. He was sure PC Western was friends in some way with Lord Rothwell. Andrè had said that anger was only useful if you needed aggression. It clouded thought. Hector took a deep breath.

'I think I need to confess,' said Hector.

PC Western remained quiet. PC Somerscales was listening intently.

'Sludge was really working to recover stolen art. Lord Rothwell told me to kill Sludge if I could.'

'Hector, Hector, come on now,' said PC Western.

'It's true. I can even show you where Lord Rothwell keeps his stolen art.'

'This is rubbish Hector,' said PC Western sharply.

Hector pointed to PC Somerscales.

'Can I show you where Lord Rothwell has his stolen art?'

'No Hector,' interrupted PC Western.

'Yes, Hector, you certainly can,' said Annette Somerscales, pleased that she could finally seize control.

By ten o-clock Lord Rothwell was in a police car en route to the station for further questioning. Hector was pulling faces at PC

Western through the window. Dad was making no attempt to stop him.

The sun was bright and Otto was complaining about a lack of food in his dish. Andrè had returned from hospital with a black eye and his arm in a plaster cast. Henry was being kept in because of the amount of blood he had lost.

Andrè had messages from France. Mrs Warp's creator, Monsieur Ballingrow would be arriving to collect the remains of Mrs Warp.

'I know she was hit with a taser, but does anyone know how she lost her head?' Andrè asked.

Hector and Kate exchanged glances.

'It fell off, all of a sudden,' said Hector.

'So you were there,' Andrè confirmed, an eyebrow raised.

'Probably enemy fire,' said Kate.

'He seems angry,' said Andrè, 'He said something about video evidence, a shotgun and the safe room.'

'Hard to say for sure,' said Hector confidently, 'There was a lot going on and it was very dark.'

As Nana served freshly cooked buns in her slightly burnt out kitchen, Edward Grantham appeared at the window. He seemed to be waving a dog lead.

Bandit rushed in. He greeted everyone by wagging his whole body rather than just his tail. He seemed wildly excited. Bandit worked his way around them all, pushing and shoving and wriggling in delight. Even Mum and Dad seemed pleased to see him.

'He had a helicopter,' were Edward's first words as he walked in, explaining Irvine Deeds' successful escape.

As Edward and Dad turned to a discussion of Irvine Deeds, Bandit briefly sniffed Otto, and then licked him full in the face.

Otto hit Bandit hard around the face, but kept his claws in. Bandit ignored the blow and licked Otto again.

Then a sound or smell caught his attention. Bandit turned and launched into a wild gallop in one movement. Once outside the door, there was a dull thud and a yell as Bandit barrelled into someone's legs and knocked them sprawling to the ground. As Kate and Hector looked out of the window they could see PC Western struggling up. The air was filled with furious shouts of rage. The path to the lake was filled with dust as Bandit accelerated towards the ducks.

The End

If you have enjoyed this book then please
tell your friends about Hector Trogg,
and please do write reviews.

Book Two
Hector Trogg: Fell Heights

The tick of the clock left small echoes in the darker corners of the hall. It was past midnight. For a school that prided itself on its early start, this was very late. Judging from the lights in the windows, only the headmaster was still up.

The clock seemed to tick louder, as if to remind Hector that he should not be out of bed. It also reminded him that Kate was late. Hector was in small part annoyed with his sister, but this was overwhelmed by a fear that she had been caught. His ears strained for the sound of approaching footsteps. He already had an escape route in mind.

For once, Hector had planned. If he was caught his excuse was going to be correcting the clock and sleep-walking. He knew it sounded feeble, but he could think of nothing better. As Hector waited in the cold silence of this most forbidding of halls, he hoped Kate was not, at this very moment, explaining her sleeping-walking to the deranged deputy head.

The unwelcome tick, marking every second, seemed to stretch each minute until it was an hour. Hector noticed the clock's tick always seemed to grow louder, and yet objectively it had to remain at the same volume. Hector hated that clock, and yet now so much of his destiny was tied to it. If Hector wanted a future the clock had to keep ticking.

Find out more about the next Hector Trogg book...

fellheights.com